Burning brought up the sling-gun pistol he and Souljourner had stripped from the first Unconquerable, faked a shot at the Diehard's face, then aimed for his upper leg. The pile bolt tore into the gap between the top of his greave and the bottom of his tasse plates, and the Ean screamed. Burning moved in with the captured targone on his left arm, parrying the sickle sword with his ka-bar, and slammed his shielded forearm into as much face as the Diehard's cheekpieces left exposed.

The soldier reeled, but Burning couldn't afford to settle for a nearly bloodless win that might allow him to get back into the battle. He jammed the ka-bar into the Diehard's unprotected armpit, in and out so fast that his hand was clear before blood spurted from the wound. Then he shoved the young praetorian down the ladder at the men behind him . . .

TO WATERS' END

Book Four of GammaLAW

Brian Daley

A Del Rey® Book
THE BALLANTINE PUBLISHING GROUP • NEW YORK

A Del Rey ® Book
Published by The Ballantine Publishing Group
Copyright © 1999 by The Estate of Brian Daley

www.randomhouse.com/delrey/

Library of Congress Catalog Card Number: 98-96786

ISBN 0-345-42211-2

Manufactured in the United States of America

First Edition: March 1999

10 9 8 7 6 5 4 3 2 1

In memory of my father, Charles Joseph Daley,
and of meteor watching on warm August nights

ACKNOWLEDGMENTS

The author wishes to express his heartfelt thanks to the following people, who aided and abetted him over the many years: Officer Michael Kueberth and Cpl. Garland Nixon of the Maryland DNR Police Hovercraft *Hunter*; Dr. Yoji Kondo of Goddard Space Flight Center, Greenbelt, MD; Calvin Gongwer of Innerspace Corp., Covina, CA; Ray Williamson, formerly of the Office of Technology Assessment; Professor Conrad Neuman, Oceanographic Department of the University of South Carolina; Drs. Frank Manheim and Allyn Vine of the Woods Hole Oceanographic Institute; Masaaki Hirayama, for the crash course in Korean history; Skipper Richard J. Severinghaus and the men of the USS *Annapolis*; the boys and girls of *sensei* Tom Fox's "American Rock and Roll Karate," for massive intrusions of reality; physicist Dr. Charles Melton and the late Dr. Al Giardini of the University of Georgia; Drs. John Camerson and Eric Seifter, for both their concern and their efforts on my behalf; and Lucia Robson, Owen Lock, and Jim Luceno for their love and support.

Some features of the LAW 'chetterguns are drawn from the research and recommendations of Lt. Col. Morris J. Herbert, formerly Assistant Professor of Ballistics and Associate Professor, Department of Ordnance, U. S. Military Academy, West Point.

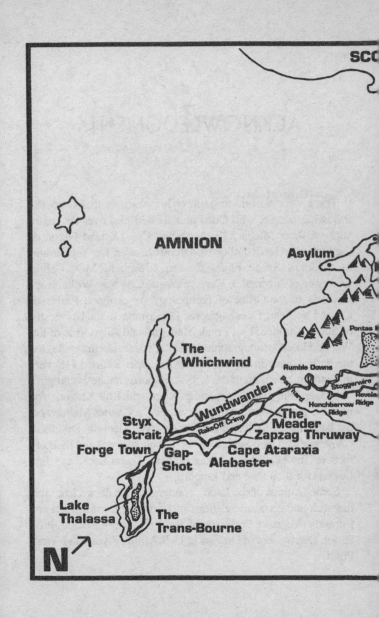

LANDS

Passwater

Washdown
Heights

Gumption

Dunrovin

rice
Square
Deal
eenth
en
Rainbows
End

AMNION

pure landing stag

Wall Water

Fluter Delve

Heaves

Hangwitch

Hardbound

Flyaway
Island

Lighthouse at
New Alexandria

SCORPIA

AQUAMARINE

CHAPTER
ONE

The swell of muddy water and tangled wreckage surging east from the burst Optimant dam heaved the *GammaLAW* upward far more effortlessly than had the tetherhook that had snatched her off Periapt. The great hydrodynamic buffet canted the SWATHship's triple bows ten, then twenty, and finally twenty-five degrees into the air. Insufficiently braced despite Captain Chaz Quant's orders, people in the pilothouse were sent struggling and staggering against the aft bulkhead. Quant, clinging to the rail under the forward windows, felt the ship being hurled up the mounded face of the waters as if something alive had bucked her free of Aquamarine itself. Having had a few minutes to think through this latest crisis facing the LAW mission, he understood that even if the rising waters failed to claim his ship, other, more daunting hazards awaited her downriver.

The *GammaLAW*, trembling and straining, took the monster swell threatening to overcome her helm regardless of the three people fighting the wheel. Loose gear went crashing; rigging, equipment, and repair tackle overlooked in the rush to secure the decks rang and beat like rioting inmates hammering at the bars of their cells. As never before, Quant thanked the structural strengthening that had been done to reinforce the vessel for the tetherlift and transport to Aquamarine. Sewage-dark water carrying fishing boats, bodies, and everything the turbulence had stirred up from Ea's bottom broke around the bows,

1

splashing against the pilothouse windows and wetting the very top of the signal mast.

GammaLAW groaned and thrashed like an animal resisting quicksand, but at last the bows topped out and began to depress once more, biting deep into the waves and sending more spray aloft. Quant held his course for the teeth of the flood and called for twenty knots, all ahead standard. A reassuring compliance came from the engine room telegraph, and there was a quick feeling of response as the mains sent steady power to the actuator-propellers. Quant knew it was an illusion, however, and in moments others on the bridge realized it as well.

"Navigation reports that we're making *sternway*, sir," Eddie Gairaszhek relayed. "True speed and direction do not correlate with relative readings of inertial tracking gear and positioning radars."

While the *GammaLAW* was moving at speed through the water around her, the entire volume of the descended Pontos Reservoir was moving in the opposite direction at an even greater velocity. His ship had triumphed over the initial bludgeoning of the flood and had marshaled her engines in the nick of time, but against being flung backward she was powerless. To the southern end of the lake and the land beyond she was being carried. It was there, Quant understood, that the brute physics of the contest would be played out. If the volume of water was of sufficient size and force, if Ea and the river headwaters that drained it could not divert enough of the stupendous spill, the *GammaLAW* probably would be washed high and dry. And hard aground—if indeed she lived through the grounding at all—she would be easy pickings for the Aquam and impossible to refloat with the limited resources left to her company.

Settling into the contest he had foreseen from the moment the dam had burst, Quant called for additional turns on the actuators, racing to position the *GammaLAW* safely for the inevitable receding of the Pontos flood. He pitied any

Aquam caught along the southern lakeshore or the river when the waters began to scour their way toward Aquamarine's single ocean, the Amnion, yet he hoped against hope that outlets downriver would provide vents for the deluge's energy and mass.

The ship was still being battered and shaken, as if fighting her way against some spring thaw in Hades, as all around her washed debris, wreckage, and drowned Aquam bodies stripped naked by the force of the waters. Quant called for ten more knots, but the *GammaLAW* remained trapped in the flow.

Eyewash descended slowly from the zenith. All through the long afternoon the ship fought her lonely battle, frothing the brackish, debris-laced water, while Quant stood at his post and watched out for turbulence-borne debris that could foul or damage the actuators.

Unspooling the aerostat to its maximum length had allowed him to keep an eye on the outgushing at the broken dam, but the camera failed to supply him with an adequate view of the falling water level of the Pontos Reservoir itself. A regional map suggested that the floodplain south of Lake Ea would absorb most of the vented waters. The *GammaLAW* would be safe there, but reaching the floodplain would require squeezing through the narrows at Fluter Delve, where the Dynast Piety IV ruled, much as Grandee 'Waretongue Rhodes did at Wall Water.

As dusk yielded to evening, the ship continued to be pushed kilometer by kilometer toward the place called the Lowdowns at Ea's southern extremity. Quant supposed that many aboard wondered why he didn't simply drop anchor or even put both hooks in the mud. Not only was the bottom treacherous, however, digging in the ship's heels would make her a target for sizable chunks of debris turned into hydro-missiles by the vicious propellant of the Pontos.

Two hours after midnight inertial tracking reported that the ship had officially crossed the demarcation of what had been

Ea's shoreline only that morning. The SWATHship was still pushed deeper inland, with trees and human bodies more common in the water now. As difficult as it was to get a reading through the particulate filth and floating wreckage, it became clear that the bottom was shoaling out. Bowing to the inevitable, Quant countermanded the forebodings of engineering by ordering an increase in speed.

Pushed stern-first toward the so-called Dales, where the ship was in real danger of being set aground, she waged her battle in good order, and within an hour she appeared to be making headway.

Quant noticed Gairaszhek on the starboard wing of the bridge, training vision enhancers on the water. Moving next to him and following his glance, Quant spotted what the lieutenant had been watching—another drowned Aquam. This one, though, was a child, its gender impossible to discern, the current quickly bearing it away.

"We came abreast and left it behind fast, sir," Gairaszhek explained with a gulp. "I, I believe we're gaining on the current. MeoTheos. Forgive me for being so happy to report that."

He was right. Meter by meter the SWATHship was forging back through the aroused waters. Ea was still rising, but with less force.

At dawn, when the ship had recrossed the now-imaginary line of the lakeshore, Dextra Haven requested a moment of Quant's time with a gratifying acknowledgment of how busy he was. Quant teleconferenced with her over their special command circuit from the port wing of the bridge.

"I know it's early to ask your conclusion, Captain," she began, "but we need to be thinking about mission contingencies. Is it all over for us on Lake Ea?"

Recalling the deep V in the dam, he answered with little hesitation. "Affirmative. For this year, at any rate. Once the flood subsides, there'll be insufficient reservoir to keep the lake levels up. Halfway through the dry season Ea will be a string of shallows dotted with sandbars and islets. We're bound to run aground if we stay."

"So it's downriver, then?"

"There'll be hundreds of kilometers of navigable water there—even in the last of the Big Sere."

"You realize that that means traversing the narrows under the Dynast Piety's stronghold?"

"It's literally unavoidable," Quant told her.

"His nephew, Knocknet, was killed during the insanity at Wall Water. The dynast may very well consider himself to be in a blood feud with us."

Quant grunted into the headset. "Then I wish you all success with diplomatic efforts, Madame Commissioner. But we'll need to move soon, the risks notwithstanding."

Haven was silent for a moment. "Captain Quant, exactly what happened to the dam?"

"Zone, madame. For my money, Colonel Zone happened to the dam."

"Why in God's name would General Delecado open fire on the dam curtain?" Quant was asking the rawboned colonel himself later that morning.

Zone was standing at the far end of the CIC conference table, looking bored by the proceedings. Shortly past dawn a rigid inflatable boat had returned him and some dozen others to the *GammaLAW*. Except for Delecado, Senior Captain Feelie Shumakova, and two of Zone's severalmates, it was the same group that had left for the dam the previous day aboard the general's Hellhog helo in response to a WHOAsuit beacon that had been observed in the lake.

"How many ways do you want me to say it?" Zone told Quant, Haven, Major Lod, and the rest. "We spotted a bunch of Aqs in a small floater throwing someone overboard. When Daddy D saw the Ext uniform, he snapped and went to triggers. Strafed the raft, then planted both pods of missiles into the dam. There would have been no way to stop him even if we wanted to.

"Thing was, one of the missiles went off short while we were still within burst diameter. Knocked the Hellhog out of the air just before the dam let loose. Daddy D, Captain Shumakova, Digger Taraki, and Strop never made it to the RIB. We managed to ride out the flood and conduct a search, but no bodies were recovered."

Zone didn't look bereaved or regretful, which, Quant suspected, was very canny of him, for it would have been out of character. It was too early to know how the rest of the Exts felt about the story Zone had brought back from the dam, but Dextra Haven certainly wasn't buying it.

"I want it on record that I don't believe a word of this," she told the table. "Three days ago Colonel Zone found it necessary to kill Wix Uniday, and now General Delecado is missing under dubious circumstances."

"Uniday was trying to commo with our enemies at Wall Water," Zone said, giving her a measure of his NoMan stare.

"So you've stated," Haven said, holding his gaze. "But we have no more proof of that than of General Delecado's firing on an Aquam raft."

Zone shrugged. "Ask my teammates."

Haven contorted a face that was showing more fine lines each day as a result of suspended rejuvenation treatments in the wake of the destruction of *Terrible Swift Sword* not a week earlier. "Wives don't often testify against their husbands, Colonel Zone. But rest assured, we will get to the bottom of this. In the meantime I want everyone concerned to fill out *individual* reports and have them to me no later than 1700 hours. You're dismissed."

Zone didn't move. "Begging the commissioner's pardon, but aren't you forgetting something? With Allgrave Burning still missing and Daddy D probably sucking mud, I'm next in the Ext chain of command."

Quant realized that Zone's reminder hadn't taken Haven by surprise. After their face-off on the beach below Wall Water it was unlikely that she would ever again lower her guard in Zone's presence, and now she gave him her answering broadside.

"In the first place, Colonel, any change of command, even among the Exts, is subject to my approval. But more to the point, there's an Ext of direct lineage to a bastion family, and as such he outranks you." She looked at Lod. "Major, you are now in command."

Still bristling from his most recent run-in with Zone—while escorting the Manipulant Scowl-Jowl belowdecks—Lod clearly savored the moment. It was Burning's fatalistic conviction that someone eventually would have to execute Zone or fight him to the death, but just now Lod was content with humiliating him.

Dextra was giving Zone the kind of smile people choked other people for using. "As for you, Colonel, you are relieved of duty pending a full investigation into the deaths of Wix Uniday, General Delecado, and the others."

If indeed it was Haven's line drawn in the dirt, Zone decided not to cross it for the moment. When he left the CIC, Haven showed Quant a warning look to keep him from making an issue of it. He admitted to himself that she was right and dropped the matter. It took an effort to do that aboard his own ship, though he had good practice in diplomatic silences during his servitude under Hallowed Hall back when the *GammaLAW* had been the *Matsya*. Besides, there were even more important issues than Colonel Zone. "Madame Haven, I think we should satellite all other topics to the fact that we have no more than ten hours to make the passage downriver."

Haven looked at him aghast. "Ten *hours*? But I thought—"

"The flood surge took away most of the seasonal silt deposit that builds up at the river's headwaters. With the silt washed away, the lake's water level is declining more rapidly than originally thought. Of course, we can't be a hundred percent sure until we send in a ROVer or a submersible, but my recommendation is that we get under way immediately. Allgrave Burning, Ghost, Mason, and Dr. Zinsser, wherever they are, will undoubtedly learn what happened here and anticipate our decision to make for the floodplain."

Haven gnawed on her lower lip. "If they weren't casualties of the flood," she said, mostly to herself. "What are our options for dealing with the fortress at Fluter Delve?"

Quant laid his hand on a stack of briefing materials. "Assuming that we can navigate the narrows themselves without incident, we'll be under Dynast Piety's guns—his catapults, steam cannon, whatever he has—for approximately thirty seconds. With the loss of General Delecado's helo, we have no air strike capability, and our Close-in Weapons System was destroyed during the Nixie attack. In sum, no effective long reach outside of what the Exts can deliver in the way of boomer rounds, fireball mortars, RPGs, and so forth. However, even those arms will be of limited use against the fortress itself, since rocks and shallows will keep us outside the range of most light infantry weapons."

He gave it just a hair's-breadth pause to see if Dextra Haven was going to suggest the obvious, but she waited him out. Too smart to try to play in somebody else's arena, he told himself. Good.

"We could send the Exts ashore to create diversions, perhaps insert sapper teams, but only if you're willing to accept horrific losses. Fluter Delve has apparently been the key to the power of the grandee controlling it, and it's heavily booby-trapped and manned. There have been five major battles fought there over the years, and the ruling grandee has upgraded his defenses after each one. Our best strategy lies in trying to slip past the fortress without engaging Piety's troops. If we succeed in that much, we have a chance of reaching the floodplain without encountering anything that can do us long-range damage."

"Except the Roke," Lod muttered.

Having wiped out the mission's spies in the sky, the aliens were still dug in on the larger of Aquamarine's two moons but had yet to demonstrate that they were interested in the *GammaLAW* herself or indeed in venturing any closer to the surface of Aquamarine.

"We can do even less against the Roke than against Fluter Delve," Quant answered after a moment.

"And Grandee Rhodes?" someone asked.

Quant shrugged. "For all we know, he remained at Wall Water."

Dextra vouchsafed him a somber nod of agreement, then squared her shoulders. "Captain, there's *nothing* we can do to bolster ourselves?"

"Only the mutha-guns," he said, referring to the twin 240-mm naval rifles that constituted the Turret *Musashi*. "They're enough to blow Fluter Delve completely off the scans, but the turret is three decks below the main deck and halfway across the ship from its barbette. Without heavy transport gear, even a jury-rigged installation is going to take hours. If the turret is going to be of any use, we have to begin moving it now and make it our priority.

"Additionally, we lack the necessary propellant and live ammunition. I've ordered every available machinist's mate to work on refitting our remaining few target-practice shells to carry explosives, but quite frankly, I don't know if they can accomplish the job in time. Even if they do, the shells won't pack anything like the kind of power a real live round would."

Haven had brightened somewhat. "It seems to me, Captain, that *any* round would be preferable to none."

"Without question. But every effective aboard is going to have to bear a hand." He leaned toward Haven. "Your noncoms, officers, aides, and deputies will have to be drafted for labor details. You and I will be getting our hands dirty, madame, along with those casualties who can be of use to us."

As if to underline Quant's remark, everyone in the CIC felt the vibrations as the *GammaLAW*'s engines were restarted after having been shut down for damage inspection. After a moment, however, they pulsed with an irregular thrumming and then quit, leaving them all to stare at one another in doubt.

CHAPTER TWO

Claude Mason had had a Scorpian day to contemplate the realization that the *GammaLAW* was imperiled—imperiled by his former friend and *Scepter* teammate Eisley Boon, whom the Oceanic had mysteriously resurrected—spit back onto dry land—twenty years earlier, only to become the object of Boon's vengeance. The Oceanic had to be brought down to size, Boon had told Mason, for Boon's sake as much as for the sake of the Aquam. The means of that downsizing was a synome antagonist developed by Aquamarine's original colonizers, the Optimants, and *GammaLAW* was to be the vehicle that would deliver it into the Amnion.

But Boon's plans to commandeer the SWATHship had been derailed by an unexpected development. The bridge he himself had masterminded to span the Styx Strait had been closed by a gang of Gapshot mutineers led by Kinbreed. Boon's army of muscle cars and Anathemites was stalled on the Trans-Bourne side.

Now, however, both mutineers and builders had had many hours to ponder the demands and counterdemands, and Kinbreed himself was staring down from the Forge Town barbican of the bridge, waiting for word of an accord or the first salvo of sling-gun darts.

On the sidelines, as ever, Mason was almost amused at Boon's dilemma. The new war cars Boon had developed were no threat to Kinbreed's club-clover faction, but access to the bridge rested finally on Boon's agreeing to destroy the very cars he needed to head north.

Boon and Mason's Aquam son, Purifyre—whom Kinbreed and others knew as Hammerstone—were standing on the cobbled circus below the Forge Town barbican. Mason had fully expected them to reject Kinbreed's ultimatums and so was surprised when Purifyre doffed his elaborate war helm to Kinbreed and told him, "Very well, Brother. We concede your demands."

Kinbreed chuckled harshly, then addressed Boon by the cover name Boon had established in the Trans-Bourne. "How conciliatory of you, Cozmote."

"Never mind that," Boon snapped. "Send your inspectors to look over my cars and reopen the bridge."

The Forge Town throng had been ready for a pitched battle, but most, whose livelihoods depended on the bridge, began yelling "Hear, hear!" and "We're losing money; open up!"

"Not yet," Kinbreed yelled tightly, a wastelands-preacher gleam in his eye. Jet-black, straggly chin whiskers protruding between the curved cheekpieces of his helmet jogged quickly as he spoke. "First we set it down in writing and take an oath to it in public. Too, Forge Town grants me ten hostages to hold while the inspectors go south." He cut his eyes to Purifyre. "Brave Hammerstone will wish to be one, if I know him."

"If it would reassure you," Boon answered for Purifyre. "But first the document. I'll have it drawn up, our hostages selected, and arrangements made to take your inspectors south. We'll speak again tomorrow at midday—"

"No. Your hostages will present themselves at dawn—and Hammerstone among them. *I'll* have a compact ready for swearing."

"At dawn, then," Boon said, as if it were nothing more than a laundry pickup.

Turning his back on Kinbreed and ignoring the ruckus and the Trans-Bourne constables' struggles to keep order, he threaded through the crowd to enter the constabulary barracks that fronted on the circus. Purifyre, his bodyguard Ballyhoot, and several others went after him; Mason was close behind. The barracks had the smell of bodies, smokables, latrine, stale gooner, and old wood. Despite open shutters, the interior was as hot as a toaster oven. The few constables already there were explosively angry.

In a second-floor bunk room overlooking the circus low stools had been shoved around a table for an impromptu meeting. Purifyre waved his baton of rank at the gatehouse, from which Kinbreed was gazing, then pronounced, "Not here."

The setup was hastily shifted to the armory, which Kinbreed's men had emptied of weapons. As everyone was settling in, Mason decided to drop his bomb before the talk went veering off. "I think I can open the barbican for you, Boon."

Purifyre grew irritated, and Ballyhoot crowed scornful laughter. But Boon asked, "How, Claude?"

Mason extracted the gas propellant cartridge from his flechette pistol. "This thing's fresh and under tremendous pressure. There's a way to release it all at once—something about turning the pressure pin ring. The LAW training cadre refused to teach us civil service cunnies the trick, but if I can figure it out and wedge the cartridge between the barbican gate and the jamb or maybe underneath—"

Boon took the alloy cartridge, turning it over in hands roughened by almost a score of years of Aquamarine hard work and abuse. "Not too different from the old M-51. Slide the striker over, turn the ring to the release notch, wap it a good one with a rock, and run like hell. Only it won't solve our problem. Even if we managed to take the southern barbican in seconds flat, Kinbreed would *still* have time to signal his people at the Gapshot end. They'd chop at timbers, ignite fires, and do whatever else their lazy, greedy little parasite brains have devised, and we'd end up losing the bridge." He returned the cartridge to Mason. "It warms my heart, though, to see that you've come over to our side, Claude."

Mason had for the single reason that he had found a new identity for himself as Purifyre's father. He granted that he had become a traitor to the GammaLAW mission, but the way he saw it, the mission was doomed in any case. With the *Sword* destroyed, Haven and the others were effectively stranded on Aquamarine, and it would only be a matter of time before the Aquam united against the *GammaLAW* and destroyed it. Better, then, to put the ship to some use beforehand, especially against the Oceanic, whom Mason had feared from the first day the *Scepter* had made planetfall on Aquamarine twenty baseline-years earlier.

By throwing in with Boon and company Mason had also reneged on the agreement he had made with Yatt, the AI personality construct the so-called Quantum College had downloaded into his neurowares on Periapt. Yatt's goal in hitching a ride to Aquamarine was to search for what the AI believed would be a panacea for the Cyberplagues, which, Mason had recently learned, not only had had their beginning on Aquamarine but had been created by the Optimants themselves.

Mason was appraising the reloaded cartridge—set for firing rather than catastrophic release—when Boon's empty fist pounded the table, startling everyone. "The Horatio option is our only option," he announced, "the fail-safe we built into the bridge to foil just such an uprising!"

"Then we must first secure the northern bridgehead," Purifyre said. "Once we have checkmated Kinbreed's people there, the span will be ours once more."

"Troops loyal to us remain in Gapshot," Ballyhoot added. "And we can send reinforcements if need be."

Purifyre clenched his hands. "If we storm the southern gatehouse from both sides at once, Kinbreed won't have time to do the bridge any serious harm at this end."

Ballyhoot nodded. "He's relying on his units in Gapshot to sever the connection if the need arises."

Purifyre looked at Boon and spoke more slowly for emphasis. "That means I'll have to go across. Only you and I can trigger the Horatio option from outside the northern barbican, and it's important that you remain here."

Boon's abhorrence of the solution was plain, but its logic was inescapable. In the end it wrung a single head tic of concurrence from him. Still, Mason was perplexed. "Go across, how?" he asked. "Kinbreed won't allow you or any other traffic—"

"The Juts," Purifyre said, already pulling at the boreworm silk fastenings of his beautiful armor. "I shall have to Jut-hop."

Mason stared at his son in dismay. "You can't. It'll be dark in an hour, and the tide is already rising!"

"Then every moment counts," Ballyhoot put in. She, too, had begun to strip off her panoply.

Boon wore the look of a man sitting in some mental storm cellar. "You heard Kinbreed," he said to Mason. "At dawn he expects to have your son as a hostage. That gives us only tonight."

"You're insane! The Juts will be underwater in hours!" Mason felt his sanity being pushed to the brink. His horror of the Oceanic and the Styx Strait, where so many of his *Scepter* teammates had died, thrashed head-on against the need to accompany Purifyre and protect him if he could. He glanced at Boon, thinking of Boon's alleged resurrection, but even that wasn't enough to keep him from shaking at the thought of anyone's crossing the Juts.

"God's wounds, stop moaning, Claude!" Boon grated. "No one's asking *you* to do anything." He turned to Turnswain, who had piloted Purifyre and Mason south from Wall Water aboard the muscle car *Shattertail*. "Bring in the stand-ins."

Turnswain returned momentarily with two men wearing

only loinwraps. They began putting on the war gear Purifyre and Ballyhoot were shedding.

"Leave through the back passageway," Boon was instructing Purifyre. "Escorts will see you down to the beach. Silvio's already started across. He'll have a company or better mustered by the time you reach Gapshot. In the meantime, I'll plant myself where Kinbreed can see me."

"I'm going with him," Mason blurted. "To the beach, anyway." He looked at his son. "The least I can do is see you off."

Ballyhoot uttered a withering laugh, but Purifyre contradicted her by saying, "He can come—if he can bear being left behind." He smiled bleakly at Mason from the door to the rear passageway. "Left behind on the beach."

Mason grasped the reference immediately. Left behind as Mason had left his pregnant Aquam wife, Incandessa, all those years earlier. The point was glaring.

Once they were through the passageway, the covert route took them down a gully that ran alongside a onetime hoppers' alehouse overlooking the Styx Strait sand itself. Ultimately, Purifyre, Ballyhoot, and Mason came to the foot of the Trans-Bourne headlands at the southern end of the meandering loop of jumbled, broken rock that was the Juts. Several other members of Boon's underground—guides for the desperate crossing—rendezvoused with them there.

Highly unseasonable clouds had moved in over the strait. It seemed likely that they would slide by, but on Aquamarine there was always the chance of a freak storm, especially of the sort the Styx Strait locals called a blirt.

From the Scorpian headlands in the east to the waves that had swept around the shield of the huge island's western flank, the seas were churning and pounding. Chop was building as if leviathans were preparing to stampede. Those of Aquamarine's flying creatures that were in the air were heading inland.

Ballyhoot opened her nostrils to the wind. "A walloping blirt is moving in."

Tides there were semidiurnal—two highs and two lows per day—and the Styx Strait had one of the greatest tidal ranges on the planet. The difference between maximum and minimum levels could be as much as twenty meters. The waterline had already climbed halfway to the foot of the rocks in the short time since Purifyre's square-off with Kinbreed.

"Is this a neap tide coming?" Mason asked hopefully, meaning one of the lows that came every thirteen days or so.

Ballyhoot made her sneering chortle again, showing meat-ripper teeth. "The noyade rises to test our mettle. Why not come enjoy it, Visitant?"

Noyade: a drowning. A noyade tide and a blirt moving in. Maybe the planet really did have it in for him personally, Mason thought. He felt sick just thinking about the salt surge the living Oceanic would bring racing over the Juts.

Ballyhoot made a *phhh!* of contempt before Mason could respond to her question and then finished removing her buskins. Bare feet would give her better purchase on the Juts' treacherous monoliths and riprap. She bound her flinty hair back with a length of braided rawhide and then donned a grimy, threadbare peasant's dhoti and a chemise of whackweed jute. Her legs, furrowed and gouged by old wounds, betrayed the slackness of age but looked as strong as pilings nevertheless. The toes of her big splayed feet gripped the sand.

The veteran woman at arms buckled on sweat-stained brown pogopod leather guards that extended from knuckles to elbows—braces for rock climbing, Mason supposed, until he saw the dagger sheaths sewn on the inner side of each one—knife fighter's vambraces. Prudent Juts wear, it came to him. Back in the days before the bridge the desperate low-tide dashes drew people out onto the causeway who weren't interested in an honest profit. It was easier to jump some legitimate hoppers, take their purse and cargo, and leave the bodies where the Oceanic would dispose of the evidence utterly. The Juts term was "picaroon," though the heyday of the picaroon bands was long past.

Out where the salt water retreated only temporarily, no Gap-shot or Forge Town authority ventured. In those same bygone days and nights honest hoppers had dropped all rivalries to mete out their own justice on the Juts. But with the trade only just resuming, the law of the jungle would prevail. It was no place for Ballyhoot's meteor hammer, sunwheel disk blade, or repeating crossbow. On the rocky obstacle course conflict usually came at the closest quarters, with little room for weapons of length. Old-timers talked about smelling an enemy's exhalation as he or she died.

Ballyhoot's only other weapon was her fighting flail, which was thrust crosswise through the rope sash that held up her dhoti. She tested the retaining strap on one of the blades and gave Mason a toothy look that wasn't really a smile, merely another display of cutlery. Mason understood that she wanted to kill him so that things would return to normal between her and Purifyre.

The nascent thought of the Oceanic getting him after she'd culled a few of his organs made him gag. Regardless, he gave Ballyhoot a sickly but unwavering smile and hooked his thumb conspicuously over the rear of the 'chettergun's receiver. He had tried to befriend her; if she remained a prisoner of her jealousy, he would simply have to find another way to deal with her. On the shingle before the Styx Strait, however, his bravado rang hollow, and they both knew it.

A drop of rain made him gaze up and frown at the overcast. Eyewash was going down, and the Amnion was showing dim, deep phosphorescence, a literal sea of whites, greens, and blues, each mote a cellular bit of the Oceanic. The first long, foamy borders of the waves were already among the lower Juts.

Mason was dismayed to see several latecomers sprinting for

the causeway, bent under packs and baskets. "You're letting
more people out there?" he said to Purifyre. "Surely they can't
all be trusted."

"We control the southern beach accesses," his son assured
him, settling his turban and snugging his loinwrap. "We're
only allowing those who'll keep their mouths shut."

"What makes you think they won't denounce you? *Their*
good new days will certainly come if Kinbreed totals the
bridge. They have a vested interest in seeing you fail."

"These, or the people who vouch for them, were all
with us—with Cozmote—even before the bridge was raised.
They're loyal. What's more, we *need* fellow hoppers at the
other end so we can blend in with them in case the club-
clovers have set a watch on the beach there."

"Kinbreed's people may already hold the beach. They might
be lying in wait somewhere on the Juts."

The boy showed his disappointment and went back to arranging the weapons tucked through his belly band. "I doubt
that Kinbreed has men to spare—or that he considers rag-ass
Jut-hoppers much of a threat. He isn't aware that the Horatio
option can be enabled from outside the barbican. He has himself convinced that he is vulnerable only to a direct assault."

Purifyre was stowing his jabber, a combination parrying and
ensnaring weapon and armor-penetrating spike. In addition to
that and a basket-hilted bowie-bladed shortsword, he carried
his stubby detonator-cap shooter with a supply of rounds in a
buckled pouch.

Mason drew the 'chettergun and offered it grip first.
"You've seen me use it. Your life could depend on it."

Purifyre had already rejected the Manipulant bloopguns
captured at Wall Water, and he rejected the 'chettergun now.
He simply didn't have the experience to use the rather unselec-
tive weapon safely, especially on the Juts.

"You may need to fight for your own life before this is over, and that's all the weapon you're familiar with." Purifyre smiled unexpectedly. "But thank you just the same."

Mason pondered numbly how a smile could be so winsome coming from such a jug-eared, flat-nosed, almost chinless face. He doubted that his own smile could have been that winning in the precosmed treatment days when he had displayed those same features. He looked out to where the Oceanic was making its inevitable advance to lord it over the Juts, and for the first time he understood, *really* understood, how an Aquam could come to pray to it. "Please, spare my son," he mumbled.

CHAPTER
THREE

After more than a day of scenic corkscrewing above the arctic wastes of the western Scourlands, the Optimant Flying Pavilion *Dream Castle* was finally turning south toward Scorpia and the peninsular city of Gumption. Concealed in a dusty utility space in the inner hull, Ghost, Zinsser, and Old Spume had passed most of the time nursing the wounds they'd suffered during the skirmish with Testamentor and the rest of Purifyre's Human Enlightenment operatives. All were dead now, though their mission of wreaking havoc in Passwater had been accomplished. The Scourlands city had been thrown into turmoil by the death of the DevOceanite prophet Marrowbone, whose followers believed that the yest of the rapture was at hand, when all the faithful would find peace in the embrace of the Oceanic.

Ghost lamented that she hadn't been able to get a closer look at Passwater, but she had moved on to more pressing concerns. While it was impossible to know with any certainty just what was going on in the Laputa's wooden outerworks, she had opted to assume that the supercargo and his saffron-robed guards had not been fooled by the knotted rope Zinsser had left dangling in the stateroom's window and that the search for her, Zinsser, and Spume was still in progress. Since there would be no escaping the Laputa when it touched down in Gumption, they had no choice but to attempt to commandeer the thing while it was airborne. To that end Ghost had found what she was sure was a route into the pavilion itself, the realm of the so-called Insiders, though even that wouldn't guarantee their being able to steer the *Dream Castle* from the circuit of travel it had been following since the Cyberplagues had disabled Aquamarine's Optimant technocracy two hundred years earlier.

Access to the Insiders' domain was via a hatch Ghost had discovered at the top of a helical ladderwell that cut through the utility space. Zinsser had balked at the idea of revealing themselves to the Insiders until she had laid out to him just how limited their options had become. Spume, his quick-fix *GammaLAW* rejuvenation rapidly unraveling, was content to keep watch in the utility space.

Trailing after her now through the stairway's green gloom, Zinsser was trying hard to control his apprehension. Despite everything they had been through since Wall Water, or because of it, the things he'd seen had only made him want to study the planet more, make sense of it wet and dry, and perhaps do his bit to try to bring some sanity to it. He was, however, at least managing to wield the cocked sling-gun with what would pass for lethal purpose.

"I know you don't want to hurt anyone unnecessarily," Ghost whispered to him short of the hatch, "but we Exts have a saying that might apply: 'In the frenzy of a firefight, you'll shoot your own mother if she walks across your field of fire.' "

"That's supposed to *calm* me?" he asked her, wild-eyed.

Ghost shook her head. "It's supposed to prepare you."

Without a further word she threw the hatch and found herself bounding into a long curve of compartment that seemed to be all sky and carpeted deck, like a patchwork of farmland, pressurized at something like surface normal. Spacious and airy, it appeared to be some kind of salon or solarium. The long waters of the Amnion stretched out to a far horizon, with Eyewash's oblique rays raking a billion golden chips of light across the waves.

In Flowstate, though, she was mostly ignoring irrelevant sensory findings to lock in on three people who were pivoting their heads in nascent alarm. As they glimpsed her springing from the open hatch, the terror in them became transparent.

"Move and I'll shoot," she said clearly. The two men and a woman were tall and graceful enough to be Periapt aristocrats, sharp-featured and thin-lipped, all sharing a peculiarly long upsweep of nose and a heavy liddedness that made them look supercilious. Their skin tones were the faintest tan, and they were turned out in intricate kimonos of some gauzy stuff like silk organdy that rendered the details of their bodies quite visible. Their headgear was as elaborate as rattan sculpture, holding lacquered windings and coils of auburn hair. Barefoot, they wore gewgaws and bangles on ankles, feet, and toes.

As they looked Zinsser up and down while he charged in behind Ghost, their expressions went from fear to somewhat vexed surprise of the sort that usually had self-righteous anger bringing up the rear. The older of the females had evidently lost or rid herself of eyebrows and had replaced them with slender arcs of blue tint. Now the arcs went even higher.

"*Whhat?* Dungfeet!" She made the *whh* sound like she was trying to blow out a candle. "*Whh*at are dungfeet doing in here? Kayam, summon the Implementors! You two . . . creatures! Remove yourselves from that carpet instantly!"

Zinsser turned a glance at the blood, grime, and dust he had tromped into the thick-piled off-white shag, but Ghost kept her eyes on the Insiders. Kayam seemed to be more flustered than either of the women, but he moved to obey his elder in an uncoordinated way, hurrying off around the curve of the compartment.

Ghost fired the detonator-cap gun that had belonged to Testamentor. The shaped charge sent a warning jet of blinding, superheated gas across Kayam's path, and he fell back with a shriek, arms flung across his face but not hurt. Shrinking back, the two women squealed in anger.

"Shut up," Ghost told them without rancor. Her eyes roamed the compartment while she reloaded; then she glanced briefly at Zinsser. "Are those controls?" she asked, gesturing with her chin to an instrument array along the starboard bulkhead.

The younger woman moved to Kayam's side while the one who had given the order was suddenly casting thoughtful looks at Ghost. Rumors that Visitants had boarded the *Dream Castle* at Wall Water had obviously reached her, and she plainly recognized that the det-cap gun was no Aquam weapon. Zinsser looked around the huge, posh promenade deck or whatever it was. The place was sparsely furnished with a mixed hoard of strange sculptures, hangings, couches, and such. Following Ghost's gaze, he hastened to the starboard bulkhead, where he found an instrument console covered by a beautifully inlaid armored hood.

The younger female Insider cawed. "Stay away from that, you shit-foot vermin! Your low little groundling brain couldn't possibly, possibly . . ."

Her words trailed away as Zinsser's whatty, using the LAW hacking algorithms, conned the hood latch. The hood swung away into the bulkhead, and a heavy shielding plate moved aside to expose a large holographics tank.

Zinsser was about to bring the console on-line when a voice rasped from hidden speakers. "Beware! Beware all! We have reports that groundlings may have entered the interior. There are indications that they have somehow accessed the sealed spaces and are moving through them even now. People, arm yourselves and form security groups. Report to mustering stations for a top-to-bottom search."

The three Insiders crouched, blinking in confusion. The woman who had chewed Zinsser out began trembling uncontrollably, though he could hardly blame her. Intruders in the interior . . . Even worse, in the sealed spaces. It had to be one of the Insiders' worst nightmares, right up there with midflight fusion failure. Below lay a world of ambitious local tyrants, desperate have-nots, and bloodthirsty war bands of all persuasions, whose heart's desire would be to commandeer a Flying Pavilion. Zinsser was learning to keep other people's problems separate from his own, though. The savage behavior Ghost had displayed since boarding the *Dream Castle* was making that easier and easier.

As Zinsser worked at invading the Laputa's nav automatics, Ghost kept her weapon trained on Kayam and the others. "How many are you?" she asked the elder woman. "How many Insiders?" She raised the det-cap gun and drew a bead between the woman's eyes.

The Insider tightened her lips as if she were going to take the hit rather than answer, then burst out, "Fifty-three! Though old Fassmass is on his deathbed and Lyrah's baby isn't twelve days old, that is our present number."

The total seemed low, but Zinsser guessed that it made sense. Though the *Dream Castle* was large, its inhabitants spent virtually all their lives inside, and overcrowding would be a disaster. He surmised that Ghost was thinking she might be able to handle all fifty-three, given some kind of trump card.

"Zinsser, talk to me," Ghost said, wrinkling her mask of facial scars.

He took stock of the whatty's readouts. While talking to the sky palace's computer presented little difficulty, he had reservations about convincing the Laputa to alter course. "I'm no intrusion expert, but it looks to me like the basic operating instructions are hardwired in the power section. The Optimants must've wanted the pavilions to fly even when no one was aboard."

"Try the archeo-hacking 'wares. There has to be some leeway."

"No go. *Dream Castle* will steer clear of dangerous weather or, more precisely, from what its radars and other equipment *tell it* is dangerous. But I can't access the nav automatics."

"Can you get inside the meteorological programs?"

Zinsser cocked his head at her, impressed. "You mean steer this ship by feeding it false weather data."

Ghost nodded. The Insiders were trading horrified looks.

"Even if I can manage to override the meteorological programs, Wall Water is a helluva long way from here—"

"No." Ghost cut him off. "We're going back to Passwater. The rioting there will provide the distraction we need to make it off this thing alive. Once we've done that, we'll find some way to contact the *GammaLAW*."

"It'll mean *erasing* the existing programs," Zinsser cautioned.

"Just do it, Doctor."

Since he had already accepted the fact that they had no alternative, the issue was beyond debate. Even partial control of the Laputa would give them a card to play—Ghost's trump. He began by stripping away the meteorological feed, permitting him in effect to fool the airship into acceding to his prompts. He was confident that he could improvise convincingly false weather data but found that he didn't have to. It happened that the automatics themselves had certain basic parameters that initiated course changes, and all he needed to do was select from and position them so that they would urge the pavilion back to the Scourlands.

Ghost was apparently making up her mind whether to take the three Insiders hostage or get them out of the way—by releasing them, shooting them, or sending them over the side. Knowing Ghost, it was all one to her. But the Laputa's other inhabitants would react differently to each option, and the subtleties evidently warranted a bit of mulling. While she decided, she backed over to the promenade deck's single conventional hatch to see if she could secure it.

Zinsser felt the *Dream Castle* sway as it rotated through another turn. He shifted his weight as the Laputa came about to a new heading—back toward Passwater.

The older woman was nearly hysterical. "You don't know

what you're doing! The ships must fly their programmed routes!"

"Keep quiet!" Zinsser shouted, noticing distractedly that he was taking on Ghost's toneless edge of unaffected menace.

No sooner did he return to his reprogramming efforts, however, than a commotion broke out on the far side of the main hatch. All at once the hatch was straining against its own frame. Ghost had set a metal pedestal crosswise in the frame, and someone was plainly unhappy about its preventing the hatch from opening. Yells and pounding issued from the other side.

"What's our status?" Ghost yelled.

Zinsser held his sling-gun uneasily. "We're headed more or less straight for Passwater—at a greatly increased speed, I might add. How we'll get down once we're there remains to be seen."

"You're going nowhere," one of the women said ominously.

Zinsser knew even without looking that things had changed. As he glanced at the captives, his first thought was, Now, where did *those* come from? Standing now and looking much less victimlike, the three were holding short, double-muzzle sling-guns.

It occurred to Zinsser that the Insiders' constant fear of attack had inspired them to stash weapons all over the ship. Not that there was much point in wondering about it now or blaming Ghost for not having kept a closer guard on them.

"Lay down your arms," Kayam ordered. "And you, *Doctor*— undo whatever it is you have done or I shall cast your scar-faced companion to the Oceanic."

Zinsser knew that no matter what, he'd do anything to prevent Ghost from coming to harm and would be additionally compliant because she herself wouldn't bend a hair's breadth if it was his life on the line.

As he was contemplating just how to go about reversing course, the head of the older woman jerked around, headdress jingle bobs chiming and a dark hole appearing in her temple. Her eyes were completely unfocused as she began to collapse, her weapon falling from her fingers. At the same time there was a roaring in the compartment, coming from Old Spume, who seemed to fill the hatchway to the utility space stairwell.

Ghost reacted instantly, firing her sling-pistol even before the woman hit the carpet and nailing the second woman with a dart that entered her rib cage right above the heart. But Kayam, blocked by the falling body, had time to shoot, more by reflex than by intent, at Old Spume.

The Insider's small, close-fighting sling-gun was loaded with barbed metal darts, some of which struck Spume in the groin, others in the throat. The Sense-maker went flailing backward into the hatchway and out of sight, though Zinsser could hear him tumbling down the helical stairway as Kayam bent to grab one of the dropped guns and fire again.

He was out of range of Ghost's det-cap gun, but without thinking, Zinsser had the sling-rifle's strangely contoured stock pressed to his cheek and his finger on the trigger. The weapon's long pilehead quarrel went completely through Kayam, ricocheting from the clear material of the viewpane to rebound lazily toward the ceiling. It fell back, rotating through a leisurely half turn as Kayam jerked once, clutching his wound, and keeled over, crying, "I have been slain!"

Ignoring Zinsser, the wounded woman shrank back as Ghost came springing at her wearing a look of stony finality.

"We may need her!" Zinsser blurted. "Maybe the Insiders can't be leveraged by hostages, but we know nothing about the rest of the interior!"

Ghost pulled her knife nevertheless and grabbed a handful of the woman's rococo headdress. The Insider showed her a round-eyed look of terror but didn't move. Before Zinsser could loose more than a strangled cry, Ghost stroked deftly with the blade and cut the woman's throat, cataracting blood. The woman fell back, gurgling and convulsing.

Ghost neatly avoided it all, wiping the bright red blade on the white carpet. Then she turned, with a contemplative look, to the compartment hatch, which was still receiving quite a pounding.

Zinsser found enough of his voice to whisper, "You—*animal!*"

For once Ghost's face betrayed some sign of reaction through the symbols she had incised into her flesh: a fleeting look that mixed vague disappointment with a trace of impatience. Then, with a single kick, she knocked the dead woman's hand open. A tiny, expensive wound-spring dart gun rolled across the carpet.

Ghost glanced at Zinsser, but he was unswerving. "I was out of range, and you weren't in her line of fire," he rasped. "You could have knocked her cold with the pommel of your knife."

Ghost gave the barest shrug, picked up one of the two-muzzled sling-guns, and moved quickly to the hatch.

The butchered woman's body had stopped moving. Zinsser stared down at it, feeling hollowed out. Something went out of him, and he knew it was whatever fascination Ghost had held for him for the better part of a baseline-year. He couldn't think of her as human any longer, couldn't think of her as his unobtainable object of desire—

He was still staring down when he became aware of a rising sound and an increased buffeting of the *Dream Castle*. Like a sleepwalker, he crossed to the wide arc of viewpane, skirting a pool of blood that had drained from the younger woman. Streamers of cloud ripped along, making the *Dream Castle* dance an ominous jig. Vibration was walking loose items along horizontal surfaces in the compartment, and fixtures were swinging about.

Scatters of rain shotgunned against the viewpane by violent air wiped away much of Zinsser's numbness in a flush of stark fear. A moaning sound was rising—as if from everywhere—through the structure of the *Dream Castle* itself. It was in a deeper register than it had been when he had heard it previously—long ago during a Periapt arctic trip—but there was no mistaking the howl of a beast hungrier than any living organism. The sky was quickly blackening to a pall, and as Zinsser gazed out, he was sent reeling against the viewpane by a demonic gust. The blood-sodden body of the woman Insider was hurled brutally against the pane, then fell to the floor, leaving a bloody Rorschach on the clear stuff.

Ghost, too, had been sent headlong. It gave Zinsser a curious satisfaction to see her knocked off her feet even though she was unfazed. "They're gone," she yelled with a toss of her head to indicate whoever had been assaulting the hatch. "What have we flown into—a squall?"

Zinsser had an insane impulse to laugh. "Williwaw," he told her, and just when he'd disarmed the automatics of all real meteorological input so that he could con the pavilion.

CHAPTER
FOUR

Crouched in the stern of *Racknuts*, Souljourner was rubbing her thumb across the drawstringed neck pouch that was her grandfather's soft-tanned scrotum and whispering to the Optimant dice in her palm. Burning watched her from the helm as the muscle car rattled south along the Zapzag Thruway, closing on Gapshot and the Styx Strait bridge. Every so often he would crane his head to the sky, hoping to see aircav helos vectoring in on him. There had been no sign of LAW forces since his brief meteor-burst contact with the *GammaLAW* two days earlier, and he had had no success in reestablishing contact with the ship's Adaptive Retrodirective Antenna Array. To make matters worse, *Racknuts* would have been in Gapshot already if a treadle shaft had not required a day and a half to repair. Burning suspected that Manna had had her boys, Spin and Yake, malinger on purpose in the hope that he would lose patience and switch to another car.

The route from Hunchburrow Hill had been a kaleidoscopic gallery of disparate slices of Scorpian life, often freakishly contrasting thumbnail scenes from subcultures insulated from one another for generations and only recently nudged toward reintegration by the effects of the hugely profitable muscle-car trade. Burning had been too consumed with worry about Ghost and the *GammaLAW* to play ethnographer, but he supposed whole university departments would have held round-robin elimination duels for the chance to experience what he had.

Just beyond Hunchburrow he had watched the ritual exposure of an Anathemite newborn on a hillside. At another stop women from an outlying hamlet had walked among male wayfarers in head-concealing basket hats and meter-high stilt shoes, their bodies and genitals exposed for inspection and use. Because the men of their own hamlet were afflicted with an infertility problem, the village elders had sanctioned a desperate exogenous campaign to keep the community from dying out. The Aquam were deeply superstitious about reproduction-related bad juju, however, and the women hadn't attracted many volunteers.

In the deep-rock tunnel the Optimants had driven at Gasser's Bore, Burning observed the remnants of the once-powerful tribe that had established a curious, largely subsurface culture in the planetwide breakdown after the Cyberplagues. The Gassers had used control of the sole convenient passageway through their mountains—along with a gritty militancy—to create and maintain a hardscrabble little independent domain. Unfortunately, they hadn't been able to resist the temptation to milk the muscle-car trade with absurdly overblown tolls, and in the end a coalition force with stakes in the car-trade profit had seized control of the tunnel and broken the Gassers' power for good. Now their dwindling descendants huddled in the shadows of their onetime redoubt, rattling alms bowls and staying as drunk as possible.

There and elsewhere Burning and Souljourner drew enough cold predatory looks from wayfarers and other members of the autobahn food chain to convince them to invest another of Burning's precious cuff buttons in upgrading their means of self-defense. Souljourner, who had learned how to handle a sling-gun at the retired Descriers' cloister at Pyx, had gotten herself a serviceable old carbine-format weapon whose galvani stone, elastic slings, and thews Burning judged to be in passable shape.

The problem with his own 'baller was that few Aquam recognized it as a lethal weapon, which robbed it of its deterrent power. With little confidence in his swordsmanship or ability with a sling-gun—and with an eye toward economy—Burning had settled for a stout quarterstaff of ax-breaker wood capped at either end with iron ferrules, plus he still had his big Ext-issue ka-bar, and Souljourner her wide, short potmetal knife.

Just then Boner was at the car's schoonerlike wheel, while Spin and Yake maintained an almost sleepily confident vigil at the grabs levers. Amidships, Manna was obsessively check-ing over her jugs of Analeptic Fix, calculating and recalcu-lating the heady profit she hoped to turn at the Gapshot parking mounds. Her announced intention was to canvas the most powerful trading and carwright companies on both sides of the bridge in search of development capital and distribution deals —with Manna retaining sole knowledge of her fix's se-cret formula, of course.

She had been no less sulfurous and perhaps even more para-noid in the wake of Burning's ploy to keep her in line with the threatened compromise of the muscle-car-juice formula. But she and her family crew still struck him as markedly more re-laxed since their rickety old six-wheeler had crossed the fron-tier into southwestern Scorpia. Their home village, RakeOff Crimp, was only a few leagues away to the east, along the coast autobahn. Significantly, the village stood only a short distance over some blighted hills from Alabaster, the walled and storied utopia for which Souljourner had a Writ that appointed her to serve as the city's new Descrier— its seismic diviner.

Watching her with the dice—the so-called Holy Rollers—Burning knew what she was thinking: Alabaster would offer them safe haven from the praetorians who had been sent south in pursuit of the muscle car Purifyre had ridden to the Trans-Bourne; along with his captive, Ghost, whom Burning was cer-tain he had glimpsed on Wall Water's dam crest road.

As much as he wanted to get a glimpse of the Styx Strait bridge, he decided to confront Souljourner instead and nip in the bud any hopes she might be nursing of abandoning the quest for Ghost in favor of the alleged sanctuary to be found in Alabaster. She was preparing to cast the Holy Rollers as he made his way aft to her, prickled by the certainty of the cleromancy she was seeking, and more, pained at the thought of what he was going to have to do to negate it.

After all, she could not have been a more cooperative and helpful traveling companion, often in adversities that had taxed Burning's self-control to the limit. Her attempts at flirtation had presented an unexpected challenge, but thus far he had managed to keep her at arm's length. Now, however, after days spent in close company and so near to Alabaster, she seemed to be drawn against her will to the wish that events could be brought more in line with the romantic fantasies she had evidently subsisted on at Pyx.

"My cousin Lod says, 'Death and the dice level all distinctions,' " Burning remarked as he squatted alongside her. "Besides, I thought the Holy Rollers had already answered your questions."

Souljourner opened her eyes, her thumb pausing in the invocational thumbing of the pouch. "I need to know why the Wyrds would have brought us here, so far south, Redtails, if not for transcendental purposes related to the destiny I've so long wished to fulfill."

He drew a weary breath. "The Wyrds didn't bring us here; *Racknuts* did. And only because I paid Manna to make that so."

She gave him one of her open, undeterred smiles. Whatever else she'd learned at Pyx, she had acquired a stubborn brand of confidence in her own opinions. "Worldly details are only the apparel the Wyrds don to effect their overriding purposes."

"I'd be more interested in hearing the Wyrds' view on the best method for locating Ghost."

Eyelids lowered in concentration, Souljourner continued to rub the pouch. Burning forced himself to ignore the guileless sexuality of her strong young body. With her big-jawed grin

and single white-blond curvilinear eyebrow, she sometimes
put him in mind of a novitiate who'd happened across the
Kama Sutra and was feeling a gleeful urge to experiment. On
Concordance, at Bastion Orman, where he had grown up, she
would scarcely be old enough for her first formal presentation.
And if he brought her aboard the *GammaLAW* as his away lay,
the sniggering among his fellow Exts would be merciless.

"The Wyrds have their own inexplicable way of making
things come to pass, Redtails," she announced while still marshaling her magic.

"Meaning what?"

She began to rub the dice between her close-cupped palms,
bobbing her head and rocking in time. "As my companion,
Alabaster would accord you respect and full hospitality—as it
would your sister and any other Visitants who might be with
her. We would have a good respite from our travails."

He couldn't much blame her for trying. A cloistered nube
who had been accorded little respect and attention, she was
suddenly afforded the chance to play queen bee as opposed to
having an uncertain future aboard a stranded vessel that might
well become a lightning rod for Aquam resentment . . . It was
Souljourner's bad luck that she had been passed off to Burning
at Rhodes's Grand Attendance. He forced down a spasm of
guilt at the need to thwart her longings and tightened his grip
around the touchcard that controlled the dice she didn't realize
were rigged.

Racknuts had slowed enough in the thick traffic converging
on Gapshot for Souljourner's cast. As she threw the Holy
Rollers, Burning keyed the ultrasonic device by feel. Having
studied the various dictates coded to each combination, he
tapped out his selected outcome: red die, four; white, six.
Kneeling over them, Souljourner froze in arrant dismay while
he turned his eyes to the Zapzag, to Gapshot—anywhere but
her gaze.

The combination was called "closing the arc." For the sake

of harmony—the presage ran—and in honoring and yielding to the ineluctable shapings of the Wyrds, which gave the Holy Rollers their power, current charges and duties had to be seen through without diversion or delay.

Souljourner thawed with a sigh he could hear over the squealing of *Racknuts*'s axles and the slow tattoo of the treadles. Burning could tell that she wanted a retoss, but that simply wasn't done. Ignoring the Wyrds' given portent, trying to impose one's own will on the dice that way, invited the loss of all divinatory power.

"Bad news?" he asked, slipping the control chip back into his tunic pocket.

She tossed her dirty-blond forelock in an Aquam shrug. "We hew to our present course of action," she said somewhat haltingly, "to succor Ghost and return to the ship. And it promises to all come good."

"*Great* news, then. Thanks."

Refusing to allow her morale to flag, she covered her disappointment with a broad smile, the sight of which made him feel unspeakably low.

"Clear the way, you cod-banging suckfannies!" Manna yelled suddenly, shaking her fist at snarled traffic on the roadway leading to the Gapshot barbican. "Get moving or get out of a lady's way, you purulent sacs of festered gall!"

Burning could second the sentiment if not the gratuitous abuse. Having gained the lead, Purifyre's car—*Shattertail*—was certainly already in the Trans-Bourne. But aside from venting her frustration, Manna's bellowing did little to improve their circumstances. Not only had the traffic stopped moving, but as they watched, the Gapshot gates began to swing shut, pressing back muscle cars and barrows, people, palanquins, and livestock, threatening to nip in half those who didn't move smartly.

Something was happening at the ramparts, as well. A pair of heavy chains was being lowered via sets of mollywood shear legs that had been moved into what appeared to be their accustomed positions. From each one hung a lifeless human body. An execution, Burning assumed, until he noticed that both men wore identical pieces of armor—gleaming black *cuir bolli* shaped to imitate body musculature. Even before the chains stopped paying out, flying things—obviously conditioned to find carrion there—veered in hungrily from the strait.

Word was rippling back from the gates through the closely packed crowds. "Trouble on the bridge," an ample-figured midwife in a sedan chair relayed to Manna. "A conflict between the Gapshot Legion and the Trans-Bourne Bridge Constabulary over which of them controls the span."

The uproar in the lake of humanity was like grievance night at the Tower of Babel. Burning jumped onto the aft rail, looking for ways in which *Racknuts* might extricate itself from the jam and proceed to some other crossing point—assuming that such crossings even existed. But what he spotted a short way back along the Zapzag made him forget his preoccupation with the Styx.

From the rails of two muscle cars—an eight-wheeler and a ten—mixed groups of Ean praetorians were gesticulating at *Racknuts* and at Burning, their hue and cry pealing forth from brayophaunt, bellows-bugle, and the pounding of tympanossos.

CHAPTER
FIVE

It was a clear, warm evening. Eyewash had set behind stupendous horizontal brushstrokes of gold, royal purple, dense gray, and greenish black. Lake Ea was eerily calm, and the screeches of the skipflats and jack-gliders sounded less grating and more disconsolate in the dusk—that was appropriate somehow. As fine an evening as any sailor could ask, Quant thought. Gazing out from a belowdecks bay, he felt a moment's poignancy that he wasn't going to be able to spare even a moment to admire it.

Along with causing a host of major and minor problems in the *GammaLAW*'s engineering spaces, the flood surge had damaged the engine-cooling systems and bent the actuator shafts. Engineering wanted time for repairs and replacements— at least a day—but Quant could give the pit snipes only unskilled helpers and an ironclad deadline. By midnight at the latest he meant to try his luck on the river that drained Ea. The lake's water level was continuing to drop, but he felt that darkness would at least provide the ship with cover. He had moved her into deeper water, hoping that whatever Aquam might be massing on the shore would think that he intended to anchor there.

In short order engine power was restored—without promises as to how long it would endure—but Quant didn't allow himself to dwell on eventualities, not with Turret *Musashi* occupying nearly all his attention. He would have preferred to leave the twin naval rifles belowdecks, but recently acquired intel data about the fortress at Fluter Delve had firmed his resolve to elevator the turret to its barbette come hell or high water. Popular accounts had it that Dynast Piety IV's siege engines were capable of hurling stone missiles clear to the low cliffs that rose from the far shore of the river.

The *GammaLAW* wasn't some warship belted with thick armor plate, and the chances of her surviving a bombardment of boulders were slight. Quant had considered employing the catapult sleds, as he had against Rhodes's steam cannon, but the cats' accuracy would be negligible and, more important, the river wasn't broad enough to permit bringing the ship bows-on to the fortress for a shot. It was Turret *Musashi* or nothing.

Looking up at the mutha-guns now, he had to keep reminding himself of that. Even with the heavy equipment that had been blown to dust with the *Terrible Swift Sword*, raising the turret and setting it into its barbette loomed as a daunting challenge.

"How's the deck look, Eddie?" he asked.

Lieutenant Gairaszhek, who had more engineering experience than anyone aboard, was glowering at the turret as if it had done something personal and insulting to him. "We're adding more bracing to the port torsion box overheads, Captain. We've already used every jack, lift, and worm gear we could locate. I've got people shoring the decks with I-beam sections cut from the replacements and snugged in with wedges." He shook his head resignedly. "Christ, sir! Hand-hammered *wedges*!"

Quant didn't much believe in pats on the back, but he tried to make his voice sound like one. "It's all right, Lieutenant. Never been on a cruise yet that didn't involve a little improvisation."

He wasn't at all as blithe as he sounded, and he supposed Gairaszhek knew it. He had walked among the forest of makeshift supports—jacks and beams smelling of oil and acrid metal—and he had experienced firsthand the heat, spatter, and aroma of welding torches as load-bearing frames were reinforced with hastily cut plate and braces.

GammaLAW's flight and hangar decks had been designed to handle hundred-ton aircraft in flight operations that included landings that amounted to controlled crashes, but the turret weighed in at five times the SWATHship's rated safety limits. Even though the load was to be spread out across the broad treads of its carrier beams, Quant understood that he was taking a terrible gamble.

The elevator was rated for something over half the turret's mass, but no one knew how much it could lift in a pinch. It was being reinforced, as well, and rigged with auxiliary hoists, lifts, and servos. As for installation into the barbette, no one expected a perfect fit or even a good one. It would suffice to lower the gun onto its tracks so that it could be traversed. Quant didn't need to be able to shoot a sniper round up a bug's ass; all he wanted was the capability of lobbing a couple of heavy shells at the fortress—*if* it began firing on his ship. All he wanted out of the whole sorry privyload of adversity, in fact, was the thirty seconds or so that it would take the *GammaLAW* to feel her way past the river's choke point.

It was enough to make a sailor pray to the Oceanic.

Unexpectedly, one of the special detail people bumped him from behind. Quant turned and saw that it was Kurt Elide, evidently recovered from injuries sustained when the Nixie attack had blown the CIWS gatling all to hell, straining—along with a half dozen others—under the weight of an I-beam section. Quant stepped aside, wondering if Elide blamed him for the debacle the mission had become. But Elide was old enough to know what he was doing—years older than Quant had been when he'd first gone to sea. In any case, there wasn't time to feel sorry for anyone, and even if there had been, Elide would have been low on the list.

* * *

Dextra accepted the fact that the Commissioner's Coordinating Center wasn't the eye of the storm any longer. It was as if the dam burst had thrown the *GammaLAW* back in time—in naval history, at any rate—and the bridge was now the center of things. Determined nonetheless to assess the ship's situation in person, she had set out from the CCC after summoning Tonii to accompany her.

Tonii had been initially resistant, insisting 'e was needed elsewhere, and Dextra had come close to yielding the point. There was something both surprising and moving about Tonii's dedication to 'ers shipmates and determination to help. For once in the gynander's life, 'e felt needed and at least somewhat accepted. Even so, Dextra wasn't about to go wandering around the *GammaLAW* on her own, not with so much uncertainty in the air, and Lod—having had his authority formally noted and announced—was off organizing the Exts. Something new and distant in Lod's manner told Dextra that she'd lost a canny aide for good, but better Lod in command than Zone, who, despite his skills, she would sooner see dead.

Dextra and Tonii's first stop was the aircraft elevator that had everybody chewing his nails. Just then it was being reinforced with odd-looking contraptions tinkered up by Piper and the Aggregate, a few of whom were also assisting with the installation. They had apparently cannibalized stuff from all over the ship, producing sleeves for the hydraulics, augments for the servos, and clever reinforcing pieces for mounts and fastenings. Some of the tools and machines they were using were familiar to Dextra, but many weren't, and she suspected the Aggregate had built them.

Piper herself was directing operations with an understated air of command. Somewhere during the subjective months of the voyage out from Periapt the pale young woman had reconciled herself to her role as leader—nexus—of her extended organism and had assumed a subtle assuredness any good officer would have admired. Orchestrating the work, she uttered commands in the clicking, glottal-stopping, shorthand-word language the Aggregate used, but only when she couldn't rely on the peculiar spasms of gesture and tics of facial expression the group mind knew as Othertalk.

As she drew closer to their work site, Dextra inhaled the aromas the constituents gave off to augment communication. The smells weren't unpleasant, merely strange and vaguely evocative. Close behind Piper, like a faithful dog, stood the Manipulant Scowl-Jowl, sole survivor of the personal guard AlphaLAW Commissioner Starkweather had taken to Wall Water. When Piper reached out to reposition a heavy I beam, Scowl-Jowl was there in a second, shouldering her aside gently and lifting the iron into place. Piper made Aggregate-style hand signals and click glottals, and Scowl-Jowl wrestled the ponderous beam over, arranging it as she directed.

That the creature understood Piper's orders came as no surprise. The Manipulants had been developed by the same man who had created the gynanders and forged the Aggregate—Byron Sarz, whom Piper herself had had a hand in killing before the GammaLAW mission had even come into being.

Dextra went to Piper, speaking low for confidentiality. "I want your opinion of Quant's plan to move the gun turret. Will it work?"

Piper didn't show any wonder that Dextra would come to her with the question—not that it was easy for an outsider to tell what an Aggregate member was thinking. In the wake of the catastrophes that had commenced with the destruction of the *Sword*, the Aggregate had become the most versatile and technically capable organizational entity in the entire mission TO&E. Under Piper, the constituents had turned themselves to each new crisis with protean genius, displaying what amounted to a hive mentality. Recalling, though, that she'd brought them along to help in communicating with the Oceanic, Dextra couldn't help but wonder how mission priorities had gone so far afield in so short a time.

Thinking over Dextra's question, Piper fluttered a gesture at a spray unit, and Scowl-Jowl obediently began muscling it over to where it was to be hooked up to a jury-rigged power coupling. The Aggregate was going to reinforce some of the critical structural members by pressure-coating them with an exotic carbon-vapor deposition composite.

"Madame Haven, if I could run a hundred-gigaflop computation with an illegal, I might be able to apprise you of the likelihood of success within a few decimals. But—" Piper glanced at the elevator, then across the hangar deck to where improvised roadbed sections were being laid down near the gun turret, "—it is impossible to tell for certain." She seemed to hedge for a moment, debating, then added, "I would say that the telling factor will be the people involved."

With that, she gestured in a way that took in herself, the constituents, and Scowl-Jowl, as well as the rest of the workers. Dextra wondered what Quant, among others, would think of Piper's notion of people.

"There's nothing new there, hon," she started to say, when a furor erupted from over by the turret. As she peered down the long and now poorly lighted hangar deck, Dextra's face fell.

Zone, of course.

Zone relished the feel of the ship now that she was in peril, battered, and at bay. The air people exhaled in times of crisis had a kind of charge other atmospheres lacked, and he took fierce delight in drawing it into himself. *This* was being alive, he told himself.

Zone had nothing but contempt for people enslaved to sex kinks or the rush of drugs. He maintained the most extravagant habit of all, and there was his fix, on the *GammaLAW*'s decks. People who were dazed, wounded, shambling hollow-eyed zombies from lack of sleep were preparing in a frenzy to fight for their lives.

An Ext sick-bay case with her right arm in a pneumocast was laboring in tandem with some humanities entitlement art-education dipshit to haul over the hitch from a tow motor. Three REMF CIC officers were working like coolies under the tread of the big, squat flatbed transporter on which Turret *Musashi* rested, monitoring deck stress while they crept along beneath the moving undercarriage. A detail from planetologi-cal studies, most of them with injuries of one kind or another, were dismantling sounding charges for use in the massive 240-mm shells—and they were doing it with hand tools be-cause the explosive ordnance disposal equipment had bought the farm with *Terrible Swift Sword*. A man with his face streaming sweat was delicately hacksawing through the shell casing, while a woman poured teakettle water on the cut point to keep sparks from blowing the whole ship clear back to Periapt.

Relieved of duty, Zone reveled in the focused grimness the ship's company brought to the work. By and large, and no matter what they thought, they were doing *his* work: preparing the ship for the float downriver to New Alexandria and the Op-timant lighthouse there that housed an AI, or perhaps merely a program, known as Endgame, which was thought to be a cure for the Cyberplagues that had put the fear of machines in hu-mankind for two centuries now. All the scheming of the past few days—the concealment of Burning's ARAA message from the Scorpian hinterlands, the murders of Wix Uniday and Daddy D Delecado, the blowing of the dam—had been geared toward getting the *GammaLAW* downriver, for the person who found and controlled Endgame would have not only Aquama-rine but dozens of human-colonized worlds in his pocket. Zone was determined to be that person, and no one was about to re-lieve him of *that* duty.

Shouldering his way through the press of people working on

the turret, Zone, backed by the members of his several and other allies, deliberately collided with the humanities entitlement civie, whose name tag read FORTUNA. "Forget the tow-motor hitch and get in under the elevator hoist. Sound off if you see any structural deformation."

Fortuna and the woman working with him stared blankly at Zone. Fortuna swallowed hard, then said, "But I heard—"

Zone cut him off, raising the tonfa club he was carrying. "Forget what you heard, you little spirochete,"

Fortuna scuttled back from the tonfa but somehow avoided being herded under the turret. Zone figured correctly that the civie had a phobia about cramped places and pressed his attack. Something in Fortuna snapped, however, and he tried to fight his way past Zone. Zone could read in the man's eyes that a brutal clubbing was preferable to being forced under the turret and flattened to a bloody stain, but Fortuna was like a blind puppy attacking a mastiff. Zone knocked him down and was about to crack his elbow with the tonfa when someone blocked his way, holding up a mechanic's creeper to ward off a blow from the club. Zone reared furiously, surprised that anyone would intervene.

It was one of Haven's errand boys, Kurt Elide.

"Colonel, stop!" Elide was saying. "I volunteer. I'll go under the turret."

Zone's trained his NoMan stare on Elide, then laughed. "What the fuck?"

"I'll do it, Colonel." Elide glanced at Fortuna. "He's got this thing about cramped places, you know."

Zone's smile turned to a sneer. He was bringing up the tonfa for a strike at Elide's skull when a roar and the squeal of treads made him step back.

Rocking from its sudden stop was what looked like the remains of a tank. But Zone recognized it as the lower hull of one of the incredibly tough full-track hauler units with its turret removed. Perched lazily near the driver's hatch was Lod.

"Some motivational training for the troops, Colonel? Perhaps you'll allow me to suggest a less strenuous method."

Zone gave the little major a death's-head leer. "You just don't get it, do you? I'll say this only once: go play dress-up in front of a mirror or find some bitch to hold hands with. But *you* don't give *me* orders."

Lod slid down the prow of the truncated robot hauler. "Here's one I'll give, Zone. Put the club down and hand over your sidearm. I'm placing you under arrest, pending trial for murder."

CHAPTER
SIX

On the rapidly diminishing beach below Forge Town, Purifyre and Ballyhoot's half dozen escorts gathered around. All those whom Boon had been able to round up were both loyal members of his organization and experienced Jut-hoppers. They wore tropical guttersnipe outfits, as did Purifyre and Ballyhoot, but other than that they were a very mixed catch. Four of them, Mason thought, were almost certainly Anathemites.

One—a hopper from the prebridge days—was a spidery woman whose face was a sagging network of creases and whose limbs stuck out from her rags like flagstaffs wrapped in burned and holed battle pennons. Her very bones seemed flexible. The young man with her, a moonfaced, immensely muscled puncheon cask of a fellow, was her son—something of a jolt, given their physical dissimilarities. The other two were twins, a postpubescent boy and girl, almost elfish in scarecrow-castoff clothes. More gracile than graceful, they were perhaps fourteen baseline-years, with angelic faces, blue-white eyes, and full cupid's-bow lips. Their platinum hair floated weightless and fine where it escaped clublike queues.

For appearances' sake all the hoppers wore lightly packed haversacks and slingbags. None appeared to favor walking staffs, crampons, or climbing claws. Mason would have wished for a hundred fighters, but speed counted for everything, and a large body of Jut-virgin soldiery would not only have hindered Purifyre but attracted the attention of lookouts on the bridge and the Gapshot shore.

"Let everyone understand," Mason's son was telling his companions, "once we've started, there'll be no turning back."

Mason followed Purifyre's sweeping gesture and saw the truth of his statement. The lowest stretch lay off the sandy shore below the Forge Town headland. It was a fairly safe, fast, level run—what the hoppers called the Trapdoor, especially in reference to northbound hops. The macabre joke was that as the tide raced in, the low leg would be the first to be engulfed by the Amnion. If Purifyre's band ran into trouble farther along, there would be no turning back because the Trapdoor would be under water. Gapshot or ghastly death; no third option existed. But no one, in any case, gave voice to reservations.

To better his grip, Purifyre began dusting his hands with granulated resin taken from one of several pouches of the stuff the group carried. "Then it's Gapshot for us. Point walkers first."

Before Mason could settle on something to say, the twins had set out for the Trapdoor. Offering last-minute advice, Ballyhoot had one arm draped around Purifyre's shoulders. Without his noticing, she paused to throw a malicious glance at Mason, as if to say: See? He belongs to me, not to you.

Mason wanted to follow, but waves were already licking the base of the Trapdoor, and he found himself backing away for higher ground. Surging, pounding water echoed off the headland and the distant Gapshot promontory, sending salt spray in his direction. Although the Oceanic never resided in its own mists, the mere smell and feel of the stuff was enough to unnerve him.

Purifyre's band began double-timing across the sand. Behind the twins went the spidery woman, Purifyre, Ballyhoot, and the woman's dwarf-Samson son. The two constables took the rear guard, intending to move up later as flankers. Mason noticed contrasts in their styles, from the spider woman's rubbery sureness to Purifyre's power and precision, from the twins' simian dexterity to the constables' deliberateness. Farther along the shingle three other last-minute entrants in the race for life and riches gazed at the Juts, packs sagging from their shoulders, then reconsidered and turned back for Forge Town. The better part of valor, Mason thought.

The blirt was moving in, windy and wet. Somewhere out around the Forge Town headland, lightning broke over the Amnion and rain began to fall.

Mason knew that the first feature waiting for Purifyre was Styx's Teeth, a close grouping of misshapen geological projections resembling canines, tusks, fangs, and incisors, all canting up at various angles. Still backing away from the incoming tide, he watched until his son was out of sight among the teeth; then he, too, turned to run. A hoped-for last glimpse of Purifyre, however, caused him to look over his shoulder in time to see the two constables die.

Figures plying short spears and hack knives had sprung up from crevices in the Juts, though the constables had been shot from ambush by sling-guns or crossbows. Picaroons, Mason told himself—highwayman predators of the Juts. Perhaps this was a new generation drawn by the sudden upsurge in potential quarry. Splotches of blood brightened the drab green-gray of the rocks as well as the pale threadbare rags the constables wore.

As the picaroons were ridding their victims of backpacks, Mason leveled the 'chettergun and fired a burst, as much to sound a warning as in any hope of hitting his faraway targets. But the high belching of the gun was swallowed by the crashing sea and the gusting blirt, and the flechettes spread like bird shot, registering as puffs of rock and dust leeward of the Juts. Two of the picaroons jerked and spasmed, but neither went down, and the rest were untouched.

The few people still on the strand were staring at Mason,

confused by the nature of the gunfire. He glanced at the ammo indicator to find that he had expended seventy of the cassette's hundred rounds in one sustained squeeze of the trigger. And the picaroons were already vanishing among Styx's Teeth, heading north, the way Purifyre had gone. Mason grasped the fact that he had inadvertently driven them after his unsuspecting son.

In minutes the waves would be breaking over the Trapdoor stretch. He let go of his fright and anguish, looked up into a sudden peppering of droplets, and charged down the beach and out onto the Juts. Lightning struck again, and the blirt hit in earnest. Chop rose as if preparing to kick the Juts apart.

Mason railed silently at the caprice of nature that had made the Juts a long, meandering roundabout loop somewhat resembling an ohm symbol. If the collapsed arch of primeval stone simply stretched straight across the Styx Strait—directly under the suspension bridge—the run would have been so much shorter, faster, easier, safer.

With flechette pistol reholstered, his arms were free for balance and grappling with the rock. Despite what he knew of Aquamarine, Mason wasn't surprised to discover that the rocks supported neither lichen nor algeol and were merely wet from spray and storm. The Oceanic wouldn't tolerate intertidal lifeforms any more than it would suffer land creatures to enter the Amnion. Twice-daily immersions stripped the stone jumble of surface organic matter with a molecular thoroughness. The Juts were pitted and seamed but bare aside from traces of salt deposit being washed away by rain.

Before he fully accepted what he was doing, Mason had lurched and hiphopped a third of the way across the Trapdoor. The initial stretch was already under water. There were no trail signs to guide him, since the Oceanic tended to eradicate any the Jut-hoppers hadn't removed to thwart possible competitors. It seemed to him that he could hear every shift and grind of stone against stone, every crack and strike as water boomed and gurgled through openings already submerged by the tide. He forced himself not to glance at the sea. If any manifestations were taking shape there, he didn't want to know. A few meters more to his right, north by northwest, came a breaking wave that flung foam high. It was probable but not guaranteed that the foam wouldn't harm him, but if one of those waves caught even a part of him, he'd be finished. He wasn't Boon, after all. If the Oceanic had the ability to sense fear, it would certainly sense his.

Suppose the Oceanic didn't simply kill him outright by sundering him into constituent molecules. Suppose it pulled him, intact and alive and still aware, down to the bottom of twenty kilometers of pitchdark water and kept him there, alone and alive forever. Better, infinitely, to be obliterated.

He had footed carefully up a long, slightly tilted granitic oval and was about to jump to a couch-size boulder beneath it when the sole of his rope sandal slipped on a combination of the wet surface and the beach sand and street crud it had accumulated ashore. His voice broke shrilly, even though the fall only unbalanced him a meter or so in the direction of the edge. Still, the shock of the misstep sent an almost painful adrenaline heat flash through him, and in its wake Yatt's Buddha face genied up before his mind's eye.

"Come to your senses, Mason! Turn back; this is suicide."

Months earlier, on Periapt, in exchange for Yatt's promise to return Mason to Aquamarine, Mason had allowed the counterforce AI to download some of itself into his neurowares. Only recently he had learned that the cybervoice of the so-called Quantum College had also been in communication with Eisley Boon, apprising him of the GammaLAW mission, as well as providing details on the *GammaLAW* itself, which Boon planned to use in dispensing his synome antagonist into the Amnion.

The mere fact that Yatt was trying to appeal to Mason's sanity spoke volumes, reinforcing the fact that the AI had no real power to seize control of his actions and could issue no threat that would outweigh his concern for Purifyre.

"The tide is rising rapidly! Retreat before the Trapdoor is closed to us. Your son is more than able to protect himself. He is experienced in this, where you aren't."

Mason didn't waste energy on a spoken reply or a silent debate. He simply pictured Purifyre cut down by the picaroons as the rearguard constables had been. Even so, Yatt was in a position to know emphatically when he was being overruled.

"Enough, Mason! Concentrate on what you're doing before you break your neck. You are our vehicle, after all." The moonfaced *uberpresence* faded from his mind to avoid distracting him. *"Onward—quick, now. The sea is nearly upon us!"*

"Those who can't do, coach," Mason muttered aloud as he resumed his climb.

Another forty-five seconds of bounding and kick stepping put him up into Styx's Teeth, hearing the flush and gutter of waves churning in crevices deep below. There was no sign of the picaroons or the constables' bodies, however. Mason waffled between unholstering the flechette pistol against a possible ambush and keeping both hands free. From the teeth on, the scrambling would be challenging.

"They have fled," Yatt's phantom voice advised. *"You are more likely to fall than be attacked here. And should you fall, you will lose the gun and perhaps end up as raw molecules in the Amnion. It is crucial, therefore, that you not fall."*

Mason resented the kibitzing, but it made sense. He worked his way up a cleft in the teeth. The plutonic rock was worn by eons of watery erosion but still had its seasonal cracks and breakages, making for edges and coarseness that punished his soft hands. His rope-soled sandals only complicated the scrambling, so he paused halfway up to fumble them off and tuck them into the back of his stomacher.

At the top he scouted the way forward but couldn't see anyone—all too understandable, given the rocky helter-skelter of the features, familiarly named by the hoppers and other Styx inhabitants the Overpot, the Highgable, the Three Cuckolds. Some formations, for whatever enigmatic reasons, the Oceanic had seen fit to reshape from disarrangements left in the wake of its last shuffling of the Juts: the Volutes, the Hypercurve, and the Arabesques.

Mason called to Purifyre but got no response. Peering back the way he'd come, he let out a strangled sound. An abrupt jump in the sea's reach had sent waves breaking over the Trapdoor stretch.

It was a storm surge, he realized, his rib cage suddenly feeling too tight for his chest. The blirt was crowding noyade tidewater up the strait.

He couldn't for the life of him recall details of Styx tides and weather, but he was certain that the Juts could be submerged in minutes—seconds, according to some old-timers. In either case Purifyre didn't have as much time as he had counted on, and neither did Mason.

"Ogling it won't do you any good," Yatt chided him.

Mason hauled himself through the cleft, slipping and banging his shins, scraping skin off his fingers and toes, and barely feeling any of it. If Purifyre and his hardened band had ratcheted their pace, he might never overtake them. For the moment, the rain had slackened to a thin drizzle, but night was coming on.

Belly-crawling up over the top of the Overpot, he was seized by the front of his camise. His wrists grappled, someone pounced hard on his back, and then his head was held fast and a dagger point was pressed into the skin under his right eyeball.

"Witless arse-berry!" Ballyhoot eased her knife point back a hair's breadth. "A shank through the eye would've served you right! What're you doing here?" Holding a handful of Mason's hair, she shook his head angrily, bumping his chin on the rock. "Let him up," Purifyre said from behind her. To Mason he added, "What's happened to my rear guard?"

Ballyhoot dragged Mason down off the Overpot rough-handedly with slightly more charitable assistance from the spidery woman and her bulked-up son. The other two near-Anathemites—the elfish twins—were watching from perches among the higher monoliths a little way ahead. Rubbing the bump on his chin, Mason explained what he'd seen from the beach. It was obvious that the picaroons hadn't overtaken Purifyre, after all.

Replacing her dagger in one of the forearm sheaths attached to her knife fighter's vambraces, Ballyhoot studied the surrounding rocks. "Maybe they clawed their way up over the Lean-to or squeezed around the outside of the Three Cuckolds to get around us when we doubled back."

Lacking a better theory, Purifyre tossed his forelock in what equated to a shrug. "They'll tell us when we hunt them down ashore and run hot wires up their cock slits. Let's therefore *get* ashore before the One Who Watches has too close a look at us."

Without a glance at the Amnion, Purifyre moved out, with everyone following, including Mason—accelerated by a shove from Ballyhoot. He was too relieved to find his son unharmed to give the shove much thought. A short distance along, the order of march was adjusted, with the twins taking the point and the long-limbed woman coming third, Purifyre and Mason behind her. Ballyhoot and the little Samson brought up the rear. A few minutes of scrabbling, however, brought another halt. The twins were poised at the flat top of an outcropping of rock and pointed questioningly in different directions. All of them could hear the waves, the living body of the Oceanic, slamming against the lower battlements of the Juts.

"The quickest way is to the east," the long-limbed woman said in a calm alto. She looked as flexible as a child's balloon animal but kept her balance easily in the gusts. "Fast and fairly level along the windward side. But it's low. This surge will cover it first of all." She indicated the other way. "The west leg's higher but harder—more risky."

Purifyre was still gazing east. "Aren't there rungs fitted into a chimney on that route?"

The woman nodded. "But a very difficult one. If the picaroons pulled out the rungs behind them as they climbed . . ."

"Then we go west," Purifyre said, unflappable. "And precious little time even for that. Stay at close intervals and alert for trouble. Hie off!"

Lightning rifted the sky again, and thunder threatened Mason's hearing. He steeled himself to ignore all of it and fought flashbacks to the day twenty baseline-years earlier when the Oceanic had risen in vengeance to take out half the members of the *Scepter* survey team.

CHAPTER
SEVEN

There in the jam-packed throngs before the locked gates and chain-hung corpses of Gaphot, Burning hadn't been the only one to spot the pursuing praetorians and realize that *Racknuts* had in turn been spotted by them.

"Missy! Pelta! Wet the pullers! Make ready," Manna called to her two little daughters, who constituted the engineering division belowdecks aft. To the crowd in general she yelled, "Out of our way! Stand clear, you gaping herd of dumplapping whistle-dicks! Coming through!"

Some of the elite grandeean guards were already dismounting from their immobilized cars, flourishing sling-guns, swords, shields, and polearms. But Manna obviously planned to make a run for it, which in turn meant a run away from Gapshot and perhaps Burning's only chance of crossing the Styx Strait. He considered slipping overboard and taking his chances—with or without Souljourner—but knew full well that he had been marked back at the Jitterland Heights parking mounds by informers and would doubtless be marked by Gapshot onlookers, if not by grandeean spies. With little chance of eluding the elite troops on foot, in any case, he decided to cast his lot with Manna until she could shake off pursuit—assuming that was possible. Watching the praetorians beat and wend their way through milling humanity, he put his hand to his pistol, opening the holster's thumb break.

He had his doubts about Manna's being able to force her

way through the press, but no sooner did the six-wheeler lurch into motion—with a bang that threatened to wring another treadle shaft in two—than hapless bystanders swarmed aside in a frantic close-quarters stampede.

"Move or I'll grind you into flurrow fodder, you lumpish horde of humpscrunchers!"

The muscle-powered treadles kicked again and again, advancing the fleximobile a meter at a time, as if it were being kicked in the stern by an invisible giant.

Two porters bearing tump-lined packs, their vests daubed with the ideograph of the freight company for which they worked, found themselves directly under the lead starboard wheel and barely managed to dodge it. To port, a richly decorated palanquin, deserted by its bearers, toppled and cracked open, spilling a floridly dressed merchant and two young women in advanced states of undress who somehow scrambled clear of the high mud-cutter wheel as it crunched through the palanquin's wreckage.

Racknuts began to veer to the east, its cut-under front wheels greatly reducing the turn radius and the need for a wide swing through the crowd. Gapshot legionnaires on the ramparts blew warning notes on their trumpets but seemed disinclined to venture outside the gates to intervene. The grandeean elites hadn't missed Manna's effort to plow free of the crowd, however. Burning felt rather than heard a hard impact nearby and saw Manna staring down at a broadhead sling-gun quarrel that had penetrated a centimeter into her repoussè-carved ivory peg leg, the shaft slanted up like a semaphore arm.

But Manna didn't waste time gawking or yanking at it; instead, she bawled orders to Boner, Spin, and Yake, who immediately snatched up the improvised wicker shields they had used in the getaway on the Jitterland Heights. Burning got into what cover the scant deck cargo provided, drawing Souljourner with him.

"Beware the stall!" Manna yelled, lurching to help Boner

wrestle the wheel through a half turn, apprehensive that the fried frutter stand would hang *Racknuts* up but seemingly oblivious to the stall's ample-bellied proprietor and the pair of tinkers patronizing it. All three threw themselves in different directions, and Boner succeeded in slipping past with only a glancing collision that toppled the stand, sending grease-fed flames leaping.

Hampered by struggling masses of travelers, the chase had the nightmarish feel of a pursuit through waist-high mud. But *Racknuts* was slowly beginning to gather speed, and bystanders were yielding the way. Resecuring his 'baller, Burning left cover to hike himself over to Manna's sling-gun harquebus; that he could use without compromising himself as a Visitant to everyone in sight.

Manna's prodigious, beautifully crafted musket was the size of a longboat oar, but he had no trouble muscling its forestock to rest on the port rail. Squeezing the firing tiller, he sent what turned out to be a stone pumpkinball round winging toward the grandeean eight-wheeler that had pulled out in front of its companion cars. Souljourner, meanwhile, had moved up to the bow and was yelling and motioning madly at some obstruction ahead. Tucking the harquebus under a lashing, Burning scrambled forward as a spiked-pellet round stuck in the deck close to him.

Souljourner was gesticulating to a cluster of men, women, and children gathered around a spinning jigajig wheel atop a ground cloth, all gripped by bettor's fever. As fanatic wagerers as any Ext, the Aquam were dividing their glances between the slowing jigajig wheel and the muscle car bearing down on them. Burning was braced to bear witness to a bloodbath, but as soon as the wheel stopped, winners snatched up their payoffs and people launched themselves every which way like frightened fish. One mendicant monk, spilling scudos from his clenched hand, had to roll between the muscle car's wheels to avoid being halved.

Breaking into the clear, *Racknuts* rolled for the coast road—the Wundwander—which curved east, overlooking the crashing Amnion. Gapshot legionnaires on the ramparts were yelling and firing—albeit beyond effective range—at *Racknuts* and the grandeeans' vehicles alike. Boner bounced the car through a shallow sewage ditch, almost tipping over on the shoulder incline, then righting again so quickly that Burning and Souljourner never had a chance to think about jumping for the outriggers. Wobbling back to an even keel, *Racknuts* began pumping hard, but the grandeeans, too, were gaining momentum. Burning's gut clenched at the thought of how played out *Racknuts*'s pullers were.

Goddamn Wyrds, he thought darkly.

For once Manna wasn't stingy with her Analeptic Fix or obsessively protective of her car. Given the kind of formidable commotion she could create, traffic in both directions made way as the ramshackle six-wheeler mustered its best speed, treadles sounding like trip-hammers trying to beat the undercarriage loose.

The praetorians' determination to close the lead came as a shock, given that they were far from Lake Ea. Burning could only conclude that events at Wall Water had turned the Ean grandeeans implacably vengeful. The praetorians had probably been issued orders to pursue Burning to the ends of Scorpia and beyond, if necessary.

Still, he wondered if they were out to fetch him home as a hostage or had simplified their mission to straightforward retaliatory murder. He was looking around for Manna's expensive baldric with its quiver of sling-gun shafts and shot, meaning to reload the piece for her, when he realized that she'd left off helping her husband at the wheel and had Boner's clapped-out old sling-gun pistol pointed in Burning's general direction.

"Slow to the top of this next uphill," she told her children. "We're disembarking passengers on the fly!"

Burning gave her an emphatic no—a rolling nod of the head. "I paid you well, Manna. We have a deal!" He thought about adding that in the open country into which the coast road was fast delivering them there would be no hope for an escape on foot, but the old termagant was crafty enough to have figured that out.

"I made no deal to lose my family and *Racknuts* and everything I have," Manna reminded him. "This is strictly between you and the elites—*Visitant*. And don't tell me you're not. Besides, our pullers are fatigued. On Gojand Hill flee, fight, or give it up as you wish, but I mean to be shut of you."

Burning eased his hand for his 'baller, but instead of targeting him, Manna swung her husband's horse pistol at Souljourner's unprotected breast. Spin, too, had his light hunting slinger aimed at the Descrier, and Yake had leveled the stubby carbine-format thew gun he used.

Manna plainly wasn't worried about his revealing her Analeptic Fix formula, Burning realized as he moved his hand away from his sidearm. Under the circumstances it was absurd to think that he could do her business prospects much harm. But the formula gave him a sudden idea that sent him back-stepping for the aft hatch even while holding Manna's gaze. He was reasonably confident that she wouldn't let fly until and unless she understood what was going on and was counting on confusion to checkmate her for a few crucial moments. With *Racknuts* shedding speed on the upgrade and Manna bawling at him to face his fate like a man, he scooted across the deck planks, shoulder rolled, and dropped through the aft hatch into the car's medieval engine space.

Missy and Pelta shied out of his reach but remained at their posts, as staunch in a crisis as the rest of Manna's extraordinary family. Fortunately for Burning, their slingers happened to be somewhere out of reach. It occurred to him in passing that the sisters might make effective counterhostages, but in the course of the trip they'd won their way into his good opinion—insofar as any children could—and Manna just might be inclined to call his bluff.

Ignoring the girls, he squirmed past the pumping treadles to root among the panniers and hampers for the particular bundles he'd seen days earlier. Above, Manna was ranting and stamping her peg leg with such force that dirt was sifting between the deck planks.

"What are you about?" Missy shrilled. "Put that back!"

"Leave Mama's fixings alone," Pelta chimed in.

Burning chucked aside precipitate of metaflux and concentrate of pithpod and reached for what he was after: a translucent fish-gut bag of decoction of Nixie. If he understood correctly, it contained some extract or concentrate of the acetylcholine-rich electrolytic jelly found in the ghostly Lake Ea creatures, which reacted with amazing intensity to the prompting impulse of the muscle car's galvani stones. Whatever the specifics, Manna used the stuff as sparingly as if it were nitroglycerin. This, however, was no time to be thrifty.

The fish-gut bag was sealed with a narrow, petcocked wooden spigot. Bracing himself, Burning used his ka-bar to punch a hole in the overhead blivet that fed the portside pullers. Then, opening the petcock, he squeezed pure decoction of Nixie into the blivet as if squirting icing from a cake decorator. With half of it gone in seconds, he turned to give the starboard blivet a booster shot.

Her eyes as big as hubcaps, Missy screamed, "You're BRAINFUCKED!" She and Pelta were already edging for the hatch.

Burning tossed the collapsed gut bag aside and began to wriggle back aft. "Stay at your posts!" he warned the girls. "There's no place to jump to." He felt bad about putting them in harm's way, but it was Manna who'd brought the whole thing to a head.

By the time he'd drawn himself clear of the clashing wooden engine, it was obvious that something was happening.

The pullers, stretched vertically between treadles and the overhead support beams, were thrashing and halting in unpredictable surges. Trying to establish a new timing patter, Pelta worked frantically at the galvani-stone distributor. The treadles slammed arrhythmically, tearing ominous creaks from the gears; then, all at once, a fierce pile-driver flurry shot *Racknuts* forward in a series of jarring leaps, knocking Burning off his feet.

Missy snatched up two galvani handset clackers and took over control from the distributor box. Gnawing her lower lip in concentration, she began clenching out swift galvanic impulses in broken time, foreseeing each spasm and co-opting its violence into the power train by means of piezoelectric zaps.

Acceleration jolted and banged *Racknuts* like a polo ball being socked along by mallet shots. Manna's wails for the punishment inflicted on her vehicle came through the deck planks seemingly unmuffled. Averaging out the kicks and intermittent lags, the six-wheeler was already traveling at a better clip than Manna had dared in all their days of travel. Short of whanging the bevel gears asunder and halting, thus placing everyone at the mercy of the praetorians, there was nothing the muscle-car troupe could do but hang on for the wild ride.

Burning popped up through the hatch to see Manna and her crew laboring mightily to hold the road. Souljourner was helping Boner at the wheel. Loose deck items were flying overboard every time the mud-cutter wheels whammed the pavement, and the crude suspension was lamenting each blow. The grabs hissed and whined, and smoke was swirling from the brake pads. But the grandeean troops' buggies were falling far behind.

Manna found a moment to glare at him. "You purulent sack of festered gall. You'll be the death of us! Any second now the pullers will expire from shock and exhaustion!"

"Then you'd better be ready to fight," Burning shot back.

Manna spat phlegmy slackwort juice straight at him. "You

expect us to engage Lake Ea's best head-on? *Pah!* That's not the way the likes of us do battle on the autobahns. Far better, we never close with them."

"Then we see eye to eye."

Despite Manna's claim, the car's muscles gave no indication of ODing or playing out. *Racknuts* rounded another curve. While its speed had fallen off somewhat, Burning could still feel the portside wheels leaving the road surface as the car heeled. Given that whatever safety barriers the Optimants had installed had long since been scavenged and that the grassy downhill slope fell steeply away into the Amnion, the pucker factor of overturning was an order of magnitude higher than it had been anywhere along the road from Wall Water.

Burning began casting an apprehensive eye ahead as well as astern. The coastline thrust an expansive curve out to the south a little farther along, and the Wundwander road veered off to keep the sunset swells in view—an Optimant sight-seeing feature of which Burning disapproved as much as did any latter-day Aquam but one that offered no option short of hopeless off-roading. Also Manna's home ville of RakeOff Crimp was not too far off, and when *Racknuts* reached it, the tactical situation was likely to shift dramatically.

As *Racknuts* swung into the long curve, Souljourner sang out, " 'Ware! One breaking from the pack!"

Perhaps it had newer pullers or galvanis or a better batch of fuel, but the pursuing eight-wheeler had left its mates behind and was making a sustained move to overtake *Racknuts*. Kilometer by kilometer it closed as the cars tore past open fields and tiny hamlets where peons stopped to gawk at the road-walloping old crate pounding as if it were about to fly apart.

As darkness was falling, they came to an uphill stretch where a segment of the Optimant course had been destroyed—broken or swallowed up in a quake from the looks of it. Repairs had been made in the form of a series of cobblestoned switchbacks, but the detour showed inferior latter-day Aquam workmanship. Burning saw Manna making a grapnel ready, its line secured to a stout frame member.

As *Racknuts* slowed to take the last switchback, this one shored up on the outer side by a pile of unmortared rock, she leaned from the car and deftly threw the grapnel. It hooked an odd looking stone—nearly J-shaped—that projected partway from the pile. The line snapped tight, and the J stone was ripped tumbling from the pile, bringing several smaller boulders with it but leaving the road's surface undisturbed.

"Local hospitality?" Burning asked, swaying as *Racknuts* recovered speed on the downhill.

Manna's round face took on the appearance of an evil, waxing moon. "Behold and enjoy, you broken-snouted titlap!"

The praetorian car wasn't long in reaching the spot and—to Burning's eye, at least—seemed to come close to dodging the booby trap. Then, however, the outside rear wheel fell through the crudely repaired course, and the road itself caved in. A second later the car went smashing and self-destructing down the long slope to flatter ground, crushing armored men under or hurling them clear.

Welcome to Mannaland, Burning reflected as he watched it go. Be alert for treacherous curves. The other praetorian cars halted when they reached the wreck, possibly because someone important had gone down with the eight-wheeler or, even more likely, one or more officers in the crash car had in his keeping a good-sized wallet of operating jing to fund the long hunt south.

Whichever, *Racknuts*'s expanded lead had Manna exuberant as the car topped a last rise and was about to drop out of sight over a high hump of headland. "Let that be a lesson to northern limpwicks who think to bully their way along the road to RakeOff Crimp," she began, only to curtail her bragging by exclaiming, *"What the frozen, fruity FUCK?"*

She delivered the words as she struggled toward the wheel, where Souljourner was still helping Boner. Too late, everyone realized that with all eyes diverted aft, no one had been paying close enough attention to the treacherous curves ahead. Whether some unknown person had left another booby trap set from a previous encounter or simply had enabled one on general xenophobic principles, there was no telling. There was no time to wonder, either, as *Racknuts* fell victim to a similar roadbed cave-in and went slewing ass-first off the downhill side off the Wundwander for a sheer drop-away into the sea.

CHAPTER
EIGHT

With the *Dream Castle* caught in a williwaw, Zinsser again floundered toward the control console, only to be flung back the way he'd come. Then, all at once, the Laputa shifted and he found himself thrown headfirst toward his target. He fully expected to crash through the display screen, but the Laputa shifted again while he was in midflight, allowing him to cushion himself against the console hood, the breath knocked out of him but otherwise unhurt. His whatty was still on-line with the array, but the problem of how to keep from being tossed back across the solarium remained. Winding one leg around a stanchion, Zinsser grabbed the edge of the hood plate and clung grimly to it.

Ghost was making her way to him by lurches and falls. He might have told her to stay put if he had thought for a moment that she would listen to him. When, in any case, his eye happened to fall on the blood she'd spilled—now pitched and jounced every which way, along with the holed bodies of the three Insiders—he cast out any pity for her.

His first thought was to attempt to reenable the Laputa's weather sensor programs, but he could find no backups for the protocols he'd been forced to delete. Having created false and furious weather hemming the sky hall on every other side, he had left the navicomputer no choice but to steer the *Dream Castle* through the storm despite the terrible pounding it was taking. He contemplated the possibility of abandoning the perilous return to Passwater—of somehow skirting the williwaw and striking south for Scorpia—but the thought of crossing so much open ocean dissuaded him. Something visceral in him cried out to be back on land, any land, by whatever means.

The console's indicators were malfing left and right, but Zinsser judged the wind speed to be close to a hundred knots. The Laputa had been seized like a toy in the hand of an angry child and was being whipped back and forth, sideways, and up and down. Horizontal rain struck the viewpane with blasting force. He could hear the sudden g-loading wring torment from structural members and cracks like gunshots as unseen components snapped or parted. Over it all howled the wind, seeming to rejoice in its own fury. Zinsser wondered what marvels the williwaw's elemental rage had worked on the surface of the Amnion, then decided he was probably better off not knowing. He would have been willing to bet, though, that the pavilion was losing altitude.

The heavy sideloads and especially the vertical motion made for chaos in the compartment. Ghost had been obliged to stop struggling, wedge herself under a well-secured table, and ride it out. Zinsser was considering what the storm had to be doing to the outerworks and its passengers when powerful vibrations suddenly traveled up from the Laputa's inverted-bowl base. He was reluctant to leave the console, but as the airship's self-appointed pilot he had to determine the cause of the vibrations. He waited for a relatively quiet moment, then lurched for the viewpane. A staggering fall brought him there, nearly landing him in the blood and gore that now slicked much of the carpeted floor.

Gazing down through the cantilevered windowpanes, he realized in dread that immense, standing storm waves were rearing, falling, and rearing up again not two hundred meters below. The blare of the *Dream Castle*'s fusion drive told him that it was straining to raise the ship against what had to be a supremely powerful downdraft.

Strange, grating quavers resounded through the ship once more, and all at once it gave a great lurch. Zinsser saw what he thought were bulkhead planks blown loose from the outerworks by the ripping wind. More followed, and suddenly a great hunk of the outerworks plummeted toward the sea, all in a piece, though ravaged and dissected by the winds that had sucked it away. Articles of clothing and furnishings twirled in the sky, and human figures were flung like hurled marionettes.

Before Zinsser could cry out, another huge section broke away from the vessel's side, leaving people clutching stanchions and frames even while they were dropping through midair. A spilled firepot left a comet trail of sparks. Zinsser couldn't suppress wretched sobs as he grasped what was happening. The Insiders had cut the outerworks loose in an attempt to halt the Laputa's descent.

"Bastards!" he screamed.

The ship was tugged and whirled by a force other than wind as one part of the outerworks hung up and dragged for a moment; then the pavilion jolted free. Zinsser saw a huge wooden half doughnut go plunging down, bearing flailing figures with it, some in the saffron uniforms worn by the ship's hirelings.

Then the pounding gusts slackened enormously, and the *Dream Castle* trimmed itself for a stately reascent. Zinsser understood, however, that the jettisoned outerworks had nothing to do with it; the airship had simply come by chance into one of the narrow avenues of relative calm between the bands of storm that radiated from the williwaw's center.

Hands trembling, he reeled back to the console and keyed in instructions that would send the Laputa higher still—above its usual ceiling—now that there was no one outside the pressurized interior to worry about. The ancient drives bellowed, and *Dream Castle* rode aloft, spinning gently.

The williwaw was less forceful when it attacked the pavilion again. Zinsser could see what he took to be the eye of the storm bearing southeast. The pavilion pulled and bulled its way to the outskirts of the fury like a dowager emerging from a free-for-all. He took a moment to glance at Ghost, then at the hatch to the interior.

The Laputa's tossing not only had loosened the pedestal she'd used to jam it shut, but had flung it somewhere out of sight. There were plenty of scraps lying around in the wake of the storm, though, and Zinsser helped Ghost resecure the hatch with a length of timber. Haunted by the sight of the sacrificed outerworks, he dreamed of how satisfying it would be to arrange something similar for the Insiders—deep-water grave, perhaps. But when it came down to it, all he wanted was to return to land, even the frozen tundra of the Scourlands.

Even as he thought it, the *Dream Castle* seemed to balk and buck. To a hair-raising sound from the depths of it—the sputter of the fusion thrusters—it plunged for a second or so. Standing nearby, Ghost began marshaling the available weapons.

"Will we make it?" she asked.

Zinsser checked the diagnostics but could only shrug tightly, begrudging her even that gesture. "We'll know soon enough."

The two of them stood in taut silence, glancing between the control console and the horizon, tension winding tighter and tighter—in Zinsser, at any rate—until it seemed the past was all hallucination and the future nothing but myth and all there had ever been was their interminable trip on the pavilion.

Dream Castle began to shake in accordance with the fluctuations of engine power; one particularly bad sputter lost the ship a half-klick's altitude in seconds. Then a shadow fluttered by to port. They looked quickly to see a south-Scorpia-style glider go by, a robed Insider at the controls, taking her chances on the storm rather than the ship. As they watched, the fragile kite was flipped over, one whole side was torn off, and the wreckage went plummeting from sight, putting Zinsser in mind of both Icarus and Dante. Either it was the only flier aboard or the other Insiders were too horrified to risk their luck, but no other gliders followed.

* * *

"You're placing *me* under arrest?" Zone said to Lod, plainly amused by the idea.

In fact, he had been counting on a confrontation, but not there—not on the hangar deck, with Turret *Musashi* lording it over everyone. He had figured that the showdown would take place in Ext councils in a legalistic power grab Haven and Quant couldn't veto. But instead, here was little Lod, coming after him in a popped-open robot hauler.

Wetbar and the rest of Zone's severalmates and allies had jumped back with strangled curses, half expecting to be mashed under and between the vehicle's treads. Zone stood his ground, but Lod, looking smug, didn't seem to have a care in the world.

"Turn to!" he yelled in the voice Ext drill instructors used, a voice Zone had never heard from Lod before. And with that, a dozen figures in Ext battlesuits surfaced in the open hull of the hauler, bringing 'bommers and 'ballers to bear on Zone and his inner circle.

Unshockable, Zone still felt a twinge of irritation, which was transmuted instantly to cold anger. The lower hull wasn't crammed with normal Exts; it was loaded with Discards—Ghost's group of pubescent ex-POW savages, the most alienated and nonpartisan fighters the Concordance War had produced. The children gazed down with solemn, utterly pitiless stares—stares Zone had seen before, stares that rarely changed when they pulled the trigger or even afterward. Zone also realized that he and his group were being covered from another angle by the Manipulant Scowl-Jowl, a bloopgun in its claws.

As he was coursing with the Flowstate, it was all the more luminously emphatic to him that he had seriously misjudged the situation. Lod, of course, was hoping that Zone and his mates would simply open up, but Zone wasn't about to give him the satisfaction of an easy win. In fact, he was about to acquiesce to the major's demands when loud voices broke the tense silence.

"Put those guns away!" Dextra Haven yelled, arriving on the scene in a breathless run. Quant was right behind her with a bellow that was probably heard clear to the crow's nest. "Everyone freeze!"

Zone raised his hands, leering triumphantly at Lod, his coven following suit. When she realized what was going on, Dextra astonished herself by feeling regret that she'd interfered. As much of an asset as he was in the field, Zone had become a threat to the mission. To have him cleanly eliminated without giving the ship's company—especially the Exts—time to polarize over it would have been a stroke of luck, but it was too late. Zone and his bunch were surrendering; Exts and others could see that. A massacre now would very likely fragment the GammaLAW mission beyond repair.

"Major Lod, order your people to stand down," she barked.

Lod relayed the command, then motioned to his designated apprehension team to secure and search the arrestees. The Discards went in warily as Zone's clique leaned against the turret and permitted themselves to be frisked. The children were as cautious as animals, and Zone tolerated their actions mutely.

"I hope you have an explanation for this, Major," Dextra was saying to Lod.

"Madame, you'll have it," he told her.

"It will be your behind on a hook if you don't," she assured him, hoping fervently that Lod could make his charges stick. God knew, she would do her best to see that the formal hearing turned out that way. So much for bringing impartiality and enlightened justice to Aquamarine.

She wondered how Lod had acquired his new allies, especially Scowl-Jowl. Then the answer became clear as she noticed Piper standing next to the engeneered Special Trooper, her expression a swirl of the gamine and the robotic. Dextra told herself that she should be grateful, but there was something disquieting about it. With Lod clearly entranced with her, a host of lines of power suddenly met in Piper. The Aggregate was allegedly immune or indifferent to mundane political power, but who knew for sure?

By then Zone was facedown on the nonskid deck and cuffed. He had even suffered the Discards' search of his cheeks in case he carried a spit needle. With their leader neutralized, the other would-be mutineers were meek in yielding to the Discards' manacles. Kurt Elide, meanwhile, had emerged from under the turret, a quivering Rim Fortuna in tow. Elide was no longer the carefree rich kid he'd been on Periapt, tagging along on Dextra's mission out of boredom. She wasn't sure just when the transformation had taken place, but Kurt had begun to act like an earnest seaman since she'd released him from duty as her assistant.

Arms akimbo, Quant studied Elide for a moment before asking, "Why is it that whenever I see you, there's shit to windward?"

Elide surprised Dextra by looking stricken. "Seems to be my lot in life, Captain," he replied.

CHAPTER
NINE

When Mason had been younger, he'd tried talus running, high-impedance cross-country, and rock gymkhana. The main thing he remembered about those sports was that they had exhausted him quickly and left him with contusions, abrasions, sprains, and chipped bones. He had vowed never to subject himself to that kind of merry, masochistic assholery again. Now, however, his impulse was to tear across the so-called Toes at hysterical speed, to subsume his terror in an all out effort to hang on to his life regardless of the punishment to his body. But instead he toiled diligently behind his son over a succession of rain-slick boulders as big as tanks.

Purifyre's file wound its way off the Toes and up over the Lean-to, where Mason wore through the seat of his wringing wet pantaloones and lost the proverbial skin off his ass sliding down the other side. In the lee of the steepled monoliths Ballyhoot and the others took brass and crystal lanterns from their packs and lighted them with sparkwheels.

"I dislike signaling our whereabouts," the spidery woman told Purifyre worriedly. "But I suppose we've little choice."

The group moved out again, along the foot of the Highgable and through the crevice behind Snoid's Beak, where Mason left swatches of shoulder flesh, and on around the curving face of Wasties' Leap. They passed close to some of the transformations the Oceanic had wrought for its own incomprehensible reasons: the irregularly perforated globe called the

73

Whiffle, the grove of rather Art Nouveau shapes dubbed the Arabesques, the transdimensional-looking metageometric Hypercurve. Once thought to be Rosetta stones to communication with the Oceanic, they were nothing but shadowy scenery now.

Mason was bleeding, dehydrated, trembling from exertion, and aching with fatigue when the band reached the Tall Lonesome, an off-kilter crag that was the highest point on the Juts and two-thirds of the way to Gapshot. Purifyre offered to lend him a stabilizing hand, but Mason grimly refused. Spiderwoman and her son heaved him fore and aft over the hump. He made it past the Seesaw on his own, then negotiated another tight squeeze called the Hanging Buttress, on and on around the great ohm symbol of the Juts.

More often now Purifyre was casting glances at the Styx Strait bridge, high above and to the east. Mason realized that he feared that Kinbreed would smell a trick and destroy the span. They paused on a slanting ledge under Mushroom Cloud, where Mason heard a distant, inhuman hiss that made the hair stand up along his arms, neck, and upper back.

"What word on the tide line?" Purifyre called.

"Coming faster," the dwarf called back, shining his lamp down. "But we'll make it. D' you hear the Hoo-Holes?" He cocked an ear with one sinewy hand. "Just past them is the Arras. Then it's a hop and a skip."

"Nothing's sure," Ballyhoot muttered, "until we've got ground under us."

The Hoo-Holes. Mason had heard of them, and the fact that the winds were moaning through them, as through natural organ pipes, meant that they would shortly be awash. The Arras, on the other hand, was supposed to be a sheer, vertical cylinder, like the inside of a chimney, with one last cramped crawl tunnel leading to the home stretch. That wasn't, though, what Mason found when he followed his son into the uneven footing of the place. Instead, there lay a slab of boulder as big as an imperial-size mattress, freshly fallen from somewhere above.

"One of the Flakes of Wrath," the spidery woman remarked. "Toppled on purpose, I'd say."

"Then we'll have to go back and take the other way," Mason said.

No one responded to the remark. The rising tide was modulating the dirges of the Hoo-Holes. The spidery woman's son attempted to worm into the crawl tunnel between the fallen slab and Arras, only to slip back after almost becoming wedged. Purifyre tried three shots with the detonator-cap gun. While the three-meter tongues of plasma made the rock glow and even crack in places, the det caps made no real impression on the mammoth flake. When the twins failed to find purchase on the fallen flake and fell back, the sister announced plaintively, "No way forward and no way back."

No one expected Mason to speak again, much less to say, "Give me a leg up. I'll need a light, as well."

Ballyhoot scowled, but the spidery woman urged her son ahead gently. The small man stood braced against the toppled Flake of Wrath, and Mason stepped up onto his proffered shoulders, the deltoids as round and hard as dumbot ball joints. Trying to recall what Boon had said at the Forge Town constabulary barracks, he removed the propellant cartridge from the flechette pistol and nearly ripped loose a thumbnail trying to figure out how Boon had made the little neck ring turn. Purifyre held one of the travel lanterns so that he could see.

Reverse the striker, Boon had said. *Slide the neck ring around so that the indicator and the last notch are aligned.* Or was it the *first* notch?

"Bring me some bits and pieces of rock. I have to tamp this thing in." That much, at least, the LAW military cadre had let slip to the despised civil service types in the abbreviated fundamentals training cycle Mason had been put through.

Even Ballyhoot pitched in, gathering fragments from among

what Jut-hoppers called "skiffles"—rock debris anywhere from the size of landscaping gravel to chunks bigger than pieces of furniture. Mason, meanwhile, marveled at his luck in finding a cranny between the flake and the Arras that was perhaps half a meter deep.

He examined the cranny carefully, even though he knew he was going to have to gamble. How long he'd have to get clear once he set the cartridge for total release, he didn't know; thirty seconds, he seemed to remember, but he hadn't been paying much attention at the time. *Whomp the striker and run like hell,* Boon had said—or words to that effect.

Purifyre held up the nine det caps he had left. "Will these help?"

Mason declined with a tic of the head; the explosion he was hoping for would essentially be expanding gas, with no charge to set off the caps. If he lived, Purifyre would definitely need them. Clenching the propellant cartridge in his teeth, Mason arranged hunks of rock and handfuls of pebbles along the top of the flake.

"Take cover," he advised. "Hands over your ears, mouths open." To the boy holding him up he added, "And you, get ready to run!"

The dwarf grinned in the lamplight. "I look forward to it."

The Hoo-Holes' lamentation was rising; there was no time for finesse. With a chunk of rock, Mason bashed down on the striker, half expecting it to blow his hand off. Instead, something gave. With unsteady hands, he lowered the cartridge into the cranny, counting off the seconds at the same time. Set into the niche, the 'chettergun cartridge promptly slid sideways and disappeared into a fissure he'd missed in the poor light. He could hear it clink and scrape as it went, sounding as if it were going to drop clear down into the Hoo-Holes and the rising seawater.

"Fire in the hole! Shield yourselves!" he yelled, struggling off the little giant's shoulders.

"Over here!" the spidery woman called.

Mason joined her behind a boulder. He'd left the lantern up on the flake, but he wasn't about to double back now. Counting off the seconds once more, he remembered too late that he could have used the stopwatch function on his whatty.

. . . thirteen universal, fourteen universal, fifteen universal . . .

Thirty came and went, then thirty-five.

I botched it somehow, Mason told himself. He started to lever himself up when a vibration traveled through the broken stone of the Juts as much as through the air, jolting him and making it feel as if cupped hands had been clapped over his ears. The tamped skiffles disappeared, and stone dust shot upward and outward. He could see where bits of rock had gone rebounding from the Arras and the flake itself as the huge fallen slab was rocked back from its resting place, passing the vertical ponderously. It gained speed as it fell to crash flat among the Hoo-Holes with an impact that Mason couldn't hear very distinctly but that nearly knocked him off his feet.

The lantern was gone, but there were others whose light shone on the exposed crawl crevice at the base of the Arras. The elfin twins crowded each other to be the first to wriggle through, the girl winning. Waiting his turn, Mason reinserted the original propellant cartridge in his 'chettergun; it read empty but perhaps had enough puff to fire a few more rounds. His hearing returned in time to catch the finish of the spidery woman's remark.

"—through now!"

Mason looked to where she was pointing. From the lower Hoo-Holes, back the way they'd come, tiny wavelets were beginning to splash, their interiors dancing with curling filaments of phosphorescence. The Oceanic was all around them, surging up from beneath. The wind was rising again, the rain was resuming, and more stupendous Aquamarine lightning was splitting the sky in zigzag cascades.

Having followed his sibling into the crawl space, the boy

twin yelled something that alarmed Ballyhoot. "Trouble?" Purifyre asked, a hand on his basket-hilted longknife.

"Can't tell," she called back, crouched by the cramped crawlway.

Without waiting for his go-ahead, she squirmed in, her leathery splayed feet kicking a bit as she strained and contorted herself into the close confines of the hole in the wall. Purifyre hovered anxiously, then followed when the way was clear.

Mason was leery of new dangers in the tunnel but took comfort in the faith that the terrain on the far side sloped upward. He became aware of the spidery woman's hand on his shoulder. She was glancing around worriedly, though it took him several seconds to fathom what she was saying. "Scantlet!" She saw his incomprehension. "My son! He took cover and hasn't reappeared!"

He was cautious following her through thickening rain because their way took them down an incline, and anything that brought them closer to sea level could be deadly. She shone her lantern around, but they didn't need it to spot Scantlet. A sky bolt ripping the night and vaporizing seawater with a quarter of a million amps revealed him to be lying flat on his back on a hump of stone five meters away. The Amnion had risen through low-lying gaps in the Juts all around where the boy lay.

Scantlet's mother made to run to his side, but Mason caught her thin wrist and encircled her waist with his arm. "No! The water—"

"He'll be killed!"

She was thin but impossible to hang on to; it was like wrestling with a nest of wet rock-eels. Just as Mason was about to lose hold, the woman went rigid in his arms.

"Scantlet, no! Don't move!"

Mason turned. Scantlet had sat up, blood from a scalp wound streaming down his face. Some crumb of rock flung by the explosion had evidently found him through blind chance.

Dazed and bleeding, Scantlet didn't realize that the rising, shimmering Amnion was nearly upon him. Struggling off the hump of stone, he put his foot in it.

Scantlet stared at the lapping wavelets and the radiant whorls and volutes the Oceanic had chosen as its manifestation, the glow brightening about his bare immersed foot. His face had gone slack, and the freely flowing blood was thinned by the rain—or at least that was what Mason thought was happening. Then he realized that the blood running from the scalp gash had *turned* to water. Water was pouring forth from the little man's forehead, too, and from his eyes. It welled out of the pores of the powerful body, trickled from his ears, streamed from his mouth in rivulets.

"I love you, child!" the woman screamed, weeping. "Remember, your mother loves you!"

Scantlet lost form and became like a wax figure melting and shrinking before fire, converted to what Mason assumed was seawater. What wasn't H_2O must have been dissolved and borne away as particulate matter because he saw no floating teeth, no tufts of hair, no scraps of clothing. The Oceanic was a past master at mobilizing matter on a molecular lever when it chose to. All that had been Scantlet became sea brine and merged quickly with the Amnion as Mason and Scantlet's mother stood locked in a tableau. Another close lightning strike made Mason start. He began pulling her toward the crawl tunnel in the Arras.

"Scantlet wouldn't want it to get us, too!"

She didn't resist.

It was a troubling sign that no one had doubled back to look for them, but there was nothing to do but proceed. The steepling wavelets were still rising, the submerged burrows of the Hoo-Holes glowing from below. The crawlway ran uphill, but the tide was coming fast.

He pushed the Anathemite woman to the hole in the Arras. She'd come back to her senses, however, and insisted that he go first. "I'll bring up the rear, push you, if needed. No time to argue. The tunnel dips before it rises!"

The news made Mason's knees feel weak. Lantern in hand, he let himself be steered to the dark cleft in the rock on all fours, moving like a toy dumbot. The rock closed in around him. He heard the woman moving agilely behind him in spite of her height.

The way angled down. The tunnel was a shifting, irregular triangle in cross section, its long apex slanting to the right. Mason hitched and belly-crawled, scarcely registering projections that banged his shins and scraped his scalp, wild-eyed with the awareness that he was still moving down, unavoidably, toward the rising Oceanic.

The passageway leveled and widened, but Mason stopped short when he saw and heard what lay ahead: a tiny gallery with a little subsurface basin, that was heaving and phosphorescent with the incoming tide.

"Haste, take the ledge to your left!" the woman said, pushing his feet. "We've only moments, and the narrowest part lies ahead still!"

Mason exploded into effort, strawberrying large patches of his body and hunkering nearly-prone along the ledge, as far from the turbulent seawater as he could. He knew carelessness equated with death in the Juts, but he couldn't restrain himself from rushing. The woman was admonishing him about something, but he couldn't seem to make sense of it.

When he reached the far side, he found consternation instead of relief. The stone flue there went uphill, but the gallery exit was small and convoluted. Nevertheless, he twisted and wriggled himself up into it, gouging furrows in his shoulders and feeling warm blood fill the injuries. He spotted a vent leading almost straight up, but it was so narrow, he didn't see how Ballyhoot and the others possibly could have squeaked through.

Setting the lantern aside, he corkscrewed up into the crevice, only to jam himself. Slowly he became aware of what the woman was saying to him.

"You took the wrong turn! The way out's to the *right*!"

"I'm stuck fast!"

"Cease struggling. I'll get you free."

He felt her levering his leg, but he had so twisted and wedged himself into the convoluted space that he couldn't be moved. Water lapped in the background as the basin filled. He wanted to beg her not to leave him, but a sudden feeling of defeat overtook him. Maybe this was the punishment fated for him from the start—since he'd abandoned Incandessa and his unborn son. A first and final meeting with the Oceanic. Maybe he had it coming.

CHAPTER TEN

Sliding toward the Amnion on the disabled *Racknuts*, Burning found himself caught between an urge to surrender to the embrace of the Oceanic and a desire to jump free of the muscle car and laugh uproariously as Manna and the others rode it down into oblivion.

Whatever Missy and Pelta were doing below, they had the drive wheels spinning furiously if futilely, since the mud cutters couldn't find any purchase. Wooden gear teeth were cracking and splintering; the brake grab levers were on the verge of shearing off their wooden stops. In one motion Yake kicked an aft drag stave loose and flipped it over the stern, but *Racknuts* had gathered too much momentum, and the warped old stave snapped like a stick of chalk.

In the grips of a Flowstate calculation, Burning scrambled across the tilted deck for Souljourner, figuring that he could grab her and still get clear. But his fine reckoning was thwarted as the teetering car pitched forty-five degrees, threatening to spill everyone over the side. Quick thumps under the bogey wheels, however, told him that Manna had released the drag shoes in a final bid to halt the car. Made of iron and chained to the undercarriage perch pole, the shoes were spike-bottomed skates with V-sloped sides that actually lifted the wheels out of contact with the ground while the spikes dug in.

As the car lurched to a halt, *Racknuts*'s cargo was sent flying. A hamper shot past Burning, with Souljourner right behind, clawing to hang on to the deck. He caught her by the wrist and waist as if he'd been practicing the move all morning. She clutched him as he pulled her to the rail.

"You stayed aboard for me," she said. "I knew you would!"

Burning said nothing and glanced aft. Another three meters and the car's rear wheels would have rolled into empty air. Far below the waves seemed to be grumbling and salivating.

Spin and Yake brought rope, stakes, and a maul over the side with them and set about making sure that *Racknuts* would slip no farther. The car was salvageable, though not without a good deal of help. Manna, Boner, and the girls were picking through weapons and personal gear they had tossed to the ground and preparing to clamber up the slope to the caved-in road. Their willingness to abandon *Racknuts* surprised Burning, but what with the carloads of pursuing grandeeans, he supposed they didn't have much choice. Leaning into the slope, he and Souljourner ankled their way back up to the Wundwander.

From there his pistol scope found the praetorians returning to their vehicles after scavenging through the wreckage of the eight-wheeler. Burning calculated that once they were under way again, they would reach *Racknuts* in ten minutes.

Manna and Boner were peering in the opposite direction, toward a small ville surrounded by a log and stone stockade. Some of the folk easing out of a longhouse were armed with scythes and brush hooks, pitchforks and polearms. Manna primed her harquebus sling-gun with a broadhead shaft but kept it pointed to the ground as she gave Burning an unconvincingly maternal smile. "You'd better take sanctuary in RakeOff Crimp, Visitant, until all this is sorted out."

He didn't bother to conceal his leeriness; if there was a gene for altruism, Manna's genome lacked it. More likely, she wasn't sure her troupe could take Burning and wanted to get him inside the stockade for eventual surrender to the praetorians.

"I'm thinking I've caused you enough trouble already," he drawled. "But thanks for the offer."

Manna stamped her ivory peg leg. "You limp-wristed scum pump! Then at least pay what you owe. I care not a frozen fruity fart for your poxy sister, and you've wrecked my muscle car!" She brought the harquebus to an uplifted, vaguely threatening position.

Burning didn't wait for the muzzle to descend his way. Raising his 'baller and peering right-eyed through the big scope, he put its bead dot on the harquebus and blew loose the top twenty-five centimeters of its forestock in a burst of shattered lionwood and whanging slip elastics.

From Manna there ripped a discombobulated *yawp*! Missy and Pelta emitted screeches that spiked into the ultrasonic, while Boner, Spin, and Yake fell back a step with eyes as round as weather balloons, weapons nearly dropping from their faltering grasp.

Burning ripped four gold buttons from his tunic and tossed them at Manna's feet. "For the car—and your harquebus."

Without taking her eyes from him, Manna squatted and collected the buttons. Then, jabbing the docked and mangled muzzle end of the sling-gun into the ground, she pulled down her lower eyelid and spit. "Go to the salt water, then!"

Souljourner seemed to draw amused composure from Manna's discomfiture. "No, it'll be Alabaster for us," she retorted. "If the maps at Pyx have it right, it must lie near to here." She indicated the saddle between two rises due east. "That way, I think."

Manna was all but frothing at her. "Yes, absquatulate your overupholstered fanny over yonder hills—to your doom! Across the haunted heights and the Ghoul Grounds, where Anathemite runaways wail to play pain games with your tenderest parts, where the cannibal vines hunger for flesh, the vampire slugs long to wade with you, and the leper fungus lies in wait to caress white skin!"

"Better still than trusting your rapacious hospitality," Souljourner said pleasantly, "or making closer acquaintance with them." She jerked her thumb at the two remaining praetorian cars, which were slowly and laboriously gathering speed on the uphill grade. "Moreover, I should be the last one to tweak of rounded moons if I were you, whose bloated arse is surely of such a magnitude as to influence the Amnion tides."

Stumped for a comeback, Manna lost her dander in a snort of involuntary laughter. "Again you give me to suspect we must be related, you sly little gland packer."

Burning glanced at the pursuit cars and took hold of Souljourner's wrist. "Time to lam ass."

He had no idea if Manna's jabber about Anathemite hobgoblins was scare talk, but escape and evasion sounded better than making a stand in the open or surrendering himself to Manna's cronies in RakeOff Crimp. As for Alabaster, he'd have to wait and see. With a little luck they'd be able to work their way back to Gapshot, and somewhere along the way he would try for another meteor-burst transmission to *GammaLAW*'s ARAA.

Even so, staying a jump ahead of the grandeean troops would take some doing. Pressed for time, he abandoned all thought of recovering his iron-ferruled staff from wherever it had ended up aboard the precarious *Racknuts*. Souljourner had her carbine-size sling-gun on her right shoulder; cross-slung to rest against her left side was their water bota.

Burning directed a grin at Manna. "Madame, I bid you long life and prosperity. May your Analeptic Fix become the fuel of choice, and may *Racknuts* survive to see better days."

Begrudgingly, she allowed a faint smile. "And better days to you, Redtails—on Aquamarine or on whatever world from which you hail."

Souljourner fell in to match Burning's dog-trot pace for the saddle. They leaned into the uphill, climbing winding pathways between paddies and fields. Spying figures out among the crops, Burning wondered if any would take up the hunt and cry once the praetorians arrived.

The pressures of population on Scorpia were such that most of the arable land was tilled to the margins; nevertheless, when he and Souljourner crested the saddle, they confronted a virtual wilderness to which the diligently maintained farmland yielded at a frontier as sharply defined as the end of the *GammaLAW*'s flight deck.

Seeing it—overgrown and overhung, dense and dark— Souljourner stopped short. "Blighted lands," she muttered. "Anathemite-cursed."

Burning considered it. Given Aquam hysteria where Anathemites were concerned, the land was probably lousy with mutagens and sodden with pollutants and carcinogens, possibly even residual radiation, but he had a lot more immediate concerns than whether any entirely hypothetical fruit of his loins would require DNA redaction.

"Then maybe it'll put *them* off," he said, gazing back down the hill.

Elite troops were already piling off the first grandeean car, which had stopped above the stricken *Racknuts*. Manna and her family had retreated to the safety of a phalanx of RakeOff Crimpers. A standoff was played out while Burning and Souljourner watched, with the elites' diverse officers gesticulating with cutlass, sword, swagger stick, and flense whip and the RakeOff Crimpers answering with pitchforks, bows, and machetes. Eventually, however, Manna's swollen bolster of an arm extended to point straight up at the saddle.

Burning was already on the move, pounding for the forbidden tree line. Skirts tucked through her girdling belt, Souljourner caught up with him in five paces, sturdy young legs pumping high. He'd considered making a stand on the crest and picking off praetorians as they came within range, but long-distance pistol accuracy was problematic even with a .50's reach. While the Ean troops were aware of Visitant handguns' effectiveness, they were undoubtedly under with-your-shield-or-on-it orders not to let offworld weaponry deter them.

Aside from that, his ammo supply was severely limited and the open fields offered far too much ground for flanking maneuvers and fire volleys from cover. No, better to delta V while they could.

As the wilds loomed up over them, even Burning could see that the forest there was different from other woodlands *Racknuts* had passed on the way south. At first it was only the odd carbuncled growth on a sponge tree or the digitlike appendages flexing and wavering slowly on a wilm malm melon—things he barely registered as he hotfooted along, doing his best to keep his bearing. Farther into the green, blue, and black twilight of the wood, however, the indications were everywhere: trees, flowers, scrub, and ferns all showing signs of mutation.

Burning had the passing thought that it didn't square with what he knew of Aquamarine ecology, that local mutagens affected the genetic transcription of *Homo sapiens* far more than they did that of the native stuff. But perhaps the place had been plastered with some kind of biowep detonated by the Cyber plagues. He was at a loss to recall one whose effect would be so tightly confined to the so-called Ghoul Grounds and not spread to RakeOff Crimp's paddies or the underlying aquifer. There was no time for second thoughts about contamination; from behind came rally cries and the brassy prompting of a brayophaunt.

It was Souljourner who spotted a relatively open way that might once have been a broad trail. As they dodged onto it, Burning's boot sank into black and silver rot that had consumed a crosswise length of log—one in a seemingly endless row of them—and he understood that they'd struck a slowly decaying corduroy road. In among the lowering wildwood and its aberrations were signs of Post-Cyberplague habitation: a canted stela furry with orange lichen, a disintegrating *tori*-gate spanning a side path choked with purple briers and mottled white and pea-green lianas, irregular mounds humped up here and there in the bracken that suggested tumbledown huts. But there was nothing that offered plausible refuge, and so the two plunged on while the intermittent blares of martial instruments let them know that the Ean soldiers had picked up their trail.

Burning wasn't in boot-camp condition, but the desperation of the hunt goaded the best effort from him, whereas Souljourner seemed not only tireless but elated by the flight. He offered to haul the sling-gun, but she insisted on bearing it, so he settled for relieving her of the water bota's weight. As night closed on the afflicted wilds, they leapt and sidestepped obstacles and did their best to leave as little sign of their passing as possible. But for all of that, they couldn't gain a decisive lead on their pursuers. Burning suspected that the elites had included top trackers in their manhunting expedition.

Kilometer after kilometer they bush-raced through the dark and hollowly reverberating Ghoul Grounds. To either side were what had been cleared farmland, completely reclaimed by the misshapen forest. Burning began to hope that the corduroy way would eventually intersect the Wundwander Parkway, but his hopes derezzed as they descended into a small glen, only to find a fork in the overgrown trail and the way ahead blockaded by a thorn jungle that appeared to go on for acres.

"Veer away south," Souljourner panted. "That way should lie Alabaster."

Burning listened to the Eans' cries and horns. From the sound of them, some of the troops were fanning out to either side, possibly positioning themselves for an enveloping move. When he cupped his ear to the north, however, he caught the thicket crash and far-off panoply clank of running men. Perhaps they'd figured out that he would shoot for Gapshot, Burning told himself. Whichever, Souljourner had caught the faint sounds as well, and was again gesturing to the south fork.

"We can swing clear of the broadcast net," she insisted, voice pitched low. "Earlier I saw the gleam of moonlight on the sea. The very ground slopes away toward it. If we reach the gates of Alabaster, so much the better, as we shall be able to claim sanctuary." She paused for a moment, then added, "Even though the Holy Rollers said we shouldn't alter our course."

Burning suppressed a grimace of regret at the dice throw he'd manipulated. " 'Hobson's Heading,' " he relented, a swipe of his hand signing for her to lead the way.

CHAPTER
ELEVEN

Ship's engineering calculated that all the cranes, overhead hoists, deck jacks, and winches they'd been able to rig had a combined rated lift of something under six hundred tons. The levers and forklifts Eddie Gairaszhek had masterminded raised the lifting capacity a good deal, but there had been no time to run precise calculations on how well they'd work, and Turret *Musashi*, even shorn of some of its armor, weighed an inescapable eight hundred tons—almost five percent of the *GammaLAW*'s total displacement.

The original plan had called for a crawler hoist to move the turret into place through special hatches retrofitted in the hull, but the hoist was a complete wipe, along with the starship that had brought it to Aquamarine.

The last component of Gairaszhek's crazyquilt "transporter" was in place. Since the ship lacked dumbots trustworthy enough for the delicate work, several human-piloted vehicles were standing by. Giaraszhek was waiting for Quant's go-ahead. Quant understood that his presence on the hangar deck amplified the lieutenant's nervousness but felt that he couldn't afford *not* to be there.

As he was about to give Gairaszhek the nod, he realized that Haven was standing nearby, Tonii at her elbow, but he fought down his usual objection to their presence. The commissioner and the gynander no longer seemed like outsiders. Hardship was weeding out the extraneous and the dispensable factors in their lives, fusing all hands. With the exception of Zone and his deranged severalmates and cohorts, the ship's company was free of dissenters, gawkers, or dead weights. Chaz Quant's ship was as important to them now as she'd been to him all along.

Haven was eyeing Quant with frank confidence when he turned to Gairaszhek and gave the go-ahead. "Whenever you're ready, Lieutenant."

Eddie stood like an orchestra conductor, shooting commands to the people positioned around the massive twin rifles. Power was slowly delivered to the hoists, cranes, and low-lift jacks. Eddie began circling the turret one way and then the other, sheepdog style, stooping to peer under it. Quant heard a creaking from the hangar deck and a distinct gunshot sound as a rivet went shooting from one of the crane arms, but he held his silence. Everyone knew that minor mishaps were likely. Then a section of deck sagged under the biggest crane. Its arm, laboring under half again the strain it had endured in its most extreme test lift, bent visibly, its double-strung cable tight as a banjo string. If it or any of the other lines snapped, it would become a lethal whiplash capable of cutting through solid metal.

Gairaszhek's talker relayed orders to the damage crews on the decks below to shore up the sagging section. Perhaps they managed it, perhaps not, but the subsidence of the deck stopped, in any case. Watching the turret rise by millimeters, Quant had to force himself to breathe.

To disperse the weight as much as to spare the deck, Kurt Elide had backed his robot hauler under a corner of the wide cargo bed itself, while other tractors, flatbeds, and transporters were easing into place under the guillotine weight of the rifles. The flatbed corner covered so much of Elide's dumbot's hull that he had had to duck down into his cupola, with only his head in the clear. If anything went wrong, he had no means of escape. But it was already too late: Gairaszhek had given the signal, and the turret was descending.

The suspension of Elide's vehicle complained as it was

pressed unmercifully down. There was a shout from someone as one of the manual levers shifted somehow, and two people were ground back against a hauler. The main battery dropped a sudden centimeter and a half, as if resolved to carry men and robots through the deck, through the bottom of the *GammaLAW*, and down into Lake Ea's muddy bed. Instead, however, the turret came to rest. A blast from Gairaszhek's whistle told the lifters to ease off their strain a little at a time. When the signal came to move out, Quant was ready; like the others, he started down the hangar deck for the aircraft elevator at an agonizing twenty meters per hour.

A bridge messenger hurried to his side. "Bridge officer's compliments, sir. You asked to be notified when it was time."

Quant nodded. It was almost 2100 hours, time to come about for the river's headwaters. Hampered by the absence of weather stats, the meteorologists had run their computations nevertheless and had made their forecast: clear weather conditions would prevail throughout much of the night. More, Aquamarine's two moons would be out. Quant glanced at Gairaszhek, who was just then studying the time display. The lieutenant was well aware that things were soon going to have to move a lot faster if Turret *Musashi* was to be of any use in defending the ship against Dynast Piety IV's steam cannons.

On his way back to the bridge Quant passed two dance therapists Haven had conscripted for the mission to avail herself of funding under some arts grant. Only now the husband and wife were working a composite applicator, repairing structural damage to what was supposed to be a watertight bulkhead. The woman raised her breather mask and gave Quant a thumbs-up. "Skipper! Keep 'er rolling!"

Quant responded with a self-conscious wave, assuming that she meant the turret. Gestures of support from crew members and other mission personnel had been on the increase since Quant had taken the ship safely through the dam-burst flood. It was a bonding process he'd observed previously in times of extreme common peril. Ironically, they all were behind him now as they might never have been if he'd somehow managed to avert the crisis altogether. But he knew from experience that solidarity was a fragile thing and that its loss could bring even greater hazards to one and all.

When he returned to the bridge, his first concern was to take the ship to full blackout. He took it as a given that Dynast Piety IV would have sentinels posted in Fluter Delve's watchtowers, but it was also possible that the grandee had dispatched ships to spy on the *GammaLAW*. The entire Ean region was doubtless wondering what the Visitants' next move would be.

The last thing Quant wanted was to go lights-out all at once. In accordance with his orders, therefore, the ship's company began dousing some sources of illumination and merely dimming others. People on all decks, all three hulls, donned IR goggles and snooperscopes; at least there were plenty of those to go around.

At length the *GammaLAW* was running without a single visible-range source showing, not even the tiny display screens of wrist whatties. Lighted areas such as the skeleton-crewed CIC were sealed off. Infrared illuminators rigged in haste that afternoon were switched on, and work went on in their eerie light. The ship could be spotted against the sky, of course, or in moonlight reflected on the water, but there was nothing anyone could do to alter those factors. And though she was making only twenty knots, she was still leaving a phantom trail of phosphorescence in her wake.

Ext snipers with sound-suppressed rifles scanned the waters. Orders were that any Aquam millship or floater that refused to heave to was to be sunk. There'd be no time to put out pursuit craft or risk raking potential spies with sonics and trusting that everyone aboard had been knocked cold. The Aquam had their own light-signaling systems, and a blinkered message passed along to the river fortress might precipitate a hail of steam cannon fire. Closer to shore, the sounds of the ship would carry—especially the work on the turret—but that was yet another unalterable.

Quant nursed the trimaran through her change of course like a man driving an ambulance in which emergency neurosurgery was being performed. The slightest deviation could send the turret off kilter, perhaps even hole the ship or make her broach to. Updates from the hangar deck said that Gairaszhek had increased the turret's speed to a hair-raising sixty meters per hour.

Quant also received reports that Zone and his gang were under close guard in the brig, damage control had repaired the greater part of the wounds inflicted by the flood, the turret barbette had been made ready, and the level of the lake was continuing to fall. Then, at 2300 hours, the calm was fractured by a distant groan of metal and the ship seemed to heel to port. Voice tubes whistled for the bridge's attention, but Quant grabbed for the hardwire phone to Gairaszhek's talker.

The poor kid couldn't keep the fright out of her voice. "Captain, the elevator's jammed! Weight overload caused a cutoff on the pistons, and we can't reactivate!"

Leaning out onto Vultures' Row, Quant could see what she was talking about. Nightmarish in IR, the huge naval rifles were poking precariously out over the rushing waters, preventing the turret from clearing the hangar deck as it was raised to the flight deck. From Quant's angle it looked as if the gun barrels were in danger of toppling the turret overboard with the first heavy roll of the ship. From the mount's positioning, Quant knew, Kurt Elide's dumbot had to have part of both tracks out over the water. He heard a clear rending of metal. Gairaszhek's talker's voice had a tension like a crane cable.

"Sir, main aircraft elevator's giving way."

Land hove into view in the eerie arctic light—the southern tip of the Passwater peninsula. The storm, the damage, or some interaction of automatics and counterfeit weather input had sent the pavilion elsewhere than the town, perhaps along its original approach vector from the Flyaway Islands.

Ghost had spent hours reinforcing and barricading the hatch, assembling weapons, collecting anything of use. Satisfied, she finally turned to Zinsser. "Can you lock down the automatics and the hood so no one can access the console?"

"You think the Insiders will be back?"

She motioned out the viewpane. "Unless the engines pick up. We may be over dry land, but that won't make a long fall any easier. Besides, the Insiders have as much reason to be nervous about the Scourland Ferals as they do about the Oceanic."

Zinsser thought briefly about the savages he had glimpsed from the Laputa days earlier, then rechecked the readouts. "I'm not sure that we *will* land. We might go off on some new heading or return to the old one."

Just then a tearing sound came from the hatch, along with the pounding of hammers and the distinct whine of a drill. As Ghost launched herself back at the doorway, the *Dream Castle* hobbled again, changing course. Zinsser's hackles rose as he realized that the airship was headed back out to sea.

At the hatch, Ghost paused only to hold a taper to the breach of her appropriated sling-gun, setting the special rounds' igniters burning. She waited until she saw a crack appear at the door, fired a blasting cap through the breech, then let go with both muzzles of the over-under double-shot weapon. Fire licked through the space at her, and cries issued from outside. In addition, a serrated, wickedly barbed boarding-pike-like thing jabbed in, accompanied by a vicious hooked weapon, both of which failed to snag her, thanks to the furniture she'd piled in the way.

Ghost dropped the two-shot, grabbed another, and let go with twin charges of glass flechettes. Even so, the Insiders kept hammering at the hatch. A flaming quarrel zipped in and buried itself in the bulkhead, singeing Ghost's face as she ducked aside.

"They're making progress," she said levelly as she backed away, letting fall the empty sling-gun and reloading the hybrid pistol.

Zinsser tried to remain focused on his tasks, but he had doubts about what he was doing. "I *think* I've got us headed back, but—"

"Down!"

No sooner had Ghost barked it than he saw the muzzle of a harquebus being wedged into the gap in the hatchway. As they both flattened themselves, the compartment filled with the buzzing of pellet projectiles that dug nasty wounds into furniture and bulkheads and even etched streaks in the tough material of the instrument facings.

Zinsser didn't waste a moment ordering the console to close itself. Ghost passed him in a low crawl, headed for the interior hatch through which they'd entered, stopping only to grab a bag of sling-gun ammunition.

"With luck, they won't be able to raise the hood," Zinsser told her as he followed, scrabbling on his belly, over the hatch coaming. As he did, he could hear the main hatch yielding to forced entry and could feel the heat as fires in the compartment burned higher.

Returned to the stairwell landing, he had to roll aside fast as Ghost hit the closure control. Once the hatch was secure, she started back down the helical stairs. Zinsser was bright enough to work out that without chutes or jetpacks or even lifelines, their best chance of bailing would be from low in the ship. The bottom of the hull, weighted by the fusion engines, would almost surely touch ground first. But where, or under what dynamics, was another question.

Descending, they passed other sealed-space hatches to unknown parts of the interior. Water, steam, and hydraulic fluid were spurting from broken pipes, and raw sewage was spraying freely in several places. There were sounds of rending metal and snapping stanchions and supports, hissing gases, bulkheads and frames crying out like mortally wounded behemoths. For all they knew, they were already walking dead from radiation poisoning, but they wouldn't have stopped even if they had known it was true.

Ghost halted to point out the hatch through which they had entered the interior from Testamentor's first-class stateroom in the outerworks. "That one."

Zinsser could see the marking she'd left on it and estimated that they were in the lowest part of the sealed spaces short of the engine area. He reached for the hatch controls, but Ghost stopped him.

"Only a quarter way!" She had to yell to be heard, yet her voice retained an eerie imperturbability.

Of course, Zinsser realized. There was no longer a gate, ramp, or railing on the other side, and now there was no outerworks either. He complied, easing the door open a slot. The pressure was minimal from the ship's interior, owing in part to the fact that the structural integrity was shot but in the main because the pavilion was flying so low.

"Oh, *Mother*!" Zinsser exclaimed.

He was looking out on breakers lapping the Passwater peninsula and at the onrushing town itself—its higher rooftops *above* the level of the hull bottom. The landing area was off to the right, out of *Dream Castle*'s current course, and the pavilion gave no sign of slowing or coming about.

The engines were surging and falling silent in broken time, making the whole vessel jerk and carousel. Seeing the coming air crash, Ghost braced herself in the hatchway, the wind ripping her hair loose from its tight chignon and whipping it around her scarred face. The lead edge of the hull didn't strike Zinsser as a good place to be. He began to struggle back up the passageway, but Ghost caught his arm.

"This might be the best place to jump. Anyway, there isn't time to reach another."

He shook his head. "We're not slowing. And we're too high! Best to brace ourselves onboard."

"And be crushed or trapped or rad-poisoned if the fusion engines rupture?"

He saw the wisdom of it. Even though the fusion was clean, the pavilion's containment housing had to have reached lethal levels of contamination decades earlier.

Dream Castle was spun as it hit some solid impediment, a steeple or spire, perhaps. Thruster balance was knocked out, but the ship careened on, canted forward. Ghost and Zinsser piled up in the angle between deck and hatch, in peril of falling out. As they helped hold each other back, Zinsser looked out on the rooftops of Passwater; on its balconies and streets, people of all ages were running every which way.

Another rooftop, this one lower, came at them but slid under, too low to hit. A slim minaret wasn't so lucky, however, and colliding with the hull, it reversed the Laputa's spin. Zinsser poked his head out the hatch in an effort to find the landing area but could no longer see it.

He did see something that made him shrink back like a turtle pulling in its head: the looming, massive stonework of the great peninsular wall. His last visual impression was of a metal and wood emplacement, a strangely designed affair of bellows, tanks, and wooden spokes. Instinctively, he threw his arms around Ghost, and she suffered it as the *Dream Castle* spun again spontaneously. The concussion seemed intent on driving them *through* the hull itself. Their section of the hull was spared the brunt of the collision, though it nearly killed them.

Surprised that he was still conscious, Zinsser glanced down through the hatch and saw the landscape swinging by underneath—the desolate black-gray gritscape of the Scourlands proper and, briefly, the glacier head that wound down out of the heights, just beyond the city wall. Another swing back, and the surface of the Scourlands was closer, the thrusters suddenly coughing to vigorous life, the Laputa determined to right itself despite the fact that systems were blowing open.

As the *Dream Castle* touched down in a monumental initial bump, a wash of hydraulic fluid, water, and sewage flooded down the passageway at them, bearing assorted debris and the lifeless body of Old Spume. Ghost instantly hit the hatch release as the airship struck again and began to furrow the ground. The hatch rolled open just as the flood was reaching them, and they were carried out the opening into nothingness—but only for seconds. Something solid stopped them without smashing them to jelly, and Zinsser realized that they'd fallen no more than a meter.

CHAPTER TWELVE

Scantlet's gracile mother was apparently of a different mind about the death sentence Mason figured he had earned twenty years earlier. Having worked her way up behind him and freed his left leg, she was now tugging at his right foot, slowly getting him unjammed.

"There's no time," Mason told her. "Save yourself." Spindly as she was, she could slide past him into the real exit route. But the woman ignored him, much as he was ignoring Yatt.

"Purifyre needs you," she said. "He'll need you even more now."

Wet and sweat-slick as they were, it took three tries before she freed up his right foot, as well. Pain made the breath explode from him as she pulled his hip free from where it was lodged.

"Stop," Mason yelled.

"Won't!"

The same all-out pull on his elbow that liberated him yanked her thin slippery fingers loose and sent her lurching backward. Mason heard her mournful cry and the splash that punctuated her fall into the Amnion. Heaving himself clear, he saw by the light of the lantern and the rising phosphorescent flood tide that what was left of her was impossible to reach. Deliberately, she had spared him the death that had overtaken her.

Unlike her son, who had been turned to water, she was slowly slumping into the basin pool and shrinking in on her-

100

self, as if the bones had been spirited from her body. The last Mason saw of her were her narrow, kindly features floating in the water like a face preserved in a specimen jar. The water churned higher as she disappeared in a swirl of hair and turbulence.

Beyond screaming, he rolled himself over into the proper exit route and forced himself to ascend in a panicked overhand backstroke, kicking with his heels even as his head struck various obstructions. Again he'd left the lantern. At length he flipped onto his stomach, clawing and thrashing uphill like a madman. Flashes of lightning guided him. With what breath he had, he yelled for Purifyre and Ballyhoot, but neither was there to lend a hand when he surfaced.

As he wormed his way free of the tunnel, his waning panic turned to shock. Sitting half-sprawled on a boulder at the foot of a vertical rock face five meters away was Ballyhoot, wounds in her side and temple leaking blood that shone black in the harsh flicker of distant lightning. In the aftermath of the fire stroke came dim illumination from another of the iron travel lanterns, this one lying on its side, crystal mantle panes shattered. By it Mason saw that the open area around the tunnel mouth was another cul-de-sac, though smaller and not as sheer-sided as the one formed by the Arras. Someone had installed wooden slats as ladder rungs in a narrow crevice to the right, but all except the top and bottom ones were gone.

Two men were lying spread-eagled and unmoving at Ballyhoot's feet. Mason recognized them as picaroons by their rogues' tatters and tentacled hair. Both Juts cutthroats were dead; one with his skull hideously staved in and the other with a hole burned through him by Purifyre's detonator-cap pistol. The wind was driving rain and salt water with hurricane force. Mason hoped that the Oceanic was adhering to its own rules of engagement by dissociating those portions of itself carried on the wind.

Ballyhoot's fighting flail slipped from her lap, its chain

snapped and the swingle missing. Mason had no doubt how
the one dead pic had gotten his skull crushed. "Purifyre," she
started to say. She couldn't get any more words out, but she
found the strength to point to the summit of the rock face on
which she was leaning. Scantlet's mother had been right: Purifyre did need him. But with the steps ripped from the crevice,
the quickest route up was gone.

Mason didn't even try to apprise Ballyhoot of his plan. Arms
pistoning, he charged straight for her. She intuited what he had
in mind but was too weak to do much more than plaster herself
to the face behind her, digging her fingers into handholds and
bracing herself in a seated crucifixion.

He left the ground in a leap, taking one step off the rock between her legs and planting his foot, without qualm or apology,
on her upraised face. He paid no attention to her gargling grunt,
the feel of her nose giving way, or the pain of her filed teeth
piercing his bare heel as he launched himself as high as he
could, clutching for handholds right and left. Air-pedaling until
he found toeholds, he finally drew himself up into wailing.
With a final kick, he breasted the top, thrashing all the more furiously when he saw what was occurring there.

The elfin boy was down with a sling-gun quarrel protruding
from his belly, while his twin sister was squaring off with a
picaroon—he with a short jabbing spear, she with a polearm
that had a cutlass blade. Behind them, three more pics were
pressing Purifyre back against a stone, all locked in squirming,
straining battle, blades bared. Two more reavers were lying
dead on the rocks.

Ignoring the girl's peril, Mason unholstered his flechette
pistol as he rushed to save his son. Pinning the boy by sheer
weight of numbers, his assailants were about to carve into
him. Everyone was too intertwined for Mason to risk a shot;
worse, it was too dark to tell exactly who he was shooting at
or where, precisely, he was putting his feet. He stumbled to
all fours, losing the pistol among the canted rocks. He would

have thrown himself into the fight regardless if a cold, green-blue aura hadn't come creeping over the Juts, the picaroons, the elf girl, and Purifyre—even over Mason.

His skin prickled, but he experienced no pain. Some automatic retrieval function in Mason's brain threw up the explanation: Yahweh's Fire, a charge-separation phenomenon even less common than a Big Sere blirt. The phosphorescence mantled everything and everyone on the Juts, coating the bridge, high and to the east, with what looked like luminescent ice. Its glow made the picaroons ease off and screech in fear. The effervescing Yahweh's Fire also danced along linear outlines in a dark pocket of rock, revealing Mason's 'chettergun. He snatched it up and whirled to bellow a warning to his son.

Purifyre heard him and instantly dropped between the legs of the picaroon in front of him. He couldn't get clear, but he was crouched low and they were still standing. Mason held down the trigger, and the air cracked with the sound of high-velocity minidarts. The gun fell silent in a quarter second, its propellant cartridge exhausted, but all three pics were dead.

Mason helped Purifyre drag himself free. The elfin girl had overcome the other picaroon. Purifyre tugged a grapnel and line of knotted climbing rope free of one of the corpses.

"I'm going back for Ballyhoot," he announced. "Did you see her?"

Mason nodded wearily, then changed it to a head tic. "She's alive . . . just below, there—" He stopped as he heard voices coming from the direction of Gapshot, calling "Hammerstone!" into the wind. He raised the empty gun, but Purifyre pushed it down.

"They're friends."

The members of the Gapshot contingent were dressed in rags, but they carried themselves with martial bearing. More constables in mufti, Mason decided. Inside an hour they had the Jut-hop survivors ashore and sequestered in a room at the back of a warehouse. Mason, Purifyre, and the elfin girl were wrapped in blankets around a fire pit, and Ballyhoot was laid out on a small, grubby cot.

The rendezvous group's leader explained that his delay in reaching Purifyre had been due to other picaroon freebooting posses. Purifyre, however, had little time for it. Instead, he busied himself reloading the det-cap shooter, donning body armor and garments Mason couldn't place, and calling for updates on the planned bridge barbican assault. His subordinates had procured a hooksword and rope dart. The parrying weapon that had served him so well against the picaroons he transferred to one of his arming belts. From his pack came his baton of command with its four-winged male figurine cap.

By midnight rushed preparations were in place. All that remained to do was trip the bridge's Horatio option—and Purifyre was the key to that.

The Horatio gadge was a perfectly mundane Optimant voice-recognition unit concealed within the barbican and secreted outside it. It had been taken from a wrecked garage door, and Boon had repaired and mated it to a solar power pack, keying it to his voice and Purifyre's only. Its simple function was to activate a solenoid, which in turn would yank a release. After that a system of counterweights, levers, motors, and worm gears would lock down the bridge's critical structural members—those a holding force would theoretically remove to sever the bridge in times of invasion. The Horatio option also disengaged portcullis bolts and gate jamb bracings. Boon had managed to keep the fail-safe system to himself and a few trusted engineers and artisans, though it alone wasn't enough to stop a determined force from wreaking havoc on the span.

Purifyre's gathered lieutenants were gearing up as well, waiting to convoy the young man they knew as Hammerstone to join with other countercoup units gathered in hidden staging areas scattered around Gapshot. Purifyre-Hammerstone heard out a report confirming that most Gapshotters, the municipal legion in particular, had hung back from rallying around Kinbreed's call to arms; their reluctance stemmed from the main-landers' forebodings about the Trans-Bourne's militant posses-siveness and genius for revenge. Analyses by several observers suggested, however, that if Kinbreed held the bridge to the dawn deadline, the day would see hangers-on and opportunists flocking to him—another reason the mutiny had to be sup-pressed immediately.

Mason was about to point out that the Gapshotters might all take up arms if they saw invading constables streaming to the attack through their city streets. Then he realized that the troops preparing to liberate the bridge weren't wearing con-stabulary armor but that of Gapshot legionnaires or in some cases civilian war gear. Each wore a homemade badge with a black cross against a white field, the symbol having two hori-zontal arms like an Old Earth patriarchal cross.

Catching Mason's gaze, Purifyre tapped a badge with his baton of command and its double-wing-set figurine. "A winged man—to let us know one another and to set us apart from the club-clover wearers who support Kinbreed."

"Where's mine? I'm going with you."

Purifyre gestured to the fighting men and women awaiting his orders, and they repaired to the other side of the room. "Your legs are injured, and your gun is useless. You'd only be a hindrance and endanger people." The boy suddenly seemed older than his eighteen years and spoke as if Mason were the son and he were the father. "Unless that is what you wish, stay here and look after Ballyhoot." He nodded to the corner where local poultice slingers were attending to Ballyhoot's wounds. Purifyre had had to threaten to strap her to the bed frame to win the concession that she was hors de combat.

Mason frowned. "And get my head gnawed off?"

Purifyre rose, deadpanning, "Word of advice: don't waste your time punching to her body." Then he was off, trailed by men and women who were older, larger, and hardened by combat and campaigning yet were showing respect for him.

Their footfalls had no sooner stopped shaking the warped floor planks than Ballyhoot gave a cough and reached for the handle of a dipper sticking up from a firkin cask just out of reach. Her wounds had been sewn up with some gut strings from a dulciphone, poultices bandaged on with rags that looked like they'd seen a lot of dirty pots and pans. One eye was swollen nearly shut, and her nose had ballooned, fractured when Mason had used her face for a springboard back on the Juts. Her lips were slashed and puffed up from his foot mashing them into her filed teeth. One fang was missing, having broken off after it punctured his heel. She still wore the knife fighter's vambraces, but both sheaths were empty; under the bed lay the haft arm of her fighting flail, its pivot chain broken and the swingle lost out on the Juts.

Since the attending herbalists had left with Purifyre, Mason very reluctantly got up and limped over to the cask, which was half-filled with gooner. What the hell, he thought. The medicine phials she'd been given probably contained the same stuff. He filled the dipper for her but hesitated when he took stock of the stare she was giving him.

"Were Tinella's last words anything we should pass along to those who knew her?" she slurred through inflated lips. She sounded tired rather than hostile.

Scantlet's mother, Mason assumed.

"She was one of the most devoted to our cause," Ballyhoot added. "From the early days, one of the best-hearted. We can at least make remembrance of her final words." She took a long slug of gooner.

"She said how awful it felt to be a parent who'd outlived her child."

"I expect that's true." Ballyhoot looked to the door through which Purifyre had left. "I expect we could find that out for sure before daylight, you and me."

From the pain in her voice and the look on her face, Mason expected her to finish the gooner with one swig, but instead she offered it to him. When he hesitated, she told him, "No worries, Claude Mason. You're all right by me now."

He sank cautiously to a stool one of the healers had used and swallowed a mouthful of the Aquam drain cleaner. "Because I stepped on your face?" For all he'd known—when he had used her so ruthlessly—she was dying and he was finishing her off.

"One way of putting it. Now I know you're not all weakly overnice, with honey water in your veins. You've got surpassing cruelness in you when you need it—which a father to Purifyre will."

Mason couldn't think of anything to say, so he spit into his right palm. She did the same—weakly, with strands of blood in the spittle. Then they clasped hands; her skin like a rasp, her grip like a power shackle.

"So now we just wait to see if he survives? I did that for years; I can't do it again."

"Nor I. Hence, I passed word behind my hand for a palanquin. We'll follow at a distance. Help me up, Claude Mason, and fetch our gear. And be sure to refill the dipper while you're at it."

CHAPTER THIRTEEN

Hearing and feeling the elevator shift under him, Kurt Elide fought panic and paralysis. The mountainous main battery was above and behind him; Lake Ea's waters were below, foaming in the ghost colors of his IR goggles. His first coherent thought was to wriggle to freedom through the small gap in the cupola even if it meant breaking a collarbone. The alternative was to be driven into the lake bottom mud by about twelve hundred pitiless tons of transporters, naval cannon, armor, and rigging, perhaps still alive and struggling against death when the cold muck enfolded him, maybe even to be fed upon by the ravenous, alien things that lived down there.

Then Kurt realized that Gairaszhek was calling his name over the hardwire earphone. "Elide? I said sound off!"

The lieutenant had obviously been commo checking with all the in situ transporter drivers. "I hear you," Elide managed after several false starts.

"All right, everybody listen up," Gairaszhek said. "Stay put—and I mean don't even twitch. The elevator's jammed, and it's gonna take us a while to get things moving. The last thing we need is any of you climbing around out there, and we *will* need you at your controls. So maintain an even strain, and I'll sitrep you as I can."

Kurt had thought ahead enough to bring along a canteen. But now he found that his most urgent need was to empty his bladder even though he'd hit the head before boarding the dumbot. There was no convenience tube or other latrine arrangement in the cupola, of course. He thought it over, gazing around the weirdly lit interior the IR goggles showed him; then he eased his head up out the cupola hatchway, which was now mostly blocked by the corner of the turret flatbed. Surely the weight of one man wouldn't mean anything in relation to so many tons of dead weight, he told himself.

The slight, slow roll of the ship and the distant thrumming of engines carried through the deck. He could hear the rush of the waters against the *GammaLAW*'s hulls. He wriggled one arm out of the cupola, following with his head and then pushing against the operator's seat with his feet. It was a tight fit, and he was starting to turn ever so slightly to the right when the elevator groaned. Kurt knew that he was crazy to think that the shift had had anything to do with him, but he froze where he was nonetheless.

"At ease, people," Gairaszhek's voice said in his ear. "No problem. Just stand to and be ready to move the second I tell you to."

Kurt hung in the hatchway, thinking. Even if he succeeded in extricating himself from the dumbot, he was going to have to struggle all the more to get back in—if that was at all possible. That would mean long minutes away from his controls, with the dumbot in a crucial position.

He felt stymied in more ways than one: the disastrous turn of events for the GammaLAW mission, the ire of the population it was supposed to be helping, the Nixies, Lazlo's death, Zone's rebellion, and now this suicidal attempt to move the immovable. It wasn't at all what he had signed up for.

At length he squirmed back down into the operator's seat, opened his trousers, and pissed in the least bothersome place—down to the left of the foot pedals—figuring that the urine would seep through the deck plates.

He felt a little better for having relieved himself, but not much; all of a sudden he needed to take a crap.

* * *

Quant took the update from the hangar deck in person, relieving his talker of the need to relay it. "Just give me the burst-twix, Lieutenant. Yes or no?"

"Then I'd say yes, Captain," Gairaszhek told him, "in about two hours. We're moving in additional reinforcements as well as rigging deck hoists to help raise the elevator—"

"I haven't got two hours, Eddie," Quant said, cutting him off. "The lake water level's not going to wait." He was interrupted by a yeoman passing along a hard-copy message, which he quickly scanned and got back to Gairaszhek. "If you can't raise or lower the elevator, at least belay it so that it won't shift on us." He'd already had to order some counterflooding in the port sponson to offset the weight of the turret and its carriers. "Weather center says we can expect extreme fog conditions and cloud cover by dawn, and I mean to take advantage of that."

A mist was already rolling across the lake. With proper satellite and remote data, he'd have been apprised of the cloud cover hours earlier, but now he was like some old-time ironclad skipper relying on the senses God had given him.

Gairaszhek's voice sounded cautious. "What are your orders, sir?"

"Rig for silence. Our priority is to sneak ourselves past Fluter Delve. We'll worry about Turret *Musashi* when we're in the clear."

With hundreds of kilometers of navigable water downstream to give her deep, wide protection from Aquam attack, the *GammaLAW* could ride out the remaining days of the dry season in relative security. The breather would give the ship's company time for repairs and reorganization, time to improvise or construct new weapons and vehicles, and most important, time to evaluate the new situation and find a way to carry out the mission.

The Roke were the only tormenting unknown Quant had to

push aside for the moment, because there was simply no way of knowing or even guessing what the Roke would or could do from Aquamarine's lesser moon. All the previous supposition about the planet's immunity to Roke inroads seemed to be out the window. But since the Roke had yet to show themselves, it was perhaps true that Aquamarine held some secret power over them, one that could be discovered and exploited. But the aliens weren't Quant's problem now; the fortress was.

"We may have to jettison that turret before we're through," he told Gairaszhek, "possibly the whole damn elevator with it. I want teams in position with heavy cutters."

"But the vehicle drivers, sir. They might not have time—"

"Pull them back for now, but keep them standing by."

Giaraszhek was tentative. "Sir . . . Captain, even our heaviest cutters might be too slow in a contingency situation. I don't like this any better than you do, but—"

"What, you don't like the idea of an eight-hundred-ton turret running the ship hard aground?"

"Sir, I think we should rig demolitions—just in case."

Quant felt about as comfortable as he would have with his prick laid out on a slicer, but he nodded to himself. "Rig them, Eddie."

By the time the *GammaLAW* reached the headwaters of the river, the fog had settled in so thickly that Quant couldn't see a half meter out the bridge windshield without vision enhancers. The surviving ROVers had been deployed on umbilicals to probe the river bottom. Sonar and radar and every functioning detector scanned the haze.

He took his ship slowly into the deepest passage, just off the northern bank and the bluffs. The fortress was on the opposite shore, protected by shallows and cliffs but not sufficiently far away for Quant's comfort. IR and radar showed it in considerable detail: bigger than Rhodes's stronghold, mostly Optimant construction, built along lines that suggested pillbox, bunker, and hardened weapons emplacement.

Perhaps the Optimants had had their paranoids, too. There were projections and other design features, unclear in the scopes but uncomfortably evocative of cannon, missiles, and directed-energy installations. Quant had to keep reminding himself what all the evaluations said about it being impossible for any advanced weapons to have survived two centuries, yet he couldn't help but think of the antenna array at Wall Water that might have brought down Commissioner Starkweather's *Jotan*.

He ordered the *GammaLAW* to dead slow and entered the gauntlet of the headwaters.

Under the wan light of Aquamarine's two moons Burning and Souljourner moved with fresh energy through the lush wildness of the Ghoul Grounds. The remains of tumbledown huts, outbuildings, and cottages began cropping up more frequently, lifeless as rotted teeth. Moss grew everywhere in thick pelts of green, yellow, and blue. In many cases strangler vines and ivy made it impossible to discern the basic shapes of the structures they'd overgrown, and in places it was tough to tell what had been lane or alley, shed or domicile. They double-timed through what had once been a village square, judging from the two-story-high fountain that dominated it like a tiered centerpiece of flaking, free-form botanical decor.

Burning had the creeping sensation that mold was taking root in his exposed skin and that fungus spores were lodging themselves in his gullet and lungs. His misgivings about what lay ahead had weakened his Flowstate to the point where an Ean man at arms came within a pubic hair of nailing him just as he was exiting the village square.

All that saved him was the fact that the abrupt head-on took the Ean by surprise as well. The man had come bounding around a huge, flora-engulfed pile with too much momentum to organize an effective attack. It was Burning's dumb luck that the solider had sheathed his pata-style gauntlet sword to take up his horn, though that didn't leave him unarmed. As he charged to close, he struck with the targone shield on his left forearm.

Such Skills as Burning had cultivated by the outbreak of the Concordance War probably wouldn't have saved him; it was the years of combat since then that enabled him to raise his forearm in time, meaty inner part presented to cushion the targone's backhanded swing. He ignored the pain and the numbing impact, praising his good fortune that the shield-club lacked cutting edges, spikes, or similarly nasty customizing.

The praetorian's uniform marked him as an Unconquerable, one of the select troopers of Grandee Fabia Lordlady, the only woman among the Ean rulers. A hefty man of medium height, he was armed with a sling-gun carbine as well as the short-sword, and high on his right forearm rode a sharp-honed crescent of knife. His signal horn was a single coil brayophaunt, which he let fall as he made a tentative slash at Burning with the armlet, only to be hampered by Burning's seizing the targone in a two-handed come-along. The shield-club was a long slender oval of wood-reinforced leather, its wide, rounded end protecting the elbow and its slightly truncated tapered end extending a few centimeters beyond fingertip length. Slightly peaked along the long axis of its outer surface, it was highly polished and hard to catch in a solid grip.

How a weapon from the bloody Pisan Renaissance sport of giuoco del ponte had cropped up on an Aquam arm was an illustration of Post-Cyberplague desperation lost to history. Burning, however, was too busy to contemplate the oddity. His hold on the targone failing, he yanked hard as if to pull the Unconquerable to his knees. Resisting automatically, his opponent wrenched upward, and Burning instantly shifted from pull to push, jujitsu-fashion. The man's arm flew up, unbalancing him and exposing his entire right side to attack. With no time to reach for his ka-bar, Burning cocked his left knee up to his right shoulder and drove a heel-first side kick into the Unconquerable's rib cage.

It was even less effective than he had anticipated. Included in the Unconquerable kit was brigandine sewn with small metal plates and cushioned with that damnable quilted Optimant cargo padding. The gel-filled padding had rendered lots of Aquam fighters highly resistant to Ext sonics and now helped the Unconquerable shrug off Burning's kick.

By then, though, Burning had put two meters between himself and the Ean and was holding his 'baller in a cup-in-saucer grip before the man's hand could so much as find his sword hilt.

"Stand fast or die," Burning told him. If ammo had not been in such perilously short supply, he might already have shot. Dextra Haven's diplomatic guidelines carried elaborate injunctions about indig life and limb, but the meltdown at Wall Water had changed all that. With the manhunt hubbub coming from many directions now, there wasn't time for any rule-book disarm. "Turn around," he added, motioning with the hardballer's muzzle for emphasis.

The soldier shuffled his feet as if about to comply, but it was all a smoke screen; shielding it with the targone, he was cheating his right elbow closer to his left hand. Burning decided it was worth a .50 to finish the whole unavoidable situation. But just as the Unconquerable was plucking his armlet knife, Souljourner's unexpected spasm of motion voided the script. She listed against Burning and straight into the path of the expected blade.

The Ean flicked his weapon loose with a twist and cast it. Burning realized that Souljourner meant to take the twirling knife stroke for him if she couldn't block it with her carbine or drive them both out of the way, so he let her muscle him sideways, adding his own momentum to their evasion. At the same time he reached over her shoulder and grabbed hold of the sinuously curved stock of her sling-gun. As the armlet whickered past, close enough to stir his Hussar Plaits, he pushed the carbine down and squeezed the trigger.

Skills weren't infallible, however, and Burning had had only brief familiarization fire with indig weapons. The quarrel passed well east of the Ean and vanished into the wilds, but by then Burning had reacquired a sight picture down the 'baller's barrel. The Unconquerable was springing, sweeping his patasword free, when Burning shot him in the center of his mass. The shaggy buildings fronting the plaza echoed the monstrous pop of the .50, drubbing Burning's ears and startling an involuntary yip out of Souljourner.

The Ean's dashing brigandine vest was no use against a parabellum slug. A hole appeared in one of the little oblong plates above his sternum, and the armsman let out a shriek, throwing his arms wide. He fell forward to his knees instead of being borne over backward by the impact. Even so, Burning kept his head dot on the man, ready to deal another round if necessary, but only until the Ean teetered sideways into the weeds, blood spilling from his mouth to mat his beard.

The sound of an ululiphaunt close by tugged Burning from a moment's contemplation of his act; any safe margin for lingering was gone. He stooped to retrieve the Unconquerable's sling-gun and targone, while Souljourner, choking back queasiness, tugged at the man's baldric, perhaps trying for the quiver and maybe a spare sling-gun as well.

"Leave that. There's no time!"

She glanced at him, then began to yank at the strap that held the Unconquerable's brayophaunt. When the horn wouldn't come loose, she took out her potmetal knife and sawed through the piece of braided pogopod hide that secured it. Burning's follow-up entreaty that she hurry was underscored by a quarrel that hissed past them.

Two Diehards of Dynast Piety IV appeared from the southeast, the direction that he'd thought was open and in which

Souljourner claimed that Alabaster lay. The second Diehard loosed another missile while the lead man reloaded, but that dart, too, flew high by a meter. Burning raised himself in a prone firing position, gripping the pistol with both hands. But while the Diehards were obviously winded from the cross-country run, they weren't brain-trussed; the pair flattened themselves in the bracken, safe from him unless he was willing to squander ammo in a recon by fire.

Burning's plan to break contact, even if it meant going to ground in one of the tumbledown houses, went inoperative when voices and clarion notes ushered additional pursuers into the square from all directions.

"Up! Delta V!" he yelled to Souljourner, whose arms were cradling the Unconquerable's brayophaunt and shortsword. Only one halfway hopeful shred of cover remained. When she stared uncomprehendingly, he added, "The fountain! Kick out!"

CHAPTER
FOURTEEN

Awed by the enormous weight of the *Dream Castle* hovering over her, Ghost refused to let herself pass out. With its rounded hull, it seemed to be hanging on a precipice, poised to roll her deep into the Scourland grit. Panting for breath that wouldn't come, she seized Zinsser and began dragging him along a meter at a time. He was stirring by the time she got them out from under the looming hull.

Ghost wiped blood, *henjo*, and hydraulic fluid from her eyelids. When her vision cleared, she was looking across some five klicks or so at the Passwater wall. *Dream Castle* had bashed a huge section of stone blocks onto the wasteland floor, opening a gap that reached nearly to ground level. Lying among the stones were the pieces of the rampart flame cannon, its volatile oil leaking darkly into the sands. Towering over the wall was the so-called Backbone Keep—a key element of what was to have been the Optimants' 150-meter-high visible physiology unharmed by the *Laputa*'s passing.

She was hurting all over, but she willed the pain to retreat; it was a discipline she'd used a thousand times as a POW. Her overriding concern made her scan for the hoist that, until the crash, had been the sole means of crossing Passwater's bulwark. Willing it into focus, she saw that the platform was being raised. That was no surprise; the Passwaterites understood their terrifying situation and were withdrawing behind the wall.

What had her more concerned were the Ferals encamped

around the redoubt, but just then no bounders or whip-plying wild men were racing toward the wreck of the Laputa. Its crash had to have been seen, however, and surely it was only a matter of time before they appeared.

"MeoTheos."

Ghost looked around at the sound of Zinsser's voice to see him staring at the horribly mangled corpse of Old Spume. Spume wasn't just broken-shapeless; his robes had been ripped off, and a vast section of his torso simply had been eaten away. Recalling the acid squirtgun he carried, Ghost ventured that Spume probably hadn't been in any condition to feel the acid by the time the *Dream Castle* had gone to ground.

Zinsser was struggling to his feet. "Are you well enough to climb? Perhaps we should start at the top and work down."

"What are you talking about?"

"Them! Are you deaf?"

She could hear the faint screams, moans, and pleas for help or mercy from God coming from inside the *Dream Castle*, but they simply didn't enter into her calculations. "No," she answered tonelessly. "Are you blind?"

He turned to see what she meant and said "MeoTheos!" again. Raising ellipsis-line puffballs of dust across the wastes as they came, a small band of Scourland Ferals were racing down from the distant highlands on their bounders, bearing straight for the wrecked Laputa. Ghost studied Zinsser curiously, waiting for him to realize that any effort to help the Insiders would ultimately land them in the hands of the Ferals. She watched him heave a sigh and cast a last guilty glance at the broken *Dream Castle*. "Should we head for the hoist or the gap in the wall?"

"The Ferals would ride us down before we could reach either." She couldn't help but grunt as she came to her feet, but she refused the hand he extended.

"What, then? We can't fight them—and there's no music to dance to."

She tilted her head with a hint of fey amusement he would have opened his wrists to see only a few days before. But all she did was indicate the glacial terminus off to the northeast. Then she turned to count her remaining blasting caps, which amounted to four.

When it occurred to Zinsser to ask what she had in mind, Ghost had already started off, so he simply hurried after her. Noting the rapid approach of the Ferals' dust cloud, he gradually took the lead. Ghost nursed a limp but kept pace without complaint as they dogtrotted across the windblown pumice.

"What's our . . . plan?" Zinsser puffed at last.

She was about to answer when the blast of a hunting whistle sounded from the faraway Ferals. Their bounders were eating up the ground at a frightening rate. "Hope for mushrooms," Ghost threw over her shoulder at him, pointing at a forest of serac glacial structures and legs stretching into a flat-out run.

The grit made for tendon-tearing footing, and when they finally reached the middle heights, flakes and fragments of boulder made the ground even more treacherous. Another whoop from a hunting whistle made Zinsser stop and turn. A splinter group of Ferals had reached the edge of the scree field. The bounders were negotiating the rock debris with great dexterity, hardly slowed by it.

Gasping for breath, Zinsser stopped. "Give me the gun. I'll try to hold them here—"

"No." She was as calm as ever. "Our luck holds, see?"

He did see, and he understood then what she had been talking about earlier. There, where great rock hunks of fluvioglacial drift had shielded the ice beneath them from Eyewash's rays, ice mushrooms had formed, grit-speckled formations as low as ankle height to as high as forty and fifty meters, holding aloft flakes of stone ranging from hand-size to house-big.

When they reached the glacial terminus with its bizarre sculpture garden of frozen water and naked stone, Ghost spun and readied her pistol, only to find herself staring into a face she knew. Leading the pack, drawing rein now that he thought he had his prey at bay, was Asurao, the Feral whom she had seen from the *Dream Castle* and who had returned her look.

Ghost held her gun high. "Turn back or I kill you all!"

The threat drew wild laughter, and several of the Ferals rose up in their stirrups to make obscene gestures, flaunt their penises, or yell taunts and counterthreats. But Asurao waved his toothed war club and thumped his chest, crying, "You should be grateful for your luck! For today you become the concubine of the slaughterboss of the Massacre Cirque Polis!"

Ghost motioned Zinsser out of the way and took aim at a nearby ice column. Divining her intent, Zinsser didn't need any encouragement to dive for cover. Ghost pressed her thumb down on the detonator, and a red-hot jet of blasting gas ate through the column in an instant. The ice exploded in steam and glittering shards, plucking at her uniform and tearing at her face. She'd chosen her point of aim carefully, and as the column shattered, a boulder as big and sharp-prowed as a whale boat dropped to rumble down the slope, touching off a minor avalanche as it went.

The triumph on Asurao's face had already been transformed to puzzlement; now it showed astonishment, if not the apprehension she'd hoped for. The Feral threw his mouth wide in a kind of mayhem-loving glee and spurred his bounder hard, leaving his companions to escape the narrow defile as best they could. Ghost reloaded and dashed to another serac stone.

The huge granite fragment continued to hurtle downslope, breaking another ice-mushroom column along the way. Some of the Ferals had followed Asurao's lead, but others were slower on the uptake. One man and his mount fell directly under the rampaging stone without influencing its course; a second barely missed being crushed against an even bigger boulder, but his bounder's right leg was pinched off, leaving a red-spouting stump.

Ghost didn't pause to admire her handiwork. She shot

through a second ice pedestal on which teetered an even bigger monolith. Rounded and plump, it required a second shot. The blasting-cap detonator was hot enough to blister her hands, but her shot sent the second boulder leaping and plowing and skittering down on the Ferals like an Olympian curling stone, initiating a rock slide that became a general land slip. With bounders screaming and Ferals crying out in anger and confusion, the whole slope seemed to surge, and a flash flood of rock was bashed into motion.

Ghost's fourth shot blew apart the highest serac in the vicinity, throwing a giant javelinlike obelisk at the Ferals. Out of blasting caps, she regarded what she'd wrought. The hillside was on the move, seracs collapsing, ground debris sliding, boulders knocking other boulders loose. Dust had risen in clouds, and the ground was shaking. It seemed, in fact, that the slope might slide right out from under her.

In time, however, the landslide played itself out and the dust began to settle, coating everything below a uniform black-gray. There was nothing to be seen of the Ferals except for one rider leap-galloping back the way he'd come. Zinsser picked himself up, spitting stone dust and dabbing at his eyes.

"He'll be back with reinforcements. I say we head for the wall."

Picking their way down through the debris, they saw a second figure moving. Gray-black as a statue, Asurao was limping clear of the devastation. He'd lost his war club and bounder, and his proud rope suit of piezoelectric nodes appeared to have been torn from him. Ghost gazed down at him and on impulse put two fingers in her mouth and let out a sharp whistle.

Asurao glanced back matter-of-factly, studying her with a different sort of calculation. He coughed out dirt and dust and showed white teeth in a slit-eyed leer. "Well! My goddess of the pavilion. What a temper you have! I was wrong about you. I'm not going to put you in my harem; Asurao shall throw all the others out and make you his only bride!" He reached down and waggled his muddy penis at her amiably.

Injured, unarmed, and afoot, he didn't seem to have a fear in the world. Ghost wondered if he, too, counted himself dead. Odd, she thought, that he could be so contemptuous of death yet find such zest for living.

"I'll give you your own war band to lead," Asurao added. "I'll even change my name to yours if you like!"

Ghost pointed the blasting-cap gun at him and thumbed it in a bluff. Then she faced toward the gap in the Passwater wall and started off. Asurao stayed put, aware that he'd be at a disadvantage if he came at her. Instead, he cupped his hands to his mouth and shouted, "You'd make a good Feral, you know! Perhaps a great one!"

The palanquin that arrived in response to Ballyhoot's summons was retchingly smelly, coming apart at the seams, and probably infested with fabric fauna. But it was roomy enough for Ballyhoot and Mason, and its carry poles were borne by four hard-eyed bruisers who weren't afraid to take a fare to the Styx Strait bridge. It was a chaotic, joggling ride through a predawn Gapshot alive with fire gongs, riot, and the sounds of battle.

The huskies cuffed and kicked their way through flocking humanity until the palanquin stopped near the span's northern barbican. Watching the upheaval through a window slit, Mason saw that the barbican portcullis was down, it and the ramparts guarded by a mixed company of heavily armed soldiery. Some were Purifyre's assault troops in ersatz Gapshot legionnaire garb; most were black-armored bridge constables from the Trans-Bourne rather than club-clover-wearing mutineers.

Townsfolk milled in angry confusion, calling challenges and obscene threats while maintaining a wary distance. Cobbles of the traffic circus before the barbican were dry after the blirt rain, but blood smeared the stones or was draining away into the. seams between them. The palanquin bearers who'd been so free with their buffets and shoves among the Gapshotters balked at moving within range of the cocked sling-guns of the aroused southerners. Rather than argue with them, Ballyhoot alighted painfully from the passenger box, handing the team-ster honcho a silver scudo. The team about-faced at the poles and thrashed back the way they had come.

Ballyhoot was leaning on Mason, and Mason on her some-what, when a constabulary officer approached to shoo them away. He held a baton of lesser command but lowered it, changing his tone, gaze, and stance as he took in her flaring shock of salt-and-pepper hair as well as the remaining half of her fighting flail. Even without her helmet—and even with her swollen nose—Ballyhoot was easily recognizable. She silenced the officer's protests that the trouble wasn't over. Then—after commandeering two sling-gun rifles to use as crutches—she pressganged him to clear a path to Purifyre.

Hobbling through the small fortress that was the barbican, Mason carefully stayed within Ballyhoot's charmed sphere of influence; the countercoup forces were edgy and unappeased. There were bodies of club-clover wearers piled along the walls, confiscated weapons stacked in corners, signs of hand-to-hand fighting everywhere, and the coppery smell of blood. They passed out the gate onto a bridge still dripping rainwater and lit by leaping bale fires and budding sunlight. Far below and to the right the Juts had disappeared under the noyade tide. The Oceanic had manifested itself as burgeoning upwells, swiftly running locobrates, and spiraling phospho-rescent swhorls.

On the bridge, trussed-wristed prisoners were being sub-dued with flails, fists, sling-gun butts, and whatever else came to hand. Ballyhoot and Mason's unwilling escort officer opened a course through the crush and collision of friend and foe with whacks of his scimitar despite being nearly gutted by a long-handled moonsword in the hands of one of his own men. They moved farther out onto the span until Mason felt it swaying under his feet. The officer made it into the open just in time for Mason to glimpse Kinbreed leaping out of a coffle of prisoners, a choke noose around his neck trailing a hacked-off lead. He was armored but helmetless, hurrying to the railing with a cutlass he'd either seized or been passed. He poised at the edge, one hand clenching a jute suspender cable.

After him came Purifyre, displaying his command baton and shouting to prevent a dozen Trans-Bourne fighters from having at the mutineer with axes and polearms. Ballyhoot, too, had brought up one of the long guns she'd been using as crutches. She pressed the galvani stone to recock it, then pulled a pilehead dart from the hip quiver of a constable next to her and fitted it into the sling groove.

"I call in your debt to me, Hammerstone," Kinbreed's voice rang out. "I reclaim my life! When I saved your life on these very ropeways, you said it made you beholden to me for an ultimate favor. Your words, not mine. Remember?

"Here and now I invoke that pledge, Hammerstone! Spare me and let me lead into exile those who stood with me. We were only trying to help our people, who gave much and lost kin and loved ones bridging the strait." He was speaking to the crowd at large now. "If we took lives yesterday, we lost many more last night—the score's more than even. The Trans-Bourne has its precious mastery back, nor will it slip away from you again; we all know that now. You've won, so let us go."

Without Kinbreed's usual desert-prophet intensity, the words sounded almost sane and fair. But Mason intuited that he wouldn't truly foreswear revolt and subversion—*couldn't,* by his nature. Somewhere down the line Kinbreed's zealotry would return him to the Styx for another go-round. He looked to Ballyhoot, waiting for her to use the sling-gun, only to find that her mauled features had gone lax. He recalled her fondness for Kinbreed, who, like Purifyre, was something of a surrogate son to her.

"Haven't I taken wounds to defend this crossing and thus the Trans-Bourne?" Kinbreed was saying to everyone. "Every man and woman who wears the club-clover once stood as comrade with you other constables, Hammerstone. Lives are owed back and forth. To show us clemency now would balance accounts and leave good air between Forge Town and Gapshot instead of feud winds."

A lot of troops on the winning side were listening hard, but Kinbreed had failed to convince someone who pressed forward from the massed listeners on the southern side.

"Until you convince yourself again that books don't balance?"

It was Boon, leaning on a cane of pogopod bone and lion-wood. He had his detonator-cap shooter at his side but was too far away from Kinbreed to use it.

"Coemote!" Kinbreed said. "Your hands have overmuch blood on them. Does mine truly need to be there, too? I revered you once, as you loved me as family."

"Yes, Hammerstone was like a brother to you," Boon retorted. "But you would've put his blood on *your* hands this morn to make yourself the deliverer of Gapshot, eh?"

As you'd be the deliverer of Aquamarine, Mason thought. But Boon's resolve, too, drained away, and his hand moved from the det-cap gun.

"I'd have died before I'd have harmed him," Kinbreed said in a low voice. "But now that I'm undone, you've nothing to fear from me. Therefore, in the name of peace on the Styx Strait, I ask only to take my leave forever of—"

He made very little sound as a quarrel's bodkin tip drove through his black-lacquered armor, penetrating just between the floating ribs. He uttered no yell, only a surprised gasp as he swung to face his executioner.

Mason was already handing the sling-gun back to Bally-hoot; she accepted it as mutely as she'd surrendered it to him a moment earlier, still not meeting his eyes.

Collapsing backward, Kinbreed lost his grip on the suspender cable and began his long fall into the Amnion. Watching him, Mason recalled something Burning had said about the Exts' last stand at Anvil Tor, on Concordance: *Eventually you don't feel anything. You do what you have to do. And that's when you're finally, truly at war.* Nothing mattered except that Purifyre was alive. Everything else was irrelevant.

"Everything?" Yatt's voice drifted silently in his ears. *"Including Endgame, Periapt, the Roke Conflict?"*

"We'll see," Mason muttered under his breath.

"And what becomes of Boon's plans to sunder the Oceanic?"

If the synome antagonist works, good riddance to the Oceanic, Mason thought, so long as Purifyre wasn't harmed in the process.

Yatt let the stillness hang in Mason's mind for a long moment. *"And your mission mates, whose ship Boon and your only begotten son so desperately desire?"*

Mason shut his eyes, thinking, I am without mates now.

But Yatt said: *"Wrong: you have us. And now we have you."*

CHAPTER FIFTEEN

Souljourner took Burning's injunction to heart, her square feet flying as she sprinted, bent nearly double, for the plaza's encrusted fountain. A capture quarrel with a head like a little jasperwood champagne cork bounced off the fountain's main basin, its impact used up on the thick moss there. A lead sling-gun pellet ricocheted from the arm supporting one of the upper tiers. It occurred to Burning again that the praetorian contingents had mixed opinions about taking him alive.

He and Souljourner vaulted, clambered, and bellied their way to the upper basin, clenching hanging fungal elf-locks and throwing themselves flat in the thick-smelling loam that had built up. Darts and quarrels hissed overhead or rebounded from the basin's rim. Hugging the dirt and waiting for the volley to peter out, Burning consolidated the 'baller's remaining nine rounds.

The sound of Souljourner's sling-gun recocking made him turn. She was loading a broadhead missile. Nearby lay the dead Unconquerable's brayophaunt signal horn and basket-hilted shortsword. "I should have let you get that quiver," he told her.

He sneaked a quick peak over the rim, between bobbing sassgrass blades. There was movement at the edges of the plaza, but no one was feeling rash enough yet to try a frontal assault. He turned and crawled low around the vertical support that held up the basins and the unrecognizable carved figure at the very top. Another flight of quarrels made him plow a path

127

in the spongy dirt. From the far side of the basin—only four meters from where Souljourner kept watch—he could see men rustling the malformed weeds and undergrowth as they jockeyed for position and adjusted the set of their weapons.

"They're reluctant to test their mettle," Souljourner remarked in a stage whisper.

No sooner did she speak than various horns took up their pealing again. Battle calls rose up from Unconquerables, Diehards, Militerrors, Fanswell's Fanatics, and the rest; then, yelling wildly, the elites charged the fountain.

Resolute as they were, it was plain that the Eans hadn't worked out practical means of dealing with offworld firearms. In their place Burning would have had half his sling-gunners move up stealthily and maintain as heavy a volume of fire as possible from stationary positions. But the praetorians were loosing their quarrels and darts as they ran, some trying to recock on the fly, others letting their slingers swing from strap and baldric to be able to draw close-quarters weapons. Their scissoring legs kicked up spores and leaf tassels as they rushed in, eight men at arms from three different elites in Burning's immediate field of fire alone. He put the 'baller's bead dot on the lead man, a Militerror who had stripped off part of his blue-lacquered *cuir bolli* armor in the heat of the southland Big Sere but was still wearing his musculature-imitating breastplate. Burning put a hole creditably close to the center of it.

Without taking time to watch the man fall, he tracked the lighted bead to the next target—a Fanswell's Fanatic—and squeezed off another shot. There seemed little point in conserving ammunition. If he couldn't break the charge, the Eans would have him and Souljourner both long before dawn. He fired on a second Fanatic, then another Militerror.

Four down, and the rush was coming to a ragged halt. Burning rolled and scrabbled ninety degrees to watch Souljourner wing her second broadhead at a Killmonger guardsman of the Dominor Paralipsio. The whistling shaft missed, but it passed close enough to the Killmonger to make him stumble, and he crashed noseguard-first into the wildsward, bone and rattan breastplate clattering.

Burning spied a Diehard covering ground with tremendous bounds, waving his kite-shaped shield and sickle sword and gathering himself to hurdle the rim of the fountain's lowest basin. A hardball slug took him dead center, and the sprint became a spastic loss of balance and momentum, then a sideways collapse into ivy and bracken. He was shrieking like a damned soul even before he landed and howled even louder as he lay thrashing ineffectually.

On to an Unconquerable who was firing as he blitzed and then to a Fanatic dashing flat-out to get in under Burning's field of fire. Souljourner, meanwhile, turned back to the arc of their meager rampart and fired a bolt at a target Burning couldn't see.

"Get clear!" he yelled even as he was swarming across her legs.

Two more Militerrors, tall and broad-shouldered like all of Rhodes's select, were driving hard for the fountain's base. One-two, Burning shot them. The first went rubber-legged and collapsed against a sapling, bending it halfway to the ground; the second, hit in his shoulder pauldron, fell back with his arm dangling by a few strings of red gristle.

And that was it—the 'baller's last round was gone. The weapon's ambidextrous thumb safety had flipped to its unloaded position to confirm it. Burning laid the sidearm aside and drew the ka-bar from its boot sheath with his left hand.

The Militerror he'd gotten squarely was improbably dragging his nearly amputated buddy away by the legs. Around the plaza's edges, horns and coarse commands were rallying the Eans to form up. Burning listened for the clarion calls and rebel yells that would signal the next charge. Instead, however, sounds of metal biting wood echoed from somewhere out of sight, eroding his momentary bliss at having triumphed.

"They're not through with us yet," Souljourner said.

In minutes harassment bolts were being lofted almost blindly from the roofs of the collapsed houses fronting the plaza. The praetorian marksmen were obliged to fire in such high arcs, however, that none could find them where they lay curled against the basin's rim.

Burning mumbled to himself. "I know how to call in air strikes, control artillery, fire and direct an armored assault, and I end up with siege warfare in some gene-fucked jungle on the pimpled ass cheek of nowhere!"

Souljourner showed him frowning incomprehension. Like him, she rested on her side, conforming to the rim to present the smallest possible target. She gripped her sling-gun and stubby work knife, while his hands held the ka-bar and the basket-hilted shortsword, ready for the storming the soldiers were obviously preparing.

The sounds of tree chopping ceased, but the horn blowing and harassment fire continued. With a thin birr and a soft thud, a quarrel dug itself into the fungused loam near the fountain's vertical support column; that made eight sticking out of the soil at contrasting angles. Perhaps to celebrate the near miss, an aeoliphone honked a battle flourish. The various elites seemed to be having a battle of the brass sections, each trying to blow individual signature calls louder by turns. He knew it for the crudest kind of psywar, but he couldn't help saying, "Goddamn bugles."

Souljourner patted the confiscated brayophaunt. "Will you sound your own call in defiance?"

Burning shook his head. "My instruments are spoons and kazoo. Why'd you grab it, anyway?"

"I thought to trumpet the clarion call of the Descriers when at last we stood before the gates of Alabaster."

That again. She just wasn't going to give up on her pipe dreams of Elysian Fields, but there was no point remonstrating with her. She licked her lips, puckered experimentally, and coaxed a surprisingly mellow blat from the horn.

"Not so different from old Tusker's dulciphone back at Pyx," she commented.

She drew a breath that strained the seams of her blouse as Burning put his fingertips in his ears. She winded the brayophaunt with such force that he expected to see leaves falling from the mutated Ghoul Ground trees. Four ascending notes, repeated. When she finished, there was a moment's stillness, then a quick scornful counterblast from an unseen Ean. Souljourner threw out her broad-ribbed chest again and drowned out the soldier with the Descriers' flourish.

Burning suffered the racket without grousing. *Poor kid's always wanted a fanfare once in her life, and this could be the closest she comes,* he told himself. *And he was the one who'd brought her there.* She began the call again but stopped halfway through it to peer out over the rim of the basin.

"They must be music haters."

He eased up to hear men's voices lifted in war cries. From three sides knots of intermixed praetorians came at the run, weapons raised, carrying makeshift scaling ladders fashioned from saplings they'd cut down. A few somehow found the breath to blow horns on the charge. Souljourner defied them with another Descriers' flourish.

"Enough!" he barked. "Get set!" They'd worked out response scenarios and contingency actions, including some worst-case tactics that were optimistic at best.

Rather than come in at equidistant points around the rim of the basin, the sortie teams veered so that two made for the side that presented the best purchase for escalade, while a third team made for the opposite side to divert the defenders' attention as much as possible or strike the coup de grâce if the attack succeeded.

Burning counted eleven men—not enough to detail slinggunners to lay down covering volleys and still have sufficient numbers for a mass rush. He held the 'baller high, where they couldn't help but see it, on the off chance that the sight alone would break someone's nerve. The Ean grunts had their shoulders hunched, steeling themselves for hardball rounds, but the flaying and swearing of the officers kept the attack in motion.

He took up position to the right of the basin's statuary, while Souljourner stood to the left, both crouched to elude quarrels that were in the main poorly aimed. "Stay staunch!" Burning told Souljourner out of the side of his mouth. "It's on."

The sortie team on his side was a little ahead of the others. Burning smelled the sharp-sweet perfume of yussawood sap from the cleft wood as the scaling ladder's upper end slammed against the basin, muffled by the dense shag of green-gray mold on the rim. The first man up the ladder was an Unconquerable, sparsely bearded for all his size—young and gung-ho, thinking to earn honors for himself and win glory for his grandee.

Burning heaved the weighty service pistol squarely into the man's face. At the same time, he heard quite clearly the snap of Souljourner's carbine as she launched a quarrel at the men fumbling a second ladder into place. As the stricken Unconquerable sagged, blood gushing from his nose and his grip failing, Burning kicked at the ladder but couldn't dislodge it.

Abandoning his post, he leapt across the basin as a third ladder hit nearby, a little off kilter but solid enough. A Diehard was just topping it with sickle sword and kit-shaped shield in hand. On level ground the armor and shield would have provided good protection, but clambering up the ladder had required him to break his defensive posture. Burning brought up the sling-gun pistol he and Souljourner had stripped from the first Unconquerable, faked a shot at the Diehard's face, then aimed for his upper leg. The pile bolt tore into the gap between the top of his greave and the bottom of his tasse plates, and the Ean screamed. Burning moved in with the captured targone on his left arm, parrying the sickle sword with his ka-bar, and slammed his shielded forearm into as much face as the Diehard's cheekpieces left exposed.

The soldier reeled, but Burning couldn't afford to settle for a nearly bloodless win that might allow him to get back into the battle. He jammed the ka-bar into the Diehard's unprotected armpit, in and out so fast that his hand was clear before blood spurted from the wound. Then he shoved the young praetorian down the ladder at the men behind him.

He had already pivoted back to where he'd left Souljourner, who was slashing at an ascending Apocalyptic with both short-sword and work knife. She was determined but inexpert, and the Apocalyptic's hilted mace was bound to find an opening sooner or later. Burning threw the ka-bar straight at the Apocalyptic's wide-open mouth. The resistance of the man's jaws and the big knife's momentum torqued it flatwise so that it penetrated far into the Apocalyptic's throat, slicing open his right cheek and exposing teeth that showed all the way back to the molars. The ladder he had been riding teetered away as cleanly as the swing of a garden gate.

"Reload!"

Souljourner heard Burning and hurried to comply, passing him the shortsword. He swiveled around the basin's vertical support to go in low at the Unconquerable from the first group, cutlass in one hand and fighting hatchet in the other. But the Ean didn't have his balance back, his momentum gathered, or his attack formulated, while Burning had all three. With body language and eyes indicating that he planned to strike at his op-ponent's groin and legs, he shifted suddenly to a high line of engagement, lunging fencing style and thrusting the parrying blade over the top of the Aquam's gorget and into his throat.

Behind him Souljourner's sling-gun slapped again; then she cried out in anger and pain. The sight of her left calf hatcheted open sent Burning wheeling across the basin as two enemy teams joined forces to overwhelm her. He absorbed it all in a Flowstate flicker: a Militerror clinging between ladder and statuary had dealt her the calf chop, an Apocalyptic had his kris sword raised for a strike; more men-at-arms were swarming up one of the ladders—

He was straddling Souljourner before the Apocalyptic's kris sword had moved a centimeter. The Apocalyptic was easy to fake off balance with a bit of broken timing with the targone, followed by a backhand smash to the face. To the Militerror who had meat-axed Souljourner's leg Burning gave steel. He picked up the hatchet Rhodes's elite had dropped and sent it spinning, to bury itself in the chest of a Fanswell's Fanatic. Sensing movement, he leaned aside to avoid a thrusting spear flung like a harpoon; then he threw his shortsword into the man who'd hurled it.

The praetorians began to fall back; the outcome of the attack was as well known to Burning as a story he'd already heard . . . That only proved that even Flowstate could lie.

Something prodigiously fast and hard whapped off the side of Burning's skull. He saw it for an instant out of the corner of his eye: one of the champagne cork–shaped capture rounds, now rebounding. His miraculous coordination frozen, he sagged back to feel his head come hard against a projection of the central support column unsoftened by moss. The sheer, rude physical impact seemed to rattle the words of an old Skills instructress to the surface of his mind: *Flowstate's just a mental climate of peak experience, not the birthright powers of planet Krypton. Screw-ups happen.*

As precise as his body had been seconds earlier, it was that unresponsive now. He heard Souljourner's gasping breath as she clenched her wound and swiped futilely with her stubby knife; and he watched as an Unconquerable cleared the ladder with gauntlet sword bared. If the praetorian was intent on taking the two of them alive, he meant to carve them up a little first, perhaps hamstring them or put out their eyes to make them easier to handle. The pata-sword lifted for a swing at

Souljourner's knife hand, more than heavy and keen enough to take it off in one blow.

The big gavelock iron that suddenly punched through the Ean's belly and brigandine was the greater of the two shocks visited on Burning just then, though the lesser shock was just as inexplicable: the Descriers' flourish being winded from somewhere below on a booming instrument that resounded like the trumpet of doom.

The gavelock was no sling-gun round but a toggled javelin; the Unconquerable fell like a stalk of threshed grain. Souljourner, who had a better angle than Burning to see what was happening, laughed through clenched teeth.

"The Varangians! From Alabaster town. The Varangians have come to save their new Descrier!"

In all her blue-skying about the walled utopia, she hadn't mentioned anything about Varangians. He placed the word after a moment's groping among long-inactive memories from his data diving into Old Earth history: invaders of Russia who had subsequently become bodyguards of the Byzantine emperors. But what was it about Alabaster that required so much hired muscle?

CHAPTER
SIXTEEN

In the ship's brig, Wetbar, Roust, and the rest of Zone's confederates held their silence. Murderously angry, Zone himself glared into nothingness, contemplating his next move. The smooth, heavy roll of door bolt solenoids came so unexpectedly that everyone jumped, shaping hands and feet into lethal configurations and groping for weapons that weren't there. But except for Zone they kept their places with the same mix of vigilance and allegiance that alloyed their brute courage.

One moment Zone was sitting in a last-defense corner, and the next he was through the hatch, even before it was halfway open. On the other side, however, there was no one to attack. The others followed, squinting in the minimal illumination and moving guardedly. Wetbar stopped to examine the door, trying to determine who or what had shot the bolts.

"Had to've been opened by the security computer," he pronounced.

"But no alarms," Zone pointed out. "Security isn't aware we've been sprung by a glitch."

"A trap," someone suggested. "Lod setting things up to make it look like a breakout. He means to take us down."

Zone glanced in both directions down the dimly lighted passageway. "Even if, it's an improvement over our previous situation. A chance to right."

He gave them hand signals, and they deployed silently along the sides of the passageway, wary of security pickups and alert to the appearance of any intruder. Zone had already spent malevolent hours sifting through his options, though he hadn't expected a break of this order. Escaping the ship would probably mean abandoning it for good, but there would be other ways to get downriver to New Alexandria and Endgame, the only power base on Aquamarine that meant anything.

He took the point himself, and they moved out.

Dextra and Tonii arrived at the jammed aircraft elevator just as Kurt Elide was wriggling out of his flatbed cupola, the last driver to get clear. Gairaszek was still supervising the work details, though he'd delegated the placement of Ext demo charges to Periapt navy demolitions specialists. Three other teams were trundling heavy laser cutters into position, seeing to power connections, and making ready for do-or-die jettisoning of the elevator. To cut down on noise, the work crews were using muffled tools and tackle, their boots and shoes shod in silencing swatches of nonskid.

Dextra felt the same loathing-longing toward the gun turret that Quant did. Dangerous beast that it was, it was still their best hope of defending the ship at long range. But irreplaceable or not, there'd be a certain relief to cutting the bastard loose and sending it to the bottom.

She was glad Kurt was in the clear; just then he was clambering around on the risky assemblage that was the gun turret and its carrier, silhouetted against fog. She couldn't make out his face very well but could tell from the way he moved that he was nervous. She recalled that he didn't like deep water, yet he hadn't retired to safety. He had forced himself to remain with the dumbot and pitch in. She longed to feel so uncomplicatedly *game*, feared ever having the ship's company learn what she was really feeling and thinking, the calculatedness of command.

Because she was watching Kurt, it seemed to her in the

first instant that he'd simply lost his footing through carelessness or overtension. But then she realized that others were suddenly losing balance, clawing for handholds, or forgetting the absolute-silence orders and crying out. Strangely, it came to her only then that she, too, was falling.

A long, dragging shudder ran through the ship, transmitted up through the very decks. Every part of her seemed to find a different voice with which to sound its distress: the tolling of unsecured gear, the squealing of joints, the shriek of the great torsion girder box that held the sponsons together.

The *GammaLAW* had struck bottom.

As Dextra toppled, Tonii grabbed her, somehow managing to keep 'ers own balance. It was more than the sudden loss of equilibrium that made Dextra feel sick to her stomach, and she understood then why sailors dreaded the thought of a ship being murdered by the land instead of borne up by the waters.

Tonii got Dextra to the rail, to which they both clung while lines whipped and danced and unsecured objects clattered across the deck. As little time as she'd spent aboard, Dextra at once registered the eeriest thing of all: no alarms, no shouted orders over the PA. Quant was apparently still hoping to slip past Fluter Delve undetected or at least keep any listeners from getting a definite fix on the ship.

Still the wrenching and torment of composite and metal reverberated through the hulls. In the din Dextra could hear a cry of "Hand overboard!" It came to her in a panic that the ship was still under power. Insanely, she was thrusting herself deeper onto the riverbed!

The lee helmsman sounded very scared. "No response from engine telegraph, sir."

Quant took a steadying breath and used a tone that was quietly vexed. "Keep trying. Helmsman, come over to two-seven-five." Whether it was or wasn't a sandbar, it hadn't been mapped by the ROVers, and the chances of powering off it without ripping the bottom out of the hulls were slim. With the engines refusing to answer, however, there was nothing to do but bull across the bar and pray that the strength of the SWATH's composite would hold.

At least three people had been lost overboard, but Quant couldn't afford to think about them now.

A young red-haired Periapt woman whose mother had been a destroyer captain, the helmsman said in a dead voice, "Helm still not responding, sir."

Quant felt the flesh around his heart go icy, and suspicion suddenly blossomed in his mind. Days earlier it had been a glitch in the anchor chain, and now the engines. The analysts back on Periapt must have been correct: the *Terrible Swift Sword* had carried a cybervirus to Aquamarine, and the *GammaLAW* had caught it.

As she held her broken arm, Kino's angular face mirrored the incomprehensible whirl of recent events: arrest, reprieve, hazard, and now pain. No need to think anymore—simply react, simply survive. Roust and Wetbar were helping her strap the arm to herself, while Zone, fancying himself the only stable thing in a ship that had gone berserk, took a final kick at the dogged hatchway that blocked their escape route.

Roust yowled as the deck rose far up to starboard, tilting them all against the portside bulkhead. The ship rode grindingly across some obstruction in the river that threatened to rip the decks out from under their feet. The lurch confirmed what Zone already knew in his skin and gut: no friend or potential ally had opened the brig door for them. Against every countermeasure LAW had taken, a cybervirus was loose in the ship and many systems were down, hence the hatch that had thwarted their easy escape by sealing itself. He didn't have the same fear of viruses that most technophobic Exts had, but he knew now that there'd be no easy way off the ship, no red carpet to mastery over the mission and Aquamarine. The PA was still mute, but it was clear from the vibrations and the traffic in adjacent passageways where the action was. A feeling of savage anticipation went through Zone. Disaster had come calling, and he suddenly knew what had to be done.

Quant fought an impulse to rattle off commands one on top of the next and assume the controls at all consolidated bridge positions. Steadying himself, he began giving measured orders, and the months of drilling on Periapt and in transit paid off. His bridge crew reacted virtually by reflex, avoiding panic because Quant had drilled panic out of them.

They swung into action, rigging the ship for collision and hull breach, preparing for leakage, assessing damage. Gairaszek's people hurried to cut away the elevator and the immense gun turret. Engineering worked frantically to bring manual control on-line even while the ship grated along the shallows. But for all the efforts, the slaved controls wouldn't yield to the manuals, and all attempts by engineering to reverse engines or provide minimal steering with engine power proved fruitless.

Quant fell victim to a feeling of depersonalization. Everything he knew about his ship and about viruses paraded before his eyes, and every detail of the tactical situation and the river and Aquamarine raced through his mind, coherent for all the blurring speed. He found words without realizing he was speaking them.

"Shut down all nav systems, all detectors, compass, radar, inertial guidance. Scramble all data input. Everything! I want the steering controls completely blinded."

The bridge crew leapt to it as the lee helmsman passed the order to CIC and engineering. In moments the ship's guidance and navigational system was shorn of every input—lobotomized. The steering controls had no idea where the ship was or on what heading, how much time was passing or what external conditions prevailed.

"Fucking damn!" The helmsman didn't even seem to realize she'd spit out the profanity. "Manual controls responding."

Quant called for hard left rudder. The book said the best procedure would be to stop, assess damage, perhaps lighten the ship, and try either backing her off or gently rocking her free. But the book wasn't talking about a run beneath enemy guns with the water level falling beneath the keel. Quant saw momentum as his only chance of forcing the ship into deeper water. Even as the steersman brought her helm over, Quant could feel the *GammaLAW* lose speed to the riverbed clutching at her. He gazed at the fog-enshrouded Ea, calculating by guess and instinct that the ship could not rip herself free. A whistle from the speaking tube and the lee steersman's relayed words made Quant's heart leap.

"Sir, engineering has engine control back!"

"Full speed ahead, all props!" Quant fired back before the last word was out of the lee's mouth. Engineering must have been expecting it; almost the instant the order was relayed, the *GammaLAW* surged against the riverbed, rocks grinding at her, muck grasping. The port sponson swung clear; the bow, to starboard. Quant continued to rattle off orders as the steersman swung the twin rudders even harder to port to compensate.

Followed closely by his talker, Quant hurried out onto Vultures' Row in time to see the ship swing dangerously close to the rocks that lay between it and deeper water. She would have cleared them—barely—under ordinary circumstances, but now the great barrels of Turret *Musashi* were projecting out off the elevator, over the water.

Quant heard shouts and orders from the elevator, though he couldn't make out any words. He called for helm amidships as he watched the rocks seem to rear up at him from starboard-side. Gairaszek had seen the danger, too, and had somehow managed to elevate one barrel of the turret, hoping to lift it clear of the rocks. How the engineers had gotten even a trickle of power to the gun servos, Quant couldn't imagine.

He held his breath as the first barrel rose to maximum elevation with maddening slowness. With the *GammaLAW* moving faster, finding fractionally deeper water, he wanted to switch on the bottom-following sonar but feared the virus would seize control of the rudders again. The raised gun barrel brushed past a great jut of granite, breaking loose a shower of small stones. The second barrel was just beginning to rise when it struck one stone fang, sending a shudder through the ship and shifting the entire turret on its flatbed. The aircraft elevator moaned. The barrel bounced free with the rocking of the ship, only to bash down once more and lodge itself between two looming fists of rock. As more rocks fell to wedge the barrel tight, Quant barked for reverse power.

Securing lines creaked with tension, one of them snapping like a gunshot, and the elevator complained like a shoulder being wrung from its socket. The ship wailed in agony and was wrenched around to starboard, abruptly tilting and jamming the gun's barrel deeper into the cleft as the starboard sponson struck something. Quant clearly heard the crunch and crack as the sponson was staved in like an eggshell.

CHAPTER
SEVENTEEN

Descending the slope in the wake of the landslide was tricky, but Ghost and Zinsser managed it without incident. That no one pursued them hardly mattered, since word of the yawning breach in Passwater's defenses was undoubtedly spreading at top bounder speed across the Scourlands and it wouldn't take long for various Feral hordes to assemble.

Passwater's trading platform had been hauled up to the top of the cleaved bulwark, but numerous figures were glancing down from weapons emplacements, and fright was on every face. Men were running back and forth, preparing for attack. There being no gate, Ghost and Zinsser made for the breach, since no one seemed inclined to throw or lower a rope. As they drew nearer, they saw young and old, male and female furiously attempt to refill the deadly gap in the city's defenses. Labor crews were trying to barricade the hole with fragments and debris, anything that would serve, while other Passwaterites were working bashed-out blocks back into place, using crude levers.

The impact of the *Dream Castle*'s armored bottom had knocked out one weapons emplacement, and it was clear to Ghost that the fields of fire of the pozzes to the left and right wouldn't cover the vulnerable point. As Passwater's inhabitants were plainly aware, the city lay wide open to attack.

A bearded man in DevOcean vestments and a lacquered leather war helmet was trying to impart order to the frantic efforts. He had obviously seen Ghost and Zinsser coming from a long way off, as harquebuses, spears, and other weapons were aimed at them.

"Hold your fire!" the old man yelled through a brass megaphone to those on the wall. "They aren't Ferals!" He looked hard at Ghost and Zinsser. "They're from the *Dream Castle*."

Ghost only nodded, but Zinsser felt compelled to point out that Ferals were closing on the city. "You're next on the looting list when they're through with the Laputa."

The man gave a face tic of acknowledgment. "What caused the crash?"

Ghost stared at the DevOceanite until the silence became uncomfortable for everyone but her. "How should we know?" Zinsser replied at last. "We were passengers in the outerworks."

"But we saw no outerworks."

Zinsser traded looks with Ghost. "Uh, precisely."

A lookout screamed, his voice cracking in fear; then others took up the cry, pointing. Horns blew and gongs were struck as everyone scanned the wastes. Pouring down from the far heights—first from two little clefts between high crags, then from a broader defile—came the black dots of Scourland Ferals on their bounders. More came from hidden ravines and over broad ridgelines—thousands, more than it seemed such hostile barrens could support.

It was more than Ghost could believe the savages could muster in such a short time. Perhaps the Ferals had always had reserves waiting in concealment, Ghost thought, against the day when Passwater lay vulnerable and the lure of raiding and pillaging overruled the need to trade for mandseng, which was essential for minimalizing Anathemite births among the hordes.

"Can't you swing the guns to cover the breach?" Ghost heard Zinsser ask the DevOcean elder.

The DevOceanite did the half-arc head rolls that meant no.

"The war engines are set in permanent emplacements. We haven't time to move them."

"Then gather all your oil or pitch or whatever it is you burn," Zinsser told the man. "Pour it onto the barricade and set fire to it when the Ferals attack. Shoot any who get through. It might convince them to retreat, and at the very least it will buy you time."

Ghost heard a note of determination in Zinsser's voice and was mystified. Zinsser had no military training; where were those command decisions coming from? Was it about Asurao? Zinsser had been acting jealous since she'd first glimpsed the slaughterboss from the *Dream Castle*. Was he thinking of the coming showdown as a fight for *her*? Was he thinking that he could put up with her not responding to him but not with her responding to someone else—at least not out here in the Scourlands, where violence came to the surface so readily? Jealousy she understood, but not to the point where it had compelled Zinsser to take sides in a battle that didn't concern him.

She thought of the knife in her boot. What he didn't realize was that she'd sooner carve him up than allow him to take power over her life, the way men had taken power over her life in the POW camps—back when she was, after a fashion, alive. But he hadn't given her sufficient cause to kill him and might never, so she left the cold executioner asleep at her shin for the time being. Moreover, Burning would be vexed if she unnecessarily executed a member of the GammaLAW mission.

The DevOccanite wasn't especially taken with Zinsser's suggestions, in any case. "There are many who feel we'd just be delaying the inevitable—that we'd be going against the wishes of the One Who Watches. Is not what has already happened here the fulfillment of all our chronicles of the revelations?"

Ghost remained silent, allowing Zinsser to ask the question that was in her own mind: "Are you saying that Passwater has no option but to yield to the Ferals?"

The old man swept a hand at the wall, but it was clear he meant something that waited beyond it. "To be accepted into the Amnion, to be accepted at long last for the great sacrament of the waters, to leave behind the unbelievers and the pain and woe of soil and sky and merge at long last with the Oceanic."

"You're talking about flinging yourselves into the ocean," Zinsser said slowly, shakenly. "But you can't—"

"Some of the faithful are already preparing to do just that," reported another Passwaterite. "The followers of the late Marrowbone. But there are still divided opinions."

"It's *insane!*" Zinsser shot back furiously. "It's mass suicide!"

The Passwaterites were looking at him oddly, some angrily. Ghost walked away, farther into the gap in the wall, preferring to put some distance between herself and Zinsser in case he gave away his offworld origin.

Instead, he shut up and followed her, as she thought he might. They had to thread their way through sharpened impaling posts that had been sunk into the ground as a second ring of make-do defense. Heading for the Backbone Keep, they clambered up over a barricade, where from the top, it was easy to take in the wrecking-ball swath the *Dream Castle* had cut through the town—the broken buildings, toppled steeples, shattered skeletal modules of the planned visible physiology that had been commandeered for use as a shelter. Men and women of all ages were rushing to help in the defense, carrying weapons and anything that would serve as a weapon.

"Seems that some of the faithful haven't enough faith for a wade into the Amnion," Ghost commented.

"What do *we* do if the Ferals break through?" Zinsser asked in a carefully neutral tone.

"Die, I suppose. Unless we can come up with a contingency plan."

Adding to the confusion and suffering, fires were spreading through Passwater. Ghost and Zinsser heard DevOceanal chants commingled with the wails of the living, the moans of those wounded in *Dream Castle*'s passing, orders and shouts by those trying to rally the defense. Groups of people dressed in Puritan robes were marching in the direction of the forbidden waters that thundered unceasingly against the peninsula.

"There's no telling how the Oceanic will react to so many human beings invading its domain," Zinsser muttered absently, "We have to get out of here."

The *Dream Castle* had bashed the top off the Skull Bunker, in which were housed many of DevOcean's holy relics. The so-called Buccal Portals hung from their hinges, and the interior was a nightmare of debris. Far behind Ghost and Zinsser now, a portion of the bulwark was ablaze. Combatants could be seen silhouetted against flames and thick smoke. As they watched, a bounder came springing straight through a curtain of fire, parts of its pelt and trappings aflame, its rider wrapped in a smoking skin blanket. The bounder cleared the piled stone fragments only to impale itself and its rider on two of the stakes planted there.

Defenders rushed in to finish off the writhing Feral. But even as they did, another wild man came soaring through the flame to die on stakes nearby. In minutes a dozen and more Ferals hung gruesomely on the stakes, their impact having flattened many. It was clear that the barricade wouldn't hold for long.

"If you have a contingency plan, I'd like to hear it now," Zinsser urged.

She pointed west, where the huge wall supported an altar that projected out over the sea. North of the bulwark the tundra rose gradually to glacial heights. Carved paths leading up to the headland there were beginning to fill with DevOceanite faithful preparing to cast themselves into the Amnion. None had yet, but once they did, the route probably would become impassable.

Zinsser's brow was furrowed. "Into the highlands! To where? And then what?"

"Short of the miracle of a search plane from the *Gamma-LAW*, our best chance is to hide out in the Scourlands until the next Laputa arrives," she told him. "Though we may have to contend with Ferals in the meantime."

Zinsser drew a deep breath.

"Keep your eyes open for rope or line as we go," Ghost told him. "We'll need it to rappel down the far side of the wall."

They started off with the cries and sounds of battle in their ears. The drifting smoke carried the retching stink of burned flesh. As they neared the switchbacked path to the altar, they saw behind them that the Ferals were now riding safely inside the wall on the bodies of their impaled fellows and their bounders. Bands of them were pouring through, fanning out in skirmishing parties, riding down anyone in their path. Swords and other weapons gleamed. War whistles and roars of triumph drifted to Ghost and Zinsser with the smoke, as did the screams of Passwaterites.

They were past the town's last structures, and still they hadn't spied any line. The footpaths were becoming more and more choked with suicidal DevOceanites. "That way," Ghost was saying when a war whistle sounded behind her.

Bounding through the last few rows of houses came Asurao, waving his war club high.

CHAPTER
EIGHTEEN

It blunted Souljourner's joy that the Varangians automatically assumed that Burning was the Descrier they'd come to rescue, but only a little. Like Burning, she was too relieved at having been spared the Eans' steel. She was also in too much pain to concern herself with details.

When she explained to the Varangians that they had in fact raced to the rescue of Aquamarine's only known female Descrier, they were quite accepting of it, if somewhat chagrined on learning that she had been assigned to Alabaster by the Praepostor of Pyx. Two Varangians hunkered down like solicitous squatch bears to attend to her hatchet wound, but Burning hastened to intervene despite being woozy from the skulling he'd taken in the final moments of the battle. The gunky poultice one of the guards was about to slap on Souljourner's butchered calf probably would have done more harm than good, whereas his belt medkit pouch contained items that would speed her recovery.

An anesthetic pneumo deadened sensation enough for him to irrigate the wound with some 150-proof patho-gin taken from one of the dead praetorians. He followed it up with an antibiotic spray and a field dressing of paraderm synthetic skin—the best he could do for the moment, given the persistent blurring and doubling of his vision. The cleanest thing he could find for use as a protect bandage was a Militerror flax-silk banneret.

The Varangians' overman, Pondoroso, made a pretense of believing that Burning's healing wonders had come by way of a Laputa trader who'd carried them across the Amnion from Passwater.

Like all his men, Pondoroso was burly and oversize, shaggy-bearded and shaggy-haired. They wore corselets of Optimant-alloy scale armor and billed helms of ivory and leather. Their leggings, breechclouts, and arm protectors sported long fringes and a host of silver conchs set with semiprecious stones. Their weapons were similarly outsize, including sling-guns as big as split-fence rails. The smallest among the Varangians would have made a credible bouncer at the roughest rage bar on Concordance. Like Manipulants, they gave Burning the novel feeling of being average height or even on the short side.

However, they were neither slow nor stupid. Their stealthy ambush of the Eans was clear evidence of that. True, they had the advantage of numbers, but the way they plied their gavelocks and curved long-handled broadswords told Burning that one-on-one they were more than a match for any praetorian.

Pondoroso even had a sense of irony. As dawn was breaking, he toed a dead Diehard who looked peaceful and untroubled in death despite having been cut almost in half at the waist. "Had they not been winding their horns across the countryside, sounding an outland hue and cry, our patrollers would not have been drawn close enough to take heed of the Descrier's flourish. Although—" He gave a casual glance at the depleted 'baller in Burning's holster. "—sounds of quick-barking thunder attracted their attention as well."

He gave Souljourner a deliberative look. "Most unwanted, I must say, for Alabaster to be sent a female Descrier, and at that, one with a male companion. For as you may have heard, only a Descrier may pass through Alabaster's gate. Other strangers are kept without to preserve the tranquillity of those within."

"He is more than my protector," Souljourner corrected. "Being espoused with me, that is."

Staving off another attack of the spins, Burning wanted to object but decided it was wiser to hold his tongue for the time being. Presumably, she knew the lay of the land, whereas he certifiably didn't.

"Espoused or not, he's forbidden to pass beyond the pale," Pondoroso was saying.

"Ah, but since it stands so in need of a Descrier, Alabaster will surely offer my Redtails haven."

"You may find, young miss, that Alabaster doesn't need you so compellingly," Pondoroso replied with a half-lidded smile.

Souljourner shook her head. "Wrong again, noble warrior. Alabaster needs a Descrier worse than it knows. And soon."

Pondoroso's "Ah" hinted at a reappraisal.

Burning blinked, trying to make the world steady down. A few quick Skills mindflexes helped somewhat. "How far?"

Pondoroso pointed with his green-shafted gavelock, its tip still stained with the blood of the Unconquerable who'd been about to pay back Souljourner with a gauntlet sword. "Four kilix thataway. My lads, prepare a pole hammock for our lady Descrier." His gaze returned to Burning. "Will you need to be carried as well?"

"I'll walk."

It wasn't a point of pride; walking would help him stay awake. His Hussar Plaits and thick locks had spared him a lacerated scalp, but the capture quarrel and the fountain statuary had both done him damage. With a double jeopardy of concussion, he didn't want to take the chance of falling asleep—even on a litter.

Gentle probing of his swollen wounds didn't reveal any obvious fractures. He wasn't bleeding from the ears or mouth; there was no cerebrospinal fluid in his nose. A hammering headache had him nauseated, but his pulse was even. He'd simply have to cope. If he had sustained a brain injury, Aquam medicine would be next to useless, as would the medkit's odds and ends.

"We're away," Pondoroso declared.

Everyone moved out in single file, with flankers, point, and rear guard deployed. Souljourner's hammock, improvised from dead Eans' cloaks, was slung from a pole shouldered by two Varangians, who handled it as if she were an anorexic jockey. The bodies of the praetorians, stripped of arms and other items, were left where they'd fallen. Burning figured that only a few had managed to flee with their lives.

Now that they were freed of their threat, Burning's first impulse had been to return to Gapshot, but the nagging aftereffects of the head shots had overruled him. Keeling over in the middle of the Ghoul Grounds probably would be a crash from which he wouldn't wake. Better to catch his breath at Alabaster and improve his odds by hiring some Varangian muscle, even if it meant sacrificing more time.

An hour's moderate marching brought them out of the Ghoul Grounds' oddities, out of the woods altogether, to within sight of the Amnion and Alabaster. Burning knew from conversations with Souljourner that the hook of land curving away before him to dip into the forbidden ocean was Cape Ataraxia. The wall separating it from the Scorpian mainland was a pristine barrier of white blocks, functional and well maintained. He caught sight of Varangians patrolling it on raised walkways in a cleared surveillance strip—what an Ext would have called a killing zone—that ran the entire arc of its landward side from water to water.

On the far side were tilled fields, paddies, orchards, gardens, and copses of woodland looking as groomed and landscaped as a theme park shire. Many of the city's white buildings consisted of joined domes, both broad and narrow, as if the opposite ends of assorted immense eggs had been used for molds.

The two-kilometer wall held only one gate, set dead center,

a double-door portal no larger than the entrance to a medium-size ground-truck garage. Stretching out from it in good military order was another town, this one with the drill and training grounds feel of a military post. The Varangians' digs, Burning assumed.

Pondoroso had his herald sound the oomphaphone as he led them in. In response, off-duty guardsmen appeared and Varangian dependents streamed out. The latter were women and children who shared the bulk, affable vigor, and coarse looks of the men at arms.

"I will apprise those beyond the pale of your arrival," Pondoroso told Souljourner. "I've no doubts that you'll be ushered into Alabaster amid great welcome, but we will first conduct a customary comparison of the seal on your Writ to the certified example we keep here."

"Both my husband and myself will be ushered inside," Souljourner said with a trace of warning. Slung backside-low in a pole hammock, she suddenly had the air of a woman sitting in the CEO's swivel chair.

Even so, Pondoroso refused to yield the point. "As I told you in the Ghoul Grounds, only an assigned or elected Descrier can be accepted within. Once or twice over the generations a healer may be permitted to enter, but then only when the Alabasterites are without one. Otherwise, no outsiders can be suffered to pass beyond the pale. And certainly not a man of violence, as I know your Redtails to be, howsoever much his violence owed to defending you."

Souljourner motioned to her dressed leg. "Redtails *is* a healer."

"He is a bandager," Pondoroso countered, "a fellow who's purchased some outland medicaments; so he himself has confessed. Moreover, Alabaster presently has a healer—an adept, at that."

"Then perhaps this adept can Descry as well," Souljourner

retorted. "For that's what Cape Ataraxia requires now. And if my mate is denied entry, I'll neither enter nor serve."

Pondoroso bowed. "In that case, we'll have no choice but to summon another."

"There's none other available. What's more, there's none so gifted as me; that's simple fact. Too, I repeat that Alabaster will need a quake sniffer long and long before any entreaty of yours reaches Pyx."

The overman's miffed expression suggested a shrubby escarpment fixing to avalanche. "Enough of hints, young woman! Say what you mean!"

Souljourner fluttered her fingertips in dismissal. "Until the hire is worthy of the laborer, I divulge nothing."

Pondoroso knew when to stop pushing. "I'll set your demands before those beyond the pale. In the meantime our camp followers will provide amenities." He started away, then pretended to have an afterthought. "Where, by the by, are your betrothal bracelets? Or binding rings or whatever talisman of matrimony is observed in the north country?"

She was only a half-beat slow in returning the serve. "Lost, with so many other belongings, when we fled our disabled muscle car on the Wundwander."

Burning was certain that Pondoroso hadn't missed Souljourner's brief spinning of wheels. Regardless, the Varangian headed for the wall's single gate without a further word.

Immediately Alabaster's camp followers—women and youths of the Varangian base—took Burning and Souljourner off to separate chambers of the public bathhouse. Burning accepted a rinse and soak while his outer clothes were being sponge cleaned and his boots and pistol belt buffed up. A Möbius chant and some focusing meme-pushes helped him regain a measure of Flowstate clarity, enough to know that setting off alone for Gapshot in his current condition was out of the question. Even if he had to let Souljourner find her destiny in Alabaster while he quartered at Camp Varangian, at least he'd be alive and able to vector the aircav in when they came looking for him.

Burning declined the offer of a Varangian chirurgeon who wanted to drain "maleficent humors" from Burning's skull with a large-gauge needle and drawing tube. At his request, one of the matrons fetched him a small rectangle of Optimant polymer with a reflective film, in which he assessed the size of his pupils and the slight droop to the left side of his face. The nausea was still with him, as well.

Attendants fetched refreshments. Burning passed on the gooner, opting for water, along with some salted biscuit that he hoped would settle his stomach.

The fire-heated bath lulled him into feeling secure until a messenger boy brought word that Pondoroso was calling for him. The staff started hustling him back into harness. Wherever the sling-gun pistol he'd stripped from the dead Unconquerable had gotten to, no one was offering it back, or the targone, or the basket-hilted shortsword. It probably was bad manners for bridal party members to go heavily armed.

Pondoroso was waiting for him at the Alabaster gate, along with a bathed and coiffed Souljourner, now arrayed in a glittery wrapgown and decked with flowers. She was getting around, determined but unpracticed, on a pair of lionwood crutches as beautifully carved and ergonomic as a brace of abstract-sculpture lightning bolts. The overman obviously knew enough about head injuries to notice the sag in Burning's face. "A brain wound expansion, mayhap," he remarked. "At least the healer beyond the wall is a good one."

"Does that mean I get in?" He needed to lie down, rest, see what the next few hours would bring.

"In a moment. The kids are bringing a flower garland for you. Customary, you know, for the exchange of wedding vows."

"Vows?" Souljourner said. "But we're already espoused!"

"A mere formality required by those beyond the pale,"

Pondoroso explained. "In the absence of documentation—to ensure tranquillity." He turned as the kids appeared with the garland. "Ah, here come the proclaimers, the attestors, and our saintly chaplain. Let's quickly ensure that you two be married."

CHAPTER
NINETEEN

Dextra had to jump back to avoid Lieutenant Gairaszek's size-EEE shoes. The giant exec was trying to be everywhere at once, to do everything himself. She couldn't blame him for feeling that way, nor could she blame him for failing.

Tonii had come to her aid once more when the starboard sponson had staved, but now the gynander and Dextra both were looking for Kurt Elide, who'd vanished from sight in the first impact. Dextra's fear that he was one of the overboards was quickly put to rest as she spotted him at the base of the wedged gun barrel. Instead of climbing to safety or working with others to free the gun, he was pointing at the overcast sky, a spectral figure with a finger raised like an Old Testament prophet, yelling, "Look, look!"

Then Dextra saw what he was motioning at: a swirl of fire, brightening the fog in fitful flares and dimmings, following an arc of lift from the southern bank of the river. Hypnotized by the implied trajectory, she watched it climb, hearing the distant flutter and sizzle of angry flame. The flame drew its parabola over them, falling with increasing speed to port, where it suddenly spread, making a furious orange nebula in the fog.

"Incendiary," Tonii said over the soft murmurings and curses. "Crudely fashioned. It must have hit the bluffs and splattered."

But not gone out; that much was clear. "They know we're here," Gairaszek said, watching the fire on the bluffs. He turned to the work crews. "Snap to! Get your charges in place and bring those cutters up!"

Nobody had to be told that the ship was a sitting duck. People scrambled to obey even as a second fireball lofted up from the fortress at Fluter Delve. This one seemed brighter to Dextra, but it occurred to her that perhaps the fog was lifting. The fireball landed astern, producing a huge splash and vast hissing clouds of steam.

Gairaszek had his talker pass the word that he was making ready to lighten the ship. If the work crews could cut the elevator and turret loose without damaging the *GammaLAW*, she'd ride high enough to float free of the impediment under the starboard sponson.

Dextra switched over to the command channel in time to hear Quant say "—meters of hull ripped open, Eddie. We can't float her free until we patch those breaches or we'll sink. A scuba team and some of Zinsser's people are preparing to assess the damage."

"What about the gun turret?" Gairaszek asked.

Quant sounded as calm as if he'd spent all evening thinking it over. "Use the cutters on the snagged barrel. Maybe that'll be enough to float us free."

"Sir, it might be easier to dump both tubes," Gairaszek pointed out.

"No. We need that other rifle more than ever."

As Quant said it, Dextra saw another fireball fly like a meteor from the fortress.

When the ship had been tetherdropped on Aquamarine, Quant had insisted that emergency repair and shipfitting equipment and supplies be onboard. Dextra had backed him to the hilt, and even Starkweather and the logistics people had been forced to do as Quant asked.

Therefore, the teams sent down to cope with the hull damage were carrying some of the navy's best salvage and repair gear. Still, Quant realized it wouldn't be enough. The star-board leading quarter of the main hull had sustained a long tear, and the prow of the starboard sponson had been crumpled as if it had been forced into a thresher. The sponson also had stress fractures that ran past several watertight bulkheads, and some riverbed outcropping had punctured two horrific holes amidships.

Even so, Quant refused to allow the albatross to alight. *This* was his command: this bridge, this deck. His because he'd asked for it. Someday he'd take the *GammaLAW* across the long waters of Aquamarine, as was her fate. He turned his at-tention back to matters at hand. "Say again, talker?"

His talker drew a breath. "Sir, damage control says there's no need to sound the call for additional divers. They've already got more volunteers than they can use."

Somewhere in sludge so dark that they couldn't see what they were doing, a grab bag of old salts and semiadults was trying to reconstruct a considerable portion of his ship. Quant understood that it was more cussedness and self-preservation that had people suiting up to go into the murky water than any sense of loyalty to Captain Chaz Quant. He wasn't used to feeling grateful to his fellow human beings, but he knew he owed those people something he'd never be able to repay.

Somehow one volunteer's transmission got bled back over Quant's line. "Wanna know how dark it is down here, even with lights?" a woman was asking. "Shut your eyes tight. *That's* how dark."

On deck, bulky flotation packs and first-echelon reconstruc-tion kits were waiting to be taken below, pumps standing by to raise the ship from her impalement. Briefly, it was SOP: patch and reconstruct, pump shipped water like the devil, inflate flotation packs in flooded spaces or force-pump aerofoam in.

They'd get her afloat all right, but—

Quant looked out across the sea of fog that now crested somewhere around the level of the signal bridge. Linked to the ship's IRs and microradars, he could see Fluter Delve not quite six hundred meters away, perhaps ten points off the starboard bows.

As he watched, another incendiary went up from the fortress. Quant hadn't met Grandee 'Waretongue Rhodes, but he had no doubt that the man had had something to do with egging on Dynast Piety IV. No doubt Rhodes had decided that even a burned and damaged *GammaLAW* in Ean hands was better than nothing.

The fog was evanescing in an almost coy dance of tendrils and swirls. Quant looked to the fortress again and saw more clearly the hot spots of the fire throwers. He signed his talker to silence and raised Gairaszek. "How long before I can have that barrel, XO? It's our only shot, Eddie."

Dextra had forgotten how abrupt and rude weather could be in real life. When the veil of fog blew away and left the ship's company gaping at Fluter Delve, it was almost like being pushed from a changing room onto center stage at the Abraxas Grand Opera. People gasped, and Dextra wondered if she shouldn't have worn moisture-breathing pants again, because this was the sort of thing that could make a girl have an accident.

The morning air was full of the yells of the emergency crews, the ring of the heavy-laser cutting rigs as they were jockeyed around, and the frying-fat sounds of the severing of the number one gun tube. The sound that hit her strongest, though, was the basso whine that was traveling through the ship—the straining song of the ordnance elevators. She knew that the three rounds cobbled together by shipfitters and ordies for the 240-mm rifles were on their ascent to the hole in the deck that was the top of the turret's barbette. Whether the main battery would be there to chamber them, however, was still open to speculation. The Heaves and the safe if swift waters below Fluter Delve were within sight but as far off as if they were on Periapt.

She considered infiltrating groups of commandos ashore to knock out the threat to *GammaLAW* but dismissed the idea. Even conceding the overwhelming power of Ext small arms, sensors were showing a lot of movement and metal along both riverbanks. The Ean grandees would have their troops waiting for anyone who left the ship.

Tonii had left what had become 'ers accustomed place at Dextra's right hand to help two demo specialists clamber back on deck from where they'd been rigging charges to sever the aircraft elevator and gun turret in a worst case. The pair were still weighted with all kinds of explosives in bricks and cans and what the specs sometimes called "cake decorators," some of them riding carabineers on the specialists' body harnesses. Gairaszek's shooter—and his talker—stood connecting detonation hardwires to a handheld det unit.

Despite all the furious activity at a distance, Dextra had an abrupt sensation of being in a fire base or strategic population center about to be blown to motes by one side or the other.

A wind came up, stirring Dextra's hair. Now that the *GammaLAW*'s position had been compromised, the shipfitters felt no compunction about sending great fantails of sparks arcing out from the gun turret in their efforts to slice number one away. The spectral feeling of the scene made Dextra's hackles rise. She was about to say something—she didn't know what—and move—though she didn't know where—but at that moment the vibrations of running feet on the flight deck drummed some ominous message into her brain.

Not that the footsteps were loud; quite the reverse. They carried the unwilling breach of absolute silence that attended a final pounce. Dextra was no brawler, but some preternatural instinct she seldom accessed made her spin, dip her shoulders, and hold up suited forearms and gloved hands to protect herself as the footsteps reached her.

Someone, flying past her like a black wind, missed with a blow that might have broken her neck. She wanted to peal a warning, but all she could manage was a mousy-sounding squeak like a nail being pulled. Gairaszek heard her even so and for all his renowned lumpishness, whirled as lightly as a ballerina to find Zone bearing down on him, with Wetbar and the rest rushing in behind.

Knowing better than to let go of it, Gairaszek managed to shift the detonator hot box to his left hand and mobilize to a fighting stance. While Dextra was still falling, the lieutenant's big, knobby right fist flew at Zone but missed. A kick, however, caught Wetbar in the stomach.

Dextra had no reach-for-the-gun-that-isn't-there Ext reflexes; she was *used* to being unarmed but paralyzingly unused to danger so close and personal. Her residual reflex was to glance around for Tonii, but Tonii had lowered 'ermself over the side to help laser number one gun loose. With the ship's company so depleted, all available hands were on lookout or repair detail, bearing a hand with the wounded, or standing watch at some essential station. Dextra realized in that moment that the flight deck was empty.

Wetbar turned expertly as Gairaszek's kick caught him, but he was sent back as if hit by a catapult sledge. Zone was in past the XO's guard, though, and Gairaszek's sheer size and strength offered scant protection. Zone's feet left the nonskid in a flurry of kicks. His handwork was all feints and blocks. A right-leg hook off a roundhouse caught the XO before he could set the det unit safely aside and recover from the shot that had laid out Wetbar.

Dextra had no doubt that Zone had broken more than one neck with that same wicked hook. Gairaszek's chin was snapped around, flesh abraded right off it by the ball of Zone's foot. The thick muscles of his neck saved him from death, but he tottered back off balance in a way that let Dextra know he'd lost contact with the here and now. As Tonii had taken pains to impress on her, loss of connectedness was the preliminary to a kill.

Dextra recalled her face-off with Zone at Wall Water and cursed the depleted weapon she had meant to fire at him.

Gairaszek's return to awareness came a split second later; Dextra saw it while she was staring at the det unit with dismay and gathering what she regarded as the minor physical courage with which she'd been endowed. The XO threw a snap-fisted blow, middle knuckle cocked, where he thought Zone would be, but Zone had become an airborne demon and the hook kick had upset Gairaszek's sense of orientation and sequence. Dextra had never actually heard a fist make a sound through the air before, but Gairaszek's did, missing by a hair as Zone tucked for a landing. Pivoting, Zone brought his right hand down almost overhead, heel outward, at the XO's right temple—kill or be killed.

Wetbar was still down, but Roust and the others swarmed in, all eyes on the det unit. Closing on the thing herself, Dextra suddenly realized that people were stepping over her—running, fighting. Her right hand was bleeding badly inside its glove, but she couldn't feel any pain.

Zone's blow to Eddie's temple hit with a thud like an executioner's ax on the block. Dextra saw his eyes begin to roll up into his head and knew they'd go the rest of the way. Still she managed to crawl for the det unit, even while Eddic was falling back like an empty vac suit and Zone's confederates continued to grapple with her. With eyes fixed on the thing, she never saw the foot that slammed into the side of her head.

CHAPTER TWENTY

"I can't *marry* you," Burning muttered while festive Varangians were preparing for the nuptials.

"Remarry me," Souljourner corrected, looking a bit pole-axed herself. "To keep you safe." Her single contour of white-blond brow lowered, and her slight prognathism became more conspicuous. "Am I such lowly goods that it demeans you to pretend espousal? Lip-serve the vows, placate the guardsmen and the Alabasterites— where's the harm?"

There wasn't time to lay it all out for her even if he'd been willing to. He shrank from the thought of explaining his aversion to wedlock, to declarations of love—an antipathy that had taken deep root after his fiancée, Romola, had broken their engagement while he was fighting Periapt's "legal annexation" of Concordance. Romola had bailed in favor of Tonne-Head Gilead, a LAW quisling and counterfeit Allgrave, despite the fact that she herself had been a war heroine at Santeria Corners.

"I can't do it," he told her. "Leave it at that. I'll explain everything to the Varangians. I'll tell them I asked you to lie—"

"Are you dementiate? After accepting their bread and salt and the protection of their swords?"

"So be it, if they turn me out."

"Oh, they'll make you leave town, right enough. They'll scourge you down a gauntlet between two lines of guardsmen with chain-whips and nunchucks! And if you think your belfry's ringing now, wait until they strike a tune from it!"

Burning had his mouth open to reply as Pondoroso stepped over to them. "What's this, spatting under the very wedding arch?"

"You know how we married folk are," Burning replied in a monotone.

As the Varangians brought on the matrimonial censers, the plighting cups, and the sacramental unguents, he tried to take comfort in the fact that his hosts didn't practice the genital-piercing rites of some Scorpian cultures with a symbolic joining of the newlyweds' hardware by chain. When his turn came to make the vow, Burning obediently echoed the cantors. Nobody remarked on his fumbling of the lyrics; it was plain to one and all that Alabaster wasn't exactly his neck of the woods.

He and Souljourner fed each other confarreational saltbread and sipped water from the same chalice. The ceremony slid him into a strong mindfulness of being he couldn't fend off. No one had ever taught him how to use Flowstate to *avoid* Flow-state. The Varangians played their rattles, jingle-gloves, tam bourones, and didgeriphones. Burning performed shuffling dance steps as shown, and he and Souljourner dabbed each other's foreheads with fragrant attar. They exchanged donated bracelets and the pledging kiss, tasting each other. Like most Exts, Burning was heedful of his Flowstate the way an Anchorite monk was of devoutness, and he perceived a powerful bond forming. All the ritual and role-playing was carrying him into a real connectedness to Souljourner. She, on the other hand, looked startled in the wake of their kiss, as if the reality of it all were just hitting her.

Whatever second thoughts were rocking her came too late. With an abbreviated shivaree of pan banging, the Varangians hastened them over to the single two-door gate in the middle of Alabaster's great white wall. A vertical cylindrical fixture built into the left one suggested a lazy Susan crossbred with an auto-bank drawer—a handy way to cut down on undesirable contact with the outside world.

Burning caught the sounds of a ponderous bolt being slid back as on-duty armsmen turned an auger-size key in a crude lock. He smelled fish oil and saw fresh stains where someone had lubed the portals' hinges. The doors' hesitation in swinging open was an indication of just how infrequently people were accepted beyond the pale. An ancient IRA motto came to him: "Once in, never out." Flowstate let him fend off apprehension; white battlements might spell insurmountability to an Aquam, but he'd take that fence when it came time—even if he had to do it straight up on a chopper extraction line.

He took Souljourner's hand. Usually firm and dry, her grip was limp and clammy. The gates opened a crack, and Pondoroso motioned unsentimentally for them to get going. Burning released Souljourner so that she could handle her crutches, acquiescing to the unavoidable as he led his new bride beyond the pale.

In passing through the gate, Burning realized that he'd unconsciously forged a mental image of those who dwelled in the alleged utopia. The gatherers of the mandseng, the eschewers of the coarse and the violent world outside Cape Ataraxia, would be ethereal botanist-lamas or maybe white-robed elfin demigods, fairer and finer than mere mortals.

But no sooner had the Varangians all but slammed the portals on their heels than his preconceptions evaporated like a dream. The reception committee might have convened at any Scorpian crossroads or ville plaza. On closer glance, though, the two dozen or so looked better fed and less leery than the usual chance-met locals. Even so, they were dressed for labor in loinwraps and lavalavas, frond bonnets and sampan hats. Several moved in behind Burning and Souljourner to rebolt the gates from their side; at the same time there was the sound of the great key being turned in the cylinder lock on the Varangians' side.

Burning had time for only a few strategic split-second

glances at his new surroundings. Cape Ataraxia struck him as well husbanded, even luxuriant for the Big Sere, but the Elysian Fields it wasn't. Two men—one in a gaudy floral-print sarilike garment, the other in black flowing hakima trousers and matching headband—stepped forward. They started simultaneous, elaborate bows to Alabaster's new Descrier but quickly curtailed them to exchange even more elaborate obeisances with each other.

"I stand abashed," the sari said, "unworthy to interrupt the conscientious Hungerford, except that my obligations as healer compel me to, otherwise—perish the thought."

Hungerford was equally decorous. "My chagrin is past all reckoning, Roundelay! Nothing short of my sworn duty as an Injunctor could cause me to intrude on your salutations to our new Descrier under any other circumstance—inconceivable!"

The doctor and the local official were a study in contrasts. Where Roundelay was short, bellied, shave-skulled, whiskerless, and merry-eyed, Hungerford was Burning's height, bearded, and powerfully muscled.

"Hence, I interpose myself," Hungerford finished, "to learn what hazard to Alabaster our new Descrier hinted at to the Varangians."

"And all have confidence you'll find it out," Roundelay simpered, "once I've ascertained that this power poses no peril to us, however inadvertent."

There ensued the weirdest little crypto minuet Burning had ever seen. The healer and the Injunctor managed to kowtow to and obstruct one another at the same time, even while continuing to trade niceties, as if their tacit struggle were not occurring.

"How I wish I were free like the rest of the world to defer to your all-consuming loftiness of purpose," Hungerford said, agilely avoiding having his toes stepped on.

"I'm wretched," Roundelay countered, nimbly escaping

being shouldered aside, "being at a loss for the superlatives by which you deserve to be hailed."

Burning fully expected them to start throwing fists, but somehow it never came to that, as if there were some threshold that couldn't and wouldn't be crossed. What did intervene were a few Alabasterites off to one side going *"Hissst, hissst!"*

It happened that there was a mandseng plant growing among the gnarled roots of a nearby yussa tree. A homunculus of mandseng, Burning knew it was called, and growing in plain sight—whereas reports gathered by the *Scepter* survey team indicated that the stuff seemed almost sentient in its perverse ability to hide itself from would-be harvesters. The mandseng in question was young, half the size of his hand, but for a peasant on the other side of the white wall it would have been a major windfall, a tenth or so of a decent year's income, not to mention protection against dozens of Anathemite births.

"Lest it wither," somebody whispered piously.

Roundelay and Hungerford broke clean as fighters headed for neutral corners, proving that strictures about disturbing the ville's sustaining crop took precedence over everything. Burning had always assumed that etiquette in utopia would be unconventional, but out and out queerbombed, he hadn't foreseen. Both had more to say, but Souljourner cut them off by whacking one of the gates with the tip of a crutch.

"Shall we wait outside? Before long you'll miss me more than I will you."

Bystanders took the decision out of the leaders' hands, bidding Souljourner enter her new home and rest. She was magnanimous in victory, telling Roundelay, "I understand your concern that we bring no ill germ to bedevil Alabaster. But rest assured that both Redtails and I are hale and uninfectious."

"Then, as to these hazards of which you speak," Hungerford said with smarmy good grace, "of what nature are they that you should claim Alabaster to be in such dire need of your abilities?"

Souljourner caressed her forehead absently. "Before dawn, so far over the horizon that it's practically back the other way, the floor of the Amnion hove in what we Descriers call an up-lift, which presages a water surge of some size, due sometime later today, I would venture.

"But there is something else at work, which even I am at a loss to identify. The Amnion is severely troubled in the north. How far north I cannot say, though perhaps as far as Passwater. You here on the south coast would normally have no reason to fear, but what troubles the Amnion in the north is rapidly spreading in all directions, and I fear that Alabaster will not be immune to the sea's actions."

The Alabasterites had begun to mumble to one another. Hungerford was distinctly impressed and somewhat intimidated. "Lacking a Descrier, we've been forced to keep most tackle, trays, and truck well up and dry, but we'll make double sure of it all this night."

Burning eyed Souljourner. She had to have known since sometime before their battle at the Ghoul Grounds fountain, but she had said nothing about the prescience. That explained some of her urgency in getting to Alabaster, where she knew that her tsunami warning would win her instant credibility and acceptance. Injured leg or no, the day had turned out favorable for her, but Burning refused to think of her as anything more than a local nube with a tweaked neurophysiology. After all, he'd successfully manipulated her on two occasions already by controlling the throws of the Holy Rollers.

Most of the Alabasterites trotted off with Hungerford to check the preparations against high water. The ones who stayed steered the two newcomers toward what would be their quarters. Along the way, Burning took in Alabaster.

On the highest point of land on Cape Ataraxia, hard by the gate, was a longhouse. "Our high-water refuge," Roundelay explained, "and route of emergency escape. Should Amnion engulf the lower elevations, we would wait out the flood there."

"Ever used it?"

"Twice. Once when I was a young sprout, but only to err on the side of safety. The cape is sheltered by the foreland at Oread's bust—a Beforetimer construction that houses a mysterious machine thought to have once been alive. Storm pushes and quake waves have never come any higher than those drying racks you see down there at Queller's Enlargement.

"Fortune favors Alabaster. If ever the waters imperiled our refuge, why, we would wait them out behind the pale with our Varangian protectors, then begin anew."

Burning checked himself from asking the obvious: What about big water that didn't stop at the wall, the once-a-five-hundred- or one-thousand- or five-thousand-year-cycle deluge, the one that was bound to come over the horizon sooner or later?

Alabaster was growing a little bit of every conceivable subsistence crop. Why the locals needed them when their mand-seng trade had to be extremely profitable was something he decided to wait to ask. The place was clean and well kept, though not overprettified: fields, groves, orchards, paddies, walls, and the egg-tip dome buildings he had noticed from back on Scorpia proper.

Roundelay led them by tidy footpaths to a medium-large structure consisting of two smaller, rounded tholi and one larger peaked one, a rambling split-level bungalow made up of vaulted ellipsoids.

"Your predecessor's place, Souljourner," the Injunctor explained. "We've kept it as he left it, albeit—" He eyed Burning. "—it will hereafter be less spacious than he preferred."

There was no lock on the Dutch front door. The place was musty but neat, spartanly furnished by some standards though offering all the usual Aquam comforts. Modest gift baskets and bentos of food had been set out, along with beverages and a few plain-wrapped housewarming presents. Posts and beams were hung with wreaths of dried peppers, clusters of herbs, and tea-bag-like sachets of spice and incense.

The villagers clearly wanted to press questions on the newcomers or just ogle them, but with a sea surge and perhaps more on the way there was work to be done. The conscientious drew their less dutiful neighbors with them when they left. Roundelay insisted on making a cursory inspection of Burning's head bumps. The healer then got pushy about opening Souljourner's bandage for an examination of her leg wound, but he left when word arrived that a woman had gone into premature labor while straining to move trayfarming gear to higher ground.

The peaked dome included a kitchen, a living space, and a workroom; one rounded chamber was a storeroom and larder, while the other was both bedchamber and study. The house was as well crafted as a yacht. Sunlight shone in coronas off beautifully joined and finished wood, and even in the Big Sere heat, shade trees and traditional architecture made the interior quite bearable.

By unspoken agreement, Burning and Souljourner zeroed in on the futon bed. He opened windows to air the place out. She hobbled over to the big floor mattress and set aside the abstract lightning bolt crutches. Pro forma adjurations from the departing Alabasterites—"Now you are one of us" and "May you keep Alabaster safe for one hundred years"—had left her thoughtful rather than jubilant. In what amounted to a moment of triumph, she settled onto the mattress, rubbing her farmertan brow.

"Another headache?" Burning asked.

"And fatigue—of an equally novel sort. I wish I could see clearly what troubles the sea. As well as what it will mean for Scorpia." She tried to brighten a bit by sheer willpower. "But at least we're safe for now."

"And where you wanted to be."

She seemed to deflate a little, then rally. "It's true that I have long desired to be a recognized Descrier, honored and rewarded and trusted—as I'd have long since been had I been born a man-child." She gestured broadly to their surroundings. "I wanted a taste of this—if only for a day. But I never meant to coerce you to vows or trap you here."

"I'm not trapped."

She looked confused, then resentful. Burning left the room while she got ready for bed. By the time he returned, she was on her side, facing the wall, a thin sheet drawn over her. Possible concussion be blowed, he told himself; he needed to lie down and shut his eyes. He undressed in the kitchen, then lay down on the futon as quietly as he could. He was just slipping under the sheet when she said, "Burning, will you fly off and abandon me?"

He wanted to say, "This is where you belong." But what he actually said was, "My wings're your wings."

She turned over onto her back, her hand groping for a moment before finding his and covering it. It was no more and no less contact than he wanted, so he remained still with his eyes closed. He heard her begin to snore softly and drift off, until a break in her breathing and the tug of the sheet being pulled away brought him awake. Her lips were parted slightly; she might have been listening to a concert with her eyes closed. Her right leg was uncovered from the hip down. One breast was exposed, surprisingly small and slack on such a Rubenesque body. Burning hesitated, then reached to replace the cover. Light filtering through the opaque cloth put soft highlights on curls of pubic hair in the shadowed stillness under there.

He lay back with a quiet, sighing grunt, pulling the sheet back over himself, waiting for exhaustion and the need for recuperation to feather him down into sleep. A sweet languor crept over him, and he felt his penis stir. He told himself that if he yielded to his hunger for her now, in the wake of the misconceived remarriage ceremony, she was bound to misunderstand. She would feel irrevocably tied to him, and perhaps vice versa.

She squirmed slightly, stealing the sheet again. He rose on one elbow and gazed at the bruises on her leg. Her skin was so pale and smooth, lightly downed with hairs so fine that he saw them as a field of faint glints. The only thing she hadn't taken off was the drawstring neck pouch in which she kept the gaffed Holy Rollers.

He eased himself over her, with caution for her wound, settling between her legs and placing his lips gently against the exposed thigh, closing his eyes. The urgent warmth of his hard-on pulsed between his stomach and the futon cover, but he forced himself to go slowly. He kissed her again, laying fingertips on her leg, breathing in the fragrance of her. He was waiting for her to push him away, halfway hoping she would.

Instead, she sat up on her own elbows to watch him, tangling the fingers of one hand in among his Hussar Plaito. He kissed her again, a centimeter closer to the place where the cover angled across the ringlets of her pubic mound. He raised his eyes to her. She wore an expression he hadn't seen before: wide-eyed but not startled, searching but not unsure. Maybe it was because he knew a blush wouldn't be visible in the half-light, but he felt no crimson rise to his face. He set his lips to her again, closer to the juncture of her thighs.

Her breath came out a little shakily. His heart pounded with a hope so simple and powerful that the rest of the world fell away. Souljourner slid her right leg up across his shoulder as gracefully as a bird lifting its wing to preen, foot arching, toes resting almost timidly on his back. A soft grace had come into every line and move of her work-solid body. Burning took the sheet with his free hand, baring her completely. He drew the first slow silken stroke of his tongue through the moistened folds of her. She breathed more quickly through pursed lips and writhed slightly to lay back, drawing her other knee up, opening to him. He gave lingering attention to her, at the same time feeling the urgency of his swollen cock, flattened and kneaded against the futon. A maiden flight wasn't to be rushed even if it meant spending himself into the mattress cover the first time around. She wound her fingers in his hair and ran her free hand down his body. He reached around and up, along the length of her torso, to caress her breast and found her fingers already there. They shared silent knowledge of what felt best. When she thrashed in pleasure, it was difficult to hang on; when she bridged, climaxing, she nearly bucked him off the bed.

In due course she pulled him up, and they lay in each other's arms, where it was all kisses, caresses, slow liberties. At her forceful prompting, he slid atop her, entering her by degrees. The thrust that brought him up against her hymen never came. They fell to more robust driving. She was still glorying in the equestrian rhythms of it when, throwing tantric performance aside in favor of the joy of the moment, he was racked by orgasm.

Finding no sign of vaginal blood, Souljourner was distraught, thinking she'd done something wrong. The celibate retirees at Pyx had never explained to her why hymens were often not intact by the age of sexual commencement, so Burning did.

"Hoo," she said. "Am I not pregnant, then?"

"No. All *GammaLAW* mission personnel were required to undergo certain, uh, treatments during the voyage from Periapt—"

"Permanent?" she said, aghast.

He shook his head. "But certainly effective for the next couple of months."

She considered that for a moment, then huffed. "Well done, then. You're off now to eat, drink, and gamble?"

Burning laughed. "Don't judge the whole world by what happens on the high roads." He reached for her gently, touching her in a way that made her breath catch again. To his surprise, she responded in kind, if fumblingly. He put aside worries about the future. He'd made his bed and had to lie in it, but for the time being it was such a lovely bed.

Souljourner still found novelty in his penis, grasping it proprietorially. "What is your Visitant name for this?"

He put his tongue in his cheek. "Asshole with a handle."

CHAPTER
TWENTY-ONE

Zinsser had no illusions about being able to defend himself against Asurao armed or unarmed, but he also knew that he wouldn't leave Ghost to face him alone. She seemed to be rooted to the spot, in any case, gazing down at the Feral. Just then a new sound issued from the DevOceanites who were chanting and milling on the great stone gangplank over the crashing waves.

"Ghost! They're jumping!"

The first few were already falling through the air headfirst, their white robes fluttering around them like windblown flames of homespun fabric, their arms spread in supplication to the jostling whitecaps. Only some were holding the notes of the chants; most were managing only a prolonged wail that revealed less confidence and serenity than the faithful should have felt. The sound of their impact was lost in the greater turmoil of the sea itself.

Ghost knew it would be only moments before the Oceanic responded. She also knew that Asurao was capable of covering the space to the foot of the cliffs in a few bounds, probably in less generous a mood than the one he'd been in earlier. And this time there'd be no dropping ice mushrooms on him.

She dragged her attention from the wild man and began to follow Zinsser up the narrow footpath. They thrust themselves between and around DevOceanites, manhandling the numbed and droning faithful without encountering much resistance and moving too fast to suffer any retaliation.

Partway up, a much smaller trail—a ledge, really, barely as wide as Ghost's foot—veered off in the direction they wanted to go. Fortunately, the cliff had a slight inward angle and suitable handholds above. When she and Zinsser had pushed free of the insane procession and reached the start of the ledge, Ghost took a final look back at Asurao.

The Feral had taken his bounder right up the trail, the splayed, heavy-nailed triple toes of the beast pounding the faithful flat with every leap. At the same time his war club was laying people out left and right. The throngs had slowed his progress, but he wasn't about to stop.

Zinsser was standing to one side at the ledge path. "You first."

She wondered what he was thinking. Perhaps he meant to stay behind and fight Asurao for her—a perverse but not uninteresting image. Indifferent, she started off along the ledge. Two extra corpses on Aquamarine wouldn't alter things.

Zinsser followed after a last anxious glance downslope. By the time Asurao reached the fork in the trails, they were fifteen meters off and widening their lead toward the top of the wall. Irrational now, the Feral tried to coax and then belabor his bounder to continue the pursuit, but the creature was intelligent enough to see that it would almost certainly fall. The animal resisted stubbornly even after Asurao had bloodied its mouth with the bit and its head with his club.

No easy route led around the cliff by which he might head them off; the headland's ridge ran inland there, to the peninsula wall. Realizing that his quarry was about to disappear from view, Asurao vaulted off his mount with a curse and set out after them afoot.

Ghost saw him coming and picked up the pace. If it came to a fight on the ledge, perhaps all three of them would die. Where it rounded the inland curve of the upper headland, the ledge became a mere pouting lip of stone. Ghost was beginning her traverse, hugging the rock, when she heard Zinsser yell and sensed his violent movement. Something caromed off the basalt.

She glanced back the way they'd come to see Asurao racing at them empty-handed, having hurled his club in exasperation and missed. It was the wrong place for a confrontation, so Ghost finished the traverse, with Zinsser crowding her closely from behind.

On that side of the headland the ledge widened and sloped away into high dunes of talcumlike sand with the wall on one side and the relentless crash of the sea on the other. Quiescent tidal pools lay in an irregular chain along the foot of the cliff. Zinsser had told her that the water in the pools would be as lifeless as if distilled, except for chance impurities and organisms picked up from the air. The Oceanic simply didn't extend itself into landlocked pockets, or, more accurately, any Oceanic part, however minute, marooned in such a place deconstituted itself—its components presumably to become a part of the whole again when the sea touched them once more.

Dune line, sea, and wall met a klick or so northwest of where Ghost stood listening to Zinsser come scrabbling around the turn. Down below, something strange was happening in the surf. The waves appeared to have stopped. The swells had subsided, and on that side of the headland, away from the town and the battle, the air felt eerily still. The sky had taken on an odd, shifting coronal look. Twisting spears of light danced kaleidoscopically. Ghost thought she caught a whiff of ozone.

She and Zinsser watched for Asurao to appear. Ghost grasped that it would be better to face the Feral there, where they could perhaps force him off the edge. The fall down the juncture between dune and cliff might not kill him, but it would remove him from the threat column for a while. While Zinsser looked around for a rock, Ghost took her big trench knife in a relaxed grip and set herself to wait.

The Feral's grunting heralded his arrival. He sounded in pain—injuries suffered in the attack on Passwater or perhaps from the ice mushrooms. Then a thick-fingered hand appeared around the turn, greased with the gel the Ferals wore, with black dirt under every nail. Ghost could easily have loped it off, yet Asurao's insane struggle held some fascination. Surely he knew that he was vulnerable, that his obsession with her might cost him his life. Others, male and female, had pursued her and even run risks, but she'd never seen anyone strive like this, pit himself against death itself.

Asurao's foot appeared bare, lumpish, and splayed, toes wriggling for purchase almost prehensilely. Zinsser came marching into Ghost's line of vision at the same moment, hefting a hunk of scrub branch as a club. He swung it in a flat arc into the Feral's big foot with a meat-hammering sound and the crack of bone. Blood welled up, and the foot slipped from the ledge. Ghost thought absently that she might have gone for the hand first.

Even so, Asurao loosed a howl that drifted around the corner of the ledge. They both expected to see him drop, but instead, incredibly, he made the traverse in a simian sort of leap, using his wounded foot with very little impairment. Zinsser fell back, raising the club for a second shot, but he might as well have been standing in the way of a wild boar. The Feral simply kept coming, feet churning the sand as he knocked Zinsser flying with one blow of his fist. then he lost his footing and went down in a sand skid near the crest of the dune.

Asurao flailed to regain his footing. It was clear what he had planned for Zinsser, who lay stunned nearby. Knife in hand, Ghost considered the times she'd saved Zinsser's life—as well as the time or two he had saved hers. Asurao was an intriguing creature, undeformed by convention, perhaps more in harmony with the feelings and attitudes she'd taken on since becoming Ghost—since she'd died—than anyone she'd ever met. But Zinsser, comrade and shipmate, was joined to her by mutual Chinese obligations. To allow the Feral to kill him now would be dishonest, a kind of weakness that might drag her back toward life again.

She had every intention of opening Asurao up before he could regain his balance. He was on his feet in a manner of speaking, sand and gel smeared in a weird pointillism across his face and a four-vaned knife in hand. He seemed to think that he'd won despite the fact that the real fight had yet to begin.

Before they could even get into it, the world chimed like a bell. Rays of shifting color shot through the clouds, and the ground trembled, sending sand liquefacting so that all three of them sank into it. When the groundquake abated, Ghost found herself up to her ankles in sand. Asurao was knee-deep, and Zinsser was partially covered. As if God had emptied his lungs, a wind sprang up, blowing in from offshore.

Ghost pivoted slowly. The swells had returned, but now the whitecaps were marching up onto the shore in ranks and files like the advance of a conquering army, dipping and rising unnaturally fast. The Oceanic had reacted at last to the Dev-Oceanites' mass suicide, and all at once water was violating its own oldest maxim: it was running uphill.

The tidal pools below began swirling and filling. A brackish rill of subsurface runoff from the wall area thickened and roiled murkily. A drainage/benjo ditch at the upper end of the devastated town rose to overflow its sides, floating weeds, feces, blood, ash, debris, and dead bodies in all directions. The Oceanic was angry, and it was coming ashore to punish human impertinence.

A shudder ran through the entire scarp. Sheets, streamers of water, and vast fields of droplets crashed off the face of the headland by the altar. By then the faithful had to have realized that they hadn't attained a state of grace, though the revelation was a bit late in coming.

Asurao threw his head back, chest expanded, and bellowed

a cry of defiance at the sea; then he glanced at Ghost and the half-conscious Zinsser and thumped his chest. "The town goes under. It is time to leave!"

They were still holding knives, but now Ghost let a small smile show, at once demure and seductive, out of place among the wicked scars. Asurao gazed at her dumbly, returned a sly grin, then turned to finish off Zinsser.

Depersonalized, she watched herself step over with a lithe, bent-legged, low-center-of-gravity move and plant a foot on the Feral's naked rump, launching him off the edge of the dune before he could react. He went head over heels, skidding sideways, plowing ass-first, cutting great wakes of sand.

She moved to Zinsser's side while Asurao was still tumbling. "Get to your feet." She extended a hand. "Water's coming."

Zinsser shook his head to clear it and winced in pain. He gazed at the sea coming to have at Passwater, and his mouth fell open. The surf was running higher in the place where the dunes ran lowest on their way to the wall. If the water closed over the dunes before they could pass, they'd be cut off, and from the way the ditches were overflowing and the wells were gushing forth, Zinsser concluded that the waters had already inundated the area on the far side of the headland scarp.

He looked to where Asurao had disappeared and gave Ghost a searching look as she resheathed her blade. Then he set his jaw and slogged off through the sand at the best pace he could manage. Ghost double-timed determinedly at his side, fists pumping close by her ribs.

Caution jettisoned, they gained momentum on the downhill run and were soon racing against the incoming water. But the waves were shouldering higher against a dune wall that was totally incapable of withstanding them. How the Amnion was doing it, Zinsser couldn't guess.

"Don't think," Ghost said, as if reading his mind. "Run."

He did, and they went careening down the dune line. They crossed some rocks and a low-lying area moments before the waves cut through and raced triumphantly inland. Then it was uphill for a long, grueling minute that had their hearts banging in their chests. One more low point remained before a great buttress of steps that led back up to the ramparts.

Ghost saw that they weren't going to make it before the first waters crossed the dunes but thought they might be able to leap the waves. There was no going back, in any case. It was Zinsser who pulled her up short as waves thundered in over the dunes' lowest point, spilling in and spreading, as if searching for something. Shortly, they were cut off, trapped on a little mound of sand that was washing away with increasing speed.

Zinsser warned Ghost back from the water. "It's liable to dissolve you, or drag you under, or—ga-aah!" He hurled a handful of sand at the water, then another, in a fit of anger he couldn't control. "Why? *Why?*"

To her amazement Ghost saw that something else was eating at him.

"Why do you care about these idiots?" Zinsser yelled at the Amnion itself. *"Why won't you talk to me?"*

It was something he might say to her, Ghost thought. In anger, he dragged off his shirt and flung it at the rising waters, only to watch them close over the shirt and drag it under.

Somebody yelled, "Sky woman!"

It was Asurao, a sand figurine now, his foot a red, pulped mass from the clubbing Zinsser had given it. He still had his knife, which was attached to his wrist by a thong. He was lucky he hadn't disemboweled himself during his long fall.

"Sky," he croaked again. "What bad luck you bring. But then, meeting a worthy woman always spells doom, one way or another. That and being set afoot on the Scourlands—the only two things I fear."

And he *was* doomed, cut off on his own somewhat higher hillock of sand. The rush of water between him and Ghost was far too wide to cross. He raised his knife point to his cheek and said, "If we meet on the Green Battlefields later on, here's how we'll recognize each other."

And he laid open a long cut right under the high shelf of his cheekbone, in an attempt to duplicate the departed soul pattern on her face. Ghost watched silently as he shifted his knife and went to work on his other cheek.

Still exasperated by the unresponsive sea, Zinsser barely noticed. "How dare you treat me like these ignorant fanatics? Don't you see I'm different? I'm a scientist! Talk to me—here, talk to *this*!"

He fumbled his whatty off and hurled it into the waters as they ate away the sand close to his toes. When the instrument splashed and vanished, he did the same with his multiknife. Zinsser was almost in tears. His entreaties became a chant as he emptied his pockets in the Amnion, perhaps in the vain hope that some bit of technology would register with the Oceanic.

His few coins went in. Then he pawed at the catch of the Roke tissue sample case, opening it and the sealed scope slide as well, before letting everything fall into the seawater in a gesture of contempt and despair. Ghost saw that the waters were about to wash over his feet and wondered if there was any point in pulling him back.

She was reaching for his arm when the uphill-coursing runoff, the sand-carving riptide, the dancing whitecaps—when all of it came to a standstill. It was as if each droplet were suddenly quiet and listening, as if the whole community of molecules that constituted the Amnion had been stunned to immobility by overwhelming news.

Ghost and Zinsser froze. Only Asurao went on with his work, incising lines in a face that was now sticky red, the blood mixed with sand and gel. In that moment of preternatural quiet Ghost realized that the sounds of combat at the wall had faded. No doubt, Feral and Passwaterite defender alike were headed for higher ground. "The, the whatty?" Zinsser was muttering.

"Could it have accessed the whatty?" He threw his arms wide. "Yes! Talk to me! Talk—"

Ghost thought she'd already seen the most fantastic feats the waters could enact, but between one second and the next the sea rose up in earnest. Their little hump of dry sand was lifted up, water rising through it and up around their legs, and borne seaward before they could move.

Something slick and cold, like chilled oil, percolated upward along their bodies as they felt themselves drawn deeper by the water itself. In a second it had covered their faces, swept down into their stomachs and lungs, entered through ears and nostrils—permeated through cell walls. They were held fast by it, screams stifled, vision blurred.

The last thing Ghost saw before being pulled under was Asurao trying to wade out to her but held back somehow by the waters. In all the books, twovees, and holos, characters passed out when the worst came, swooned or were knocked cold. That didn't happen to her; the traditions of declaring oneself dead, of wearing the scars, said it was an act of defiance that promised to call down a horrendous fate, that it was payback for leaving behind the pain of life.

With her filmed-over eyes wide open, mouth stretched wide, and chest heaving for breath that wouldn't come, she was sucked below, Zinsser tumbling alongside, by the will of the Oceanic—for a meeting perhaps unique in Aquamarine's history.

CHAPTER TWENTY-TWO

On discovering that Gairaszhek wasn't wearing a sidearm, Zone turned from the XO's collapsing body before it hit the deck. No one on the immediate scene, in fact, was armed. Navy SOP for keeping weapons clear of demo operations, Zone surmised. That made it all the more important to get Gairaszhek's handheld demo unit armed before reinforcements showed up.

Even in all the commotion of the ship's grounding and the Aquom barrage Zone assumed that he and his confederates had been spotted and that some alarm had been relayed to Quant. Turning, he saw Haven hunching toward the fallen demo unit and revised his priorities even as he moved toward her. Get hold of the commissioner, *then* grab the shot-box.

He meant to cripple her, but before he could, he was hit from the side by a blow that seemed to come out of nowhere, astounding him. His senses were so attuned, his reflexes so fast, that such things simply didn't happen. Even as he twisted to avoid the full force of the impact, he winced from the pain of it and realized that he'd been nearly disabled by a dropkick. More, his assailant was rushing toward him.

It was Haven's gender blender, Tonii. Zone hadn't seen this side of 'erm before, though he had always assumed it was there. Zone had meant to make 'ers intimate acquaintance in a different venue of struggle, but so much for that. He stopped his fall on one knee, faking with the hand an opponent would expect him to use and then dealing a savage and clever strike off that one.

Tonii somehow detected the feint, however, and stopped just outside Zone's critical striking range with a squeal of 'ers combat boot soles on the nonskid. 'E brought one foot around and down in a strong, limber crescent kick meant to break Zone's extended arm and smash open his guard for a frontal assault. But Zone was long gone. Even in the act of rising, he got off a snap punch that nearly caught Tonii in the groin. The gynander's offensive stalled, and Zone surged up at 'erm.

Tonii was the best he'd come up against in a long time, stronger and quicker than he'd expected—enhanced, bio-engineered, whatever. Plus, 'e had been shrewd. Even though Roust was the direct threat to Haven, Tonii, recognizing the real wolf in the fold, had moved on Zone first. But he felt himself gloriously awash in the Flowstate and knew no misgivings. He flicked a look aside and saw that Haven was down, perhaps for the count, which meant that the shot box would be theirs in seconds—once he laid Tonii out.

Zone was adept at reading facial expressions, even those of a poker-faced fighter, but in a face that mixed male and female aspects he wasn't sure just what he was seeing. Tonii's look struck him as unworried and confident, but pose meant nothing. He began a series of combinations in advance, moves assembled as need and opening dictated, attentive to the twin hazards of distraction and inattention but focused on keeping the gynander from roadblocking him. He had a height, weight, and reach advantage and made the most of them. Time slowed for him; his blows went right where he intended, and there was a cold rationality to the way he put together move and counter-move, body placement and attack form.

Overhead, he heard the demon passage of another fireball from the fortress. Time was short.

He'd expected to kill or disable Tonii in the second phase of fighting, but the punches meant to accomplish that rolled off 'ers rotary parry; his kicks snapped in empty air instead of through and beyond the target; his defenses were very nearly compromised by 'ers counterstrikes. Still, Tonii didn't dare make a stand. Zone bore in, a bit rueful that he would have to kill so fine a combatant. Once again, though, his killing shot failed to score. The effect was the same as if a Zen archer's arrow had snaked away from the bull's-eye to bury itself in the dirt. Tonii performed some pirouetting move he'd never seen before—feet crossed in midair—and came close to catching Zone in the forehead with the flat of a combat boot.

He saw the corrugations and carefully sculpted purchase ridges of the boot heel, the moisture beading it, the specks of grit and ground-up nonskid lodged in the sole features. He had time to consider the images like the astronomical features of some alien moonlet even as his body was shaping for retribution. *That* was how close the kick had come to killing him; *that* was how deep in Flowstate he was.

While Tonii was executing a good defensive landing and recovery, Zone dove neatly over 'ers follow-up kick, his hands mission-adapted for a precise block-and-strike sequence. But now it was Tonii who wasn't there, open to his case closer.

The gynander had chosen the tougher way out, rolling off force absorbed in the neck and shoulder muscles, risking a snapped spine, jacking to 'ers feet and ready to fight, hands poised like sculpted claws. Zone was momentarily abashed. 'E *couldn't* be trained in the Skills; besides, 'ers fighting style was different. For the first time in his life it entered Zone's mind that there might be something equal or even superior to the great Ext secret.

Going against doctrine, he whirled for a back kick going in, aiming over shoulder and then under armpit as he spun his head and body, firing out hand fakes and misleading kinesics, the heel of his right boot tucked up over his hip for a split second, as though he were going to unload that way, only to dip and rearm, kneecap up by the sternum.

Yet Tonii managed to foot sweep him as if he was were new kid at school even while fending off all his incoming, compressed into a ball so tight that it seemed remarkable a leg could stalk out and find leverage. 'Ers hands were suddenly at the excess cloth near his right elbow, the empty grenade loops by his right breast pocket. Tonii leaned in, determined to drive the back of Zone's skull into the nonskid deck surfacing with perhaps the oldest martial arts move on record.

So he grabbed her—embraced her—and quickened his spin, landing on his feet instead of his head, feeling disappointment spread through Tonii's body. Then he sent his elbow through and through, scoring on Tonii's throat, even though the gynander had dipped 'ers chin into the hollow of the right collarbone.

A kick from Tonii found his hand, breaking the bone behind the thumb and unbalancing him. As Tonii's fingers and limbs and body tensed for another assault, it occurred to him that Haven's sexware assassin was capable of killing him. But it didn't matter much; dying never had.

Zone regained his lost balance with automatic ease, poising himself. He threw himself fully at Tonii, then changed his attack, even though it meant leaving his right side open. He could see the surprise displayed in large text on Tonii's face as he got in close. Primed with a clench of his jaws, he puffed an envenomed spit needle straight into Tonii's eye—one the Discards had missed in their cursory search.

Or so he thought. In the slowed time rate of the Flowstate he watched the spit needle, its tiny whisk tail deployed, glance away from its trajectory, leaving a minute drop of nerve toxin on a data scan eyepiece Tonii had snapped down into place with a flick of the head.

'E had been expecting the needle!

Zone shifted instantly with a close-in attack even as he became aware that Tonii had focused on his open right side—and was using some kind of weapon—a *jitte*-like Aquam "police fork." And damned if the gynander didn't know how to use the thing. Zone felt his sleeve engaged and spun, his balance upset.

The clarified senses of the Skills could make a fighter aware of all the events of a duel, every threat and opening and placement of each participant's every body part. Even a combatant of Zone's caliber had only so many hands and feet, and human balance and coordination had their limits. Too durable to be ripped, Zone's battlesuit worked against him. Tonii drove the point of the *jitte* back into the bulkhead behind him, the special barbed point digging in and holding fast. At the same time the gynander made a lethal strike at Zone's temple with the heel of 'ers left hand.

Examining his options and finding himself at a distinct disadvantage, Zone suffered the hit. But he leaned forward in the last splitsecond, distracting Tonii with a kneejolt at the same time. Consequently, the gynander's blow landed farther back along his head, and something in Tonii's body language told Zone that the failure of the gambit had once again thrown Tonii's timing off.

He lurched at 'erm as if to bite out Tonii's throat, and Tonii drew back reflexively, even though 'ers throat was protected by a heavy neck guard. Then he pursed his lips as if to spit another poisoned needle, and Tonii tilted 'ers head down to maximize the protection of the data-scan eye screen.

The defensive move put 'ers head just where he wanted it. Zone wrenched the *jitte* free of the bulkhead, broke Tonii's grip on his other arm, and, closing with 'erm, jabbed his thumb deep into Tonii's unprotected left eye, twisting it and then ripping it free in a swift, practiced evolution of motion that took less than a quarter-second. The gynander gave a tormented grunt even while tiger-clawing at Zone's face. With a harsh, wordless sound he forearmed Tonii across the throat and snapped a punch to the solar plexus, throwing 'erm flat on 'ers back on the deck, dazed.

Zone moved in to break Tonii's neck with his foot. No time to waste even on the pleasure of the kill—

—and paused, reordering priorities, as someone landed on his back. From the assailant's spine-snapping technique, Zone knew right away that it was an Ext, though a small one, perhaps a female or even one of the Discards. With an application of rangy strength, he twisted, and Lod came flying off his shoulder, hitting the deck with stunning force. Zone felt a flare of anger and a soaring triumph; his only regret was that Lod was too rattled to realize what was about to happen to him.

Lod surprised him by abruptly opening his eyes, but the prone-position attack he launched was futile. Zone slapped Lod's feeble guard open and reached for him. Lod tried to grapple, then spit at him. Zone instinctively dodged—a gob of saliva rather than a toxic needle. Knowing the delight Zone took in blinding an opponent, Lod writhed around onto his stomach and tried to squirm away.

Zone tangled his fingers in Lod's blond ringlets, using his hip to turn aside Lod's awkward back kick. Getting a better grip on Lod's head, Zone seized the little Ext's right ear in his fist and ripped it away in one brutal motion. Lod screamed and turned to fight as Zone was tossing the ear aside; then Zone rammed a big, bony fist into Lod's face.

Zone made a lightning quick recon: Tonii was still down, Roust had the shot box and was straddling a mauled and beaten Haven, the laser cutters had yet to appear on the scene. Blood ran in rivulets from the circle torn in Lod's scalp. Zone hauled him to his feet and was about to jam him down on a length of broken-off standpipe when someone stepped into his way.

"Put him down," Piper said.

She didn't say it angrily or with any hint of fright; she pronounced each word carefully, as if she thought he'd be too stupid to comprehend it. She stood before him unarmed and alone in stained and rumpled lab coveralls, her huge eyes darker-rimmed than ever.

"Stop this, Zone."

There was a hint of something tragic in her voice and something fleeting in her expression that made Zone conclude without question that Lod really had gotten to her. He motioned with his chin to the standpipe. "There's enough room for both of you, doll," he said through gritted teeth. He had raised Lod high for a body slam when yet another someone grabbed him from behind.

This one was no little man, in fact, not a man at all. Its alien stink cut through the laser-burn fumes, the reek of incendiaries, the smells of the deck. Zone dropped Lod and turned like an infuriated tiger, but Scowl-Jowl was more than ready for him.

Lod went tumbling to the nonskid, and Piper rushed to him, straining to drag him clear as Zone and the Manipulant lurched and staggered, locked in a mutual embrace, framed by fantails of sparks thrown high by the laser-cutting teams racing to sever the number one gun from the ship. Twice before Zone had fought Manipulants at close quarters and had killed them both. One he'd gotten with his bayonet, and the other with a sharpened entrenching tool. This time it was unarmed combat without any room to maneuver, but he wasn't dismayed. He willed himself into his most depersonalized state and became something of a monster himself.

Blows and strikes that would have broken ordinary human bones, crippled unaugmented opponents or killed them, hardly phased Scowl-Jowl. There was no gouging his eyes, protected as they were in the massive bone orbits, no attacking the bud-like ears that were now sphinctered shut. Whatever organs the Manipulants carried in their crotches weren't easy to hurt.

And as for Scowl-Jowl, he simply squeezed and squeezed harder without a letup. Somewhere Roust was yelling at the Manip to release Zone. "You god-fuckin' damnya! I'll blow the whole shitsack fucking ship apart!"

Veins pulsed huge and dark in Roust's throat and forehead and spittle flew from his mouth, but Scowl-Jowl carried on with the execution. There had been no time to rig more demo kits, but Zone's severalmate had passed beyond the point where rationality mattered. His thumb depressed the shot box's det button.

When no explosion ensued, Zone's severalmate pressed the button again and again, then looked down, slack-jawed. Dextra still lay between his boots, but now she had the fallen demo man's heat torch and the hardwire leading from the shotbox over the side of the flight deck to the elevator. Steadying the fired-up torch in both hands, she rammed it up into the juncture of Roust's thighs.

Roust shrieked and flailed back but then rocked forward again, shreds of his battlesuit exploding off his chest along with a red mist of blood, shards of bone, and gobbets of dark, glistening tissue.

The crash of a boomer echoed across the lake as Roust toppled forward onto her face. Sprayed with blood and gore and shocked numb, Dextra looked around to find Quant and an Ext sniper on Vultures' Row. The woman fired again—at Zone this time—but her round missed him and went on to sever a power cable, which began to dance sparks across the nonskid.

Despite anything Zone could do, he was bent backward in the Manipulant's bear hug. Dextra waited to hear the crack that would be the snapping of his spine, but she had forgotten just what kind of enemy Zone could be. Mule-kicking like a maniac, his feet struck a heavy generator dolly and—although Dextra would have said it couldn't be done—toppled Scowl-Jowl the other way. Zone knew that the Special Trooper wouldn't release its hold on him, just as he knew that Scowl-Jowl probably would land on the live power cable the second sniper round had cut. Wearing its improvised lab scrubs instead of an armored combat coverall, Scowl-Jowl took two thousand volts through its back, while Zone's battlesuit spared him most of it.

Dextra expected to see Zone fried nonetheless, or at least

immobilized, but he managed to break free of the Manip's spasming grip and stagger to his feet. Dextra had the sudden insight that Zone had struck some kind of deal with Satan, because he had the sinister luck of a demon. For a moment her and Zone's eyes met, his nearly protruding from a head overloaded with information, the accelerated processings of the Skills, the raging dark power that drove him. But he hadn't forgotten the markswoman on Vultures' Row, and he was quick to register other armed-response teams closing in across the deck from every quarter.

A .50-caliber shell blasted up nonskid and deck plate inches from where he was standing, and he turned and launched himself over the side of the deck, disappearing from sight as he fell toward the jammed aircraft elevator below.

CHAPTER
TWENTY-THREE

Somebody was yelling something, was worried about something up on deck, from what Kurt Elide could make out. But he stayed bent to the laser cutter he was manning with the Navy shipfitters, straining to cut through the last of the two huge trunnions that held the number one gun in its mount. He was fast learning that the only way to get an unpleasant job done was to bend to it, let nothing distract one, come hell or high water.

He'd had to take the brute-force task of helping belay the cutter in place when the uniflex cutting dumbot blew and burning the gun free became a priority. The enlisted rating he was replacing had been burned horribly by molten metal and laser backblast, and nothing said that that wouldn't happen again—to Kurt.

He'd heard someone mutter before the lasing started that severing number one manually was the most ticklish job any of them had ever tackled. The original idea of cutting the barrel in two had proved unworkable because of the possibility that the snagged muzzle would pry loose a boulder. With the ship aground and the muzzle hung up in the rocks, number one's immense mount had to be cut away just so, and in a particular order, so that it would swing free forward and out of the way without dropping an avalanche onto the elevator or flight deck.

Unfortunately, that also meant that the team had to bear up under superheated air and gobs of blasted scoria. Thick insulated safety boots smoldered, and even the ceramic-composite duck boards they threw down to raise themselves above the molten runoff began to smoke. Kurt felt like a draft-labor troll serving out some subvolcanic sentence. There was an unreality to it unlike even the other thousand demented things that had happened to him since he'd given in to the impulse to enlist.

It was the first time in his life he had encountered a situation he couldn't simply abandon. Kurt thought deep down that the feeling of commitment to a cause that made one do things one would much rather not do was vastly overrated. Left queasy by the danger, he tried to shut it out by narrowing the focus of his concentration to the weight of the laser cradle against his shoulder and the bright clash of the beam and the gun-mount alloy.

He was knocked traumatically out of his trance when the laser drill captain slumped suddenly, slewing the drill around so that it spattered angrily over the enormous breech lock. Instantly Kurt realized that she had been knocked cold, and there in the turret, he recognized the possessed face of Zone. The Ext was clubbing Rim Fortuna, who'd been holding up the other side of the laser cradle.

Good God, not *again*, Kurt thought even as he staggered at Zone, not at all sure what he planned to do. He knew he couldn't fight him, but he also knew that Zone could blow the starboard sponson—or perhaps the whole ship—if he reached the charges and demolitions that had yet to be placed. Certain of Kurt's relative inability to do any harm, Zone was virtually ignoring him.

Kurt almost stumbled over the power cable that energized the laser, and the thought no sooner popped into his head than he bent and wrapped a turn of cable around the breech lock's stay. The laser cradle pulled the line taut, stretching it thin, then began rotating back in the opposite direction despite Zone's efforts to halt it. Fighting to wrestle the laser around, Zone overlooked the open and merciless jaw of the naval rifle's breech lock, as big as a two-hundred-liter beer keg.

The breech lock hadn't been part of any plan running through Kurt's head until the entire left side of the improvised cradle support gave way and Zone went off balance, falling with head and chest between the dark, male-threaded tunnel of the breech and the waiting titan's plug of the breech lock. Humming but not beaming, the laser rig collapsed, automatically going off-line. In what amounted to an out-of-body experience, Kurt reached out for the gun captain's station and hit the switch that closed the breech.

The servos were powered because it had been thought they might help in freeing the gun in some extreme contingency. The breech lock swung to, turning to screw itself shut and crush Zone. It seemed so foregone that Kurt couldn't believe his eyes when the Ext somehow regained his senses and rose from the narrowing gap like some kind of resurrected Lucifer. More, he seemed to be moving faster than any human being could. Before Kurt could dodge or lash out, Zone had grabbed him and bashed his head against the whirling threads of the breech lock. Kurt saw what was coming but couldn't do a thing to save himself.

Oddly, the impact wasn't as painful as he would have thought, merely a cosmic sense of impact and darkness. Perhaps Zone had slammed his head down a second time; he couldn't be sure. But the next thing he knew, Zone was forcing him down into the gap with crazed strength, and Kurt could feel the inexorable pressure of the breech lock driving his chest and right shoulder back and back into the lock. Pain came at him like the wave surge from the Wall Water dam. He fell and heard the bones of his shoulder and rib cage crack. His breath was driven from him with such force that he couldn't even scream. Blood rushed up and spewed from his mouth while the threads continued to turn and the very lip of the breech lock prepared to crush his head.

Then it stopped. Interior and work lights dimmed, and the laser went dead. Someone had cut the power. The emergency lights came up, turning the turret into a red cave except for the area around number one where shielding and mount features had already been cut away. Enough daylight leaked in to see by.

Kurt moaned as a dribble of molten metal fell from somewhere, spattering across his chin and lips. He expected Zone to finish him off, but something was happening outside his crimson cave: noise, yelling. He couldn't move his head, couldn't even shift his eyes, but he recognized Lod's voice, shrill and hysterical as a crazed animal's.

"I'll kill you! Goddamn you, I'll fucking kill you! I'll fucking kill you!"

Lod and Zone struggled into his line of sight for an instant, Lod clinging to Zone's upper body, his brilliant blond hair matted down into a wet red helmet, his face a mask of blood that seeped from his scalp. He'd somehow gotten his belt around Zone's neck and was garroting him with it. Zone's tongue was swollen from his head, but he got his bearings and rushed backward to slam Lod against the turret bulkhead. Hands were grabbing at Zone's legs from the floor-set hatch as he stuffed Lod's limp body down into the faces there, turned, and leapt away.

"No, no firing!" Dextra used both hands to force away the 'baller an Ext ready-response trooper was aiming at Zone. A .50-caliber slug would bounce around the turret dozens of times, perhaps hundreds, killing any of the work crew who might still be alive, perhaps even ricochet right back out the very hatch it had been fired into.

How she'd gotten to the vanguard of Zone's pursuers, she herself didn't understand. It had something to do with the sight of Lod abruptly leaping to his feet, knocking the ministering Piper over, and racing off with a mindless shriek of hatred.

Coming down the boarding net someone had lowered from flight deck to elevator was something she didn't even recall doing, although she had to have made the descent. While others were searching the flatbed carriers and other hiding places for Zone, she'd gone straight to where she knew she would find him.

"Use sonics!" she finally got out.

A Discard nodded, adjusted his 'baller, and went up through the hatch, pistol in a modified two-handed grip. Hearing the scrabbling at the number one gun mount, Dextra abruptly intuited what was happening and wanted to yell to the boy to saturate the entire turret, but it was already too late.

She struggled up just in time to see a shadow disappear from the daylight by the mount. Zone had made his way out of the turret and up the barrel.

She saw Kurt Elide, too, horribly mangled by the power rammer and lying as still as death, but the sight of him somehow failed to immobilize her. She reached the gap in the turret neck and neck with the Discard and looked up the great alloy trunk of the gun barrel to see Zone dashing sure footedly along its fog-slick roundedness, headed for the rocks that gripped the *GammaLAW* as if by a handle.

"Shoot him! Shoot him!" Dextra hollered, but the Discard, calmly adjusting his 'baller, shook off her hand.

"Battlesuit," the kid snarled.

Dextra understood: the suit was capable of radiating countersonics. The kid was right to be flicking back to .50s, only he seemed to be having trouble with the handgun and kept muttering "C'mon, *bitch,* function!"

Dextra looked back to Zone, who'd nearly reached the rocks. She had no firearm, but she wasn't entirely without weapons. "Colonel Zone!" she yelled.

If she could slow him down even a bit, the sharpshooters would be able to take him. She coughed at the smell of Aquam incendiaries as she drew herself out onto the top of the number one gun breech, the light of Eyewash breaking through the last of the fog to silhouette Zone, who was searching for handholds in the rock face.

Mostly cut away, the barrel shifted under him, and Zone almost lost his footing. "Stop, you bastard!" she ranted. "I want another chance at you!"

He wavered for a moment, looking back over his shoulder at her. But she saw the controlled madness in his eyes and knew that no ploy of hers could hold him. And more, a roaring, fluttering in the air was descending toward him. Zone had swarmed up just below the top of the rock face when some new kind of Aquam round burst somewhere south of the Upcusp, throwing out burning motes and fast-moving flaming shrapnel.

Dextra cursed the devil's luck. If she *hadn't* tried to stop him, Zone would have been right at the crest, in harm's way, when the round detonated—blown to bits by whatever giant AP ball Fluter Delve had come up with.

Zone didn't spare time for anything as brainless as a look of triumph or acknowledgment, though. He was up and over the jumble of rocks in a slithering flash. Ext sharpshooters pocked the rocks near him with rounds, but none found him. Just as his trailing boot was disappearing from sight, however, another round fell on the far side of the Upcusp. Fire snaked and streamered through the air, headed for rock and the water as well as for the *GammaLAW*'s decks. Dextra thought she heard a distant scream but couldn't say for sure.

With no more than hope as her protection, she ducked away from the gouts of liquid fire as alarms sounded from all parts of the ship. Then she slid back into the gun turret, painfully aware of her rapidly aging body. In the absence of rejuvenation treatments, she was an old woman already, and it was only a matter of time before she would be of little use to anyone.

CHAPTER
TWENTY-FOUR

Inside the gun turret Piper was ministering to Lod, who'd apparently passed out, and this time there were medics on the scene. New laser teams were getting the cutters back on-line, and a few volunteers were picking through the debris strewn in and around in the turret, trying to determine what had happened. A couple of Ext infantrymen had security nailed down. With part of the deck ablaze and Fluter Delve's volleys falling closer to the ship, Quant was determined to make a break for it.

To Dextra's utter astonishment, Kurt Elide was still alive; that was to say, a glimmer of awareness showed in his eyes. A shipfitter was standing by with a cutting torch, but there was little that could be done.

"The breech lock works are all jammed up, ma'am," he told Dextra. "And he's all caught *in* 'em." When the laser drills had fired up, he added, "We have to cut the gun loose *now*, Madame Haven. ASAP. The Aqs are ranging in."

Dextra wanted to argue, but now that she'd seen an incendiary burst up close, she understood that the *GammaLAW*'s only hope of survival was to get the turret up the elevator and fire the number two gun.

Having been out on the barrel, she knew what the next cut had to be, and so did Elide. She thought that he was comatose and that death would come easily, but then, horribly, his eyelids fluttered, and from somewhere deep within he brought up a collapsed and flail-chested voice like that of an ancient talking-chip doll.

"Not the . . . water."

Dextra had to put her ear next to his crimson, bubbling lips to make out what he was saying. She could sympathize with his abhorrence of being dropped into the river like so much garbage. What transfixed her was that it should galvanize him even then, against any rational prediction. The fear in his voice was real, however, and she thought that that fear would keep him conscious long after the laser crews cut away the gun mount.

"You!" Dextra shouted to the Discard who had come close to tagging Zone with a hardball round. "Give me your 'baller!"

The kid gaped not so much in reaction to what she was about to do but because the Discards hated by reflex to surrender a weapon. As for the poor SOB caught in the breech, he was beyond any medical treatment or life support the impoverished *GammaLAW* could give him.

"I can deliver the knife," the Discard started to say, when Dextra cut him off.

"Just gimme the goddamn gun and get your little razor-blade ass out of here!"

She hadn't lost a certain theatricality; the kid slammed the smooth, outsize grip of the 'baller into her palm as he withdrew. She hefted the weapon awkwardly, recalling enough from familiarization fire to make certain that a round was chambered. Kurt was less alert when she returned to him. She slid her arm under his bloody head and thumbed off the handgun's ambidextrous safety. The sound roused Kurt for a moment.

"Madame Haven?"

"Shhhh, Kurt." She cupped his head to her and brought the gun close, remembering him as he had been when she'd first seen him on the flight deck of the *GammaLAW*—then called *Matsya*.

But he fought to say something, anyway. "Tell Captain Quant that I, I—"

It was unintelligible. Trying not to weep, Dextra brought the gun up under his chin. Maybe there were some last words he wanted to say—a brave epitaph, a vile accusation?—but there was no way he would ever get them out of that shattered mouth. She'd seen enough trauma and suffering to know that a coherent dying statement was a rarity. She was only prolonging his pain.

She moved her cradling arm out of the line of fire. At the last moment she felt someone take her hand and realign the 'baller so that its round wouldn't ricochet off the breech housing; then she pulled the trigger. There was a deafening roar, and the thing in her arms didn't even resemble a human head anymore. She felt something in her hand, something Kurt's dying hand had pressed there as she held it.

It was the GammaLAW mission patch she'd given him when Kurt had chauffeured Tonii and Dextra away from her villa in Abraxas for the last time. She wondered if it meant that Kurt had died accusing her or forgiving her.

Tonii dragged her back as the lasers fired up. Two-thousand-degree metal trickled and spit, and the last cuts in the gun were made.

The gynander somehow got her back through the hatch, as well, and into the open. Someone passed the word that Lod had been taken to sick bay but that he was expected to recover. Gairaszhek was in a coma, and things didn't look promising for the electrocuted Manipulant, Scowl-Jowl. Zone's several-mates and cohorts had been brigged.

Dextra saw Piper in the cupola of the dumbot-hauler Kurt had driven. "She's a trained machinery operator," Tonii explained.

Just now no job was more dangerous than any other. Fire-fighting teams battled to control the jellied flames that had splashed from the Upcusp to the deck. As people scrambled into the flatbed drivers, a torrent of mud-thick water began to fall everywhere. Quant had hesitated to activate the ship's wet-down systems earlier for fear that the muck in which she was lodged would foul the pumps, but there was no choice now. The wetdown system would go a long way toward suppressing the fires.

With a creaking of metal, the rush of a rockfall, and a deep, percussive splash, the number one barrel and Kurt Elide were carried to the riverbed. The ship listed to port, and Dextra determinedly held back tears. The elevator gave a moilsome groan and resumed its slow ascent to the flight deck. In moments, however, it jolted to a stop short of the flight deck by a half meter or so. With Quant's blessing and the command for haste, the engineering team decided to shoot craps.

The flatbeds began to roll, gouging parallel hash marks in the nonskid. The flight deck itself buckled, but somehow the shoring members kept it from collapsing.

Quant had thought about firing the single remaining 240-mm from the deck itself or even from the elevator, but the engineers predicted that firing outside the foredeck barbette might sink the ship. Besides, if it was to traverse for aim, the turret would have to be set into the barbette. In fact, Quant was reluctant to fire the gun at all. But heavy concentrations of armed Aquam were suddenly visible all along the southern bank of the river in what seemed to be prepared firing positions. Ext infantry weapons or not, he knew that any effort to abandon the ship under arms would probably result in heavy losses, perhaps a massacre.

The last of the heavy cranes trundled in to raise the turret off its improvised carrier and lower it into the barbette. Quant had to fight to concentrate on the ship's overall situation as the flatbed was moved under the hoists. Even with the jettisoning of the number one gun and the deployment of flotation packs, damage control reported that the ship could be floated for only another twenty minutes—twenty minutes the ship didn't have.

Quant was about to relay as much to damage control when the bridge lurched under him. He didn't need a report to know that one of the flotation packs inflated in the starboard sponson had shifted or perhaps broken through a damaged bulkhead. The jolt was followed by a string of cracking sounds as the cables supporting the turret snapped. *Musashi* was only a meter above the barbette rim, but its stupendous weight proved too much for the circular mount. Askew, the squat gargantuan plunged through the opening, staving in the foredeck.

Quant expected it to drop like a stone, straight through the hull, but it was as if the turret were satisfied to hang there, content with the damage it had done, its remaining muzzle impossible to traverse, elevate, or depress.

Utter silence fell on the bridge. Quant sensed all eyes turning to him, and a nimbus of tranquillity came to him even in the midst of yet another disaster. It was a calm that was perhaps the essence of command: the ability to accept that one had to carry on, give another order, overcome.

"Tell them to load it," Quant told his talker quietly, "and stand by to fire one."

Not a week earlier manually moving one of the three monster rounds into the turret would have struck Quant as Herculean; now it was simply something that had to be done, like trying for a breath of air when one was drowning. By his order, *GammaLAW*'s gunnery officer reported to the bridge. Before the man could protest that there was no possible way to aim the surviving tube, Quant cut him off.

"Then *I'll* aim it. Stand by to advise."

The ship was within five minutes of being buoyant enough to sail clear when another fireball fell short of the starboardside sponson fantail, splashing flame all over the stern. Word came, however, that number two had one in the spout, shell and propellant packs all in place—although it had cost fingers and toes and collateral damage. Quant ordered the ordnance elevators sealed against backblast and passed the word that everyone was to stand well clear of the muzzle. A blast of even a few dozen psi was enough to knock a person unconscious, and the 240-mm would throw out hundreds of times that much.

Dextra Haven appeared on the bridge, covered with mud, smoke, and blood. "Captain, could you find some way to fire a warning shot?"

Quant's face was stone. "Madame, I haven't forgotten the cries from the slaves on Rhodes's millship. And I understand that most of those in Fluter Delve are noncombatants. We may have only one chance at this. I will fire for effect."

She nodded, seeming to stare beyond him. "I had to ask, Captain."

Quant swung to his talker as damage control reported ninety percent buoyancy. "All engines, full ahead."

The *GammaLAW*'s actuator disks spun the river into mounds of froth as she lurched ahead by half meters, afire and wallowing, fountaining thick foul water on herself, threatening to tear her own bottom out. Quant watched as Dynast Piety IV's fortress came into full view. His gunnery officer was off in some private mental storm cellar, mumbling as he concentrated. The turret was lying partly on its side, the barrel at an insane angle; the shell would travel according to bizarre ballistics. Gunnery had generated a computerized holo model of the trajectory, but the hard data were no better than a rough guess; the fan of the possible trajectory was laughably huge.

Time had run out, however. Quant took one last look at the mad cant of the naval rifle, ordered full right rudder until the bow came over six points to starboard, and wondered why he'd never become a praying man.

"Stop all engines. Fire number two."

A second later the gun captain squeezed the trigger on the polished brass pistol grip that fired the gun, and number two erupted. A tongue of orange-white flame twenty meters long gushed from the muzzle, wreathed in blue-white smoke. The recoil ran through the entire ship, shoving her hard into the mud and pushing the turret deeper into the foredeck. A crack opened down the entire length of the reinforced barbette.

Quant clung to the rail of Vultures' Row, vision enhancers fixed on the fortress. Even though he'd done his damnedest to aim for the center of mass, he hoped to at least see one end of the fortified shore register a hit, or even the headlands beyond. Defying the odds, though, the shell scored an almost dead-center hit and detonated.

Recent masonry and centuries-old supercrete flew apart in titanic chunks, and for a surreal instant Quant could see windows and doors and other apertures, all lit by a hellish sunlike light from within. That whole section of the fortress flew outward, sideward, upward, rushing away from the explosion. An instant more, and smoke seemed to erupt everywhere, blocking Fluter Delve from view. The whole river was jagged with the impact of flying debris.

Quant looked up to see giant hunks of the fortress still flying up and up, almost lazily, while the last of the shell's propellant cooked off, belching flame and smoke from the muzzle.

"Tell everyone to remain under cover," he found himself saying distractedly.

Soon the dumbots would extinguish the deck fires, and there would be nothing to stop the ship's company from doing as proper a repair job as they could manage—further lightening the ship, pumping her dry, seeing to the injured, and at last, moving downriver through the treacherous Heaves and then into safe, navigable water. Assuming, of course, that crop fields hadn't been set ablaze to blind the ship in the narrows above the Heaves.

With luck, the example of the Fluter Delve would mean that the mission would never have to fire another round to ensure Aquam cooperation. But Quant didn't feel like exulting in triumph. He glanced at Dextra Haven, but her eyes remained fixed on the demolished fortress as debris from the explosion finally began to rain down on the tortured, burning, mud-soaked decks of the *GammaLAW*.

CHAPTER
TWENTY-FIVE

The Skills and the war had made Burning's sleep cycles shorter and lighter than most people's. He came out of a half doze in midafternoon without residual headache, nausea, or dizziness. He decided to stop worrying about a concussion and moved to one of the open windows.

There was nothing amiss in or around the three-dome bungalow, but Alabaster itself was busy preparing for Souljourner's predicted water surge. Burning began to explore the interior of the bungalow and in the course of his circuit found a ventilation port in the storehouse dome loft that was ideal for sending off another burst to *GammaLAW*'s Adaptive Retrodirective Antenna Array. Afternoon wasn't an ideal time for bouncing signals off chance meteors, but the antenna built into his plugphone touchcard was still working, and recording a burst transmission took him all of thirty seconds. After that it was just a matter of getting comfortable and holding the touchcard braced and steady at an angle best suited to getting its finder beam to rebound off a micrometeor wake and attract the attention of the distant ship.

It was the most ancient GI drill: hurry up and wait. He was close to nodding off when a chirp in his ear told him that his luck was holding. After being incommunicado for days, the SWATHship had received his signal and responded. That, however, was where the good news ended.

Someone had obviously had the foresight to have on hand a

response tailored to what he needed to hear. Necessarily brief, the message was recorded in the voice of a commo tech Burning didn't recognize. Word of the ship's disastrous losses and move downriver after the rupture of the dam left him shaken to the core. Daddy D dead, perhaps at the hand of Zone; Ghost still listed as MIA, along with Mason and Zinsser; Zone himself dead or missing; Lod appointed acting CO of the surviving Exts; the Roke dug in on Sangre . . . The entire mission was in a leadership crisis, and Burning was in the same jam as Ghost and the other MIAs—shit out of luck for aircav rescue.

There was no explanation of why the news was completely at odds with what he'd been told in his previous ARAA contact with the ship, but it gnawed at Burning that Zone had had something to do with the false transmission. Zone had somehow intercepted his burst from Hunchburrow Hill and sent him bogus hope.

He considered his new circumstance. He was unarmed, a long slog from the River Ea, and abruptly aware of how remiss he'd been in his office as Allgrave of the Exts. Priority one now was to get back to the ship by any means. Maybe Haven wouldn't forgive him for having gone after Ghost, but every Ext would understand why he'd done what he had.

Another long wait yielded no further contact with the *GammaLAW*, so he decided to try again the following morning, when micrometeor wakes would be more plentiful. He pondered the difficulties confronting him in traveling back to the lake country. The first and perhaps most formidable was the white wall that sealed Cape Ataraxia off from the rest of Scorpia. It was possible, he supposed, that the Varangians would simply let him stroll out the gate and roll treads, but he doubted it.

He climbed down from the loft in distraction. In the main room Souljourner had awakened and was sitting up on the futon. When she noticed the plugphone chipcard, she gathered the top sheet around her, leaving him the only one naked.

"What news from your comrades?" she asked after a moment, her voice raspy with sleep.

He averted his gaze. "Nothing that will help us. The ship's having problems of its own."

Souljourner let the sheet slide from the wounded leg that would keep her, at least, from hitting the high roads for some time to come. She watched him very carefully. "Lucky, then, that this is such an agreeable place to abide for a while. You *can* bear it for a while, can't you?"

He turned to show her a tight-lipped nod.

"Then come back to bed," she told him.

Lying with her head against Burning's chest, Souljourner was the first to notice that the sky was beginning to darken well short of dusk. The background chatter of the laboring Alabasterites gave way to a great outcry. Burning and Souljourner hurried to a window and bent to it, heads together, to look out at the sea.

A strange, almost red light had come into the sky. The Amnion was choppy but no higher than usual. The lower shoreline was deserted of people, though, and people were crying out. Alabasterites on higher ground were pointing to something far from shore—a kind of hummocking of the waters.

Burning heard a chilling, churning rumble, and they could both see the roiling gray wall of water surging in from the endless ocean. Without a point of reference, it was difficult to judge proportion. Burning initially feared that Souljourner had underestimated the surge and that the entire peninsula was about to be drowned, but she squeezed his hand confidently.

Too late to run, anyway.

The wave broke much farther out than others, following the universal ratio: once the distance to the bottom was one and one-third that of the wave height, it was time to fall. But while the miniature tsunami broke high across the lower shoreline, turning the place into a biochemical combat zone, the last frothing wavelets, more mud than water now, stopped short of the edge of Alabaster's hastily harvested areas. Souljourner was laughing and crying with joy at the accuracy of her Descrying, excited as a kid at Christmas, kissing Burning's neck, jumping up and down.

The second wave was so weak by comparison that it barely stopped the receding of the first for a moment. And while the mud and seawater were still draining from their sacred shores, the Alabasterites began filing into the irregular little plaza before the Descrier's cottage. Burning tensed, then grasped that everyone was singing.

Souljourner was casually reassuming her robes when he realized that he was still naked. He had his trousers in hand before his blanket hit the floor, the Skills somehow lending themselves well to emergency dressing. Souljourner gave him a conspiratorial smile, then went back to brushing her hair out as best she could with an air of important preoccupation. The singing grew louder, and there were sounds of impacts against the walls and domes of the cottage. Burning returned to the window.

"They're throwing flowers," he reported.

"Open all the windows, please."

Wondering what had become of the ego-deprived nervous child who'd come south with him, he did as she asked. Crowds pressed in on all sides of the cottage. Children were pushed forward to set gifts outside the Dutch door: more food, bolts of cloth, simple Alabaster jewelry and flower garlands, a hand mirror and ornate combs. All very touching, though Burning couldn't help but wonder where the real wealth of the peninsula was hidden.

Souljourner, however, had a sentimental thickness in her voice when she told everyone, "Thank you . . . my parish!"

It gave him a twinge of premonition. Here he was trying to figure a way back to Lake Ea, and she was sounding like someone who'd found a home. And he, blithe asshole, had just married into the place!

As dusk settled over the city, the Alabasterites began to move off, waving happily, calling out their thanks. Souljourner hugged her arms to herself, looking out on the town, the grateful people, the land that had been cleared instead of lost to the Amnion, all because of her warning.

"Isn't it wonderful, Redtails? I never knew it could be like this."

Burning had stepped back from the window into the shadows and suddenly felt as if he were speaking from a shadowy side of himself. "You deserve their praise. And mine—for everything you've done since Wall Water. But I have to make one thing clear: we didn't plan to come here, and *I* can't stay."

When she turned to face him, he could see that she was prepared for it. "Your ship might be sunk before too long, your teammates imprisoned! As we might be, should we choose to return to the lake country."

"Maybe. But I have no choice. And it's starting to look like I'm going to need your help. If you'll give it to me, that is."

As he hoped she would, Souljourner reached unconsciously for the drawstring pouch at her throat. "Will you help me leave here?"

She looked like she was off in another world as she shook the Holy Rollers from the pouch and clenched her hand around them. Palmed in his right hand, the Aggregate-fashioned control card was already programmed. She rolled the configuration he'd selected and conjured by means of the card's touchpad: LEAVE VIA NECESSITY'S GATE.

Souljourner knelt, unmoving, staring at the dice. He could see that she wanted to render an interpretation that would spare her disappointment and pain, but she was utterly guileless; she would tell the truth.

"It seems that we are to enjoy only a brief respite here, Redtails. Our journey leads us onward—or backward, perhaps." She gathered up the dice and went to the futon with a slow, troubled gait.

Burning tried to salve his conscience with a number of different ointments. He'd *had* to do it to keep from becoming mired in Alabaster, he told himself. Besides, Souljourner would be a lot better off on the *GammaLAW*; she'd have a better future there than among Alabaster's mandseng root farmers. He could leave her behind, of course. She wasn't indispensable. But the idea of a parting vexed what little heart he had. He joined her in bed, thinking to comfort her in his arms, but she turned away from him.

Burning rolled over onto his back and stared at the domed ceiling, delving into himself for auguries and weather signs, for personal Descrying. But he couldn't divine anything but vacuum. If he truly felt remorse, he would shake Souljourner awake and tell her the truth about the gaffed dice. Instead, he sighed and closed his eyes. In spite of his paralyzing exhaustion, he could find no peace of mind.

Rumbling up from the south, sixty-eight strong, the muscle cars encountered no resistance; no one along the Zapzag Thruway or in the Panhard of the Rumbledowns dared bar their way or even attempt to flag them down.

There were cars of all sizes, from four-passenger courier roadsters to medium-size corvettes mounting war engines and boarding stations, some of them hauling trailers crammed with weapons and more of the contraptions Boon had devised over the years. Toll extortioners drew back into hiding at the first sight of the strike force; local lords were more than glad to see the convoy trundle through without stopping. Uncharacteristically silent, wayside traders and merchants shut their eyes and mouths against the dry-season dust the high wheels raised.

The cars were the fastest and most powerful Boon could assemble and were loaded down with the cream of his Styx Strait Bridge Constables and Human Enlightenment agents— average and Anathemite. The convoy might have included twice as many vehicles, but word of the dam burst and the

GammaLAW's strife-torn passage through Fluter Delve had come south. If the ship moved too far downriver, it would pass out of Boon's effective striking range or, worse, escape altogether.

Purifyre rode in the prow of the lead wagon—a corvette—looking northward as he had since leaving Gapshot earlier the previous day, remaining at his self-appointed post even for meals. Mason was always nearby—standing, sitting, squatting, suffering all the discomfort his son seemingly ignored. He understood from the onset that Purifyre didn't want to talk, but Mason wanted to be near the boy, anyway.

After the Jut-hop across the strait and his killing of Kin-breed, Mason had come to an astounding realization: he had become part of Boon and Purifyre's fight to save Aquamarine from the forces of LAW as well as from the Oceanic, if such a thing was possible. Always self-centered before, he would have given Purifyre the only 'chute if their plane were going down. He had been taught what it meant to love unconditionally, and the parental instinct had him in its grip. He saw now that his previous life had lacked meaning and purpose.

He'd been offered the kind of battle gear many of the Aquam were wearing—gel-dunnage antisonics suits—but opting for it rather than his ship suit would have robbed him of what little claim to honesty he still possessed. Aft, at the helm station, Boon looked comically out of place in armor, but he wore it with the kind of gravity he brought to things that were logically necessary: Mason's communing with Endgame, for example. Boon had thought to do so himself via the cybercaul, but it made little sense, not when Mason had a better working knowledge of the whatty and its archeo-hacking 'wares and not while Mason had Yatt as a guide.

Word came from the corvette's crow's nest that an oncoming car had been spotted. The convoy made ready for battle, though one car was unlikely to pose much of a threat. And sure enough, it showed by signal flags that it was one of Boon's—a courier from the north. While the corvette was fast approaching, the smaller car came about to travel alongside, matching speeds so that a messenger could be transferred from one to the other.

Mason trailed Purifyre aft, where Boon was hearing out the messenger. "The *GammaLAW* is anchored above the Heaves for repairs. The thought is that it will pass through the Heaves on the morrow, then perhaps anchor near Gouge Deep for resupply."

Boon was animated by the news. "Then we stand a chance of reaching Yclept in time to join our advance troops."

"There is other news from the north," the messenger said. "The *Dream Castle* failed to arrive at Gumption."

"Failed to arrive?" Boon said, astounded. "Is there no news from Testamentor or the others?"

"None. There can be no word of events in the Scourlands until the *Brigadoon* arrives in Hangwitch on its return from Passwater."

Purifyre took a moment to consider the news. Boon had deferred to him in all tactical decisions since the convoy first had formed up. "Something untoward has happened. We must hasten our pace. We'll have to cover forty klicks per hour minimum."

"The *GammaLAW* won't go much farther than Hangwitch, in any case," Boon thought to point out. "Haven will want broad, calm waters where the ship can remain out of reach."

Purifyre's ugly face contorted. "But our plan . . . All our agents would have to travel by floaters. We'd lose days, perhaps more."

A subordinate spoke up. "There are at least a dozen cars that won't be able to hold to the speed you call for, Purifyre. Perhaps as many as two dozen."

"Then they'll have to catch up as best they can," Purifyre shot back. "That's my word on it. Relay the order."

Semaphores did just that, and the corvette—the *Haulass*—

increased speed, its rocker arms pounding the long, heavy wagon body. Troops returned to their stations, including Purifyre.

Something about the dropping away of car after car, cutting the war party's fighting strength so much, brought Mason's worst fears back to the surface. There was a good chance that he would be forced to go up against his own shipmates in combat. Moreover, Purifyre's life would be on the line, and Mason couldn't bear the thought of his dying—

"Worry about your own dying, Mason," Yatt interrupted, *"and consider the logic and fairness of risking an advanced life-form to service the irrational and largely emotional fixations of a lesser one."*

Mason didn't have to ask which was which. *I'll go to New Alexandria when the time is* right, he sent to the AI.

"And if you die in the fighting aboard the ship and we expire with you? What of Endgame and what it means to the future of humanity?"

Humanity or artificial life? Mason asked. *All along you've been careful to make it sound like you're toiling for our sake. But I'm beginning to wonder just whose future you're striving to safeguard.*

Yatt fell silent for a moment, then showed Mason's inner eye a schematic of the lighthouse it had to have downloaded from the Smicker's bust computer. *"What serves one of us serves both of us, Mason. Humans and machines have been partnered through history. There is no future for one without the other."*

As his palanquin was conveyed downriver, escorted by a battalion of Militerrors and Diehards, Grandee 'Waretongue Rhodes complimented himself on his supreme wisdom. He had made the wise choice in not traveling to Fluter Delve in the wake of the fighting and the subsequent flood. Wall Water's castellan, Lintwhite, had been left behind to oversee repairs to the fortress, though Rhodes had taken along Lintwhite's two sons to safeguard against a coup in his absence. Dynast Piety IV had carried out the attack Rhodes himself had decreed, but—just as his sense of self-preservation had warned him—the Visitants' ship was replete with hidden tricks.

So downriver he went at all speed—to Hangwitch, where Rhodes's cousin administered the Laputa landing ground there—even while Fluter Delve burned on the far shore of Ea. Peasants and merchants, priests, and pilgrims all hastened to clear the north bank road at the sound of his herald's clacker and the sight of his personal pennant. He still meant to have the ship, but the key to that now lay along the shores of other narrows.

The north bank road posed little risk at the moment. Clearly, and perhaps severely damaged, the *GammaLAW* wasn't likely to get under way immediately.

Rhodes's palanquin was just past the southernmost extreme of the Upcusp when something on the riverside attracted his gaze and he ordered a halt. Commoners on all sides groveled as he exited the covered litter to have a closer look, careful to keep two ranks of praetorian guards ahead of him as he approached the body that had washed ashore.

The Visitant was apparently unconscious. His battlesuit's flotation pouches had apparently kept him from drowning, but his face and hands were bruised, lacerated, and in places badly burned. Disk swords bared, three Diehards made to roll the figure over.

Seeming to come to life by galvanization, the Visitant completed the roll by himself, reaching for one of the guards even while kicking at another. Rhodes recognized him as one of the elite guards She-Lord Haven had brought to the Grand Attendance at Wall Water—an Ext, if memory served. Only this one was more like some parolee from hell.

The Diehards were having at him with swords and knives when Rhodes ordered them to stand fast. A hostage, at last, he told himself.

CHAPTER
TWENTY-SIX

As Ghost was pulled deeper, the light from the surface began to fade. The thick stuff that ensheathed her pressed in on her chest, but then—as if comprehending her danger—it lessened its grip, adjusting itself to the rhythm of her breathing. Zinsser was drifting nearby, his eyes as wide open as hers, though there was what looked like a thick, nictitating membrane over them. He resembled a man inside a protoplasm bubblesuit meant to suggest a man. Ghost concluded that she was probably similarly enclosed.

More remarkable was the fact that they were linked to one another by flexible membrane umbilicals of denser stuff, and connected to them both, like orbiting satellites, were the things Zinsser had thrown into the sea: his coins, shirt, whatty, Roke specimen container, and the rest. She tried to recall what had been said in the briefings about the wide "insular zones" the Oceanic maintained between the land and the sea proper, surmising that she and Zinsser were being transported through it.

She doubted that the DevOceanites had gotten the same treatment. If she and Zinsser were actually being drawn away from the land, the Oceanic was apparently through with its attack on Passwater. After what she'd seen, Ghost suspected that anything that had entered the sea, the faithful included, now existed as discrete molecules, if at all. Certainly Asurao was nowhere around, and neither was any other Aquam or Aquam artifact.

But Zinsser had done something—inadvertently, she was sure—to change the Oceanic's attitude toward humans—well, *two* humans, at any rate, and perhaps only temporarily. It would explain some things if it turned out that the Oceanic was capable of reading photonic computer memories, though its previous refusal to communicate with humans then would seem all the more enigmatic. Something else drifted nearby: her combat knife.

It was almost dark, but the gelid sheath around her was radiating warmth. Ghost had the impression of immense shapes moving in the distance and felt turbulence in the water. She narrowed her eyes in an attempt to see. Whatever it was that coated her eyeballs seemed to discern their function and accommodate her, for all at once she observed a galaxy of phosphorescent pinpoints moving through the water, as if drawn to Zinsser's and her sheaths.

The pinpoints of light had appeared and mobilized, as if spontaneously. In seconds they permeated the sheaths, and she and Zinsser were suddenly descending together in bulky sacs of congealed gossamer light that illuminated her pale, pressed skin and soiled clothes. They were carried on and on, two figures in pointillist light surrounded by minor pouches carrying their belongings. When she thought to glance around for Zinsser on occasion, he seemed unharmed but mesmerized.

They drifted on for hours, during which she phased in and out of consciousness. But she understood that the Oceanic had been palpating her with sounds—sonogramming or sonaring her, perhaps in an effort to learn something. The sea sounds in her ears certainly seemed like an attempt on the Oceanic's part to communicate with her. Some of the sounds struck her as human sounds, somehow stored and replayed; others struck her as what amounted to the Oceanic's sound impressions of humans. The rich acoustic interplay lulled her into a state of placidity that robbed her of all sense of time. If what she was hearing was the constant medium of the Amnion, it was certainly the most soothing Muzak she had ever heard.

The Amnion's waves, spray, and mists seemed to be parts of the Oceanic's infinitely protean extended form, a means of seeing beyond itself, of not only communicating but also managing the whole of Aquamarine's ecology.

Upon one of her gentle awakenings she sensed vibrations and realized that Zinsser was mouthing something. The stuff in their chests and the conducting medium made the sounds unintelligible, but she thought from what she could see of his lips through the blurry protoplasm that he was saying her name. Ghost didn't see any reason to respond and was distracted, anyway, by the glory of what was suddenly looming up below them.

Perhaps the Oceanic understood the human appreciation of light, she told herself, but more likely it had simply evolved to bring light into the deeps with it. In any event, she found herself looking out on a menagerie of light shapes. The water was somewhat murky, rich with nutrients and microorganisms, but within the dozen or so meters' radius of clear visibility wondrous things came into view, as if making close flybys.

They manifested in all sizes, from microscopic particles to leviathan things whose full dimension she couldn't calculate; great undulating walls of hide or surfaces of fin or vane, warted and stippled in fantastic patterns and colors; delicately translucent structures like cities of living glass, striated in neon rainbow hues; brilliant, scintillating forms everywhere, moving grandly or darting with impossible-to-follow speed.

The Oceanic's control over the very molecules of the Amnion passed all understanding, but it made for a pretty sight.

A whirling gyroscope shape floated past, making Ghost wonder how evolution could have brought such a thing into existence. A stagger-winged biplane ray banked to her left, showing an underside that looked like a huge map detailed in softly glowing pastels. As she watched, the ray came apart, elongating here and parting there, attenuating or simply emulsifying itself.

The smaller parts formed new shapes of various kinds and went their separate ways at wildly differing speeds. A thing that put her in mind of a living streamer of spotlit blue smoke, fringed with countless blurring cilia, zipped past her with unspeakable grace.

A trancelike feeling engulfed her once more, perhaps the work of the symbiotic sheathing or, again, just a natural consequence of what she was experiencing. Again time lost all meaning, though eventually she detected a thinning of the benthic traffic. She had the impression that she and Zinsser were being drawn deeper still, but without gradients of pressure and light, there was no way to be sure.

It was so easy to drift that she decided she should fight the urge to be pacified into complacency. There were unlimited questions to ponder, and most of them bore directly on the GammaLAW mission's safety and the Exts' survival. But she couldn't reach a single conclusion.

There was no way of even guessing how many hours had passed since the crash of the *Dream Castle*. She should be aching, ravenous, and for that matter losing blood, but that didn't seem to be the case. She thought of Asurao, watching her as the waves carried her under and scarring his face in homage to hers.

Another conduction yell from Zinsser roused her from what had become a waking sleep. At the same time something quick and shape-shifting moved across her field of vision, and she became aware that others had already streaked past. The water was bright with strong spears of light issuing from below, dancing and refracting everywhere. She struggled slightly, and though there was no hope of swimming in the globular masses of Oceanic plasmagel, the imprisoning blob clusters shifted around so that she could see what Zinsser was pointing at.

Another of the fast movers zipped by: an organism or object

like a shifting incandescent cobweb, flying through the water with a definite implication of purpose. And there were more of them off to every angle, bound for a convergence point below.

She wanted to gasp when she saw it, but the stuff in her lungs wouldn't let her. There were things like it on a dozen worlds, she recalled vaguely from school, but few big enough to be seen with the unenhanced eye. This one's diameter was bigger than the *GammaLAW*'s beam.

Diatom was how she thought of it from the first. It vibrated with the constant touch of conjoining cobweb things, growing, she felt sure, from nothing. And the imprisoning sheaths of plasm were making straight for it. It occurred to her to wonder why the thing under assembly hadn't been made closer to the shore and the surface. Had the events at Passwater put a heavy demand on raw materials there?

As the sheaths brought them closer to it, she could see odd indentations in the surface of the diatom, like dimples on a golf ball. Transparent spines dozens of meters long extended from it in all directions. Peculiar ripples ran in scroll patterns, like swells, everywhere across skin like flawed ice. Where one of the cobweb things touched the diatom, the web merged and was absorbed.

Closed in on one of the indentations, the sheaths went into some sort of excited state; minute bubbles of light fizzed off them, and they began shrinking. The sheaths merged with the diatom, too, with neither a jolt nor much of a sense of transition.

Ghost was steeled to be digested then and there, but instead, she and Zinsser, along with their odds and ends, were passed in and in, as best she could tell. Either that or the diatom was re-arranging itself around them. Perhaps both.

She could not pay much attention to the sensation of vast tidal movement within the translucency because the stuff that had entered her through every avenue was suddenly withdrawing. Coughing and gagging, she could barely get herself to breathe again. Not far away, Zinsser was sputtering, too.

When she wiped the tears from her eyes with a sleeve that was surprisingly dry, Ghost saw that she and Zinsser were sprawled on a level, circular surface made of what seemed to be tiny, dry pellets or grains. The air was breathable but hot, and it scratched her throat. They seemed to be in a hollow within the diatom, twenty paces or so, side to side.

Zinsser was kneeling with his ass in the air, twiddling at the tiny pellet things on the floor. "Ingenious," he remarked.

Levering herself up, Ghost brushed a hand across the ones nearest her and found to her surprise that they were rooted to a surface of the same stuff, like taste buds. She coughed again. Zinsser seemed to notice her for the first time.

"Air's too dry, eh?" There was sweat on his brow in spite of the low humidity; he wiped it off and examined it distantly. "Too hot, as well. But of course this would be the way it thinks of the surface."

He got up and flicked his middle finger off his thumb, as though getting rid of some imaginary wad of stuff. "They're scavenging out all the moisture they can with these and those—" He gave a nod to the stuff hanging down like Spanish moss from the domed ceiling. "—and cooking us slowly. Zookeepers with the wrong data."

But he didn't look like a man who was frightened of being heat-dried. He got up and crossed to where the moss hung low, to spread it in his hands and examine it. There was something different about Zinsser now. After weeks of being obsessed with her, he had suddenly forgotten her. The *carnal* Zinsser, that was. There was something closer to the core of him than even the pursuit of women, especially elusive ones. There was his fascination with the sea—the original human body in one sense, the saltwater bath that life had to drag ashore with it in haphazard fashion when it left the sea—and now with what it had brought forth on Aquamarine. The certain part of him that had zeroed in on her, even in the worst of their trials and privations was *gone*, swallowed up in this thing that had a far greater hold on him than she did.

While Ghost didn't care to have his libido back to vex her once more, she couldn't help but be impressed by the power that had been required to subsume it to this greater passion. If he had the slightest misgiving about their situation, the slightest trace of fear, he was hiding it well. Picking herself up off the pebbly deck, she decided that Zinsser's *mind* had cut in. She'd never been around a man—or many women—to whom that happened. It wasn't exactly bravery, but it was something she wanted to know more about.

He was holding the feathery moss up to the available light, the myriad luminous motes in the walls of the diatom. "I need a loupe. Do you see my clipknife around anywhere?"

She did. It was entombed like all their other things, in little hummocks of clear stuff—save one. As Ghost realized what was missing, a tremor began running through the diatom walls and floor. "Zinsser, your knife is here . . . and your whatty is, too. But there's something missing."

"Mmm? Can't you just throw me—"

A great seam in the wall opened, and something began to push forth from it. Zinsser gave a cry, flailing to keep his balance, but she could see he was still listening.

"The thing the Oceanic took—"

The rising sound of the diatom's disturbance obliged her to yell. There was something protruding from the seam in the wall, some rounded protoplasmic probe.

"—it wasn't your whatty that made them take us! It was—"

Trampoline forces ran through the sphere. Since the Oceanic wasn't accustomed to dealing with land objects aside from rendering them down to constituent chemicals, it probably didn't know much about life support. A glob of clear stuff was thrust into view on a long, incongruously rigid pseudopod—contoured but stiff as lucite. Suspended in its head was the hinged-open tissue sample dish and the floating pieces of the sample slide.

"The Roke sample," Zinsser said with a religious hush. "*That's* what the Oceanic is interested in!"

CHAPTER
TWENTY-SEVEN

Even after two days of repairs undertaken in the wake of the events at Fluter Delve, the *GammaLAW* was barely able to make headway downriver. Haste, in any case, would have risked opening one of the make-do patch jobs, loosening a rudder post, or further weakening the turbines that had been strained in heaving the ship from the shallows. With the water silty as a result of the dam flood, the underwater sponson observation dome had been a priority repair, but there was still the danger of grounding on another sandbar.

Even so, Quant insisted on staying under way as long as the engines could provide enough speed to negotiate the currents. The river was continuing to subside, and though there were stretches of deep water, he knew that he wouldn't breathe easy until they passed through the cascades at the Heaves and were safely into the lower Ea, where there would be year-round navigability.

Like the lake dwellers, those who lived along the river derived much or all of their livelihood from the waters; the *GammaLAW* was constantly encountering nets, aquaculture baskets, prawn pots, kelp-salad trellises, and more. Where she could, the SWATHship eased by without doing damage, but much as Haven despaired at antagonizing more Aquam, she yielded to logic and to Quant when there was no choice and stood by as the ship cut a path through dam nets, mowed down fish hatcheries, and smashed aside woven eel traps. The prerogatives, responsibilities, and obligations of a captain had a talismanic power that even Haven was too savvy to tamper with.

Such repairs as could be effected under weigh went on around the clock, with the ship's complement throwing itself into each task with grim commitment. With anger and fear driving people to maximum effort, Haven worried about the campaign she would have to wage with her own mission personnel in support of reopening contact with the Aquam.

Twice they came to ferry crossing hawsers with no choice but to sever them. The civic affairs people wanted to stop long enough to refasten the lines in the ship's wake, but Haven was again forced to defer to Quant's judgment that time was too critical. Other traffic on the river—dugouts, rafts, the occasional keelboats and small barges—steered well clear of the Visitants' ship without having to be warned away. Some went so far as to flee or beach themselves when they encountered the trimaran. Even those ashore hunkered fearfully. Word of hostilities upriver had apparently traveled faster than had the crippled vessel herself. Some of the intel staffers were in favor of taking prisoners for interrogation, but Haven nixed that idea. She was certain that in time they would reach a place where the locals would be willing to talk.

The one piece of good news was that Burning had contacted the ship, via the ARAA system, from Alabaster several hundred klicks from New Alexanderia along Scorpia's southeastern coast. He and Rhodes's former Descrier, Souljourner, were apparently in pursuit of Ghost, whom Burning had glimpsed in the company of Purifyre. The contents of his message had also hinted at previous contact with the *GammaLAW*, of which there was no record. It was known, however, that Colonel Zone's late severalmate Strop had spent many hours monitoring the ARAA for just such bursttransmissions.

As for Quant, he lived on the bridge with only occasional sallies to inspect ongoing work in engine rooms and hull repair locations. The acting executive officer, Edwinna "Winnie"

Ketchum, and Lieutenants Maingwaring and Broadbent became his eyes and ears, and Tonii now served as his talker. With *GammaLAW* at a modified condition III alert—Exts and others manning firing positions at all times—there was nowhere for the captain but the bridge.

Except, however, that Dextra had observed a private night-time requiem Quant had held for Kurt Elide. Dropping flowers and a citation over the wing of the bridge, Quant was heard to say, "He was high-hearted and lacked a wariness of life. Maybe that was why I couldn't let myself like him entirely. I knew that this day might find him."

Deep in a coma, Scowl-Jowl gave a rattling cough and shifted on the doubled-up bunk the shipfitters had rigged for him. Too big for any gown or wrapper, the Manipulant lay naked, like some warrior insect, under a sheet that barely covered it. Sick bay was thick with the smell of the Special Trooper's festering wounds and burns. Since Glorianna Theiss and her medical staff weren't sure which ministrations might be lifesaving and which deadly to Scowl-Jowl's strange physiology, Piper had remained by the Manipulant's side, advising Theiss about his treatment. Recuperating from the operation that had reattached his right ear, Lod had initially been merely jealous of her vigil, but he was fast growing worried about her health.

"Please try and eat something," he was urging Piper as she sat unmoving at the foot of Scowl-Jowl's enormous bed.

As far as anyone knew, she hadn't eaten in days. Other Aggregate members said that it was no use trying to force food on her by mouth or by vein, though none could explain why. The tics of gesture and odd odors they employed to get across even that much pointed up the fact that Piper was the only effective interface between the hive-mind commune and Alones.

"Now that we're through the Heaves, I'll be going ashore," Lod continued. "Most of our vac-packed meals were destroyed in the fires, and we're rapidly running out of provisions." He urged a squeezebag of broth on Piper. "At least take something to drink."

Scowl-Jowl stirred just then, and she leaned forward, nostrils flaring, to take in the Manip's scent. Throwing his head back, Scowl-Jowl loosed a sound that was more growl than groan. From a pouch slung at her hip Piper took a pneumo and triggered it into his naked chest. Spasms begun to rock him immediately, nearly lifting him from the bunk, as Glorianna's voice rang out from the compartment hatch.

"Is he dying?" In charge, she shoved Lod aside.

Piper was already stepping back. "He will recover now. The balance of humors has been shifted. Normal anabolism resumes."

Glorianna inspected the injector. "What did you give him?"

"Synthetic enzyme—at Scowl-Jowl's signal."

"That growl was a signal?" Lod asked.

Piper shook her head. "He signaled with scent."

Lod knew enough about the monitors to see that the Special Trooper's life signs were up. But Glorianna still looked puzzled. "I wish you had let me in on this."

"To what end?" Piper said simply. "You wouldn't have known what to olefact for. You lack the proper instruments."

A few days ago, Lod reflected, the GammaLAW mission's surgeon general would have been all over Piper for that, but after what she and the rest of the survivors had been through, Glorianna merely sighed. "Will he live?"

Piper patted Scowl-Jowl's scarred, immensely muscled shoulder. "He will be well in a few days. You needn't do anything for him."

That was good news, Lod reflected, because the staffers were just about dead on their feet. A lot of the med systems had never been made operative, and even with some Exts and other volunteers serving as aides, orderlies, bedpan wranglers, and the like, Glorianna's team had been hard-pressed to keep up.

The toll from the passage through Fluter Delve was nineteen dead, twenty-four WIAs.

Piper turned to Lod. "I had to purge and fast to increase my olefaction." She was all huge, anxious eyes now, worried that her Aggregate oddness had driven some new wedge between them.

"Fine, then drink this," he told her gently, proffering the squeezer once more.

She was sipping from it when the bitchbox mounted on the bulkhead announced that Lod was to report to the mustering station at the aft accommodation raft. As if he didn't know it.

Piper seemed to notice for the first time how he was dressed. "Why are you battlesuited?" She shook her head in momentary bewilderment. "You're going ashore?"

"Not because I want to. But it's either that or we start eating our shoes."

Fretfully, he tugged at the battlesuit's high collar, even though it was hanging open. As least there had been time onboard the *Sword* for an Ext quartermaster to tailor the combat regalia more comfortably for him, plus he'd gotten his hands on a LAW 'chettergun carbine—handier than a boomer for someone his size, what with its collapsed wire stock and pistol grip.

"Will you pay for provisions or simply appropriate them?"

He surmised from her expression that she wasn't making a moral judgement; she was simply asking, perhaps concerned for his safety if he was about to rob the locals blind. But he didn't want to answer the question there, even though it looked like everyone was too preoccupied to eavesdrop. He took her hand and led her out of sick bay.

"Buy, trade, barter, or beg," he told her as they headed aft. "Haven and Quant are determined to get on friendly terms with the Aquam. But if they try to use starvation as a weapon . . ."

He shrugged. Even Dextra, with her unbelievably dogged conviction that the GammaLAW mission could be carried

forward, had as much as admitted that she wouldn't stand
for petty tyrants and warlords laying a food blockade on the
ship. If Lod's foraging and procurement expedition didn't
succeed, others would follow as the *GammaLAW* moved farther downriver. Soon, however, it would be a matter of survival. The intel staff was already going over sat photos and
other data to pinpoint native food stockpiles, and ops was
drawing up contingency plans for raids.

Outside sick bay the *GammaLAW*'s belowdecks were swel-
tering. Lod's Ext combat panoply was bearable only because
of the phase-change liner that absorbed body heat. Many of the
cooling and aircirc systems had been shut down to permit repairs as well as some cannibalization of parts. Inspection plates
had been removed in deck, bulkhead, and overhead; temp
power cables snaked everywhere; parts, tools, and materials
were scattered around. Lod and Piper could hear sounds of
welding and cutting and smell burned metal, sweat, and a
sewage malfunction or leak

Maddeningly, the midges had returned. Their bites produced
nothing more serious than nettlesome itching, but that was trial
enough.

They passed two shipfitter's mate strikers—former arts-
outreach grad students—lugging a compressor turbine shaft.
They were stripped down to essentials, loincloths and head
rags improvised out of drogue-chute silk, plus a few odd dress-
ings on more serious injuries, along with scabs, bruises, and
crusted blood showing from lesser scuffs.

"It's fortunate that Doctor Theiss has so much to occupy her
mind," Piper observed, forming her words with great care, as
she always did with Alones. "If she had time to dwell on
Aquam suffering and how remote it is now that she'll ever be
able to help them, she would likely suffer a deep depression or
perhaps even take her own life. The wounded and plague-
stricken, the Anathemite, the starving, the mentally afflicted—
she'll have little or no power to help them now."

Piper pronounced it as fact. Lod had long since learned that her heightened senses told her things he might miss, but the statement angered him as well. "NeoDeos, this tour is so buggered-up—even for a *government* project," he hissed.

Piper didn't feel the need to respond. She insisted, though, on accompanying him to the accommodation float, promising that she'd get some rest back in the Aggregate berthing spaces once she'd seen him off.

It was a mercy to get abovedecks, into the relative cool and sweetness of the open air. The *GammaLAW* was anchored well below the Heaves in a place the local maps showed as Deep Gouge. Those on work detail favored forager caps, pith helmets, or something similar against the strong sear of Eyewash and thicker footgear because of the sizzling deck. Parts of uniforms were mixed in with make-do garments of tarp, sacking, curtains, netting, and more. Quant disgustedly called it "dropcloth couture" but was resigned to living with it for the time being.

Northwind, the ship's only remaining hovercraft, had been repaired and lay sighing softly, tied to a five by ten-meter accommodation raft. Lod tried to see a bright side; at least he wasn't going to have to go ashore with a vulnerable and faintly ridiculous-looking flotilla of RIBs.

The strac squad of handpicked Exts waited to one side, running final equipment checks and dragging at flax cigarettes. Each had been selected for his or her imposing size to allay any Aquam image of privation aboard the ship. Lod had also given consideration to discipline and smarts, however. The mission could ill afford unnecessary friction or violence.

Also present were Dextra Haven, Tonii, and Winnie Ketchum, acting XO while Gairaszhek remained comatose. Having put aside her commissioner's robes, Haven was wearing a balloony white tropical sport suit with a lot of venting. She did carry her staff of office, though, silent notice to the ship's complement that this was still a LAW mission.

"It's not a *bad* idea, Commander," she was telling Ketchum as Lod and Piper arrived. "But—no. It would send the wrong message."

Lod grasped that they were talking about Winnie's plan to shield activity on the ship's decks and upperworks from Aquam eyes by rigging big screens of fabric, spunfilm, or whatever else could be scrounged up.

"The locals might see it as a threat or conclude that we're more vulnerable than we are," Dextra elaborated—because Ketchum looked slightly crestfallen. "In any case, it might provoke another assault."

Winnie swiped a sweaty lock of auburn hair out of his eyes. "Yes, ma'am."

Haven swung to Lod. "All set, General?"

He was still getting used to the new rank. He'd have preferred to remain a major, but the Exts had very traditional attitudes toward fealty and promotions and had insisted on Lod's upgrade—especially in the absence of Burning and now Zone.

Not that it was by any means SOP for a general to go ashore on a shopping detail. Lod would have been much happier to risk a company commander or, better yet, a platoon leader, but—in Haven's mind, at any rate—this was no ordinary foraging mission. Lod was going ashore because she trusted his political instincts.

Ship-to-shore commo would be provided by laserphone and masercom the engineers had rigged up. Lod felt better knowing he could buck decisions back to the *GammaLAW*. In his place a lot of young fire-eaters might have been tempted to demonstrate personal initiative, but Lod found that sort of thing perilous and all too liable to shorten one's life span.

Dextra had turned to take in the milling squad members, knowing that other ears were hearing her, too, through portholes and on the main deck.

"Ladies and gentlemen," she began, "I want to thank you personally for volunteering for this duty. Today, here, we start putting the GammaLAW mission back on track. Events since the night of the Grand Attendance and the destruction of the *Terrible Swift Sword* have convinced me that a peaceful resolution to the Roke Conflict will be found on Aquamarine. Even though they now occupy Aquamarine's smaller moon, the Roke either cannot or will not follow up on their first attack, and if we can learn why and use that factor to our advantage, we'll be saving untold lives—quite probably whole worlds.

"We have our brains and our hands, the advanced skills and knowledge we brought with us. We have tools, weapons, medicines, and other resources, and most important, we have *this ship*, which gives us a vast technological edge over the Aquam. More than all that, however, we have the fortitude and the determination to make use of our strengths.

"When you cast off, it will mark the beginning of a turnaround that will eventually take us back to the stars—as well as place us at the center of the history of these times. Because we'll carry a light to drive back the darkness."

Dextra certainly felt the power of her own words, Lod told himself, but she had no idea what the hidden secret of Aquamarine was or how a battered GammaLAW mission was going to obtain it. As for his grunts, they had been around too long to be impressed by speeches; to forestall an uncomfortable silence in the wake of Dextra's sermon, Lod turned to Major Atelier, formerly a G3 under the late Daddy D.

"If you'd call the play, please."

"Mount 'em up, Lieutenant!" Atelier called out to the officer ramrodding the pickup squad.

Lod's mouth flattened. He hated gungspeak.

"If only we'd made contact with the Oceanic," Dextra muttered while Lod's dozen were piling aboard the hovercraft. "God, I'd give anything to know what Zinsser's fish trap was looking at when it got itself fried."

"Then why don't you look?" Piper said.

Dextra felt a sense of the unreal as she slowly pivoted her head. "What are you telling me?"

"Data were relayed to the *GammaLAW* before the jamming began and Pitfall was destroyed. Nearly eight hundred milliseconds worth is stored in the Aggregate computer."

Looking like he was on the way to his own hanging, Lod was giving a final wave before embarking. Dextra was suddenly too preoccupied to give him more than a cursory nod and flutter of the hand, but Piper was blowing him a kiss.

"Why wasn't I told that data were there?" Dextra demanded.

"Very few Alones bother to listen to us," Piper explained as Ketchum tossed a freed line to a crewwoman on the hover. The rpms came up, and the craft rose on its fingered skirts and gunned away, throwing up spray and turbulence.

"They don't bother to listen to you because—" Dextra began, but stopped. Could Piper even understand how weird other humans found Aggregate members? Their sometimes capricious, impractical devices, their often-meaningless words and gestures, their constant non sequiturs? There was no time to go into it, and it was beside the point, anyway.

"Well, Piper, here's one person who's going to listen to you—you have my word on it. Now, show me the data." To an Ext standing nearby she added, "Round up some of the Science Siders and have them meet us in the habitat."

CHAPTER
TWENTY-EIGHT

Zinsser's first joy of realization had worn off, and now he was wondering why a truly xenophobic benthic superorganism would care about a Roke tissue sample, unless the Oceanic's interest had something to do with the Roke's possibly marine makeup. If there was some kind of potential affinity and the two races somehow established a cooperative bond, Zinsser might well have inadvertently lost Aquamarine and perhaps the rest of the galaxy for *Homo sapiens*.

Immersed in thought, Zinsser went to examine the plasm-enclosed open sample container and slide. The walls and floor of their little corner of the diatom palpated faintly. "Now I understand why the Oceanic carried us so far into the Amnion rather than assemble this, this habitat closer to shore," he told Ghost absently.

"Short of resources there?" she asked with her usual terseness.

Her insight drew a pleased smile from him; he liked smart people, female or otherwise. But he shook his head. "I suspect it's more than that. Possibly a design problem in part and the fact that this construct couldn't exist at shallower depths. I'm wondering, though, if it doesn't have something to do with the aggregate intelligence of the Oceanic, which I now consider to be very high indeed.

"Could be that its system of memory retrieval is slower than ours—although the Oceanic reacted almost immediately to the slide, didn't it, hmm—and the necessary technical information for building this organism and communicating with us took some getting . . ."

Zinsser laughed ruefully at his inability to answer his own questions, then reached out to touch the quivering stuff of the pseudopod. "Who knows? Maybe the requisite memory was bound up inside a smear of slime cells on a fumarole out in a midocean trench someplace—"

He leaped back from the pseudopod holding the tissue container. The moment he had placed a fingertip on it, the pseudopod had begun unfolding, the translucent stuff lying back in thick scrolls like molten plastic to expose the sample container and pieces of the microscope slide resting on an irregular tongue tip of pseudopod. From somewhere they couldn't pinpoint a ray of light shone down on the pieces of the sample slide. The Oceanic was calling their attention to it.

"The last thing I want to do is touch it," Zinsser mulled, "but there isn't much else to do."

Ghost didn't see any point in hesitating and reached to take it, but Zinsser snatched the slide first, wiping his fingertips afterward. "It's like petting a slug. Oh, well, I suppose the idea of solid work surfaces is a human prejudice as far as the Oceanic is concerned."

He scrutinized the slide cover against the isotonic light. "There isn't as much sample here as there was, so I suppose the Oceanic is telling us that this is what interested it. But why?"

"Maybe the Roke are an ancient enemy the Oceanic has managed to keep at bay," Ghost posited. "Military intel is always important."

Zinsser frowned. "But *how* has the Oceanic kept them at bay?"

She shrugged. "Same way it's kept humans at bay: by atomizing whatever organism trespasses against it."

"But the Roke are most probably *marine* in origin."

Ghost frowned. "Okay. Then maybe the Roke are a new lifeform to the Oceanic, and it wants additional intel. Or because the Oceanic now connects the Roke with *us*, it wants additional intel."

Zinsser blinked at her. "I can't recall the last time I heard so many words from you at a stretch." He gestured to the amoeboid walls of their tidy cell, which was beginning to extrude turbid stalks targeted at Zinsser and Ghost. "Clearly, it wants answers," he continued. "But it's out of luck, and maybe we are, too." He returned the pieces of the slide to the pseudopod tip.

The pseudopod hung where it was, however, seeming not to know what to make of Zinsser's action. Flickering light issued from outside the diatom as things swarmed like curious zoogoers. Great and small they marshaled, swimming holding patterns: ovoid and snakelike, ice-cream cone, medusa—all radiating intense and individualistic lumin patterns, all watching, Zinsser was certain, events within.

"Water's clearer down here. You can see far," he remarked troubledly. "We're *deep*. I wonder how the hell this quivering egg keeps from being crushed." He turned away from the teeming benthic things. "God, shouldn't we be exhausted? Starved? Dehydrated? It feels like days since we were in Passwater . . ." He sniffed at himself with a certain amount of surprise. "And yet those sheaths kept us fresh in every way."

Many of the eyestalks followed his movement; the rest were trained on Ghost. There was no particular place to sit, so he sank down tailor-fashion. "Wh—" The taste bud surface was foaming up around him gently. Zinsser pressed it here and there experimentally, and where he did, the expansion stopped. He stretched full length and messed with it until it looked like he was lying on a half-deflated cocoon bag.

He reclined, head pillowed on his hands, looking at the things swimming and radiating overhead. "What d' they want? JeZeus, it's maddening! I feel like something in a freak show."

Ghost was absorbed in watching the slow mass dance of the

brilliant benthic things outside, in putting down the revolt of feelings inside herself at the scrutiny of the eyestalks. It was as if she herself were on a microscope slide, under the minutest examination for an error or flaw—the sort of thing that had once tormented Fiona. Only now it was infinitely worse than when the entire Concordance upper crust had so mercilessly monitored her. Now an entire ecology, an entire *world*, seemed to be watching her. The attention of so many eyes watching from above, around, and below was unnerving, something she'd have struck out at if she could have. Still, there were other ways of showing contempt.

Her footfalls were silent, but Zinsser looked up as he felt the vibration of her nearing him. The look on his face told her that he'd truly forgotten her, that his mind had shipped off to some cerebral otherspace where he was pursuing the enigma of the Oceanic. Ghost found it strangely reassuring, unburdening, even arousing. Zinsser watched, dumbstruck, as she thumbed open the buttons of her tunic bib front. He looked at her face in confusion, but she didn't reveal any expression through her scar mask, merely finished the right side of the bib front and started on the left.

"Now?" he stammered. *"Now?"*

"Haven't you wanted me, Doctor?"

"Of course, goddamn it, but you said—"

"I was mistaken."

Zinsser sneered and gestured broadly. "This—you find *this* erotic?"

It was hot in the heart of the diatom but so dry that perspiration was sucked off her skin almost as soon as it appeared. "Don't you?"

Zinsser leaned back, content to wait and see what she would do next. Ghost herself wasn't altogether sure, but she liked the feeling. She recalled their brief body contact on the cliff face above Wall Water. She'd had no one for almost a subjective year—not even on the Periapt-bound *Damocles*—though men and women alike had made overtures. She took great pride in the iron control of her chastity, but she enjoyed defiant abandon as well, summoned up by sheer caprice and will.

The tunic hung open, and she cupped one breast through the sheer liner shirt; it only half filled her long-fingered hand. Zinsser understood that he was more audience than participant for the moment, but he accepted it, resting on his elbows and watching her frankly. Ghost let the tunic fall open and shrugged out of the heavy military cloth and braid. She felt thin, pale, and vulnerable without it and wondered if there'd be some reaction from the eyestalks or the swimming benthics, but there was none.

The feel of her skin made her realize that the wounds and injuries suffered in the past few days had been healed, not scarred over or patched but regrown as if they'd never occurred—as if she had done time in Periapt's most advanced healing vats. She sank to her knees in the froth of welled-up flooring before Zinsser, shucking her liner shirt. A touch at the fly seam and her trousers opened to slide halfway down over her white hips. Ghost eased a caressing hand inside her liner brief as she bracketed Zinsser's knee between her own.

He seemed only slightly less remote than the strobing leviathans swimming outside. Either he'd read her wishes or he was being woodenly cautious; in any case, it was what she wanted. Her nipple firmed to her touch; her other hand found heat and moisture and promising sensations that made her breath catch.

Zinsser moved deliberately but not so fast as to deter her, pulling pants and briefs down around her knees, then lying back again to watch, drinking her in with his eyes—more restraint than most Exts would have been able to muster, or most lovers anywhere, for that matter.

Ghost rocked blissfully on the fulcrum of her own fingertips and nurtured the heat in her breasts. The more certain she was that Zinsser wouldn't interfere unless invited, the more abandoned she became. His eyes were like incendiaries, but they were all that moved. He hiked his hips off the foamed flooring casually, almost incidentally, and bridged himself there. Ghost freed a hand from her breasts and worked his cummerbund free. A flick of her nails opened the shirred codstrap he wore under his formal trousers.

She cupped him in the palm of her hand, gripped him. She bent over him while intensifying her own pleasure with her other hand, still with that infinitely precious feeling of control. Zinsser swallowed audibly, seeming to keep his breathing even by dint of concentration. She had expected to see him lose restraint by then; surely he was on the verge, and she suddenly wanted to see that. She placed her mouth on him, paused, drew back. She pursed her lips and gave him a half centimeter more. Drawing back again, she stayed close enough for him to feel her warm breath; then she encompassed him, letting him feel the gentle pressure of her teeth. Ghost kicked one leg free of her trousers and straddled his thighs, easing down so that the very tip of him entered her. She had to be meticulously careful not to go too far, because no friction would stop her now.

It was an insane and desperate game to play, there where the observational powers of an entire planet had been brought to bear, dangerous, impulsive, and intoxicating. But if the Oceanic expected to see humanity at some pretended best, it had picked the wrong set of people to spirit out to sea. For Ghost there was a third lover present: a liberating sense of truth, the dropping of hypocrisy, a rejection of sham.

With a scroll wave of her torso, she lowered herself all the way down on Zinsser, to the hilt of him. She started to rise, but he clasped one hand around her buttocks, and it was too sweet a moment to deny. On the fifth thrust he withdrew from her, leaving her panting and gulled, shocked and feeling *had*. Zinsser had come, and she hadn't—the opposite of what she'd had in mind. He didn't let go of her flank, however. More pliable now, he slid himself over her damp cleft and made some kind of unexpectedly limber pelvic move that put him inside her again. And while it felt good, Ghost laughed at the unexpectedness of it. The tolerances being so close, her convulsions squeezed Zinsser into the open so that he flopped around between them, flinging off tiny droplets of what he had passed.

Perhaps the Oceanic *was* scrutinizing them, but neither of them really cared. Zinsser rose up to take her in his arms without the kind of apprehensive look he'd long worn in her presence—without the fear that she'd stab or shoot or bash him. Ghost experienced a moment of doubt, but then she slid her arms around him and heard his deep, grateful sigh. Just for her *hug*. She wanted to think about that, but there wasn't time.

She saw and felt that he wanted her again. Ghost rode his hips, and their movements began to mesh. Once inside her, he was hard again very quickly, and that amused her and made her caress his face. Perhaps the Oceanic *was* peering closely . . .

It got a show, in any case.

"Bring the prisoner," 'Waretongue Rhodes ordered.

The grandee was seated on a throne of carved lionwood rather than the chair of living bodies he was known to favor at Wall Water. The portable throne was set in the shade of a thatched-roof pavilion Rhodes's carriers had cobbled together in a clearing alongside the river, well below the Heaves.

Zone wore his defiance like a suit of new clothes as two of Rhodes's Militerrors muscled him forward and then down onto his knees while a quartet of Diehards stood by with poleaxes and shortswords to discourage any rash actions. His broken hand was bandaged, as were the worst of the burns and contusions he had sustained in the fight aboard the *GammaLAW*. Rumor had it that the SWATHship, too, had passed through the Heaves and was anchored in Deep Gouge, twenty klicks downriver from Rhodes's encampment.

"Tell me, Visitant, was it fate that yanked you from the

decks of your gunboat, or were you purposefully ostracized from She-Lord Haven's company?"

Zone looked up at Rhodes, holding his gaze. "Neither. I took it upon myself to escape."

Rhodes regarded him with a sneer. "Much to the acrimony of your comrades, by the look of you."

"Credit Dynast Piety," Zone told him. "One of his rounds caught me on the Upcusp."

"Then you're fortunate to have survived. Or perhaps I am, in that I mean to hold you for ransom."

Zone uttered a short laugh. "Commissioner Haven would sooner pay you to *kill* me than return me, Rhodes."

One of the Militerrors made as if to punish Zone for his disrespect, but the grandee waved him back. "And yet I recall seeing you at Haven's side during the Grand Attendance."

Zone returned a stiff nod. "That was then. But things have changed—my loyalty to Haven's mission, anyway."

Rhodes sat back, steepling his fat fingers. "Explain yourself."

Zone eyed the guards flanking him and slowly moved from a kneeling position to a seated one. "Haven has forgotten why she came to Aquamarine. In case you're still in any doubt, the starship that brought us here is a memory—wiped out by the Roke or a cybervirus or maybe the Oceanic. It doesn't matter. What does is that Haven's gone from professing to want to help the Aquam to nursing ideas of setting herself up as grandee of all of Scorpia. Haven and company are stranded here, and they mean to make damn sure they're in a position to demand anything and everything from you and whoever else tries to cross them. Hell, blowing the dam was only the beginning."

Rhodes's eyes widened somewhat. "That was a deliberate act?"

Zone simply shrugged. "How else could she ensure that the Lake Ea region would suffer crop failure before the dry season is out? Plus, she was out to force you from Wall Water."

Rhodes's concern turned to skepticism. "All this may be

true, but it doesn't tell me what you hoped to gain by fleeing into hostile territory. As I say, I remember you from Wall Water—as do some of my Militerrors who had the misfortune of crossing paths with you during the madness."

Again Zone shrugged. "I was under orders to protect Haven."

"And now you've willingly deserted the ones who may soon hold the upper hand on Scorpia?"

"They only think they will." Zone grinned. "I've come into some information that could reverse things for Haven—and for yourself, if you're interested."

Rhodes glared at him. "Try me."

"The key to dominating Aquamarine, the real power, is waiting downriver at New Alexandria."

Rhodes traded glances with some of his lieutenants and burst out laughing. "Oh, I think not, Visitant. Not since my own father abandoned the lighthouse almost twenty years ago. Unless this power you speak of resides in the hands of a group of fisherfolk and squatters."

Zone waited for the laughter to subside, then shook his head. "You're wrong, Rhodes. There's a dormant Beforetimer computer in that deserted lighthouse, similar to the one that was concealed in your bedchambers at Wall Water—the one inside Smicker's bust."

Rhodes frowned. "I never got to see that Beforetimer machine. It was destroyed by some of your people after the fighting that ensued during Commissioner Starkweather's departure. But be that as it may, what could this other machine house that could reverse the course of Haven's mission?"

Zone licked his lips. "A cure to the Cyberplagues—the machine viruses that brought down the civilization of the Beforetimers and changed history on every human-colonized world between here and Concordance. Whoever controls the cure will be in a position to dictate terms to Periapt itself. Aquamarine would not only be spared any threats of annexation by LAW, it would be able to call the shots however it saw fit."

Zone gave it time to sink in. "Look, even with advances in the engines that drive LAW's starships, it's unlikely that another ship will arrive here for fifteen years—and that's assuming that one is dispatched immediately on reception of the news that the *Sword* was destroyed. That gives Aquamarine a good long time to prepare for the coming and to get the complete lowdown on the Cyberplagues. The only thing standing in the way is the *GammaLAW*. With what I know about the ship, I think it can be stopped."

Rhodes was stroking his chin. "Does She-Lord Haven know about the machine in New Alexandria?"

"No, but there are others who do—and they never returned to the ship after the Grand Attendance. That's why I was so eager to escape—to get down to New Alexandria ahead of them."

Rhodes stared at Zone for a long moment. "You claim that the ship can be stopped, yet it freed itself from the Upcusp and all but destroyed Fluter Delve with a single shot."

"A fluke," Zone said. "The gun you're talking about lacks the proper ammunition. Besides, by now the ship is almost depleted of stores. Haven will be forced to steal from the locals." He paused, then asked, "How far is New Alexandria?"

"By foot—five days."

Zone cursed to himself. "That's too long. Don't you have any wagons or muscle cars?"

"No routes suitable for muscle cars exist on this side of the river—at least not until the bridge at Hangwitch, a half day's journey from here. There, I'm certain we can commandeer what we need."

Rhodes whispered something to one of his servants, who hurried from the pavilion. Moments later several boxes were carried into the shade and opened for Zone's inspection. Inside were LAW-issue weapons and ordnance, obviously collected from ships and aircraft destroyed by Starkweather's *Jotan* and washed ashore.

"Will these help in overpowering the *GammaLAW*?" Rhodes asked.

Zone nodded. "They'll help."

"And who will see to the Beforetimer machine in New Alexandria?"

Zone met Rhodes's gaze. "You leave that to me."

CHAPTER
TWENTY-NINE

"There!" Piper said.

Dextra squinted at the spot Piper had pointed out with the cursor light, in among the readouts holoed up from the Pitfall data, but many of the scientific symbols and spectrography displays meant nothing to her. "I didn't see it. Run it back and repeat."

"Here and here and here," Piper said in her careful, nearly condescending diction. "Although the constituent chemicals are common enough, obviously, the structures of the individual organisms are widely varied. No different from most carbon-based life. Whatever genetic analysis Pitfall may have performed has been lost. But *this*, at least—the synome—is a constant and the key to some of the things we're seeing."

One of the Science Siders stared at the various displays. "Serotonin?" he ventured.

Piper was so excited that she did little Aggregate tics of confirmation, then stopped herself and nodded elaborately. "Yes. Serotonin. Common to every individual form the Oceanic assumes."

Dextra tried to make sense of it. The *Scepter* survey team had concluded that serotonin was the basis of the Descriers' sharpened perceptions—their ability to forecast or, rather, *feel* quakes and so forth—but what did that have to do with the Oceanic?

Beatrix, the head oceanographer in Zinsser's absence,

showed everyone a knowing grin. "The various and sundry Oceanic forms communicate via serotonin production."

"Can *we* talk to them?" Dextra wanted to know, way out of her depth. "And if they answer, will we be able to understand them?"

Piper showed that she knew how a shrug was done and when it was warranted. "The initial problem will be to construct a suitable transmitter-receiver. Overcoming the Oceanic's jamming may pose an even more difficult challenge."

"Chicken and egg," Dextra murmured to herself. "We have to get the Oceanic to shut up in order to open communication with it. But the jamming may continue until we're successful at opening a dialogue." Looking up, she found Piper regarding her as if waiting to speak and recalled her own words at the hovercraft's accommodation float. "All right, dear: I'm listening."

Piper cocked her head to one side. "You must stop thinking of communication in terms of the spoken word or telecom. The Aggregate can tell you that there are many dimensions to communication and many paths by which information may travel—"

She was interrupted by the image-enhancement program's signaling of a find. Dextra saw a whirling holomodel out of the corner of her eye and turned to it, skin tingling, with a strange precognition that something momentous was happening. Spying Piper's wide-open mouth, she wondered if some Aggregate pheromone had ignited the sensation.

Spinning slowly was a helix of tiny motes, resolved into data by the computers, a grand, majestic nebula of biochemical information.

Dextra found her voice. "Is that some kind of DNA diagram?"

Piper nodded without taking her eyes from the display. If it was a genetic model, it was like none that humans had come across. Dextra found a moment to reflect on the irony that Starkweather had almost certainly died before knowing what

Zinsser's Pitfall had caught. Those on *Terrible Swift Sword* hadn't died completely in vain.

"We've got one," she whispered.

Pulling away from the ship, Lod saw that she didn't look as bad as he had feared. Along with repairs, Quant had insisted on a high priority for repainting. Nonnavy personnel had been vexed about the diversion of resources, even though dumbots and sprayers made it relatively simple. But now Lod saw the wisdom of it: shining white in the midday sun, the *GammaLAW* looked majestic and formidable. Aquam who didn't know better might well conclude that she was entirely shipshape. The only jarring note was the remaining 240-mm barrel, canted at a drunken angle, its turret still lodged off kilter in the barbette.

"Greeting party's forming on the bank, Colonel," Atelier announced.

Lod turned to see four Aquam dressed in the local sarong-muumuu variations assembled on a spit of beach. They wore folded-leaf sunbonnets in yet another local style, with the present examples resembling perched cormorants. None of the four were armed with anything more hard-core than belt knives, and no backup or ambushers were visible within slinggun range. From safer distances, assorted other locals of all ages were watching the hovercraft's approach.

They backed away but didn't break and run as the hover revved down and the plenum touched ground. Lod didn't have the least objection to Atelier being the first one out, leading troops to establish area control. Then he set aside his helmet—a definite readiness infraction, but he felt he couldn't make a friendly impression hiding under its brim—and emerged into the blazing sunlight again. A light breeze fluttered his fine blond hair. Two Exts were stationed to guard the hover, and the pilot and copilot remained at the controls.

Lod was too far from the ship to see whether anyone was

keeping tabs on them. The Aquam shore delegation—three men and one woman—held their position as he started toward them with Atelier and the balance of the squad bringing up the rear. One of the men and the woman were older, no doubt ranking citizens of the town. The other two, tough-looking and suspicious, might have been in their thirties in conversion years. Lod pegged them as bodyguards.

The local gesture for peace was open hands held up before the face, edges out. The Aquam answered Lod in kind when he was within three meters of them.

"Good health to you," Lod began, "and flawless children."

They wished the same for him, though not very convincingly. The older man added, "Why do you put ashore here, Visitant?"

Lod assumed an easy, condescending air. "To learn how we might best serve your needs."

The Aquam traded looks that were difficult to interpret. Lod pretended not to notice. "And so our ships now fan out through the lakes and rivers, and our air vessels cross the Amnion in search of advice. Your village is called Yclept, am I right?" The two elders made head tics of agreement; the bodyguards remained vigilant. "My name is Lod. I'm a general serving under the She-Lord Dextra Haven. Perhaps we could sit down in the shade somewhere and discuss topics of mutual interest."

The older man shrugged. "I am called Gwong. You may come have a seat in our coolth tower if you wish." He eyed Atelier and the others. "Those would do well to wait here."

Lod responded with the shoulder hunch that meant no. "I'm hardly a grandee, but my attendants must remain by my side. You have nothing to fear from them, but we of LAW have already learned that it's wise to travel in a group."

He expected an argument, but the Aquam seemed indifferent. They led the way to the village, with Lod trying to keep the chat flowing. The people of Yclept kept prudent distances to all sides; quite a number of naked men and women, their bodies agleam with oils that reduced water resistance and facilitated swimming. Hours earlier, when the *GammaLAW* had dropped anchor, they had been tending to their nets, cages, and underwater arbors. They had apparently gained enough confidence since to return to their aquaculture work.

Unique to the area below the Heaves was a large, mostly useless hive life-form. The hives clung to sheer cliffs and, in growing, shed their outer rinds in irregular sections the size of shuttle wings and tailerons and a few smaller sections prized for use as tools or weapons. The stuff was extremely tough to work, but the Aquam of Yclept employed the larger pieces in building strange-looking longhouses, sheds, and the like. The village itself was a jumble of greenish-blue translucent shards veined in crimson and gold, laid out at mismatched angles: lean-to peaks, flat-topped boxes, shallow partial domes, and rude but fairy-looking pyramids.

In contrast to the rind structures were the native coolth towers, delicate minarets built of local materials used mainly in the height of the dry season to catch what breezes there were. After the swelter of the *GammaLAW* belowdecks, Lod could appreciate the wisdom of them.

One little girl got over her misgivings and came trotting out to meet them. She might have been eight or so in conversion years. Lod had gotten used to the fact that Aquam children often looked a lot younger than they were because of dietary deficiencies. At least this one was clean, he noted, her hair carefully fixed in a complex and tightly wound do. She fell in alongside him shyly, peeping at him between her fingers. Hoping for something like this, Lod smiled back and casually offered her a wafer of crisped white chocolate from Dextra's small personal trove, wrapped in golden foil. The kid peered at him dubiously, then hit it like a game fish, making the bait disappear. Seeing that none of the adults were stopping her, she proceeded to puzzle the wafer out of the foil wrap. Other children huddled around her, but their elders chose to look on from a distance. When she took a timid nibble of the chocolate, she let out a series of delighted yips. The rest of the kids closed in, demanding a try. Only a few got their licks in, and so the rest naturally turned on the shore party.

Lod had meanwhile given Atelier a subtle nod. The bulked-up Exts silently passed out the treats that had been carefully allotted to them. Exts weren't generally very good at making cute with children, but Lod saw with relief that they were following orders without smacking anyone's hand away.

The adults made no attempt to beg, which immediately endeared them to Lod. He spied a lush flower bush whose blossoms reminded him of swaying scarlet and gold pagodas. He'd seen their like at Wall Water and stopped to sniff them.

"Beautiful," Lod observed. He didn't dare pluck one without asking, though he was almost sure no one would mind. Gwong stepped forward to do it for him. Lod wedged the blossom through a grenade loop high on his battlesuit and inhaled its aroma again. "These would enhance the dinner table of Madame Commissioner Haven," he said loudly enough so that those standing nearby could hear.

He didn't doubt that the people of Yclept were good traders—not easy to get the better of—but he hoped the comment would at least give them pause. If the offworlders were so well provided for that they could hand out sweets and concern themselves with fresh flowers for their she-lord's table, Yclept might have little that they wanted or needed. And what, they had to be wondering, did the Visitants' ship carry that the Aquam could use? Lod looked forward to telling them. Done right, it would be a win-win deal.

Gwong's coolth tower, or at least the one to which he headed, was the tallest in the village, but there was a problem. It lay behind a huge monolith boulder, out of the line of sight to the *GammaLAW*, so that maser commo would be cut off.

Gwong was eager and open now, explaining that a feast had already been laid out there. One look at the steps leading up fifteen meters to the openwork hut itself told Lod it wouldn't be a good idea to ask the Yclepts to rearrange things. He improvised by detailing two Exts to stay behind as a commo relay point in a spot that had line of sight to both the hovercraft and the ship. Taking along Atelier, two riflemen, and another Ext carrying the phone unit, he fell in with Gwong, and together they made their way to the tower.

The steps were as unsteady as Lod had feared, but the Aquam swarmed up them like squirrels. The hut at the top made it all worthwhile, though: a small cottage, really, sitting firmly on thick tree-trunk posts and commanding a view of part of the river and virtually all the surrounding countryside.

Lod guesstimated the interior at four meters by six. It was furnished with sitting mats and low tables, elbow rests, and pillows. From the walled-off space at the far end came cooking smells that, while strange, made his salivary glands busy. The tables supported pitchers and drinking bowls of fruity-smelling gruely punch. Lod wondered morosely if the stuff had been fermented with spit, as many Aquam beverages were.

"Your stopping here is opportune," Gwong was saying as they all settled around the table, "for you as well as us."

Lod chose a seat from which he could see his relay team, giving them a subtle hand signal and getting a helmet nod of acknowledgment. He reminded himself that he would have to repeat the signal every ten minutes or so or the Exts would automatically alert the ship that something was wrong.

Since there were no individual drinking vessels, the bowls were simply passed round. Lod's head swam a bit when his turn came; its base liquor might have been 150 proof or so, and it hadn't been cut nearly enough. The Exts seemed to approve, however. He began to swing into his spiel.

"Yes, the opportunity to exchange ideas, to expand your horizons and welcome you into the realm of interworld trade . . ."

He tried to be dismissive about trade, but Gwong didn't seem to be paying attention, in any case. He interrupted Lod's patter with loud hand claps that summoned food servers from the curtained food-prep area. "And the benefits will, by far, lie with us in the main," he said as comely maidens and young men entered.

Lod wasn't wild about the way Gwong said it, but before he could figure out why, he saw the dishes the servers were carrying. He had assumed that fish would be the staple. Instead, there were wooden skewers of broiled meat, hot and spicy-smelling. He'd simply have to hope that his immunization shots had been effective and that Glorianna Theiss wouldn't have to end up cutting him open to remove some kind of local nematode.

Atelier and the other Exts didn't hesitate in helping themselves. Lod emulated them and the Aquam, taking the skewered meat and gnawing off a bit. It was tasty, if overspiced, and he suspected it had been put through a lot of tenderizing and pounding.

"Luckier for you than for us, yes," he said around the meat. "But we can both benefit." He didn't want to rush into the matter of food, but it seemed a good opportunity. He waved the skewer. "Such provender as this, for example, would give our meals variety."

Gwong inclined his head, and the sardonic look on his face was enough to make Lod tense up. "Of that we can supply you with much. We have far, far too many born to us, anyway."

"Born—" Lod managed. Realizing what Gwong meant, he felt his midsection knotting like a fist, and his gorge came rushing up his throat.

"Yes, *far* too many of them," Gwong repeated. "But at last a good and unique use for them!"

CHAPTER
THIRTY

Ghost and Zinsser lay in each other's arms, drifting and ignoring the visual and sonic probings of the Oceanic. After what they'd been through, scrutiny was hardly a concern. Red-orange light played and reflected all through the interior of the diatom, but something was coming into view below—a volcanic rift in the sea's floor.

"Now I see," Zinsser said with remarkable calm as he moved to a better point of observation. "The Oceanic wasn't delaying or retrieving memory. It was bringing us *here*."

Conduitlike structures as big in diameter as subs or shuttles surrounded the rift, arranged like so many fire hoses that led down into the boiling fury. Ghost supposed that the living thing carrying them had to be heat-resistant as well as invulnerable to the stupendous pressure it was under. Glancing to one side, she saw lava being squeezed like toothpaste from a tube, cooling and blackening almost at once, only to be replaced by more. She knew from briefings that these structures were basaltic pillow formations in the making. When she looked back to the rift, one of the great hoses was shuddering slightly and repositioning itself, apparently correcting a bad lie resulting from the formation of new pillows.

"God only knows how deep the conduits go," Zinsser was muttering, "but I suspect that they're organic. Organic lines created by the Oceanic, delving deep into Aquamarine. But why take us here?" he said to her, however rhetorically. "If they can do something like *this*—"

The diatom began to shake as it edged closer to the rift. Ghost drew a hissing breath; maybe the Oceanic knew secrets of organic building that humans hadn't discovered, but close proximity to all that fire and magma had her nervous. The roiling, smoky waters burned around them as the diatom angled to give them a direct look down into a volcanic blast furnace.

"It's deliberately showing us the power it wields," Ghost said. "It wants something from us in return. A reaction?"

Zinsser shook his head slowly.

Ghost became aware that she was standing there with his semen running slowly down her inner thigh. When a droplet fell free from her pubic hair, the floor of their cell absorbed it at once. Another jolt shook sweat loose from the lank, sodden hair plastered to Zinsser's forehead, and those droplets, too, were absorbed as soon as they struck the floor.

Moments later the diatom began to pulsate; the open space in its center compressed so that they were battered by a slight increase in pressure. Under intense light, the pseudopod supporting the Roke tissue sample quivered visibly, as if to draw attention to itself once more.

Ghost touched the semen on her thigh, smearing it with her fingertips. "Is it possible the Oceanic is interpreting our *secretions* as a response?"

Zinsser looked momentarily dumbfounded, and then his eyes lit up. He touched his forehead and flicked beads of sweat to the floor, watching them disappear. "Of course! Why didn't I see it? The manifestations of the Oceanic communicate chemically as well as visually and aurally. It has more in common with . . . the Aggregate than it does with us." He cut his eyes to Ghost, then to the tissue sample. "It's intrigued by the Roke sample, and it thinks we're answering its questions—

albeit incorrectly." He aimed a laugh at the ceiling. "God, we've got leverage with the Oceanic at last!"

"Not if we can't talk to it," Ghost countered.

Zinsser ran a hand over his mouth. "But we can. Though we'll have to begin with a simple vocabulary—the characters of which will have to be body effluvia and whatever sounds we can make . . . perhaps direct tactile stimuli to the interior walls of this very cell—"

"You're losing it, Doctor," Ghost said. "What you're talking about could take . . . well, more time than we have. We have to somehow convince this thing to take us to the *GammaLAW*."

Zinsser made a bemused escaping-gas laugh. "Oh, yes. What, chart a course to Lake Ea in earwax or shit?"

Scowling, Ghost grabbed the locket the Oceanic had returned to her, worked the clasp, and opened it. The lock of Burning's hair was still inside, apparently undisturbed. "My brother's bound to be aboard the ship. How about feeding it a bit of his hair?"

Before Zinsser could reply, the walls of their cell burst apart and turbid, questing structures grew. Ghost felt a shift of Flowstate, yet failed to avoid the things. They humped up to all sides, hemming her and Zinsser in, and sent out thin feeler filaments that began to envelop the two of them. The locket was knocked from Ghost's hand as she was fending off a tentacle. Oily gel flooded in like mounds of pudding, immobilizing her from the waist down, then rising.

Struggling did little good, but Ghost fought, anyway. She was certain that Zinsser had already disappeared beneath a hummock of the slimy nodules, but then she heard his voice off to one side.

"Put this with the locket—if you can find it!" Somehow he'd gotten his hands on the Roke tissue sample slide. "Perhaps the Oceanic will understand if you place it with your brother's hair."

He managed to toss the slide to her, just short of being swallowed by a massive gob of the stuff. Ghost caught the slide and began to look around for the locket. She saw it not three meters away, lying open, the red curl of Burning's hair glinting in the light. Her final move before the gelid stuff engulfed her was to toss the slide as carefully as she might have thrown a winning dart.

In a moment she lost all contact with the outside world. The gel wasn't at all like the clear sheaths that had carried her and Zinsser from Passwater's dunes. She was isolated from all sensations. Then, with a crash and a nova burst, the images began, and she broke her self-imposed stolidness, howling out loud.

It was as if a stranger were rummaging through her memory, projecting scenes at random. In the same way she was forced to view thousands of images from her childhood and youth, the war and its aftermath, she experienced every sensation from agony to orgasm, heard all the sounds her ears were capable of detecting, smelled a discombobulating montage of odors.

She was familiar with theories about how true interspecies communication might be established through sheer mind-to-mind contact, but there was no hint of that here, not with the Oceanic blundering around, perhaps firing neurons at random, rifling the deck, shooting in the dark. It wasn't telepathy; it was something scavenging uselessly through the data bank of her brain.

The scavenging included a flash of her experience during the Roke attack on the *Sword* on its arrival in the Eyewash system, but the Oceanic didn't halt the flow or single out the memory. Clearly, it had no idea what it was doing, yet it kept up the memory rape—showing her the demeaning times when her attractiveness had made her prey to so many wants and needs and wills, the ghastly times in the concentration camp, the horrors of the Concordance War, the rush of events at Wall Water . . . She thought her brain might burn out, though that was perhaps what the Oceanic desired: her execution.

Abruptly, however, the sensations faded, and once more she was lying on the strange, dry tongue of the diatom floor, listening to Zinsser cough and gag. The gel had gone without leaving so much as a residue on her skin, though Zinsser's come was still caked in the pale hairs on her thighs. When it came to fine-tuned finesse, the Oceanic *was* a magician in its own right.

Hoisting herself up a bit, she saw that the diatom was on the move through quieter, unclouded water, ascending and coming onto a new heading.

"It's taking us southeast, I'll venture," Zinsser croaked.

Southeast toward Scorpia, southeast toward the *Gamma-LAW*—if they got that far. Ghost disliked the warmer impulses of the living, but she couldn't help feeling a certain lifting sensation in her chest. Could they have gotten through to the Oceanic? Was it taking them to Burning? She thought again of the volcanic rift and the huge conduits reaching down into the planet's lower fires. The Oceanic had been deliberate and threatening, after a fashion. But what was the threat? What was it that the Oceanic wanted to show itself capable of doing? And how long did humans have before the planet's dominant life-form carried out that threat?

Standing out by the husk of the CIWS gun mount, Dextra and Winnie Ketchum were waiting for some word from Lod when it happened.

An eldritch mist began to roll in from downriver, creeping over the countryside as well as the water in a way in which no one aboard had ever seen a weather system behave, aberrant or not. The brume billowed and roiled, and while it moved with the prevailing breeze for the most part, the front also moved against it.

Klaxons began bellowing for all hands to take cover and batten down, seal the ship. That in itself told Dextra that Quant was at a loss for a course of action. Even at modified condition II it would be virtually impossible to seal the ship in time, what with all the ongoing repair and work details.

Nevertheless, people frantically dropped tools and materials, rushing to comply. Dextra yanked her headset jack free and followed Winnie's lead as they ran for shelter. Exts who were standing guard sealed up their battlesuits as the ominous cloud rolled in across the ship's deck and upperworks.

Dextra and the XO were caught halfway to a ladderwell. The fog had an oily, warm feel. Less a mist than a kind of vaporizer cloud, it didn't completely obscure the terrain behind it. The front appeared more tenuous than that, and as they watched, it spread thinner to blanket the entire area. On the other hand, it refused to evaporate or be left behind as the ship swung slightly to starboard.

Dextra was wondering if the creeping-flesh feeling in her lungs was her imagination until she heard people around her coughing. She replugged her headset near a hatch that was being secured by an emergency detail. Suppressing the temptation to take cover, she raised Quant.

"The biosensors aren't picking up any toxin readings," he told her hurriedly, "but this stuff is definitely not a weather phenomenon. I'm going to have to hand you over to Tonii. 'E'll keep you apprised—"

"You will *not*," Dextra corrected him coldly. "There's no need for you to baby-sit me, but I will remain on this channel and you will keep me in the loop."

"Understood," Quant returned after a moment. "Stand fast."

Winnie touched Dextra's arm and pointed at an open porthole in the upperworks' number two deck. The mist had found the opening as it had certainly found others throughout the ship—gaping deck plates and bent hatches and air intakes whose filters had been mashed by Turret *Musashi*'s passage— and was streaming into the porthole itself as if it were some curse-pall seeking out the hexed.

Tonii was on the channel almost at once. "The fog's found

entry points, Dex, but there may be no cause for concern. We have Aquam under surveillance on the banks where the cloud's already passed through, and none appear to have been harmed by it."

"Have you identified what it is?"

"Engineering reports that most of the sensors are off-line for repairs and won't be up and running for at least half an hour."

Dextra had stopped listening and was watching Piper approach like some hypnotized child. It occurred to her that the Aggregate nexus hadn't been affected by the mist and was merely aswim in a flood of data.

"It's searching, seeking," Piper announced when she was close enough.

"Seeking what?"

Piper's short, damp hair whipped her face as she shook her head. "The seekers self-destruct rather than surrender information."

Dextra glanced around anxiously, then shot Winnie a look. "Got her over here."

Winnie did, bringing up the rear with Piper in her arms as Dextra rejacked and dialed through to the habitat, putting the call on half-rez visual in her headset visor. Piper's second in command, Doogun, answered—a phantom image through which Dextra could still monitor the situation on the main deck.

Dextra could see Aggregate members moving around in the background, holding up sampling and sensing equipment, operating data units and analyzers. Maybe the habitat had its own defenses or, by being belowdecks, was spared the kind of impact Piper had sustained from the cloud. Dextra could also recognize how high-content the constituents' Alltalk was: their kinesics made them look subtly spasmodic, and there was a good deal of intensive Touchtalk taking place. No doubt the habitat was a soup of pheromones and other message odors as well.

For that matter, Dextra could pick up the exotic aromas

wafting off Piper, as well. Still holding Piper erect, Winnie flicked on the station's flatscreen and speaker to follow the conversation.

"Doogun, sound off," Dextra said. "What's *in* this cloud?"

Doogun ticced and gesticulated for a beat or two before catching himself and shifting over into measured conventional speech, his articulation slow and overly precise. Dextra could almost hear the hyphens between the words.

"It is not a cloud. It is more a megacluster of tailored microorganisms or perhaps a dispersal of dedicated, genetically engineered biobots."

"Are we talking about nanites?" Dextra asked. If anyone could cross the technical barriers that had kept humanity from realizing the Pre-Cyberplague dream of nanotechnology, she was willing to bet that the Oceanic could.

Piper was shaking her head. "Not nanites but very micro. Monocellular." She had recovered somewhat, but her arms still hung listlessly. "They're alive but not entirely complete lifeforms." To the screen she added, "There is no DNA, Doogun?"

He shook his head, then split the screen, patching in visuals from the Aggregate's sampling and testing equipment. Dextra found herself looking at a shoal of translucent things that suggested da Vinci's whirligig attached to a small cargo pod or instrument package. "Some kind of sporozoans?" she ventured.

"Easy for the Oceanic to mass-produce," Piper murmured. "Given especially its control over global weather systems."

Most of the readouts were lost on Dextra, but even she could see how the things self-destructed under direct examination or chemical testing, breaking down into their constituent components with astonishing speed.

"Any synome?" Piper asked.

Doogun narrated the readouts. "Very rudimentary, as you can see. It probably enables only crude cooperation and communication."

"But enough for their purposes," Piper mulled to herself.

"You said no DNA of their own," Dextra asked Doogun. "Whose, then?"

He rang in some graphics. "Not DNA at all. More of a model of a human genome. We believe it is linked to a chemical trigger. The model will, of course, fit only one human genotype. We are attempting to cross-check with the ship's ID files to determine if anyone in the mission corresponds, but damage to the ship has caused interface glitches."

"Couldn't these things be some noncopacetic life-form the Oceanic is evicting from the sea?" Dextra suggested.

Doogun tolerated the question but shook his head with exaggerated emphasis. "I repeat: these are not life-forms as such. But their engineering, if you will, is distinctly Oceanic."

"Swarms of microremotes," Tonii mused, "fanning out across the planet like bounty hunters."

"Except for one thing," Dextra said. "According to all our data, the Oceanic never manifests any surface-faring form."

Tonii shrugged. "Then something has changed all the rules."

The oily sheen of microorganic seekers coated everything in sight. Already some parts of the cloud were moving on, and an effervescence on Dextra's skin, a sudden evaporation of the slickness there, seemed to confirm that she wasn't the one the Oceanic was looking for. Still, she couldn't help shuddering, wondering what was in store for whoever was the object of the search.

"Dex," Tonii said, "we have action in the forward berthing compartments. Go to channel sixty-three, please."

Doogun's face was replaced by a scene of pandemonium in one section of the Exts' berthing spaces. Apparently the optical pickup was mounted on someone's helmet.

"—grease was just drifting and settling until a few moments ago, Captain," the camera wearer was saying. "Then this began."

Here and there throughout the area, pools or patches of the

deposited seekers had begun to change, frothing up, spontaneously whipped into foam. Where they did, tendrils of the cloud were drawn that way.

The camera danced as the Ext camera wearer hollered, "At ease! At ease! Put your weapons up!" The pickup focused on two Discards toting a small flame thrower, on the verge of decontaminating the walls. The blank-eyed reptilian stares they threw the camera wearer's way suggested that they might turn the nozzle on him.

Piper brushed past Dextra to key open a PA channel that sent her voice over the berthing-space bitch boxes. "Young men! Those organisms will not harm you. Please put your weapons away before someone is injured!"

Useful as they were as attack dogs, Dextra wondered again why she had allowed herself to be talked out of turning them over to Periapt child welfare. And yet, hearing Piper's voice, the boys reluctantly put the flamer aside.

"Pan around," Dextra relayed to the cameraman. "Can you tell us what's happening?"

"Just what you see, ma'am," the Ext returned. "Isolated smears of detergent is what it looks like to me. No rhyme or reason, except—"

"Look in here!"

Dextra and the others heard the call distantly through the camera wearer's mike. The scene jogged and jolted madly as the Exts went running in response. Then they were suddenly looking into a small cabin, personal quarters, where the seekers were massing everywhere. Waves of froth dripped from the desk and bedding, seeped from lockers, and ran down the bulkhead in ripples. Tendrils of cloud were drifting in, in response to some silent, probably chemical summons.

"They've got the spoor," Piper said. "Target DNA in residues of sweat, dead skin, even the film left behind by exhalation."

The target wasn't, couldn't have been anyone in camera range, Dextra thought, or else he or she would have been—

what? Encysted? Dissolved? She didn't know much about Ext country, had purposefully steered away from that part of the trimaran to allow them to conduct their own affairs as much as possible. But she had to ask, "Whose quarters are those?"

The cameraman sounded infinitely weary, dazed. "The Allgrave's," he answered.

Dextra stared at the mounding foam, recalling Burning's meteor-burst transmission to the ship's ARAA. Would the cloud or others like it find him there, in Alabaster? And what exactly would it do to him if and when it did?

CHAPTER
THIRTY-ONE

No sooner had the Oceanic's apparently Burning-seeking mist withdrawn downriver than Dextra hurried to Vultures' Row to learn if there had been any word from Lod's shore party. Why the Oceanic should be seeking Burning was a mystery she had tasked the Aggregate with solving. In the company of an Ext officer named Defeen, Quant was holding the handset that provided direct maserphone commo with Lod's relay team.

"Any reactions to the mist?" Dextra asked Defeen.

"Negative, ma'am. Everyone on shore is as puzzled as we are, but the mist didn't linger long there, and no one appears to have been adversely affected."

"And the situation in the coolth tower?"

Quant patched the maser link through a speaker on the flight obs bridge. "You can hear for yourself, madame."

"Sir, the indigs lowered blinds when the fog moved in, so we haven't been able to observe activity in the hut. Only other change is the *yodeling*."

No one could tell if it was made by human voices or some kind of diggeridoo instrument, but the ululation had started almost as soon as the mist had disappeared. For all anyone knew, it was some kind of thankfulness chorus.

Dextra had the relay team in her vision enhancers. She knew that the Exts would disregard any orders that placed them in jeopardy, but she felt that she had to say something. Besides, she *was* an honorary colonel in the battalion. She flicked on her headset mike. "Sergeant, this is Commissioner Haven. Under no circumstances are you to fire without direct orders from this end. Is that understood?"

"Understood, Commissioner Haven."

"Tell me, Sergeant, what are the rest of the villagers doing? Are there any signs of hostility?"

"No, sir, except for—wait one! Shit!"

It wasn't panicky—just another weary Ext obscenity that might or might not be the preamble to some big-bore crisis management. Dextra's enhancers didn't reveal anything out of the ordinary. Quant, Defeen, and Tonii were poised, listening and watching.

"What is it?" Dextra asked, losing patience.

"Some fuckage goin' on, Ma'am."

Dextra watched the sergeant and two others at the relay point press their backs together to form a security wheel, rifles pointing out in different directions.

"Villagers on the move," the sergeant continued. "Dozens of them, though they don't seem to be headed our way in particular. Also, movement from the coolth tower—it's General Lod, sirs. Him and the XO and the rest. They look all right. They're moving on their own, but the general is signaling for a pullback."

Dextra heard Defeen chuckle and felt the tension ease. Lod had never made a pretense about being adept at Ext warcraft. Still, something had to be wrong for the meal to have ended so abruptly. She got on the line again. "Sergeant, maintain careful discipline. I don't want anyone hurt. Break. *Northwind,* stand ready to put out from shore as soon as General Lod and his party arrive at your location."

There looked to be widespread commotion in the village, but none of it seemed to center on the offworlders. Dextra wondered if she should have sent more troops ashore, after all. Regardless, from what she could tell, the withdrawal from the coolth tower had come off without a hitch. Lod was already busy counting heads and making sure he hadn't left anyone behind. Dextra gave him points for not taking the time to chat with her. Despite the absence of shooting, she sensed that he was eager to get everyone out of Yclept.

"Captain Quant," he said at last, "I recommend you make ready to get under weigh ASAP."

"Why?" Dextra answered. "Have the villagers refused to deal?"

"Uh, no." There was something subdued and nearly despairing in his voice, very un-Lod-like. "No, they're more than happy to give us meat. Even insistent, you might say."

"Then out with it, General! What's the so-called fuckage about?"

"It's about *what* meat they eat, Madame Commissioner."

Human flesh, Dextra understood him to mean. Even if she hadn't, she would have known by the sight of throngs of scourge- and spear-wielding Yclepts driving cringing, wailing figures down toward the riverbank. What surprised her, though, were the flopping, hobbling gaits of some of the apparent captives, the outlines that were subtly wrong in some cases, less subtly so in others. Then she understood that, as well: the Yclepts ate not just any human flesh but that of Anathemites.

Through the enhancers Dextra watched a spidery man lose his footing, only to be helped up by a stout, nearly naked woman with a cluster of teats in a sort of udder down the front of her torso. Some held what appeared to be children; some scuttled along on all fours, hopped like Sourlands bounders, or had to be dragged along the ground by others. A number were bound and gagged, but most were simply cowed and terrifiedly submissive. There were also what appeared to be elderly normals—possibly Yclept residents who had outlived their usefulness.

It seemed impossible that so many could have sprung from

one small village on Lake Ea, and there should have been many adults among them. Some, perhaps, were functionals, tolerated so long as they could earn their keep. But even so . . .

Quant's voice sounded as lifeless as a computer simulation designed for neutrality. "It's no wonder meat is so abundant in desolate countryside like this. We appear to have stopped at a stockyard or trading center of some kind."

Quant's assessment sounded right. Even for the brutally practical Aquam, consuming Anathemites from one's own village or clan group would be socially disruptive, and so it would follow that places like Yclept would come into being, where the excess mutant population could be traded away—perhaps even ostensibly for slavery, to salve the consciences of the traders—in return for fish, goods, money, even the Anathemite meat of some other group. Nauseated, Dextra chinned on her mike. "Lod, alert the Yclepts that we don't *want* them—as people or meat! Put a stop to this, do you read me? No deal!"

"I'm trying, Dex, but it's no use."

They could all hear the jarring in his voice as he ran, and they could see his small, battlesuited presence among the towering Ext fighters as they made a disciplined withdrawal toward the *Northwind*.

"They consider it a done deal," Lod yelled above the sounds of angry Aquam voices. "And they apparently don't want to hear different."

Dextra knew from the *Scepter* team's experiences that matters of trade had to be handled very delicately. It was important that indications of acceptance—by word, gesture or other sign—wait until all the terms were agreed on. More, once a deal was declared done, it was tremendously difficult to back out of or alter it—and then often at the risk of initiating a vendetta.

Lod and his Exts were backing toward the waiting hovercraft even as the Yclepts continued to thrust cringing Anathemites at them and wave cuts of meat in the air.

"Disengage and return to the ship," Dextra ordered tightly. Quant was watching the shore. Following his gaze, Dextra saw that one of the villagers had dragged forward a bound figure dressed in a pitiful smock of rags and was placing a long hive-rind machete to the Anathemite's throat. The man—or woman, perhaps—had long, greasy hair though no obvious sign of mutation or defect. Dextra had no sooner focused her enhancers on the scene than the villager drew the knife across the captive's throat, then shoved the figure forward, saturating the sand not more than a meter from Lod's boot tips with blood. A second sacrificial victim appeared from another quarter, this one with its head nearly hacked off.

Dextra went on-mike again. "Lod! Belay my earlier order! Tell them it's a deal—but only if they stop the killing." There was no time to threaten or argue. Each passing moment would bring another grisly death.

"Wait one," Lod returned in a shaky voice. He went off-mike, though Dextra could see him harranguing the villagers. She felt Quant's eyes on her and beat him to the punch. "I know: I'm letting them blackmail us. But we'll worry about that once the slaughter's stopped."

"Fine with me," Quant said evenly.

It *had* occurred to her that they could simply withdraw, move downriver, and leave Yclept to its own sins and horror, whereas by remaining she was perhaps setting the mission up for further extortion at Yclept or elsewhere. Also, she couldn't imagine how the ship was going to feed several dozen Anathemites when there were scarcely stores enough for the existing company. But she simply couldn't allow herself to stand by and watch people be butchered.

Lod came back on freq. "I think I've got things stabilized, but they don't want to wait to deal. Unless we propose a trade immediately, they're going to set up a slaughterhouse right here on the beach."

"What are the terms?" Dextra asked.

"We can take one boatload aboard if we return one boatload of trade goods. That's the sum price for *all* the hostages—maybe two boatloads if we pack them in tight."

Lod sounded a little more in possession of himself. Dextra wondered if she herself would be as cool, standing there amid the horror. "What sort of goods are they interested in?" she asked.

"Cloth, simple tools, utensils—along with some of our trade trinkets."

Dextra considered it. Perhaps because the Yclepts sensed that the execution of *half* the Anathemites would be as unacceptable to the Visitants as that of all, they were willing to let Lod leave with one boatload without advance payment. Whatever their reasoning, Dextra asked Tonii to see to the ransom personally. Then she swung to Defeen, second in command of the Exts after Atelier.

"Assemble a punitive force and prepare attack plans. We'll want maximum security aboard the ship, as well." She loathed inciting bad blood with yet another Aquam faction, but a failure to respond to Yclept's savagery could prove fatal to the entire mission. "How do you feel about hanging a couple of Yclepts from your yardarm, Captain?" she asked Quant.

His vision enhancers were still trained on the shore. "There's room for as many as you'd like, madame."

Lod had overestimated. Most of the Anathemites and other castoffs managed to fit aboard the hovercraft. Even so, the Yclepts were willing to let them leave, apparently content with Lod's word that he'd return with the promised goods. Still, their faith made Dextra uncomfortable. Did the Yclepts know something she didn't? From what she caught over the tac net, the *Northwind* crew, confronted with the smell of the hostages, had been forced to adopt breathers.

Lod had prudently chosen to ride shotgun on the trip back to the *GammaLAW*. Everything happened so fast that when the hover made ready to dock at the accommodation float, no one was quite sure what to do with the newcomers; they were simply shunted to one side while frantic Exts and crew members began tossing in a ransom of bolts of fabric, knives, pots, saws, and the like.

"Hold them on the foredeck," Quant ordered when Atelier requested instructions. "Make certain that none of them wander off. We'll hose and decontam them, then confine them to one of the vacant berthing spaces."

"Offer them water," Dextra thought to add, "and food, within reason." She asked Lod if he wouldn't rather stay behind than embark on the ferry run, but he shook his head. On visual, via a pickup by the mooring float, he looked a bit green in the face but more determined than she'd ever seen him.

"I struck the deal, Madame Haven. I don't want the Yclepts to suspect a trick and go violent on us."

"I appreciate that," Dextra told him softly, "even though you're ruining your image. But I want you onboard to coordinate things. Clear?"

"Clear, madame," Lod allowed after a moment.

In all the confusion Tonii could get no reliable information about the condition of the Anathemites, and the commo nets were too busy with priority traffic. When 'e had finished expediting the loading of the ransom, 'e moved forward to check on the outcasts personally, a patch over the eye Zone had thumbed out during the fight that had preceded his escape. It so happened that the quickest way forward lay along the starboard side, opposite the focus of action, and Tonii was just aft of the island bridge when 'e spied Piper staring into the river's fairway.

"Something's not right," Piper said when Tonii asked. She pointed to deeper water. "I detect an unusual scent coming from out there. A moment ago I thought I saw something moving."

"Fish?" When Piper shook her head with certainty, Tonii became more alert. "Have you checked with sonar?"

"What could sonar tell, what with the *Northwind*'s noise? What's more, I'm not even sure that anyone's on the sonar—look! There!"

Tonii saw it then: a ripple that didn't quite break over something large, something swimming unlike any fish or aquatic life-form. Whatever it was went deeper, but Tonii thought 'e saw other forms in the murk, undulating toward the ship. Whether or not it was the Yclepts trying an end run, Tonii turned to reach for an alarm or phone, only to be hit by the weight of three bodies, which bore 'erm to the deck. Tonii had a confused impression of Piper writhing in the grasp of two or three others.

Whoever held 'erm was tremendously strong and quick, and for a second 'e thought some enhanced commando survivors from Starkweather's AlphaLAW units had followed the *GammaLAW* downriver from the lake and were staging a raid. But then 'e got a whiff of the attackers and realized that the Anathemite hostages weren't as helpless as they'd seemed—or as victimized. They had been brought abroad as part of a concerted attempt to take the ship.

All that passed through 'ers head as Tonii was snapping one heel up and back to catch the groin of the Anathemite trying to chicken-wing 'erm. At the same time Tonii snapped 'ers head back into an attacker's face, feeling the nose and teeth give.

Torquing one hand free of the grip that held it, 'e put stiffened fingers up a set of nostrils that loomed before 'erm. Another hand free, and 'e backfisted a face to the left—one that looked part dolphin, replete with a blowhole atop a smooth, glossy skull.

Tonii heard splashes near the accommodation ladder—whatever forces there were in the river were beginning to board, making the most of everyone's distraction. Why weren't the Ext sentries firing? Tonii wondered. They, at least, shouldn't have been suckered away from their posts by what was happening onshore.

'E managed to throw a snap kick to a spongy-fleshed thing in robes twice as complex as a Bedouin's. 'E shrugged and dropped and was free of the hold, regretting the fact that 'e had removed life vest and pistol earlier, to serve as Quant's talker. 'E turned 'ers head to cry out, but hands closed on it and more grasped 'erm again.

Tonii had no doubt that the ragged-looking creatures whose lives Dextra had "saved" were in fact well-trained infighters, hardened and practiced and very knowledgeable. 'E should have been more than a match for any one of them, but in spite of all 'ers enhanced strength and engineered reflexes and all the hard-won combat proficiency and meticulously honed agility, the weight of numbers bore 'erm down, darkness closing in while 'ers fingers were still a meter from the alarm button.

CHAPTER
THIRTY-TWO

Dextra had moved from Vultures' Row to the catwalk below Battle Two, from where she could observe events both ashore and on the foredeck, where the Anathemites were to be mustered and checked over by Glorianna's medics. Minutes had elapsed, however, and none of the rescued had appeared on the main deck, back in sight from the forward breakwater. She thought to mention it to someone, even ask Quant at the risk of vexing him, but before she could, his voice came over the command channel, ordering the Ext in charge of the hostage-herding detail—a CPO—to report.

A long moment passed before a man answered, "A slight holdup here, Captain. We're still processing them."

Dextra was instantly alert and knew that Quant must be, too. The man spoke with a legit Periapt accent, but he didn't sound like the CPO. More to the point, under the circumstances, no old navy salt would address Quant by his rank over commo; it was always "sir" on a duty footing, "Skipper" at less formal moments—but never, never "captain."

"Good work, guns," Quant said casually after a slight hesitation.

The alleged CPO also took another moment to respond. "Thanks, Captain."

That clinched it for Dextra. The CPO would be "boats"—a bosun—not a gunner's mate. Something was very wrong. She started looking around for Tonii, then recalled with a cold

275

spasm that 'e had gone over to starboard to bear a hand in processing the Anathemites.

Quant made no further inquiries over the channel; that was not surprising, what with unknown people on the wire. But why would the Anathemites—

The distant sounding of a signal whistle startled her. It wasn't the deep foghorn the ship used for alerts and general quarters or the shrill little pennywhistle, as she thought of it, used to salute in the harbor, signal pilot boats, and the like. Still, it gave the two shorts and a long for battle stations.

Dextra grasped the notion that Quant hoped to get his people into position before the other side understood that he was aware of them. But someone on the other side had apparently done his homework, for no sooner had the signal gone up than there was a general outcry from port midships and the slapshot sound of sling-gun discharges. At the same time a bedlam of Anathemite voices was raised forward.

Even as boomers began to sound off, Dextra spotted a group of half-naked Aquam to starboard, moving adroitly to cover and opening up with sling-guns and at least one Ext rifle. Movement on the river caught her eye, and she turned farther to starboard in time to see waves of Aquam surfacing and coming alongside to nets strung by those who'd boarded earlier. The swimmers were wearing breathing bladders of some sort—primitive closed-system devices that showed neither snorkels nor telltale bubbles. More astonishingly, they were all astride aqueons.

The aqueons were cruder than the oceanographic division's high-tech models but essentially the same devices, sprung with what looked like the same thews that powered the sling-guns. It was no wonder the raiders had been able to make the entire trip underwater; even with primitive aqueons, their speed had to be four or even five times that of an unassisted swimmer.

More and more of them were surfacing, and a great number had already clambered up the boarding nets. Dextra put the total at well over two hundred. Her first guess was that Rhodes or some other grandee, perhaps an alliance of them, had assembled the force, but the aqueons and breathers didn't square with that, and neither did the avid participation of Anathemites as Trojan horse cavalry.

Dextra was staring straight at one—an auburn-haired woman as big and burly as an Ext—when the Aquam's body shook violently and a crimson splotch appeared in her chest. The boomer's report roared across the deck, and the woman's body was pitched backward off the rail. In response, though, the raiders swarmed aboard even more quickly, and those already in place opened fire.

The Ext who'd shot the woman was taking aim at another boarder when a volley of sling-gun rounds hit him, one quarrel passing through his unprotected mouth to emerge from the back of his neck. Still, his second round hit the deckhouse corner behind which a squad of boarders was crouched, punching a neat hole in it. The next round went straight up into the air as the Ext staggered back, moaning and gurgling in his own blood. Two darts and two spiked pellets found the exposed area under his chin, and he went down.

An Ext and a vest-clad and helmeted navy rating dashed in to retrieve the wounded man; the second Ext was battlesuited, but the navy woman was caught in the side by a two-tined bolt. Another Ext ran out to give covering fire, but an iron from one of the heavy indig arbalests got him.

The arbalest had a metal and horn bow so powerful that it had to be cocked by a double-set of thews. At that range and with the enormous kinetic energy the sling-weapon boasted, a pilehead shaft could penetrate even Ext battlesuit weave. Dextra wouldn't have been surprised to see one go through Periapt hardsuit armor.

More Exts were dodging and rushing to better firing positions. Dextra drew back from her vantage point just short of a salvo of sling-gun missiles that rattled off the railing she'd been leaning on. Remembering the shore party, she shot a glance that way and hissed an involuntary curse. The second boatload of Anathemites evidently knew that the game was out in the open or perhaps that the ship had alerted the *Northwind*'s crew. As Dextra watched, in any case, the hover slewed and spun out of control, skewing off toward the opposite shore on a vector that took it within fifty meters of the SWATHship's bow. She stared, hypnotized, as it roared up onto the bank, hit a low cliff face, and disappeared in an outlashing sphere of fire and ruin.

In the meantime the deck was acrawl with raiders angling for position and keeping up a high volume of fire. Some of the Aquam carried man-catcher poles, but most bore repeating sling-guns, crank-operated magazine crossbows, and other leading-edge Aquam weapons, along with knives, toothed war clubs, and axes. Where there were Exts who could find decent cover, the raiders were stopped cold and even pushed back. The pounding of the big boomers, even set frugally to semiauto mode, sounded like strings of God's own firecrackers. Elsewhere, though, the boarders were moving fast, fearlessly, and skillfully. The very unexpectedness of their attack had given them a huge advantage; many of the ship's personnel had been caught away from their weapons.

Dextra heard a buzz-saw sound above and looked up to see marksmen firing from the starboard wing of the bridge. It was the sound of Periapt 'chetterguns—pistols and longarms both—meaning that LAW held the bridge, at least for the time being. She saw Quant up there, looking perfectly calm, dividing his attention between the shipboard trouble and the situation to either side of the ship and ashore. He was calling out instructions to his talker, and while Dextra couldn't hear them, she felt the vibrations as the ship's engines came on-line.

Tonii didn't answer Dextra's desperate shouts. The only way to find 'erm would be to walk head-on into the enemy fire, because that was where Tonii had gone—and much as she loved the gynander, body and spirit, Dextra wasn't ready to choose death yet. No diplomatic immunity or press credentials were going to hold her ass inviolate now.

As Dextra turned toward a hatch, intent on getting to the bridge, thunder and a crashing from the forest scarp off to starboard brought her around. When she saw what was happening, her mouth opened, as mouths had to be opening among all the ship's company.

The vast forest screen, impenetrable and high-rearing, abruptly gave way, toppling out into the river like a falling billboard. Coming hard atop it was some sort of immense roll or drum, flung forward as the flat hit the water and unrolling toward the ship like a thrown cylinder of carpet runner. From what Dextra could make out in a moment's frantic glance, it seemed to be made of woven vines, branches, and so forth. The attackers seemed to have built some kind of internal unwinding mechanism into it—branches and/or sling thews as springs, perhaps to trundle the giant boarding ladder toward the ship. Before it was even fully deployed, Aquam were racing out across it, holding up palisade shields and two-man testudo covers. They also carried scaling ladders because—as they must have foreseen—the makeshift pontoon bridge fell a dozen meters short of the ship's starboard sponson.

The ladders were borne forward on many sets of human legs and were walked hand over hand until they reached the deck, while the trailing ends were made fast to the raftbridge. Boarders were ascending them even before they had been well fastened, taking heavy losses from the few Ext gunners who could get full-auto fire on them. None of that deterred the Aquam, who charged in as single-mindedly as hive insects defending a nest.

Those on the boarding raft returned fire with arbalests and catapultlike mass throwers that vomited out whole hedgchog broadsides of darts and bolts. Both types of weapons were slow to reload, but the Aquam managed to gain momentary fire

superiority nonetheless. In the meantime, most of the Exts had
been forced to switch back to semiauto; at fullchoke a boomer
ate up even one of the big thirty-round banana clips in a little
over two seconds.

As Dextra scrambled for the ladderwell, she reflected on the
sling-gun quarrel that had touched off the bloodshed at Wall
Water. It had been Purifyre's bodyguard, Essa, who had fired
the weapon. She didn't see either of them, but something in her
gut told her that Human Enlightenment had at least lent a hand
in planning the raid on the *GammaLAW*—perhaps with the
help of Claude Mason, despite Burning's claim that Purifyre
had fled for the Trans-Bourne with Ghost in captivity. Burning,
for whom the Oceanic was searching. Nothing added up. Regardless, Dextra doubted that even a full understanding of the
events would help her save the GammaLAW mission.

Burning awoke to pounding at the cottage's Dutch door.
"Descrier, please attend us."

Hungerford, Burning thought.

"At your earliest convenience, if you please."

Roundelay, the healer.

Three more harsh raps, and a less genteel voice rang
out. "Come to the door immediately. That means you, too,
Redtails."

Pondoroso, the Varangian. And if he was inside the wall—
beyond the pale—something untoward had happened. Burning
leapt up and headed for the door, which couldn't be locked, in
any case. Behind him Souljourner was sitting up on the futon,
gnawing at the fingernails of one hand, the other pressed to
her head.

"More of what I've been feeling," she said by way of explanation. "The Amnion's consternation intensifies."

She had been in distress for the past two days, during which
they'd done little more than lie around the cottage making
love and nursing their wounds. Burning had tried to treat her

headaches with what pills remained in his medkit, but none of them had done the trick.

"What do you people want?" he directed toward the door. "You keep up the pounding and shouting, you're going to kill every mandseng plant on Cape Ataraxia."

"We would have a word with Souljourner, please," Roundelay repeated in a quieter voice.

Burning glanced about, unsure of the hour. Either they had slept straight through the entire day, or they had been rudely awakened to an overcast morning.

"All is not right with the Writ," Hungerford called through the door.

Burning looked at Souljourner, whose shoulders were hunched high around her head. "Anything you want to tell me?" he asked after a moment of watching her.

She swallowed and found her voice. "The Writ . . . it's forged, Redtails."

"*For—*"

"I had no way of escaping those old codgers at Pyx," she said, cutting him off. "Praepostor Sternstuff meant to keep me imprisoned there until one of us died, so I clobbered him with the seal, used it to imprint the Writ, and inked in my own name."

Burning's initial irritation turned to hopefulness. "Does this mean we're likely to be tossed out of here?"

"More likely hung."

Burning winced. The pounding returned. "What's your problem with the Writ?" he demanded.

"Our problem is not with the Writ per se," Hungerford replied, "or with the Seal per se, but with the signature, which does not match the hand of Praepostor Sternstuff, an example of which we have before us."

Burning cursed. "You're mistaken. Check again."

"We've dispatched a runner to Pyx to confirm the signature,

Redtails," Pondoroso warned. "But until we have confirmation, Souljourner—and you—will have to vacate the cottage and be remanded into custody."

"Hey, guys, who was it two days ago who saved your asses from the big surge?"

"We are not disparaging of Souljourner's talents," Roundelay was quick to say. "She will always have Alabaster's gratitude for the astuteness of her Descrying ability. But unless she is indeed the Descrier assigned to our city, she cannot be permitted to remain."

"What are you're going to do, kick her out?"

"That, Redtails, depends on the outcome of the inquest and trial."

Burning had his mouth open to respond when a collective yell rose from the beach. Expecting to see another tsunami heading for Cape Ataraxia, he rushed to the window that looked downslope, only to be confronted by a fog bank covering the foreland at Oread's bust and moving rapidly ashore. Souljourner joined him at the window, in obvious discomfort.

"Despite what you think, it is neither mist nor fog, Redtails. This has been conjured and sent here by the Oceanic."

"For what?"

Souljourner shook her head. "Although I Descried its coming, I cannot divine its purpose."

Burning suddenly realized that the pounding on the door had ceased, and a moment later he spied Roundelay, Hungerford, and Pondoroso making tracks toward Queller's Enlargement, where almost everyone else was running in the opposite direction.

He took Souljourner by the shoulders. "Get your things together. This is our chance."

"Our chance?"

"To beat it out of here."

"But the wall—"

"We'll cross that when we come to it." When she failed to

move, he took a calming breath and began again. "Look, it's either that or we end up imprisoned or worse for forgery and lying about being married. Anyway, remember what the Holy Rollers decreed: 'Leave via necessity's gate.' "

She worked her prominent jaw and nodded. "You're right, Redtails. We must get away while we can."

By the time they left the cottage, carrying only what they could wear, the mist that wasn't a mist was moving across the cape and beginning to infiltrate Alabaster itself. Burning could see wisps of it as he plunged along hand in hand with Souljourner, whose hatchet-wounded calf had not fully healed. There was no abandoning her now, no matter what.

Curls of odd blue-gray brume were snaking through the orchards and grottoes as if sniffing the air for something. He thought about veering off toward the eastern terminus of the white wall, but a single glance toward the Amnion in that direction revealed a palisade of the weird cloud rising from the waters. Downslope, people were racing for shelter.

The Sceptor team had found no evidence of the Oceanic's having employed chemical warfare against humans; every recounting pointed to a policy of strict nonintervention on the part of the marine entity toward surface dwellers. But for all Burning knew, the cloud—it wasn't a cloud, either—was toxic. With Souljourner limping but game to go, he dashed into a grove of gnarled trees that fronted a portion of the wall where it swept downward to the sea.

The mist caught up with them there and began to settle with a clammy, oily feel. Souljourner was right about one thing, Burning thought: it didn't feel like any fog he'd ever come across—though he couldn't tell if his reaction to it was at least in part due to his emotional tumult. Where it touched his bare skin, the vapor set off the same kind of warning tingle that the smell of the Aggregate's NNF precursor had set off in him during the Lyceum ball in the

Periapt Empyraeum. This time, he was sure, it wasn't familiarization but sheer instinct sounding off. He stopped and turned, still looking for a way over the wall.

"Redtails, your face!" Souljourner said suddenly.

Cold fire had begun to play across all his exposed skin. When he held up his hand, he saw that it glowed with fine blue radiance. Indescribable odors were coming off him, as well, exotic and bewilderingly complex. Some message, his mind reeled, but from what and to what?

He was about to tell Souljourner to get clear before she was exposed when he realized that she, too, was standing in the thick of it. If their positions were reversed, he might have backed away, thinking about contact toxins, but Souljourner grabbed his hand before he could think to snatch it away and tried to rub the stuff off.

They left the woods behind, but the mist clung to them. On Burning it was growing effervescent, pulsating, and glowing, and the smells from it seemed to clog the very air, as if spreading through the cloud. Motes in the vapor grew thicker, like lattices of foamy snow. Burning couldn't tell whether it was a new phenomenon or if the individual pellets of mist were combining into larger accretions. Those, too, began collecting on him as if driven by a blizzard. He had a momentary view of a group of Alabasterites who, seeing what was happening to him and the Descrier, had come to a dumbfounded halt on the hillside below the longhouse that was the town's high-water refuge.

Burning began to sway under the weight of the encasement. The foam was cohering, exerting a pull like a huge gelid mass of muscle. Not that he was observing it calmly; he howled and groaned, trying to no avail to break free of the stuff. His feet, too, were trapped in a thick drift of the froth. Once more he urged Souljourner to flee, but she refused, clinging close to him and striving desperately to keep his mouth and nostrils from becoming completely obstructed. Soon, perhaps because she clung so close, the mounting lather began to envelop her, too.

As the piles of thickening suds closed in, Burning felt a distinct tug in the waist-high stuff, as if it were flexing its muscles. The pull was in the direction of the shore. He turned that way automatically and let out another roar.

The waves were dancing tall beyond Oread's bust, though the weather was calm and the sea was flat everywhere else. The water itself was humped up as if something huge and rounded were surfacing. Burning was struck through with the most primeval of fears, the horror that something had come to eat him. He struggled wildly to get free and shove Souljourner free, but the foam wouldn't permit it. Inexorably, they were pulled from their feet and down the slope toward whatever the Oceanic had waiting for them.

Hungerford, Roundelay, Pondoroso, and the others watched as the mist and foam withdrew, taking Burning and Souljourner with it. The waters seethed up, lashing the shore, so that it was difficult to tell where one left off and the other began. But when the waters receded and the mounded lather was gone, so were Burning and Souljourner. The air was already clear of the Oceanic's smart mist, and within minutes the waves were quiet, as well.

CHAPTER
THIRTY-THREE

Notwithstanding his vast collection of paper and electronic books detailing the exploits of old-time naval heroes, Quant had faced his infrequent challenges in a rapid shifting among phones and data displays rather than with cutlass in one hand and ship's wheel in the other, though today was turning out differently.

His 'chettergun had killed a dozen raiders attacking the *GammaLAW* on the starboard side, yet more continued to stream up the boarding nets. Backing off the wing of the bridge, he handed the depleted weapon to his talker and patched into the command and control net. What with so many watertight doors out of operation, the Aquam had broken through in many places belowdecks. That they seemed to know precisely how to proceed left him flabbergasted.

His talker relayed word from one of the Ext combat teams. "Aquam are massing in the forecastle. Ext gun teams have 'em stopped down there and are driving them back. The exec agrees main deck attack on quarterdeck most likely."

Quant understood that there'd be no stopping them as long as they were willing to absorb heavy losses, but there was still a chance. "Get me ordnance," he snapped.

The talker stared blankly for a moment, as if Quant had spoken a foreign language. *Ordnance,* he seemed to be asking himself, when the only firable heavy gun on the ship was the now-single-barreled 240-mm turret?

It took some time, but at last the talker succeeded in raising a gunner's mate striker—a former comparative-dance major—deep in the damaged and cracked barbette.

"I want whatever's left of the propellant brought up on the ordnance elevators," Quant instructed his talker to relay. When the mate-striker tried to point out that there were only two jury-rigged shells remaining, Quant went on-line to snarl, *"Just do it!"* Others on the bridge were as mystified as the mate striker, but none of them dared question him now.

A muffled explosion forward was followed quickly by two more—Exts, using grenades. Quant hadn't okayed their use, but this wasn't the time to get stiff-assed about regs. Something occurred to him, and he turned to his talker. "Ask Ext C and C why they aren't using sonics."

The talker was shaking his head before he got the question out. "Report from the brigade XO, sir. The Aquam are wearing the same kind of quilted armor Rhodes's Militerrors wore. Sonics can't penetrate."

Trying to quiet a sudden feeling of doom, Quant turned away to survey the deck. Countersonics from a bunch of pre-tech pirates? He had the chilly feeling he'd been preparing all this time for the wrong kind of battle.

"Anchor is to, sir," the bosun's mate of the watch reported. The *GammaLAW* was already swinging free of the river's bottom, but now she was caught and held fast by cables carried over by the first of the boarders, and full rear rudders weren't able to pull her loose.

"Check on ordnance! Tell them to step lively with that propellant!"

Before the talker could relay the command, however, an explosion ripped open the side of the bridge. Quant saw the paint on the bulkhead crack and flake off in smoldering bits. In-bent metal turned red-hot, then opened. A wall of force hit him, along with the rest of the bridge watch, and he was suddenly floating in blackness.

* * *

For Dextra capture came more ignominiously. Searching for Tonii, she came across the body of a boarder who'd been blown through a horizontal ladder by an Ext grenade. The body had been sent backward with such force that the ladder had neatly chopped it into even rectangular sections of soppy tissue, bone, and hair wrapped in rags.

In spite of all she'd seen, Dextra puked, and that was how Purifyre, leading a sally team, found her. One of the keys to the takeover of the ship, she was treated carefully even after she tried to kick Purifyre in the crotch and gouge out the eyes of his second in command, the woman she knew as Essa.

"I thought you favored nonviolent solutions," Purifyre said grimly while Ballyhoot pinioned Dextra's arms.

"In your case I'll take what I can get," Dextra spit. "I knew Human Enlightenment was behind this, just as you were behind the firefight at Wall Water." She turned in an attempt to glare at Ballyhoot. "I saw this one fire the quarrel that started the shooting. God knows why, but you planned for things to go wrong for LAW from the start."

Purifyre's homely features assembled themselves into a grin. "God knows why, and you don't, Madame Commissioner? You would yoke the Aquam to LAW's vehicle, 'annex' this world without a thought to those who dwell here?"

Dextra was shaking her head. "My goal all along has been to help Aquam the world over. Not just the petty tyrants who rule the lake district and certainly not Human Enlightenment to the exclusion of every other religious sect on Scorpia and elsewhere."

Purifyre snorted. "Perhaps. But Aquamarine would still be under Periapt's thumb, forced to participate in *your* war with the alien Roke, forced to endure the rape of our resources to furnish construction materials for *your* starships, forced to endure the comings and goings of 'commissioners' and others of your ilk."

"The Roke may soon be your enemy as well, Purifyre. They occupy Aquamarine's moons even now."

Purifyre folded his arms across his chest. "They've had centuries to come here, Dextra Haven, and they haven't yet."

"That's precisely why Aquamarine is so important to the cause of peace," Dextra said, straining against Ballyhoot's hold. "If, as I suspect, the Oceanic is the cause of the Roke's reluctance to so much as make planetfall here, Aquamarine could become the most important world in human space. Do you fail to see that—and see that you'll need help, mine or someone's else's, in making the most of what will come to you?"

"Primitive as we are, we'll simply have to manage without you."

"What have you done with Ghost?"

His brow wrinkled. "Ghost?"

"Don't be coy. We've heard from Allgrave Burning. He tracked you to the Trans-Bourne."

Purifyre touched his lips. "Burning I saw—but days ago, near the Jitterland Heights parking mounds. Ghost I have not seen since Wall Water."

Dextra's baffled expression mirrored Purifyre's. "Purifyre, you saw the mist that moved upriver? It was searching for *Burning*. Something important has happened."

"Indeed it has," Purifyre said in an obvious reference to his victory.

Dextra laughed in spite of herself. "You actually think you can operate this ship without our help? I wish your father was here to talk some sense into you."

Purifyre didn't respond. Instead, he ordered her hands tied, then had her taken to a prisoner collection point, where she was relieved beyond words to find Tonii, Lod, Piper, and Quant. The ship's passageways were thick with smoke, most lighting was out, and the dead and wounded lay everywhere, including several of the Discards. The Anathemite insiders and the first of the boarders had moved fast to seize ammunition and other critical resources. In the end it had come down to hand to hand, e-tool against sword and sling-gun.

In short order the prisoners were moved to the flight deck, where everyone was thoroughly searched and positively IDed. Serious WIAs were taken to sick bay. With the battle over, the Anathemites mixed easily with Purifyre's common fighters, and it was clear that they were accustomed to serving together—an amazing thing among Aquam.

Dextra kept waiting for Purifyre to reappear, and when he did, he was accompanied not only by Essa—whom he called Ballyhoot—but by a short man of compact build with receding dishwater-blond hair, a long upturned nose, and almond-shaped eyes that were darkly intense. Dextra was certain she had seen him before, or perhaps his likeness, though she couldn't place where.

Purifyre was cradling a boomer and had a 'baller tucked into his belt. "We're continuing to search for stragglers," he was telling the stranger. "Division chiefs are setting watches."

The stranger nodded. "Good. Then let's start cutting out some techs and watch commanders. I want us under weigh before dusk."

Dextra followed the interplay minutely. Under weigh, she was thinking when Claude Mason appeared on deck. "I want to propose a candidate for your yardarm," Dextra said to Quant when she got over her astonishment.

Quant shook his head. "He's too dim-witted to have had anything to do with this."

"But Purifyre's people seem to know the ship by heart."

Quant nodded. "Exactly. And Mason doesn't."

Dextra watched him come to his son's side, ignoring the taunts and threats the ship's company hurled at him. But it was the blond stranger who came to stand before her and Quant.

"Let's get through the first part of this without wasting time," he began. "My name is Eisley Boon, though my confederates know me as Cozmote."

"Boon!" Dextra said in pure astonishment. "I knew I'd seen your face." She stopped, confused, then added, "But the *Scepter* reports have you listed as dead."

Boon laughed to himself. "Let's just say that the rumors of my death were greatly exaggerated."

Dextra gave her head a bewildered shake. "I don't understand. You're behind this . . . *piracy*?"

Boon sniffed. "I am. But rest assured that none of you will be harmed if you obey our commands."

"But *why*?" Dextra demanded. "You must know by now that the *Terrible Swift Sword* was destroyed. What threat do we pose to anyone at this point?"

"Why, no threat at all. Oh, I realize that LAW will eventually dispatch another mission to Aquamarine, but that still gives me—what?—something on the order of ten to twenty baseline-years to accomplish what I need to do."

"Which is what, precisely?" Quant asked harshly. "Set yourself up as lord of Aquamarine now that you're done playing Connecticut Yankee in King Arthur's court?"

Boon showed him a fey smile. "Very perceptive of you, Captain—or should I say Skipper to amend my earlier error?" He swung to Mason. "Claude, perhaps you'd care to have the honor of explaining to these good people just why I have 'pirated' their vessel."

Mason was shaken momentarily by the realization that he would have to speak directly to his onetime shipmates, but he somehow summoned the nerve. "Boon doesn't give a rat's ass about LAW or any of the grandees," he began. "He's got it in his head that Aquamarine's real enemy is the Oceanic, which he means to scramble by taking this ship into the Amnion."

Utter silence fell over the flight deck; Boon himself broke it with a laugh. "I might have put it somewhat differently, Claude, but thanks for the effort."

"You're insane to even think of taking this ship onto the Amnion," Dextra said at last.

"Ah, but it *can* be done, Madame Haven," Boon told her, "and we will do it." He looked at Quant. "Unless I'm mistaken, Skipper, the *GammaLAW*'s wetdown system is still fully operational."

Quant scowled unalloyed hatred at Boon but answered levelly. "You're not mistaken. But why would you need full-lockout protection when we're not carrying CBR weapons?"

Boon looked downriver. "Think about it."

Quant followed Boon's gaze, then lowered his head and said nothing.

"Do us both a favor and convince your people to cooperate," Boon was telling Quant a few minutes later. "It's taken too much to get to this point for me to care about a few more lives. Am I making myself clear?"

Quant was no martyr. He loved his ship, but he wasn't some head case out of a romance with such an obsession for a vessel that he was willing to get himself killed for no good reason. Furthermore, he had seen enough of life on Aquamarine to know that Boon would probably be willing to use whatever torture or coercion was necessary to have his way. He turned his head painfully, feeling rope scrape his skin, to call out for his XO. Winnie Ketchum was sitting on the deck not far away.

"Get the division chiefs to sound off and have them muster sea watches," Quant said. "Then stand ready to take supervision from Lieutenant Boon's personnel. And stress to all hands that I expect cooperation with the commandeering forces."

Quant had hoped that his use of Boon's LAW rank would elicit a reaction, but Boon was already giving other orders and his adherents were forming up according to pre-made op plans to oversee the running of the ship.

"We would appreciate your cooperation up on the bridge now, Quant," Boon said after a moment.

Quant wasn't used to being called by name, but he didn't let his resentment show. With a final info-soliciting glance at Dextra, he levered himself up and began to take a head count of those who had been herded together on the flight deck. The already-reduced numbers of the ship's company had been further thinned by the battle. They looked even fewer as Boon's reserve troops started coming up the boarding ladders, carrying supplies and weapons. Human chains were set up to facilitate the transfer of small kegs that appeared to have been sealed with some kind of epoxy or wax.

Purifyre was getting Piper and the rest of the Aggregate into motion. Quant thought hard about the sundry equipment in the habitat, wondering if there was some potential resource or weapon there, but dismissed the idea. The Aggregate was too alien, too incomprehensible, to be relied on or even understood.

An Aquam boarder prodded him with a sling-gun muzzle, and he accepted it. He was a captive, a defeated adversary, and for now he had to at least look and behave like one.

To Dextra, the irony was that the Aquam were treating her with respect. Some of it might have had to do with Boon's orders or even some intervention on Mason's part, but Dextra suspected that it was due to the fact that her age was showing. Overnight, gray had crept deep into her hair and additional lines had appeared around her eyes and mouth. The Aquam, especially the younger males, were merely being courteous.

She laughed to herself. Why hadn't she dyed her hair white and wrinkled herself like a prune *before* she had agreed to meet with 'Waretongue Rhodes at Wall Water?

Boon's pirates were leading away members of the ship's company, to be searched one last time and then confined to various compartments belowdecks. If the boarding units' knowledge of the SWATHship's layout hadn't come from Mason, who had it come from? Dextra asked herself. As she thought back to the months of mission organization she'd gone through on Periapt, a possibility came to her: Perhaps Buck Starkweather had been in contact with Boon. But how could Buck have learned about Boon when even Mason believed him dead? The two of them—Mason and Boon—could have been conspirators from the start, she supposed, though that seemed unlikely. Then she recalled that it was Yatt— the unseen voice of the Quantum College—who had suggested the then-*Matsya* for the mission. But then, how had the Quantum College learned of Boon's presence on Aquamarine? And why would it—or they—choose to align itself with someone hell-bent on scrambling the Oceanic? If the Oceanic was the key to resolving the Roke Conflict, did the QC have a vested interest in prolonging the war?

Dextra's gaze found Mason. Seeing the light of devotion to Purifyre, she abandoned any ideas of trying to work on the man and turn the mission's situation around. Mason was beyond any leverage except for whatever could be applied through his son, not that even that avenue looked promising. Purifyre strode the flight deck helmetless, long hair blowing in the wind, jaw set at an angle of command, like some trophy figurine.

No, Boon was the linchpin now. Everyone, from Anathemite fighter to Purifyre himself, looked to him as the unquestioned leader. Dextra was eager to learn how he had faked his own death, but there were things she needed to tell him first.

Focusing on him, she tried to convey a sense of earnestness. "Boon, before you strike at the Oceanic, there are some things you should know, things we've only recently discovered."

Boon seemed amused, but he did stop and give her more attention. "For instance?"

She considered bargaining with him—her own freedom first and then, somehow, cooperation with Boon's forces instead of a disastrous square-off. But she was astute at forming quick and accurate impressions, and she didn't read Boon as anyone she could muscle around. She would have to give him something, if only to get the game going.

"We obtained a readout of the Oceanic's DNA profile before the *Terrible Swift Sword* was destroyed. We have its basic genetic code."

Boon relaxed a bit. "Is that all? Hell, I could have provided you with that. Oh, but you couldn't know . . . You see, I learned it years ago—not long after the *Scepter* lifted off. If I hadn't, I assure you that I wouldn't be aboard your ship today—"

Both he and Dextra turned to the sounds of a nearby scuffle. Out of character, Piper was struggling weakly in the grip of the Anathemite who had taken hold of her arms. "Madame Haven, I must tell you," she was saying. "There wasn't time earlier!"

The Aquam was about to bring Piper to her knees with a shot to the head, but Boon signaled him to stop. Piper slumped in the Anathemite's arms as he dragged her across the nonskid to where Boon and Dextra were standing.

"What do you need to tell me, Piper?" Dextra asked.

She raised her face. "We not only have the Oceanic DNA readout, we have the Roke readout, as well—from the tissue sample."

Boon frowned. "The Roke don't concern me."

"But they *match*," Piper said, looking at him. "Not to the last gene, of course, but in too many ways for it to mean anything but that the Oceanic and the Roke are related. They're genetic *family!*"

CHAPTER
THIRTY-FOUR

The more he saw of the great diatom, its workings, and the genius behind it, the more rapt Zinsser became, until—long hours after the attempt at steering the sphere toward the *GammaLAW*—a great vertical fissure opened in the inner lining membrane not ten yards from the sampling pseudopod, and he knew in a horrible flash of insight that both he and Ghost were about to die, crushed by merciless pressures in the eerily lit depths of the Amnion.

Their prison ship–creature vibrated perceptibly, as if to some great unseen soft-landing impact. It seemed for a moment that they'd struck an undersea mountain. But Zinsser saw nothing that even approximated a threatening scarp, only the glimmer of an immense curvature that might have been an ocean-bottom dome habitat. Ghost was so intent on what was happening that she didn't bother to shake his hand loose of hers. She was watching the growing cleft and listening to the leathery tearing sounds with the avidness of a spectator at a martial arts contest. Something was moving within the diatom wall beyond the fissure, in the gelid swirls of the assembled creature's living plasm. It came to Zinsser then that the diatom had rammed into *another* of its kind and that an exchange of substance or information seemed to be occurring.

A sudden suspicion filled him, but before he could voice it, the membrane of their private chamber had parted and they found themselves staring into an open space beyond—and the two people who stood there.

"Burning?"

Ghost asked it with a kind of vast amusement but with more warmth than Zinsser had ever heard from her. The Allgrave cried out his sister's name with considerably more shakiness. In a half dozen long strides, he reached her and swept her up in a great embrace, leaving Zinsser and Burning's female companion to eye each other. It was several seconds before he recognized her as the Descrier Grandee Rhodes had given to Dextra Haven at the Grand Attendance.

Everything was confused for quite a while after that, tales and explanations piling up faster than they could be digested: the Laputa landing ground; the Jitterland Heights muscle-car mounds; the flight of the *Dream Castle*; the pursuit of the *Shattertail*; Old Spume, Purifyre, Manna, and Testamentor; Asurao and Pondoroso; Passwater and Alabaster . . . It was Zinsser who explained about the lock of Burning's hair, which had apparently given the Oceanic a garbled message. That the mist had taken Souljourner was something of a puzzle until Burning confessed that the Descrier in effect had had him all over her. He told, too, of what he had learned about the dam burst, Zone, and the Roke during his brief contact with the ship.

"All this time we thought you were on the *GammaLAW*," Ghost said.

"And I thought you were a prisoner of Purifyre's Human Enlightenment cultists," Burning replied.

He was still visibly disturbed; Souljourner, in a state of shock. But both were returning to normal with a rapidity Zinsser found interesting though not entirely unexpected, given that they were Ext and Descrier.

After an hour or so of multitrack conversation they had heard each other out and gotten their bearings. But something else was transpiring, as well, a kind of neural intercourse no one dared mention. It was as if their absorption by the Oceanic had allowed them to see deeply into each other. In Burning, Zinsser could read a certain passion and tenderness for Souljourner, undermined by a sense of embarrassment and guilt over some matter. In Ghost, Zinsser perceived that while she had always seen through his weakness and hypocrisy, she was most drawn to him—perversely—when he was at his most weaselly! She knew, too, that her violent actions aboard the *Dream Castle* had knocked her from the pedestal on which he had placed her, whereas he had actually risen a notch in her estimation by letting go of his lust.

"We're still left with the problem of getting *out* of these things," Burning remarked ruefully when everyone had been brought up to date. "How did you manage to steer yours to Passwater?"

"*Steer* it?" Zinsser said. "We don't even have the vaguest idea how to control the lights." He summarized the theory he and Ghost had developed that the Oceanic relied more on chemical messengers than on anything else. He said nothing about their lovemaking, though he assumed that Burning and Souljourner were reading his inner thoughts as clearly as he was reading theirs.

"It's not important that the Oceanic think *I* can furnish information about the Roke," Burning said at last. "What is, is that it *understood* your actions of associating the lock of hair with the tissue sample. Surely we can make use of that."

Zinsser sniffed. "Perhaps. But in fact, the Oceanic is less interested in the four of us than it is in the Roke. Frankly, the tissue is the only reason Ghost and I are even alive."

Souljourner blanched.

Zinsser glanced at her and stroked his chin. "But now the Roke are on Aquamarine's moons, you say. They're moving closer to a world they've shunned for at least the hundreds of years since the Optimants colonized the planet."

"The cloud you called the smart mist is new, as well," Souljourner interjected. "Nothing like the seeking fog has ever happened before. The One Who Watches has *never* reached out for land-walkers."

"A canny observation," Zinsser allowed. "But what follows from it?" He looked through the diatom's wall into dimness. "We've assumed that when Starkweather made use of Pitfall, the Oceanic was either frightened or affronted enough to destroy my device, as well as the *Terrible Swift Sword*. Suppose it was the *Roke* who destroyed them. Suppose they were acting *protectively* toward the Oceanic."

Burning nodded. "You said that the Roke were probably marine creatures, so maybe there's even a genetic connection. Maybe the Oceanic is a Roke experiment they've been reluctant to tamper with."

Zinsser stared at Burning for a long moment, his eyes widening with each passing second. "Burning, I think you've put your finger close to the mark, except for one thing: fossil evidence alone proves that the Oceanic evolved here and spawned the land life-forms we've all seen. What's more, the Roke couldn't possibly have been monitoring Aquamarine over eons. Their rate of technological advance just in the time since humanity met them says otherwise, not to mention the state of their interstellar colonization. But that leaves another possibility: The Roke evolved on Aquamarine."

Souljourner didn't quite understand what he was getting at, and Ghost only watched him neutrally through her mask of fighter's scars. Burning was slow and suspicious in coming at Zinsser from another angle. "But the Oceanic shows no interest in space travel. As Souljourner says, it's been content to remain in the Amnion."

Zinsser then saw a wonderful thing: Ghost broke into a smile of honest pleasure, even of surprise—of insight. "But a species that had been 'nudged up' would!"

Zinsser took pleasure in her anticipating him. It thrilled him to see her dead face brought so glowingly to life. "Interstellar travel, to such a species, would be the only real hope of taking command of its own destiny. Or, quite possibly, the Oceanic banished them."

Burning showed him a knowing grin. "Because the Oceanic would never stand for a surface life-form challenging it as Aquamarine's dominant species."

"It has long suffered *us*," Souljourner pointed out.

"Yes, but the Oceanic didn't create us," Zinsser said. "It has yet to view us as a direct threat to its dominance. Banishment might have been a natural response to one of its own creations that had developed a threatening technology." He paused, then sighed defeatedly "Even so, I can see at least one other scenario: the ur-Roke may have reasoned or known instinctively that they were one day going to have to abandon Aquamarine."

Ghost frowned. "To act as the Oceanic's eyes and ears in the galaxy?"

Burning glanced between her and Zinsser. "That would run counter to their having shunned this place for so long. And protective or not, what's brought them back now when they could easily have shown themselves when the Optimants were here?"

Zinsser licked his lips. "I'm beginning to wonder if they haven't returned for a reconciliation." At Burning's blank stare he added, " 'Prodigal son,' Allgrave. Here the Roke evolved, and they remain tied to Aquamarine in a way humans are no longer tied to Earth. Their Eden is *real*—a unity of mind and spirit with the metaorganism that is the Oceanic. Something in them has called to it now."

Burning was reduced to stubborn groping. "That still doesn't explain why they've stopped short at the moons. Why not drop down the well and have their reconciliation? What are they waiting for?"

Zinsser shook his head. "We can't be certain, of course, but let's for the moment posit that the Roke haven't come home sooner because they haven't been able to do so on their own.

Let us posit that they needed *our* help in facilitating the reconciliation."

Zinsser spread his hands. "They can no more return here than a pogofoot can jump back into the Amnion—even to douse itself if it's on fire. Not because the creature knows its fate from experience or even from observation and inference but because on a genetic and cellular level it is *physically incapable* of doing so.

"With the Roke, perhaps, there's a genetic, reflexive, and physical mandate—a governing device or fail-safe that, in Roke-Oceanic terms at least, is virtually tamperproof. Having been cast out of Eden, they are constitutionally unable to return, or alter their own physiology so that they can return, or even make direct contact with the Oceanic from a distance."

Zinsser took a breath. "I'm suggesting that the whole business with the Roke craft—the attack on the *Sword*—was a way to get this tissue sample—this message in a bottle, smart secretion, call it whatever you will—to the Oceanic."

Burning's laugh had a tinge of madness to it. "Zinsser, why wouldn't the Roke use a rocket, or a rock, for that matter? Or how about a laser, a radio, a semaphore?"

Zinsser compressed his lips. "I don't have all the answers. Something about the terms of banishment, perhaps. We're dealing with the first real alien intelligence we've contacted and, in turn, an offshoot form of that very intelligence."

"Do you think the Oceanic recognized the tissue sample as coming from the race it spawned?" Ghost asked.

"Enough to be intrigued, certainly," Zinsser answered. "But it's possible that the Roke have evolved since leaving Aquamarine—or have evolved themselves, become all but unrecognizable. Though something remains to the DNA signature that has tantalized the Oceanic."

Burning snorted. "If the Oceanic banished the Roke, it may not want to remember them."

"Is any of this going to help us get out of here?" Souljourner asked in a quiet, frightened voice.

Burning squared his shoulders in readiness. "Maybe we can get our release in return for what we know. We take the position that we won't reveal anything more about the tissue sample unless one of these globes deposits us close to shore—preferably somewhere near the New Alexandria lighthouse, since *GammaLAW*'s just upriver."

Zinsser smiled faintly. "There's still the matter of getting our point across, Allgrave. I mean, what items can we put together to spell 'New Alexandria lighthouse'? If it could understand us, you two would never have been brought here to begin with. But you're right. We have to at least try to communicate our terms and then, supposing the Oceanic concurs, impart to it what I believe this message from the Roke means."

"Which is?" Ghost asked.

Zinsser faced her, more soberly now. "That they mean to have their reconciliation one way or another. That they've been waiting for the chance to send this one plea, this message, in the hope that reunion could be effected the easy way. But if not by love, then by force. The Roke mean to make the Oceanic listen to them."

An odd, muted clicking made Zinsser glance toward Souljourner. She'd opened the drawstring of the smooth-worn little brown neck pouch. From the way she was slowly running her palms against each other, eyes closed in deep concentration, and from the sound escaping her hands, Zinsser knew from his time on the *Dream Castle* that she was going to throw an Aquam dice divination.

Burning appeared to be more than accustomed to the sound; he didn't even look up at first. But as Souljourner knelt and let the Holy Rollers gallop in a motion sequence of unconscious grace, Zinsser saw a sudden look of alarm cross Burning's face and saw his hand convulse as if reaching for something inside his tunic. There was no making sense of it.

It happened that there wasn't an opportunity to ask, for just as Souljourner was leaning forward to read the throw, a galaxy of lights sprang to life in the plasm walls of the chamber and the Descrier was suddenly standing in an angel aura of soft whiteness, ethereally and youthfully beautiful. Even more illumination spilled at her feet, however, on the dice themselves.

Each visible pip was throwing back a finely focused brilliance, and directly overhead a pattern of lights appeared. The pattern didn't replicate what was showing on the faces of Souljourner's dice throw, though it certainly suggested it: incandescent circles in a row of three and, nearby, a simple brace of two—

Zinsser laughed and snapped his fingers. "Of course! It's the die faces that are *down*—in contact with the skin of the diatom!"

Whether the Oceanic was reading trace radiation or whether the dice simply resembled some luminous deep-sea communication method the Oceanic already used, he couldn't say. An explanation wasn't the important part, in any case; the point was that contact had been made.

He went down on one knee and dropped a die on the living floor experimentally, but it produced no result, no change in the light show overhead. When he made an unpracticed throw, however, the radiance washed across the ceiling again and the pattern of the facedown pips was replicated.

"I don't know why, but it has to be a throw," Zinsser said. "This is going to complicate things considerably."

Burning began to grope for words; then, with a guilty look, he produced a small touchcard control pad. His face was redder than Zinsser had ever seen it, and that was saying a great deal. "What pattern do you want?" he mumbled.

"Red six, white three," Zinsser answered at random, one eyebrow raised. Though Burning for some reason refused to meet Souljourner's hooded eyes, he held the palm card up for everyone to see. His fingers moved over it in two swift, practiced stroke-groups, and he nodded.

Zinsser knelt and threw, and the pattern came up.

Burning handed the card to Zinsser and, unable to bear Souljourner's gaze any longer, said, "The dice are gaffed, rigged—responsive to whatever is punched into the card. The card was fashioned by some of our LAW personnel—a group called the Aggregate—who have a way with teknics."

He lowered his eyes. "I manipulated all the throws you've made since the Pellhouse. I did it because I needed every edge I could get. Even in Alabaster. There were too many things riding on your doing what I needed you to do. I didn't want to trick you, but I could never find the right time to tell you."

There was no way to tell her what he really meant without facing her, so he took a deep breath and looked up. "No, that's wrong. I did want to trick you. But I felt like a shit about it. It turned my guts, and I'm glad I don't have to do it any more."

He stopped because she was smiling at him, not very reassuringly, it was true, but it wasn't what he'd expected at all.

" 'Love is blind.' Is that what you're moaning about?" Souljourner asked. "Do you have that stupid saying, too? Well, I'll tell you something, Redtails: love is not blind. It's wise and seeing. It sometimes lets things weigh more heavily than cold logic might. But that's because it's hot with perception and soars with passion. Compared to it, cold reason is blind, selfish, and frightened. You'll never find more perception or insight than from love. That's what made me let you use me and the dice."

"Use—" He almost choked on it. "Are you saying you knew? How long?"

"Since the day on the *Racknuts* when you called the right number without being able to see it from where you were sitting. I know. I checked later."

Zinsser looked up from where he was getting the Oceanic to respond to the patterns of dots, collaborating with it on a new numerical-geometric alphabet; then he grunted and went back to his experimentation, calling the numbers as Ghost threw the dice.

The Oceanic had a lot to answer for.

"The prisoner is dead, my liege," one of the Militerrors reported from alongside the torture device on which the muscle-car driver was racked—one of several who had been captured during the raid on the parking mounds north of the Hangwitch suspension bridge. As to the scores of cars themselves, they had apparently originated in the Trans-Bourne and had been driven north in haste under the direction of an Aquam named Cozmote.

"Who is this Cozmote?" Zone asked Rhodes, who was being held aloft in a four-carrier litter.

"An artificer who himself hails from the Trans-Bourne," Rhodes said while the dead driver was being removed from the rack. "A brilliant though irascible scoundrel. An early influence on my nephew, Purifyre, in fact."

Zone's eyes narrowed. "Mason's son."

Rhodes nodded. "Cozmote is thought to have been the brains behind the Styx Strait bridge, some say the brains behind Human Enlightenment itself."

Zone glanced at the dead man. "And now this Cozmote has apparently moved on the *GammaLAW*." He looked at Rhodes. "What's Cozmote's interest in the ship? Is he in competition with you and the rest of the Ean grandees?"

"He professes to be angered by our policies regarding slavery and Anathemites and cannibalism and such, but not to the point of rivalry. His interests lie in teknics and trade."

"The *GammaLAW* is one helluva 'teknic,' Rhodes. That means Cozmote is either a fool or even more crafty than he lets on."

Rhodes shrugged and cut his eyes to the rack. "I know no more than what the driver revealed. And no amount of torture can loosen the tongue of one who cannot speak." He brought his blunt fingertips to his lips. "I wonder . . ."

"Wonder what?" Zone pressed.

Rhodes came back to himself and straightened somewhat in the litter. "Some of the violence at Wall Water was made to appear to be the work of the DevOcean prophet Marrowbone and his followers. But it strikes me now that my nephew—a sworn enemy of DevOcean—may have worked a clever ruse."

Zone mulled it over for a moment. "Claude Mason is one of the people who never returned from Wall Water, Rhodes. If Cozmote and Purifyre are in league with him, they could pose a serious threat not only to the *GammaLAW* but to what's waiting at the New Alexandria lighthouse. We can't delay in getting there."

"Most of Cozmote's muscle cars are spent," one of the Militerrors said, "but we'll sort through them once more and cull the best of the lot."

Rhodes nodded. "At the same time I want scouts sent upriver to learn what's become of the ship."

Zone was about to concur, when he bit back his words. "We might be able to save your scouts the trip."

You're not curious to know if Cozmote succeeded in his assault?"

Zone sneered. "Of course I am. But first tell me if you still have the communications headset Commissioner Starkweather gave you."

"Why, yes, I do."

Rhodes had the headset delivered to Zone, who quickly assessed it. "The mate to this was in the hands of my allies when I escaped the ship," he explained after a moment. "At the risk of giving myself away, I might be able to communicate with my people . . . if they haven't been executed by now," he mumbled.

The headset had an integral camera, but Zone wasn't interested in sending visuals of himself to whoever was in possession of the mated set; he simply zeroed the cam function, pulled the rig on, and activated it. It took a long moment before anyone responded, but Zone immediately recognized Wetbar's voice at the receiving end, the interior of the ship's brig showing up on Zone's video-reception visor.

"Are we safe to talk?" he asked.

"Colonel!" WetBar said in a harsh whisper. "We figured you for dead. Where are you?"

"You don't need to know that right now. Just give me the short version of what's going on there."

"Roust is dead. The rest of us have been locked away since you made your break." The camera panned to reveal the faces of Kino and several others. "But everything's changed, Colonel. The ship's been surrendered to a force of Aquam pirates commanded by Mason, Purifyre, and some former LAW officer named Boon."

"Boon?" Zone interrupted. "Who the hell is he?"

"A member of the original *Scepter* team, from what we hear. The indigs call him Cozmote."

"Sonuvabitch," Zone muttered in genuine surprise.

He recalled the Science Side modules Mason had brought to Wall Water, allegedly to impress his son, Purifyre. Could they, along with Boon-Cozmote, have been in collusion from the start? He recalled, too, the burst Burning had sent from southern Scorpia. Burning had thought he was pursuing Ghost, when it was obviously Mason whom he had seen in Purifyre's company.

"What are their plans for the ship, Wetbar?" he said finally. "Is Boon thinking of setting himself up as head honcho?"

"Hard to call, Colonel. All we know now is that he's planning on taking the *GammaLAW* straight into the Amnion."

"Into the Amnion? Is he synaptshit?"

"The scuttle is that he's got it in for the Oceanic in a big way. He's planning to put an end to it."

And the goddamn Oceanic knows it, Zone thought. The mist

that had swept over the land and river only the previous day, the rumors about the crash of one of the Laputas in the Scourlands, the slight but persistent tremors that had Rhodes's Descrier in a near panic . . . Zone wondered if Mason was one of the people who knew about Endgame. He had been in Rhodes's bedchambers during the Grand Attendance; he had to have seen Smicker's bust open. And soon the *GammaLAW* would be passing by the New Alexandria lighthouse on her way to the Amnion—

"Colonel, what do you want us to do?" Wetbar asked.

"Just sit tight," Zone said. "We'll be waiting for you downriver."

CHAPTER
THIRTY-FIVE

After more than thirty-six hours of reassigning duties, tinkering with the ship's wetdown system, and adjusting to his new circumstance as a captive, Quant took the *GammaLAW* downriver once more. Below Yclept, Lake Ea, fed by two tributaries, widened appreciably. If the ship had been his own, he would have greeted the surfeit of navigable water with relief and joy, but every kilometer that passed under the triple hulls brought them closer to the deep waters of the Amnion.

Quant refused to reflect on the attitude of the ship's company toward his apparent surrender to Boon and his pirates. Discipline and respect were the keys to commanding a vessel at sea, and he'd been obliged to jettison the hard-won loyalty he had earned. At Boon's request he reported to a filling station where vile-smelling synome antagonist was being transferred from kegs to the *GammaLAW*'s pumping system.

"What exactly do you expect to happen when the Oceanic gets a taste of your concoction?" Quant asked.

"It will replicate," Boon said distractedly. "The vector is a kind of virus that will invade Oceanic cells and refuse all chemical cues to capitulate. In about three weeks it will have spread to every corner of the Amnion."

"And the Oceanic?" Quant pursued.

"With luck, it becomes fish. Highly intelligent ones in some cases but discrete organisms in any event, no longer capable of the sort of recombinant operations or metafunctioning

Aquamarine has grown used to. In short, the Oceanic will do what marine life everywhere else does: swim, propagate, and feed on one another."

Quant stood rooted in the wind, thinking about the fantastic bestiary of the Oceanic going into a sudden, eventually global feeding frenzy.

"In time a food chain will shake out a new ecological balance," Boon was saying, "but the Amnion will become a human domain, just like the land." He looked at Quant. "That should appeal to you, Skipper. Just think, to be able to sail Aquamarine in this ship . . . I always assumed it was your secret plan."

Shrewd, Quant thought, though he avoided meeting the remark head-on. "Have you considered that the *GammaLAW* could be broken apart or even pulled under before this toxin of yours takes effect?"

Boon smirked. "Is this feigned stupidity? Do you think I don't know about the measure one icebreaking system?"

It had occurred to Quant that he might, but he had hoped differently. "*How* did you know, Mr. Boon? You couldn't have learned all you know from Mason. Besides, it's obvious that years of planning have gone into this operation. So who provided you with the *GammaLAW*'s specs? Was it Commissioner Starkweather or some other AlphaLAW? Did Cal Lightner or other Preservationist Hierarchs arrange this?"

Boon dismissed it with a wave of his hand. "You've no doubt heard of the Quantum College, Quant."

Quant's jaw dropped a fraction. "But—"

"A . . . representative of the college has been in contact with Aquamarine almost from the start—back when the mission was still Haven's wet dream. As far as I can figure, it was a shot in the dark by the college, but fortunately, I was here to monitor the transmissions. I've had months to work out how to make the best use of your ship."

Months, Quant told himself. Yes, a transmission from Periapt would have preceded the *Sword*'s arrival by at least that much if it had been sent just after the selection of the *Matsya* as the mission's on-the-cheap command post.

"The college saw to it that the *Matsya* was chosen for the mission," Boon continued, "in the same way that it covered its tracks by assigning the mission gamma status, which meant a minimum of peeking and poking by LAW or Lyceum oversight committees. Granted, things would have been a lot easier if a fleet of bombers or a flotilla of submersible carriers had been delivered here, but the *GammaLAW* will do nicely."

"What about the Roke?" Quant asked. "Destroy the Oceanic and you may be stripping Aquamarine of the protection it has enjoyed for baseline-centuries. The Roke will annihilate the very people you're hoping to elevate."

Boon shook his head. "Like I told Haven, the Roke don't concern me. My fight is with the Oceanic." His look hardened. "You don't know the half of it, Quant."

Quant waited, but Boon didn't explain. "I know this much: You're going to have to begin untying more of my people if you want measure one."

Boon gave him a hangman's grin. "You're the captain." He handed over Quant's command headset.

Quant managed to swallow what he'd been about to say and returned to the bridge. By the time he arrived, Boon had called for a test run of the wetdown system. On all decks, nozzles gushed and everyone hunched his shoulders, waiting for the rain of stinking compound, but Boon had his humorous side: it was rainwater that fell on everyone.

Quant began to accept the fact that Boon had seen to all contingencies. With the ship making ten knots downriver, she would be likely to slip out into the deeps of the Amnion by nightfall.

Long before the enormous lighthouse at New Alexandria came into view, the sky over the sea put on a flickering, rumbling light show, as if an artillery duel of every conceivable ordnance and energy were occurring. Immense, moaning winds rose up out of nowhere to assault the ship from every conceivable direction.

By the time the top of the lighthouse was sighted from the highest lookout position, the river's turbulence had also changed in a way Quant hadn't yet experienced on Ea. A surging, quirky chop slashed the ship as it forged through heavier water. All the while the sky continued to pulse and coruscate, filling the air with the odor of ozone and boiled-off seawater.

With the *GammaLAW* nearing the wide mouth of the river, the crew again prepared to crank up the ship's decontamination wetdown system. But first there was something to attend to: Boon had ordered a stop at an ancient road that accessed the lighthouse itself, where Mason and Purifyre's second, Ballyhoot, disembarked for reasons that were left unexplained despite a palpable intrigue surrounding their leave-taking. Then Quant took the ship under the enormous Optimant-built shrine gate that nearly bridged the river and out to sea.

Selected members of the ship's company had been confined to compartments, but Dextra had persuaded Boon to allow her to suffer her captivity on the bow. The entire mission had been undertaken to establish contact with Aquamarine's marine overseer, and because of Boon's mad scheme, she might have only one chance to do so. If they were going out into the Amnion, she wanted to be the first to feel whatever the Oceanic threw at them. Purifyre and several of his Anathemite cohorts escorted her there personally and stood guard.

Out beyond the remains of Turret *Musashi* the foredeck breakwater was a broad, flat V partition, shoulder-high to Dextra, for protection against the most extreme weather. However, one was supposed to stand in the lee of it—sternside— as opposed to squatting atop the apex like some graying figurehead.

"Aren't you being overly dramatic?" Purifyre asked archly.

"Purifyre, I still feel that we can strike a deal with the Oceanic, and believe me when I tell you that I make a *living* striking deals."

She was still unsure of Purifyre, but betraying that uncertainty wasn't going to do her much good, any more than was worrying about Tonii, Quant, or the others. She reined in her focus and concentrated on Mason's son as if he were a tie-breaking-vote holder or a reluctant news source. Having seen him in two guises now, she sensed there were others, as well. Stern as a Manipulant's sergeant-major, Hammerstone—as some of the boarders called him—wouldn't be easy to reach. But the votary of Human Enlightenment couldn't have been entirely subsumed.

"My wrists are bleeding from these damn ropes," she went on. "Have you a poultice of some sort?"

She tried to sound like an Aquam asking for his ministrations, but in fact it was her thick offworld accent that somehow took him off guard. A change came over him, and he gazed at her differently. When his fingertips went to the trickles of blood on her forearms, his hands looked gentle, as they had that night at the Grand Attendance, despite the gloves he'd worn.

"Who gave you your healing touch?" she asked lightly. "Or were you born with it?"

"I have Cozmote to thank for some of it."

"Been sort of a surrogate father to you, has he?"

"I won't deny it."

"And Mason? Have you any feelings for him at all?"

"He has earned my respect these past few days. I can never feel toward him as I would toward a father who raised me, but I begin to accept his love more each day."

"What are he and Ballyhoot planning to do at the lighthouse, Purifyre? Why isn't he here with you?"

"My father returned to Aquamarine for my sake, but in order

to accomplish that, he made a deal with others who have their own agenda."

"What are you talking about? What others?"

"The Quantum College."

"Mason?" She thought back to his daring escape from the Blades on Periapt and to the evening of the Lyceum ball, when he had been picked up by a pair of Abraxas Warrantors for possible illegal cyberinterface. And she thought about Yatt, who had done so much under-the-table work to assemble the GammaLAW mission. "What's all this about a separate agenda? What would the Quantum College want from Aquamarine?"

"An end to the Cyberplagues. They had their beginnings here, perhaps—as Cozmote believes—at the hands of the Optimants themselves, who were on the verge of doing what he will soon do: sunder the Oceanic."

Dextra tried to take it in. "What's in the lighthouse?"

"An Optimant computer that may house the cure to the Plagues." With that, Purifyre snugged her bonds, wringing a cry from her, and turned to walk away.

"You won't be able to hold all the parts of yourself together much longer, Purifyre!" she called to his back. "Healer, prophet, warlord, son. Some of them will have to go. Which parts are you willing to give up?"

He whirled on her, and the warlord in him almost made him lay the back of his spiked gauntlet across her face. Dextra couldn't prevent a scream from escaping her. But then he stopped, and for a moment his face was like a holo-screen flicking through channels. The blow never came, and he strode away once more, staggering somewhat, leaning on the breakwater. Dextra tried to think of something to say, but there was no calling him back.

Turning into the wind, she saw the open sea before *Gamma-LAW's* plunging bows, an endless landscape of black knife-edge ridges throwing off hurricanes of foam, made ghastly by the light effects racing across water and sky. And she thought, Is there *any* dealing with the creature who reigns here?

Memories of his final night on Aquamarine tore at Mason as he and Ballyhoot hurried toward the hundred-meter-high Optimant-built lighthouse, abandoned twenty baseline-years earlier, when Skipjack Rhodes, Incandessa's father, had moved his family and clan to Lake Ea to corule with his cousin at Wall Water. The fisherfolk who lived in the area had retreated inland when word had reached them of the *GammaLAW*'s coming.

Prongbush had sprung up where there had once been lawn, and glassgrass poked through cracks in the walkway. Gone, too, was the ring of shanties and lean-tos that had huddled against the lighthouse on its windward side both for physical support and for questionable security. The rains were worse on that side during the Big Drench, but the leeward face of the tower was where slops from above had been dumped.

Short of the main entrance, whose whamboo gate now swung in the wind and where—in Skipjack's days sentries had once stood, Mason stopped to eye the place where he had kicked aside the toylike gizmo Hippo Nolan had cobbled together to amuse himself: a mollywood cart no bigger than a child's wagon, propelled by slings, galvani stones, and living tissue rocker arms—Aquamarine's first muscle car.

Passing through the gate into the tower's debris-strewn interior, Mason paused again to switch on the field light he had carried from the ship. The Big Sere being in full broil, the base of the tower was a sweat box. Even without Aquam body odors and cooking smells, the air swarmed with bite-mites, bloodflits, teardrinker midges, and earborers. Air circulation from the central stairwell and two sets of gallery doors at the top did little to cool a building designed for central climate control—which had gone off-line two centuries earlier. Some relief would be found on the promenade deck thirty stories above them.

Perhaps forty meters in diameter, the ground floor, though heavily garrisoned, had housed casbahs of unhampered trade and regulated vice. Lowest in the pecking order, people of few means had lived and worked there. Images from that final night onworld came to Mason: an Anathemite child smothered to death, its swaddlings hiding all evidence of the defects or mutations that had doomed it to death; feuding women, blindfolded and left with wrists roped together, settling their differences in a fight with maoriwood bastinadoes; the ritual sacrifice of a windle yearling to propitiate the Oceanic and avoid storm surge and tsunami . . .

Skipjack's artificers had installed a crude elevator hoist where a central-shaft people mover had been sent crashing to rubble, along with its passengers, by a cybervirus. Hippo had improved the rickety contraption by installing a braking mechanism on the jute hoist cables, but both the cable and the basket had long since gone to rot. There was no option but to take the grand staircase that corkscrewed through the long axis of the place.

Mason and Ballyhoot climbed past rotundas that had been common parlors, rialtos, casinos, lovers' lanes, confessionals, musicians' tourneys, and poets' jousts. Mason recalled cooked-meat vendors offering delicacies prepared from the flesh of convicted felons; shamans making minor adjustments to the skull-deforming frames worn by infants; rings of older, married men and women, seniors in their families, masters of their trades, and whatnot shooting craps with pairs of Holy Rollers.

Mazes of living and working spaces had been built against the outside wall of the lighthouse's upper levels—subdivided by planks of mollywood, jellywillow, and yussa or weavings of cansceharl flax or whackweed jute—while the rotunda around the stairwell and hoist had been left open for socializing, haggling, and light artisanry. Mason experienced aromatic memories of gooner, sot-mead, and whomp; puffed thudgum rolled in poi-pod husks, quobacco, whackweed, bash . . . He could almost hear the voices of the *wari* players beckoning him to join in some penny-ante game. "Handsome Visitant!" they would shout to him—what with the cosmetic perfection of his face and his long auburn queue, the handsomest man on Aqua-marine, many said. Part of him had basked in the adulation, and part of him had winced at the sham of it.

When at last he arrived at the doors to the promenade deck, Mason hesitated. Outside was where he had said his good-byes to Incandessa, eight months pregnant with their child. Outside was where Hippo Nolan had come running to tell him about Boon, off at Execution Dock trying to talk a group of Conscious Voices out of suiciding in protest at the imminent departure of the *Scepter*.

"Saint Boon," Hippo had called him.

Impatient with him, Ballyhoot tugged him onto the panoramic sweep of promenade, where the wind assaulted them once more and the sky above the wave-stacked Amnion seemed to be in a dress rehearsal for the apocalypse. Fighting the wind and with scarcely a glance at the lionwood banquette where he and Incandessa had sat, they rounded the broad curve of the summit and crossed the deck's worn and fissured jasper tiles to the stairway that led up into the former quarters of the ruling family—what had once been the lamp chamber.

The chamber had been emptied of all but the cyclopean lamp itself, dark for centuries. Ballyhoot shrugged out of her backpack and handed Mason his whatty, its assortment of connectors and adapters, and finally the cybercaul Ghost had discovered at Wall Water, which Mason gingerly slipped over his head.

"We have arrived," Yatt said to him. *"It is here, before us— ENDGAME."*

Mason glanced up at the lamp, which slowly tipped toward him and began to unfold like a technological flower in slow-motion blossom.

"Endgame!" Yatt said.

CHAPTER
THIRTY-SIX

Boon's guard shifts were looking worse and worse as the waters rose. No Aquam were used to ordinary seas, let alone the kind of moil being flung at the *GammaLAW*. Even some of Quant's own navy vets looked queasy, and he himself had to consciously quell his stomach. The months-long journey from Periapt had robbed them of their sea legs. Much to his dismay, one Anathemite vomited in a corner of the bridge and on himself. Only sling-guns and sword points prevented Quant from throwing him out bodily.

Having gone into the wide mouth of Ea, the ship was obliged to shoulder her way against heavy waves. Detector sweeps and lookout reports indicated that the Aquam had fled the area around the lighthouse. Except for Ballyhoot and Mason, there wasn't a soul within kilometers of the coastline, and Quant spared a moment to wish he were one of them—just a simple Aquam hotfooting it for the highest ground he could find. Not that anyone clinging to the peak of Aquamarine's tallest mountain would be saved if the *GammaLAW*'s passage into the Amnion brought about a deluge of biblical proportions.

The ship had one thing going for it, a mere sliver of an edge: augmented by the flood from the dam burst, the flow of the river had extended the boundary between fresh and salt water. Ordinarily in the Big Sere, salt—and perhaps the long arm of the Oceanic—might have penetrated into the estuary itself, but for the moment confrontation with the Oceanic would be postponed until the *GammaLAW* passed into the littoral proper.

Even with the ship's SWATH sea-keeping abilities, Quant would have had second thoughts about attempting the seas he found waiting for him. With the ship as damaged as she was, he might not have even taken his command out. But he knew Boon wasn't bluffing about slaying mission members if his orders weren't followed.

Quant divided his time between peering worriedly through the bridge windshields and snapping orders to his talker. The crew had managed to get the ship battened down, though a problem arose when Quant ordered the rigging of lifelines across the decks. From a command terminal somewhere forward, Boon countermanded. In Quant's own terminal screen the former LAW lieutenant appeared bloodless and hollow-eyed. Quant knew instantly that he was suffering mal de mer about as badly as anyone he'd ever seen. Still, that didn't keep Quant from ranting. "Are you blind to what these seas can do to us? We have to rig lifelines!"

Boon merely shook his head. "No lifelines. Everyone stays inside, except for those required to be on deck."

"Then at least let the medics pass out anti-nausea drugs and—"

"No drugs! We don't need—"

Boon's gorge had been rising, and Quant saw the first part of his upchuck just before Boon broke the connection. Too bad, he mused. He had hoped to turn the tables by sedating some or most of Boon's forces.

With the waves sliding and clashing like black mountains, he called for measure one icebreaking pressure. The super-speed turbopumps—ironically, one of the few nonessential systems that hadn't been cannibalized—thrummed the entire ship, their aquajets supplying new dynamic and motion forces to deal with. All around the *GammaLAW* steam rose from the water as if she were sailing in her own personal thermal vent.

Engine indicators rose as the reactors burned hot. Seawater sucked in through keel vents was heated almost to boiling in moments and sent gushing from the ship to all sides and below. Quant had used the measure one system in trips to both of Periapt's polar regions, melting boiling channels through pack ice and anything else in his way, and he had given thought to what a horrific antipersonnel weapon it would make. But he had never imagined venturing into the bosom of Aquamarine's world-sea with nothing more than fire and water as his weapons.

He had tried to convince Boon of the danger of overheating the hull, particularly in warm waters, but Boon knew all about the composition of the SWATH's hull.

Farther into the mouth, in waves that had traveled the fetch of the planet's circumference, there was as much foaming dirty white as there was black. Even more astounding were the energy anomalies that began to boil across and above the surface of the sea. Whatever was going on, the Oceanic was most certainly displeased by the intrusion.

"Come about to a southerly heading and increase speed," Boon relayed suddenly. "I know you can get at least five more knots out of her."

Quant nodded to the conning officer, and engine turns were increased. The ship's bows bit into walls of swell. The helmsman fought the wheel's servos against unimaginable currents. Someone was reporting that the wetdown system was on standby when all at once the horizon was fractured by countless branching bolts of lightning. Sky and sea seemed to surge toward one another like reuniting lovers, like planets in collision, gravity pulling parts of them together ahead of the main embrace.

Yet Quant could see that it wasn't really the sea flying up from its ancient bed or the sky settling into the waters; it was some mustering of the darks and flashes in each. The sea was as lightning-shot as the clouds and as swirled with storm brume and fluxes of wrack. In moments the flows of angelfire and hellglow began to move toward the *GammaLAW*. Any doubt about the Oceanic's awareness of the ship was erased. Waves seemed to walk the vessel's way as she neared the deadly quarantine margin the One Who Watches had maintained since time out of mind. Radiant phenomena of all sorts streamed toward her like energy weapons. In among them came vast dark shadows, as well.

Beyond any come-about point, Quant purged his mind of moral concerns. No sling-gun was needed to force his hand now; indeed, he didn't even wait for Boon's word.

"Hit the wetdown," he commanded. "Everything we've got."

Klaxons sounded, and the PAs echoed his order. Boon's doomsday concoction was fountained high and shot out in great flat circles as things in the Amnion converged on the ship from all sides.

Down at the breakwater Dextra fully expected the light effects, radiation surges, whatever they were, to penetrate the superheated area emitted by the *GammaLAW*'s icebreaking system. All she could do was trust to the ship's all-too-thin insulating layers. But the swiftest-moving of the Amnion's coursing light swarms began to turn aside at a distance she estimated to be right at the kill zone of the boiling seas. She supposed that meant they weren't really pure energy at all, but living things. At the same time shadows swirled in from every direction.

The first shadow was a batlike form that mantaed through the water, followed by some sort of winged tail. While fully half the size of the flight deck, it, too, veered away from the roiling water; likewise, the creature behind it—an even larger form that seemed to be a mass of intertwined serpents or tentacles with no true center.

Dextra considered what creatures that size could do to the ship. She'd have given anything for depth charges, even one lousy pulsejet torpedo. But it occurred to her that the creatures hadn't breached—hadn't emerged even partway to purge, as a Periapt billowmat would—like an old Terran whale. Perhaps it meant that the Oceanic's avenues of attack were limited to the subsurface.

More shapes were teeming farther out from the ship: as narrow and sleek as underwater rockets, as bulbous as buoyed amoebas, floating like great lily pads just beneath the surface. They weren't merely keeping their distance; they were merging, coalescing, and rising from the water.

Out there beyond the superheated zone, shapes that put Dextra more in mind of construction towers than living entities were starting to penetrate the waves—a surfacing monsterscape of spires, domes, and multiform antenna arrays. With the waves continuing to surge and cool the fusion heaters' output, the new forms—by dint of their incredible size—would perhaps be able to overcome the measure four's liquid shield.

Dextra whirled to Purifyre, who was overseeing the wetdown system. "We've got to turn back! Whatever these creatures are, they're going to be all over us in minutes!"

"The wetdown system is up to operating pressure," Purifyre said evenly, even though his grip quaked on the stanchion he clung to.

Dextra saw that it was true. The men manning the hoses were pumping the synome antagonist in a widening pool that mixed with the steaming water and raised yellow clouds. At any other time, its thick smell probably would have made her faint.

"You think a little puddle of repellent is going to hold *those* things back?"

Purifyre ignored her and swung to one of his confederates. "Alert Cozmote: the icebreaking system can be shut down. We won't be needing it anymore."

When the pumping ceased, everyone in the vicinity of the breakwater observed a moment of silence as the still-rising mountain range of Oceanic forms was carried forward on the swift current. *GammaLAW*'s bow bounced lower into great troughs and was taking longer to shake off the water.

"Purifyre, you've got to put a stop to this!" Dextra screamed, shaking soaking-wet hair from her face. "Whichever way this goes, Boon is sealing Aquamarine's fate. If we die, LAW will return and you'll be absorbed into Periapt's fold. And if the synome antagonist succeeds in differentiating the Oceanic, all you'll have done is killed off the planetary ecology!" She groped desperately. "Human Enlightenment, Purifyre. Remember your oath!"

She could see his lips move, forming words she couldn't hear. But just when she thought she had him, he turned a look of utter fury on her and went back to honchoing the pumping operations.

GammaLAW rode one last long, high swell as the Oceanic ramparts closed in, their very bulk protecting the ship from the angry smashing of the waters. A moment's shelter, Dextra thought, from the metaorganism that would send the *GammaLAW* to the bottom or disassemble it and every man and woman aboard. Then the leading edge of the first creature—black and convoluted hide as coarse-textured and pockmarked as newly cooled lava—touched the growing swath of Boon's concoction.

The creature stopped in a way that a human might after encountering an electrical field. Dextra had learned enough about boat-handling to know that stupendous forces must have gone into halting the thing dead in the water like that—all from its first tentative contact with the killing fluid.

Where the chemical had touched the creature, an angry radiant blotch began to spread—as if a welding torch were being held to it—and the thick hide began to disappear, turning to a sloughing goo, individual globs of which were splashing into the Amnion. From the sea where the surrendered cells of the thing fell, the water foamed and seethed, shot through with occasional lights and roiling slicks of stuff, sometimes tiny individual shapes that were themselves coming apart.

Boon's mad genius notwithstanding, she hadn't really thought the synome antagonist would work. She would have bet that the Oceanic was capable of overcoming anything—even an Optimant-created toxin. But it was working. The first creature couldn't seem to coordinate any effective reaction. Dextra supposed that its nervous system was under attack, the antagonist's effects traveling along it like an explosion along a det cord. And though the Oceanic must have figured out at chemical-reaction speed what it was facing, it was apparently helpless, even with all the constituents available to it. It was as if Boon had discovered the universal solvent—an acid capable of dissolving *anything*.

Sundry parts of the Oceanic were falling back, but the first and then the second were wallowing helplessly in the yellow stuff. More, the wake of synome antagonist was spreading faster than the ship's pumping could account for. The only explanation was that the soup of catabolizing Oceanic cells themselves was producing more. The Oceanic's very cells had become its worst enemy.

Dextra knew now why Boon had been so confident and why he hadn't simply dumped cauldrons of the antagonist into the rivers or surf or even fired it far out to sea with catapults or steam cannons. The ship's pumping system was spreading the chemical faster than the Oceanic could deal with it. The aggregate intellect and godlike powers would soon be lost forever.

As she watched the myriad creatures fall back in panicky disarray, Dextra saw her plans for communicating with the Oceanic and resolving the Roke Conflict fade. She felt a sudden overwhelming grief for Aquamarine. But not Boon, evidently, and not Purifyre. The *GammaLAW* continued to surge forward, breasting waves no longer menacing her with capsizing. In fact, her bows were riding high—higher even than in calm waters.

Suddenly, however, a great shadow passed across Eyewash, and yells went up from everywhere on deck and on the openworks. Hands pointed. Even as Dextra spun to look, there was a moaning of displaced air and the throbbing of immense engines. She craned her head back to see a stupendous shape of rounded streamlines—a thing with lifting-body characteristics on a vast scale—descending majestically from west to east, headed straight for the Amnion.

That the craft was Roke went without saying.

CHAPTER
THIRTY-SEVEN

To the south, perhaps a hundred kilometers from shore, the Oceanic had thrown up a ridge of manifestations that pierced the low underbelly of the darkening though lightning-split sky. The *GammaLAW* was out there somewhere, certainly corralled, perhaps capsized and already being disassembled—unless Boon's synome antagonist was having the desired effect. Moments earlier something huge had shot across the sky, moving west to east, low over the Amnion. But Mason had no time for events in the outside world; his attention was riveted on the exchange between Yatt and the Optimant computer that had telescoped from the opened rear of the lighthouse lamp.

Sling-gun in hand, Ballyhoot watched him from the doorway to the broad, circular space that had once belonged to Skipjack Rhodes and his brood. Mason had the cybercaul masking his comely features and wore the whatty on his wrist, standing beneath the transformed Beforetimer machine as if before an altar. She could still recall the hushed conversation Cozmote and Mason had had in Cozmote's Trans-Bourne laboratory, where uncovered Beforetimer secrets had allowed him to fashion the toxin the Visitants' ship was now fountaining into the Amnion.

"The monstrous egos of the Beforetimers stood in the way of their accepting that Aquamarine's dominant life-form was and would always be the Oceanic," Cozmote had told his former shipmate. "That fact was in their faces constantly, and because of it they created the antagonist."

The Beforetimers had been in the middle of a planetwide debate about whether to loose their toxin when the so-called Cyberplagues had struck or, more accurately, been loosed, accidentally or preemptively, by some of the Beforetimers to prevent others from carrying out their plan to sunder the Oceanic. Plagues themselves had originally been developed for use against Old Earth, from which the Beforetimers feared retribution for having taken with them all knowledge of advanced teknics when they had commenced their long journey to Aquamarine.

Mason suddenly burst out laughing—a head-back, bitter laugh that was muffled somewhat by the soft hood, which, what with its eyecups and mouth bowl, imparted something of an insectile appearance to its wearer.

"Mason, what is it?" Ballyhoot asked, limping as she approached.

Mason made the eyecups transparent so that he could see her even while continuing to communicate with the Beforetimer machine. "Oh, the beauty of it, Ballyhoot," he said with apparent amusement. "I hope you're in the mood to laugh with me, because someone has to share the irony of this moment."

She hung the sling-gun over her shoulder and swung him around to face her. "Mason, get a grip."

His laughter had sent tears coursing down his cheeks. "Boon had it wrong, Ballyhoot, a hundred eighty degrees wrong. It's true: the Cyberplagues were created here. But it wasn't the Optimants who inadvertently or deliberately sprung them on the rest of human space. It was the Oceanic."

Ballyhoot shook her head in confusion.

"The Optimants were actually in contact with the Oceanic. They had worked out a kind of lingua franca that was effected by means of chemical messengers. But they had left it to their AIs to further the dialogue, and it was the AIs that were in a quandary as to what to do about the Oceanic; it was the AIs that couldn't bear that Aquamarine had an overseer more powerful than they could ever become.

"But the Oceanic saw through their envy and jealousy. Instinctually, it felt that it had nothing to fear from humans, but it worried that the AIs would machinate to release the synome antagonist the Optimants had developed. It recognized that the way to safeguard itself—as well as kill two birds with one stone—was to use the Cyberplagues the Optimants had intended to target against Earth and cripple artificial life throughout the galaxy. In contact with the AIs, the Oceanic created and dispatched a virus into the Optimants' computational ecology, encoding the already fashioned Plagues and releasing them."

Ballyhoot tried to make sense of what he was saying. "Does this machine have the cure?" she asked at last.

Mason uttered a short laugh. "Endgame isn't a panacea for the Cyberplagues. It's nothing more than a repository of data on how the Plagues came about and how they came to be spread. To save itself, it dropped out of the debate short of the Oceanic's preemptive strike. Along with the computer in Smicker's bust and a half dozen others scattered across the planet, Endgame had intuited what was coming."

"Then there is no cure for the Cyberplagues?"

"Oh, I'm more certain than ever there's a cure, Ballyhoot. But the Oceanic holds the only key."

Ballyhoot turned to gaze out the open doorway.

"You see how wonderfully ironic it is?" Mason said. "Boon hasn't a clue what he's about to do." He tapped his forefinger against the side of his head. "After all the secret scheming and intense planning, after all the messages sent across space to Aquamarine, Boon is about to scramble the answer the thing in my head came here to find. This whole mission is nothing but a major fuckup, Ballyhoot. I suppose it's possible that the Aquam will be spared LAW's takeover for another half century

or so, and Boon will certainly have had his vengeance on the
Oceanic, but I wonder how long Aquamarine itself has to live."

Ballyhoot turned from the view in time to see Mason pull off
the 'caul. "What do we do now?"

He shrugged, then aimed a glance at the huge lamp. "Go
down to the beach. Wait for the ship to return. Not much else
that could go wrong at this point—"

Hearing faint movement behind him, Mason whirled and
saw a bruised Zone standing in the door, a 'chettergun in hand.

Zone grinned. "I'll take that 'caul now, Claude."

The Roke craft was larger than any human-built shuttle or
OTV. With the fact of its appearance to absorb, Quant was
somehow further astonished by the realization that while
it looked to be under control, the ship wasn't even trying for
a land touchdown. With a flare-out of control surfaces, it
plunged deliberately into the domain of the Oceanic.

Ineluctably, his mind came back to the *GammaLAW* and the
predicament of the SWATH's complement. Hurrying out onto
Vultures' Row, he saw Boon, Purifyre, and several dozen
others cowering on the foredeck as the Roke craft disappeared
beneath the steepling waves not five kilometers from the bows
of the ship. From the look of things, even Boon was transfixed.
Quant did the unthinkable and left the bridge, if only to bask in
the pirates' utter consternation.

Spying Quant as he neared the breakwater, Boon drew the
flechette pistol he had taken from Quant himself. Purifyre, too,
saw Quant coming and barked orders to the two Anathemites
who were carelessly escorting the captain. Drilled in obedience
to the Human Enlightenment *rishi*, the pair snapped out of
their trances, steeled against additional doomsday shock
waves from the sky and sea. Even then, the sound wake of
another Roke aerospace vessel reached them. A sphere was
approaching from the southeast, flattening its angle of descent
toward the *GammaLAW* and the waves, but it never arrived.

Arrested by a conspiracy of sea and sky while it was still twenty kilometers out, the vessel came apart in a roiling of orange flame and black smoke.

Quant searched the sky for others even as the guards were taking hold of his arms. Far off to the southwest something resembling a very pregnant arrowhead was skimming and slowing low over the swells, preparatory to submersion. Straining against the hands that held him, Quant shouted to Boon, who had the edge of one hand to his brow as the Roke craft cut across the *GammaLAW*'s bows and submerged. "Boon, we have to try to come about. Secure those damn pumps and help me get this ship back upriver!"

Boon turned, shaking his head. "We keep going."

At that, Purifyre ordered his followers to return to their duties of hosing the synome antagonist into the seething waters.

"So much the better if the Roke keep the Oceanic occupied," Boon added.

"Use your head, man," Quant said. "This changes everything. Boon, *think*! The Roke have broken their moratorium. This may be our chance to summit with them and the Oceanic."

" 'Summit'?"

Boon said it with obvious revulsion. Quant knew nothing of Boon's background, but it was clear that the word had had the opposite effect from what he'd intended. He knew, too, that Boon had grown far too used to overcoming obstacles to admit error or accept failure.

A fourth Roke vessel appeared in the sky and disappeared into the Amnion. But where Quant would not have been surprised to see thermonuclear fireballs blossom from the whitecaps or great volcanoes of water spew out spacecraft debris, there was only the rising, restless water.

Raising the 'chettergun, Boon turned his gaze on some of the *GammaLAW* crew members who were helping to man the wetdown pumps. His eye fell on Tonii, who was standing near the starboard rail. Quant understood what Boon was about to do and bellowed for him to stop.

"Then return to the bridge, Quant!" Boon's face was red with rage. "Keep this ship under weigh or so help me God, I'll kill ten of your people every hour!"

Members of the crew howled angrily and almost attacked their captors, except that the Aquam were avid, in the frightening turn of events, for the certainty of a target to shoot at. The Exts simply looked on stonily, even Lod. It was only war, nothing new.

Quant eyed Tonii briefly, then whirled and stormed back toward the bridge, already calling out hoarsened orders to his crew to stand down. He was suddenly so preoccupied with thoughts of the world of hurt he would someday inflict on Boon that it took him a moment to realize who was keeping pace beside him watchfully.

"Purifyre." When Quant stopped to face him, a half dozen Aquam leveled sling guns at him. Still, Quant finished in a low growl. "Commend your soul to whatever god you worship, Son, because sooner or later I'm going to kill you and your commander."

Purifyre's grotesque features arranged themselves into a smirk. "You're wasting valuable time, *Skipper*."

Quant supposed he should be more politic, perhaps try to get Mason's son to see sane reason. But all he could add was, "You, Boon, and your bastard turncoat father—"

Quant, Purifyre, and the guards were suddenly flung forward. Quant spun around to find the bows lifted out of the water as an immense something rose beneath them. His first thought was that the *GammaLAW* had run up onto one of the Roke vessels, but he soon realized that the Oceanic was responsible—some part of it that obviously hadn't been affected by Boon's synome antagonist.

Sound and deck vibrations told him that the bridge crew had reversed the engines in an effort to back off from whatever was surfacing. But all the *GammaLAW*'s shrieking and moaning did no good. Neither did the sling-gun quarrels and flechettes fired by Boon and his cohorts.

Hulking all across the bows now was a spiked, gelid sphere whose above-water portion was already the size of the ship and whose submerged part might, for all Quant knew, fill the abyss. Its projections—opaque, seemingly protoplasmic spines that radiated in all directions—held their shape even without the support of the seawater. Darker contours and brume moved and shifted inside it in what, given more light, might have been colors.

One brave Aquam team washed a thick stream of the synome antagonist across the face of the giant diatom or radiolarian to no effect whatsoever. As it moved forward, engulfing the breakwater, Boon's men broke and ran.

Quant saw Purifyre come back to his feet after having been thrown headlong by the impact. Glaring insanely at the Oceanic form welling up over the ship's foredecks, he plucked an Ext grenade loose from his battle harness and launched himself across the deck. Tossed high, the grenade sank into the diatom, losing shape as it penetrated and then dissolving into a mist, from what Quant could make out.

Boon took hold of Purifyre before he could waste a second grenade. "No use!" Quant heard him shout.

Knocked off his feet once more as the diatom started to bear the *GammaLAW* stern-first back toward the Scorpian coast, he began to feel a certain resentment, an almost childish pique, that his vessel's excellent sea-keeping characteristics and sea-kindliness were suddenly irrelevant. On the plus side, however, the bridge crew wasn't going to have to contend with the difficult business of steering in reverse. Quant swung to Boon and Purifyre, who were leading Dextra and some of the others aft. "Seems the Roke vessels aren't distracting the Oceanic, after all, Mr. Boon," he shouted. "In fact, I'd wager to say that they came down the well to *rescue* it!"

* * *

Ballyhoot didn't hesitate for a moment. Filed teeth bared, she flung herself at Zone. Even in his damaged state, the Ext was too fast for her. He didn't bother to use the 'chettergun but relied on his feet, which caught Ballyhoot in the side of the head and sent her tumbling down the stairs onto the promenade. Mason could tell by Zone's glance down those stairs that Ballyhoot wasn't going to trouble them for some time.

"The 'caul, Mason," he repeated. "Don't make me shoot you."

Behind Zone a hemispheric bulge had appeared in the Amnion, like the rounded hump of an immense sea creature, making for the mouth of Ea.

With Yatt screaming in his head, Mason extended the cybercaul to Zone. As to what had brought the Ext to the lighthouse, Mason could only assume that Zone had observed some of the holodata Smicker's bust had displayed and had put two and two together. Still, Zone was obviously in the dark about a few things.

"The 'caul won't do you any good, Colonel," Mason said. "It's configured to my neuralwares."

Zone merely motioned him aside. "I'll be the judge of that, handsome."

Mason stepped away from the reconfigured lamp. "Besides, if you've come for Endgame, you're in for a disappointment unless you're prepared to strike a deal with the Oceanic."

Zone tried to read Mason's expression. "What the hell are you babbling about?"

"The Oceanic released the Cyberplagues. It was in biochemical contact with Optimant AIs. Some of them were plotting to kill the Oceanic."

"Like your friend Boon's trying to do now?"

Mason was confused. He had heard about Zone's bold escape from the GammaLAW, but that had occurred days before the raid on the ship. So how had Zone learned about Boon?

And who, in fact, had guided him downriver from Fluter Delve?

"Mason," Zone said, as if to bring him around.

"It was the Oceanic or the AIs," Mason said quickly. "It could have simply wiped out the Optimants, but it was more worried about the AIs than about humanity. That's why it introduced an encoded virus into the AIs, plaguing them and eventually every other computer in human space."

Zone mulled it over. "So's there's no cure, then?"

Mason shrugged. "You'd have to ask the Oceanic."

"Good thinking, Mason." He stuffed the 'caul into Mason's hands. "Put it on and tell Endgame here that we want to talk to the Oceanic."

Mason's mouth fell open. "Colonel, this machine *deliberately* broke contact with the Oceanic to save itself from getting the viruses. The one in Wall Water followed suit, then others in Passwater, Alabaster, and a few more places. There's no telling how the Oceanic will respond if it learns there are still functional AIs in its midst."

Zone took a menacing step forward. "Your buddy Boon's about to destroy the Oceanic—yes or no?"

Mason hesitated, then nodded.

"Then it's our duty to warn the Oceanic. After that it's likely to be more amenable to answering our questions about curing the Plagues."

"He's right," Yatt all but screamed into Mason's mind. *"Do as he says. It may be our only chance."*

"Put on the 'caul, Mason," Zone ordered. "Tell this fucking machine to establish contact with the Oceanic. I know it's been two hundred years, but it must have some of the communicating agent stored, maybe down in the base of the lighthouse, where it can spew it into the water."

"It's true," Yatt confirmed. *"The Oceanic can be petitioned from this very place. Don the cybercaul. We will do what's needed to convince Endgame to comply."*

Mason tugged the 'caul down over his face, only to rip it off seconds later.

Zone raised the 'chettergun to Mason's temple. "Don't even think about double-crossing me."

"It's done," Mason replied, shaking from head to foot. "It's done."

Zonc appraised him skeptically. "That fast? Who the fuck are you trying to fool?" He backed away from Mason to glance at the Amnion, where the humpbacked thing was only kilometers from shore, the *GammaLAW* seemingly stuck to it like an insect to lacquered paper.

Farther out Mason saw something he hadn't seen in several subjective years: The Oceanic was massing for a manifestation of perhaps epic proportions, much likc thc onc it had conjured in reaction to the drilling the *Scepter* team had attempted at the Styx Strait. It was about to hurl a Skyskein at the lighthouse.

CHAPTER
THIRTY-EIGHT

Among the several theories being bandied about as to why the Oceanic was bearing the SWATHship back toward land, the most troubling was that the Oceanic planned to crush her against the rocks hard by the New Alexandria lighthouse. Quant nevertheless hoped that Aquamarine's overseer was merely doing to his ship what it had done to the countless species and mutations it had refused to suffer in its realm: thrusting it—benignly—onto shore.

In light of the fantastic reversal, Aquam and ship's company had forged an interim peace; it had become abundantly clear that the Oceanic controlled the ship. Boon's Aquam still went armed, keeping LAWs and Exts under watch, but there was little or no pointing of weapons, and those who had been confined to the belowdecks spaces had been released, even the Discards. Some of that was due to the numerical advantage the boarders enjoyed, but also, beneath the headsman's ax of the Oceanic's sentence, a wary fraternity was in evidence.

Quant's optimism began to soar as the ship was edged back into the great bay at New Alexandria, but only until sensors revealed that the salt content of the entire estuarine system was off the scale. The Oceanic was taking care to keep other land life-forms from transgressing.

The tireless tugboating of the *GammaLAW* continued until the enormous *tori* gate was looming almost directly overhead, though the diatom itself had submerged, apparently flattened or reshaped to avoid touching the riverbed.

Automatically, Quant threw a look at the gate's stupendous alloy lintel. He failed to realize that anything was amiss until after he had looked away. His eyes roamed over the Oceanic-imbued waters of Ea, where clusters of dissolving materials were visible along both shorelines—what looked to be the remains of floaters, fishing boats, and corpses.

Again he glanced up, and it struck him that the things he'd taken to be weathering or protrusions were actually moving objects clinging low to the titanic crosspiece. It passed through his mind that those above might be more of Boon's people, but if so, why were they concealing themselves and seemingly preparing to rappel onto the ship?

He whirled, about to holler for stop engines and all ahead full, when he recalled that neither he nor the *GammaLAW*'s engines were dictating her present list and direction. Concerned that Boon's company might hear it as an attempt at mutiny, he hesitated to call for general quarters but did so regardless.

No sooner did the alarms sound than he was on the PA, shouting, "Stand by to repel boarders! We have hostiles on the *tori*, preparing to drop down on us. Mr. Boon, get your people to the rails and watch overhead."

Shadows began falling all across the ship's decks, and figures came plummeting in controlled falls along rappelling lines lowered like a great beaded curtain of spider silk. Confusion among Boon and Purifyre's forces weakened their initial response as a first wave of new boarders hit the decks, firing sling-guns as well as LAW-issue sidearms. A second wave was already descending before any of the *GammaLAW*'s defenders had a clear idea of what was occurring. As many as were touching down on the ship, twice that number were lying dead or dissolving in the Oceanic-imbued Ea. Why the *GammaLAW* itself hadn't been torn apart or suffered the same fate as the Roke vessels, Quant couldn't say, but it was obvious that this latest group of raiders hadn't counted on being trapped on the *tori* by the now-hostile waters.

As he watched from Vultures' Row, it came to him who was attacking his ship. In a single glance his eyes took in the uniforms of Diehards, Killmongers, and Unconquerables—the cream of the Ean grandees' elite guards. But mostly what Quant saw was the Grandee Rhodes's own Militerrors, and in short order 'Waretongue himself, seated in a woven chair, was being lowered to the flight deck.

"How good to see you again, Commissioner Haven," Rhodes said from his perch on the forecastle. Scores of mixed praetorians ranged about him on all sides, some wielding LAW-issue sidearms they had somehow learned to handle. "And Purifyre, how good to see you again, Nephew. Is that *Cozmote* I spy among you Anathemites?"

Defiantly, Boon stepped out where Rhodes could get a clear view of him, but he said nothing.

"We came across your convoy of abandoned muscle cars, Cozmote. Some of your pilots—your late pilots, I should say—allowed as how you had nursed some harebrained scheme to sunder the Oceanic. Is it true?" When Boon remained silent, Rhodes laughed. "Seems the Oceanic didn't enjoy your company, Cozmote—or whatever you attempted to feed it."

The *GammaLAW* was still nosed up on the submerged diatom, but the ship had been shoved to the south bank of the river, close to the ancient meandering path that led to Land's End and the lighthouse there. Rhodes's Militerrors were in the process of transferring Exts and LAW personnel to the hangar deck, but Dextra Haven, Purifyre, Boon, and Quant, among several dozen others, were gathered below the forecastle, awaiting confinement or whatever else Rhodes had in mind.

"I must confess," the grandee was saying, "that we came to take the ship rather than be rescued by it. How were we to know you would be bringing the Oceanic back with you? Though why it hasn't destroyed your ship as it did our rafts, I expect one of you will have to explain."

Rhodes's eyes found Dextra. "So much for your plans to rule over Aquamarine, Madame Haven."

"I have no such plans," Dextra told him. "All that transpired at Wall Water was due to a misunderstanding—and the presence of Commissioner Starkweather. If we could begin anew—"

"And will you rebuild my dam?"

"That, too, was by dint of accident."

Rhodes waved his fingertips in a dismissive gesture. "Enough of your lies. I'm well aware that you destroyed the dam to force me from Wall Water, as I am aware that your starship is no more. So don't bother pretending that you have reinforcements above. LAW sends its forces to conquer the primitive Aquam, and the Aquam end up conquering LAW—with, I grant, the Oceanic's complicity in saving Aquamarine."

When Dextra made as if to respond, Rhodes held his hands up for silence. "Hear now—especially you Anathemites—of the punishments that await Commissioner Haven and her company and of the imprisonment that awaits Cozmote, Purifyre, and all you who have rendered them service."

Rhodes was about to pass sentence, when the bows of the ship gave a powerful lurch and a portion of the diatom ballooned up in front of the ship. Several praetorians opened up with sling-guns and confiscated boomers to no avail. The diatom's extruded portion loomed higher above the ship and then it began to ooze open like the mouth of a slug. Exotic marine odors permeated the air. Rhodes's elites were about to open fire once more, when a voice rang out that was familiar to at least some of those on the deck.

"Hold your goddamned fire, you dumbass wads!"

Every shocked praetorian did. A silence like that of a battle-field after the last salvo fell over the deck. The silence lasted only a magical moment before a slime-covered shape was par-tially regurgitated through the diatom's gaping orifice.

Praetorians, Anathemites, and LAWs alike began shifting indecisively, and at least one Militerror called for resumed fire. Quant's iron command voice countermanded it, though, and the sound of him broke Dextra from her frieze so that she, too, began to shout for people to come to their senses. As dumb-founded as any of them, she had a passing thought of the an-cient myths of Jonah and others like him swallowed up by leviathans of one kind or another.

"Don't make things worse than they already are, you idiots," the squirming form added.

Astounded at the sound of the first pronouncement, Dextra realized that while the speaker's words were being amplified by the sea creature's huge body, they still had the ring of Ext-accented Aquam.

"Burning," Dextra whispered in astonishment. When Puri-fyre and Boon turned to her, she added, "The mist or fog or whatever it was—it seemed to be searching for Burning." She swung to face the diatom once more. "MeoTheos, I believe it found him!"

The shape pushing its way free of the pulsating protoplasm was growing more plainly humanoid all the time, even if it re-mained strangely bulky and cumbersome, like a person in an unpowered hardsuit. Three other shapes were visible below and behind the first, which was suddenly giving the Ext field signal gesture to cease firing.

"I'm coming out," Burning said again, perhaps unnecessarily.

With an almost coughing sound a portion of the diatom sur-rounding the maw convulsed, and all four shapes were ex-pelled onto the foredeck. Leaping back, Dextra was certain that she was about to get her first glimpse of a Roke, but the three with Burning turned out to be Ghost, Dr. Zinsser, and the Descrier Rhodes had rid himself of at the Grand Attendance. Ghost's scars had been turned into a nearly-radiant mask, and the Descrier looked positively sublime.

"Souljourner?" Rhodes exclaimed somewhere behind Dextra.

Boon, too, was utterly overwhelmed. Dextra thought him lost for words, but then she heard him mutter, "Four more resurrected. Four more!"

Burning and the rest were encased in some kind of rind or skin, trailing thick, tentaclelike leads or umbilicals that led deep into the maw. When Burning's lips moved, it was clear that he wasn't speaking into atmosphere within the exosuit but into some other medium. His voice came off the epidermis of the rind itself.

"The Roke have seen to it that whatever you spilled into the Amnion has been neutralized. They're very protective of the being that created them. That's probably why they destroyed *Terrible Swift Sword*, as well. They apparently mistook Pitfall for some sort of weapon."

Created them, Dextra nearly shouted to herself. Then Piper had been right: the Oceanic and the Roke were family. She felt light-headed with both rapture and confusion. The four returnees were already beginning to shed their rind armor and now-severed umbilicals.

"Lies!" Boon said suddenly. "These people are puppets operated by the Oceanic!"

"I resent that," Zinsser said, sloughing off the last of his rind encasings. "Face it, man: you've lost. And there isn't time to debate the matter. The Oceanic wants us back on land, where we belong. It only tolerated us—and indeed the intrusion of this ship—because it wants additional information about the Roke."

Dextra looked at Burning. "Allgrave, you said the Roke saved the Oceanic."

"Those that did have been absorbed. But the Oceanic apparently doesn't recognize the genetic material it fashioned millions of years ago. It expects *us* to provide the answers."

"Either we comply or else," Zinsser interjected.

Boon squinted at him. "Or else what?"

"Aquamarine will be drowned. This business with the Roke has torn away the Oceanic's intellectual—and I suppose you might say ethical—underpinnings. I assure you, it has the power to change the very spin of the planet."

Boon shrieked a laugh. "A billion billion joules worth of power? How, by exploding a hundred thousand fusion bombs and running them through a turbine? By putting ten trillion little fishies on treadmills for the next googol centuries?"

Zinsser couldn't keep satisfied condescension out of his voice even now. "By discharging an electrical field they've built up in a superconducting layer around Aquamarine's core—which, I may add, they empower and control via dendrites that penetrate both the mantle and the lithosphere."

Boon's teeth grated audibly, and he swung around to Grandee Rhodes. "You have the weapons to burn this abomination off the bows of this vessel, 'Waretongue. You can scald everything back for a half kilometer in every direction. Then—"

"You won't even warm its fanny," Zinsser corrected. "Good God, man, haven't you heard a word I've said? The Oceanic has developed organic forms that let it reach down through *magma*, forms that thrive in thermal vents and hot spots. Do you suppose it cares about a little warm water?"

Boon was beyond dumbfoundment, struggling to speak. At last he got out, "It's not . . . I'm not going to let it . . ."

"It doesn't matter what you will or won't," Dextra cut in. "The game's gone beyond your plans. Boon, we're in a position to make history. We can be the ones to put an end to centuries of senseless war."

Boon relaxed somewhat. The fine line she was walking made the hair stand up on the back of Dextra's neck. She turned back to Burning and Zinsser. "How can we provide the Oceanic with what it needs to know?"

"We four have been in a sort of scrambled contact with the Oceanic," Zinsser answered, "but we haven't been able to communicate anything more than basic requests. A bio-chemical interface is required."

Dextra looked at Boon. "Is this true?"

He nodded, if begrudgingly. "The Optimants knew as much, though it's my belief that they left the actual communicating to their AIs."

"But we have the Oceanic's synome," Dextra blurted out.

"How? When?" Zinsser asked in amazement.

"Your own Pitfall gave it to us. It managed to analyze the genetic structure of the Oceanic before it and the *Sword* were destroyed—" She swallowed hard. "—by the Roke, apparently. A portion of that data was transmitted to the *GammaLAW*." She turned to gaze at those gathered behind her: Anathemites, praetorians, Exts, LAWs, ship personnel. "Where's Piper? Lod, have you—"

"Overboard!"

No one had observed the rigid inflatable boat go over the side, much less the fact that Piper had seen to it. At the controls of the RIB, she was in the middle of Ea now as a manifestation of the Oceanic—a Farfeeler, Dextra thought—pushed upriver and rose to pull her under. Exts held Lod back as he went to the rail, fully prepared to throw himself over the side in what would have been a futile rescue attempt. No sooner had Piper disappeared than Doogun and a dozen constituents of the Aggregate appeared on deck.

"She injected the synome in the hope that the Oceanic would be that much more accepting of her," Doogun explained while Lod railed at the river. "If it does accept her, Piper will be able to communicate with us chemically through the water itself. She will be your human analogue to the synome itself."

A second manifestation was taking shape out beyond the

lighthouse, building as if to assail something or someone onshore.

"Mason's in the lighthouse," Dextra told Burning and the others in a rush. "There was something he needed to do." She looked at Boon.

Boon made his lips a thin line, then exhaled defeatedly. "He had some cockeyed notion that a cure for the Cyber-plagues was stored in the lighthouse's Optimant computer."

"A cure?" Dextra said. "Why would such a thing reside here?"

"Because the Plagues began here," Boon said evenly.

While Dextra was absorbing it, Rhodes said, "Claude Mason is not alone in chasing the cure. The one you call Colonel Zone is there, as well."

Without a word Burning turned and hastened for the shore.

CHAPTER
THIRTY-NINE

Fighting the lethargy he felt after being split from the Oceanic, Burning raced toward the lighthouse. The manifestation continued to build in the waves that broke on Land's End. Captured by the mist and then encapsulated by the diatom, he had experienced a wholeness novel in his life, a womblike sense of connectedness and contentment. It was as if the Oceanic had endowed him with the power not only to perceive the thoughts of Souljourner, Ghost, and Zinsser but to empathize with each of them without prejudice or judgment. Indeed, the intimacy the four had shared had made it difficult to so much as trade glances after their expulsion. If the Roke had felt as bereft at being ostracized from Aquamarine and losing the oneness they might have shared with the Oceanic, their need for reconciliation or reemergence was entirely understandable. Burning wasn't at all sure that life as he had known it previously was worth living. What the Oceanic was mostly doing, in its own way, was enjoying Flowstate experiences to their fullest, all but trivializing the mere taste of Flowstate the Exts had cultivated for two centuries.

Burning wasn't even halfway to the hundred-meter Optimant structure when living geysers and ramifications formed by the crashing waves reached up out of the Amnion, defying gravity, rising until they blocked out the setting sun and an enormous portion of sky, to literally take hold of the lighthouse summit. The temperature plunged, and a sudden hard wind ripped at Burning's clothes and whirled sand and Big Sere grit into this eyes and ears and nostrils. Enclosed in what might have been a fist of frothing water, the lamp room was torn away and pulled down into the brine. Farther out from shore the surface of the Amnion had dipped in a huge, shallow bowl that began to fill as the sea roared back from the land, carrying away what had been the object of its wrath.

When the wind permitted, Burning rose out of a nearly fetal crouch and resumed his race for the now-decapitated tower. Pure adrenaline took him bounding up the dark, helical stairway while saltwater runoff cascaded down the central shaft.

On what might have been the twenty-fourth or twenty-fifth story he discovered a semiconscious gray-haired woman whom he recognized from Wall Water as Purifyre's second, Essa. Her body was mottled with both old and fresh bruises and her left leg was certainly fractured, but she was breathing regularly and in no immediate jeopardy. Stirred to awareness by the feel of Burning's arm under her shoulders, she managed to open her eyes slightly and raise one hand in a gesture that indicated the short arc of promenade deck that remained.

Three stories higher Burning found Mason, battered but conscious, slumped against a lionwood banquette that had obviously fallen from somewhere above. In his right hand he clutched the cybercaul Burning hadn't seen since Ghost had shown it to him at Wall Water. Dripping seawater, alive with the Oceanic for all Burning knew, was puddling not a meter away, but Mason was either oblivious to the potential danger or completely beyond caring.

"Zone," he said weakly as Burning squatted in front of him, gingerly examining him for broken bones. "I don't think he made it off the promenade in time, but I can't be sure."

"And the Optimant computer?" Burning asked.

"Gone. Taken to sea. The price for revealing itself."

Burning had no idea what he was talking about and wasn't eager for details. Assuring Mason that he would return momentarily, he took the stairs to the lighthouse's truncated top and edged carefully out onto what was left of the promenade deck. By then the Amnion had settled down somewhat, and the western sky was awash in colors Burning was certain he would remember for the rest of his life. He moved to the deck's retaining wall and was about to peer over the edge, when instinct held him back. Not a second later a bandaged hand flew up out of nowhere, failing in its task to attempt to grab whoever leaned within range.

Burning moved a meter to the right before closing on the wall once more. Prepared now, he gazed over the wall to see Zone dangling by the fingertips of his left hand from the lip of the lighthouse's missing crown. That the Oceanic had nearly caught him in its grasp was evident by the fact that Zone's lower legs hung from him like softened candle wax.

"I shoulda known you'd be too smart to just look over the wall, Allgrave," he began. "But then, you've got me to thank for those smarts. If I hadn't beat the shit out of you when you were a kid, you mighta never turned into the data freak you did."

Burning compressed his lips. "Why couldn't you have let it go at that, Zone? A year of rehabilitation for me wasn't enough payback for the lashing my uncle gave you at the Wheel Weevil stables?"

Zone shook his head. "It wasn't your uncle's lashing, Allgrave. It was just who you were—born easy into Bastion Orman. You and your sister both. I knew early I was never going to get a shot at the life you two enjoyed."

"I feel bad for you, Zone. I mean that. You could've spent your time making a better man of yourself instead of wasting it on hating me."

Zone smirked. "You're still a pussy. I'm what you see, nothing more or less."

Burning returned the smirk. "I'm confident in saying that you're a bit less at the moment, Colonel."

Zone looked down at what had been his legs, then raised his eyes once more. "Oceanic threw some water on my fire, that's for sure. I don't suppose you want to lend me a hand up."

Burning touched his chin, as if in contemplation. "I'd say not if your life depended on it, but between you and me, I figure you're already gone."

Zone gazed at the rocks and the foaming sea before looking at Burning one last time. "Then I'll see you in hell, Allgrave."

He let go and fell—purposely aiming for an incoming wave, it seemed. Burning's eyes tracked his descent. Zone landed on his back and disappeared beneath the water, only to reappear briefly, jerked and whirled by the power of the sea.

Then all that was within him began erupting from his orifices as he was slowly turned inside out. Blood clouded the foamy water, and Zone's body began to shrink in on itself and then disassemble and vanish from sight.

"Why me?" Boon screamed at the retreating diatom from the *GammaLAW*'s breakwater. "Goddamn you, why *me*?"

Zinsser came alongside him, still recovering from days of immersion in the Oceanic but curious enough about Boon to attune himself to the matters at hand. "What did it do to you—Boon, is it? Absorb a lover? Foil some earlier plan to sunder it?"

Boon turned, wide-eyed and shaking. "It's what it *didn't* do to me, Zinsser. I was sacrificed to it the night the *Scepter* team went upside for the return voyage. I was under the water, Zinsser, and—" He gestured to himself. "—look at me: I'm as whole as you are. It killed me, resurrected me, then dumped me back on land like a piece of refuse."

Zinsser arched an eyebrow. "For that you've been bent these twenty years on murdering it?"

Boon's nostrils flared. "I'm someone who needs answers, Zinsser. I wouldn't expect you to understand."

"But I do, Mr. Boon. I've devoted my entire life to probing

the mysteries of the ocean. But you say you were 'sacrificed' to the Oceanic. By whom?"

"By a group that no longer exists, an all-female pacifist cult known as the Conscious Voices. A lot of their beliefs were incorporated into Human Enlightenment."

"Pacifists," Zinsser mused. "What was their attitude toward the Oceanic?"

"They revered it."

Zinsser bit his lower lip and nodded. "Then you may already have your answer, Boon. The Oceanic had probably absorbed enough of the Conscious Voices to have grasped that they were allies of a sort."

Boon was shaking his head. "I wasn't one of them, Zinsser. I went to Execution Dock thinking to stop a suicide, when all along it was a plan on their part to sacrifice a member of the *Scepter* team."

"Yes, but the women no doubt laid hands on you. Don't you see, Boon? To the Oceanic, at least, you were indeed one of them."

Boon fell silent, returning his gaze to the sea beyond the mouth of Ea, while Dextra, Quant, and some of the constituents approached the breakwater. Elsewhere, Rhodes's army of mixed praetorians had released everyone from captivity and surrendered the LAW armaments it had collected from planes brought down by Starkweather's weapon platform. Seeing the lamp room taken from the lighthouse had apparently been reminder enough of who truly reigned on Aquamarine. 'Waretongue himself, however, wanted it understood that his actions did not constitute a surrender but rather an amnesty designed to set the stage for renewed talks between the Ean grandees and Haven's LAWs as well as between the grandees and Boon and Purifyre's Trans-Bourne contingent.

"We have had our first communication with Piper," Doogun told Zinsser. "The Oceanic understands who the Roke are and is prepared to welcome them home. It has agreed to discontinue jamming the commo frequencies to facilitate our transmitting a message to those on Sangre. The Oceanic also begins to understand who *we* are—the GammaLAW mission—and will consider acting as a mediator between us and the Roke."

Burning and Mason appeared just then, supporting Ballyhoot between them. "The computer's history," Burning told Zinsser and the others when Mason and the woman had been led off to sick bay. "From what Mason told me, the computer tried to reestablish contact with the Oceanic, but the Oceanic wasn't having any of it."

Dextra loosed a weary sigh. "There goes our chance of curing the Cyberplagues."

"Maybe not," Burning countered. "Mason claims that there are other dormant computers in Passwater and Alabaster—part of what was a counterforce that took itself off-line with the Oceanic before it released the Plagues the Optimants themselves had planned to loose on Old Earth."

Zinsser had his mouth open to reponed when a manifestation suddenly reared alongside the ship and deposited on deck the pulped and pureed remains of what had once been a human. It took the Aggregate several minutes of water sampling to verify Burning's initial assumption that it was none other than Zone.

"The Oceanic wishes to know if we want him back," Doogun said.

Dextra swallowed her gorge and managed to shake her head. "Throw it back overboard. Tell Piper to tell the Oceanic that this one was the worst of us. Perhaps it can someday tell us why."

EPILOGUE

"Another holo-perfect sunset," Dextra remarked as she and Quant walked barefoot down the curve of beach at Land's End.

"Zinsser is convinced that the Oceanic is arranging them for our benefit, spewing microorganisms of some kind into the air to produce those colors."

"I'm certain the entire ship's company appreciates the Oceanic's efforts."

"No, Dex. *Ours*—as in you and me. It's grown as accustomed to these sunset walks as we have."

Dextra shuddered slightly, though more out of awe than apprehension. "I've often felt like we were being observed, especially on foggy evenings."

"Like the smart mist."

"Exactly like the smart mist." She stopped to gaze across the tops of perfect waves to the blue-green Amnion beyond. "You may get to sail these seas yet, Chaz."

"I now take that as a given, madame."

Two months had passed since the *GammaLAW*'s brief encounter with the Amnion. The Big Sere was ending, and each day brought the promise of rain. The ship was anchored several miles upriver on the far side of the *tori* gate that nearly spanned Ea, though a communications and research station had been built near the lighthouse to accommodate Zinsser and the members of the Aggregate, who remained in contact with Piper—her essence, at any rate, to which Lod sent a daily wreath—the mission's mediating sensorium at the center of human–Oceanic relations.

'Waretongue Rhodes had set up temporary quarters at his cousin's stronghold in Hangwitch while Wall Water was being refurbished. LAW engineers, under the direction of Eddie Gairaszhek and Tonii, were looking into what could be done to repair the dam so that Rhodes and the other grandees would be able to pass the next Big Sere on and around Lake Ea. It was hoped that Rhodes's cooperation would result in a like acceptance of the Visitants elsewhere on Scorpia—in Gumption and Alabaster—as well as in the Trans-Bourne and the Scourlands. Dextra was determined to be of assistance to the Aquam if it killed her. That was why she had tasked Glorianna Theiss and Boon with developing something more reliable than mandseng root to prevent Anathemite births. Their inevitable success was bound to sully the mystique of Alabaster in addition to disturbing the trade routes, but that seemed a small price to pay for what most Aquam would regard as a Visitant miracle.

Dextra had also dispatched envoys to pave the way for even greater miracles to come. Ghost and a team of Exts and Science Siders had left the previous week for Passwater aboard the Flying Pavilion *Brigadoon*. Briefly occupied by the Scourland Ferals, the town had been sacked, burned, and abandoned, but it was possible that the Skull Bunker's Optimant computer known as Akashic Record had survived. Scuttlebutt had it that Zinsser believed Ghost hadn't gone north to search for functional AIs so much as to look for a Feral named Asurao, who was rumored to have survived the deluge the Oceanic had loosed on Passwater's suiciding DevOceanites.

At the same time Burning, Souljourner, and another team of Exts and Science Siders—including Claude Mason—were en route to Alabaster to determine if the voluntarily silenced Hypatia, concealed in Oread's bust, could be talked to, much as Smicker's bust and Endgame had been.

Discovering another dormant AI was essential if the human

and Roke space was to be cured of the Cyberplagues. While the Oceanic had tentatively agreed to reconstruct the organic virus it had released into the Optimants' AI ecology, the *GammaLAW* lacked a sufficiently sentient computer to execute the negotiation and house the data. Even the Aggregate could be of only limited use, and Mason's brain simply wasn't big enough.

He had finally revealed the truth about what he had brought with him from Periapt: the personality construct of a self-generated artificial intelligence known as Yatt, who not only was the voice of the Quantum College but also had been the source of at least some of the glitches that had vexed the *GammaLAW* since its tetherdrop to Lake Ea.

The price the Oceanic had set for the cure was Dextra's promise that Aquamarine would be off limits to AIs or, alternatively, that any that arrived would be overseen by the Oceanic. Its fear, engendered by the techno-empire of the Optimants, was that AIs would eventually supersede and replace organic life. Two hundred years earlier the Optimants themselves had been in danger of becoming superfluous, in part because the artificials had been left to self-evolve in their own fashion during the Optimants' long cold sleep while journeying from Old Earth to Aquamarine.

To thwart the AIs' murderous plans, the Oceanic had made use of an encoded virus rather than any bioweapon because of its basic stricture against going topside, which it was forced to violate after discovering the Roke tissue sample Zinsser had brought downside.

A tentative agreement had also been reached regarding the Roke. Dextra would long remember her first view of the squid-like aliens who appeared for mere seconds in New Alexandria Bay, outside one of the submerging spacecraft, short of being absorbed by the Oceanic. It was some as-yet-unrevealed crisis in their evolvement that had compelled them to override their biological evolution to avoid Aquamarine, and in fact, it was that need to reconcile with their creator that had inadvertently led to the human-Roke conflict.

Aware that humans—the Optimants—had arrived on their true homeworld, the Roke assumed that humanity was in a position to expedite the reconciliation the Roke so desperately needed with the Oceanic. Time and again the Roke had attempted to deliver into human hands a sample of themselves, which they were certain would be presented to the Oceanic, and time and again humans had destroyed what was presented.

With dazzling hindsight Zinsser's team was about to point out countless examples of life on Aquamarine that were demonstrating a similar roundaboutness in acquiescing to the Oceanic, but for two centuries no one had recognized the Roke's xenogenetic compulsion for what it was. The Cyberplagues had confused things further by being misinterpreted by the Roke as an attempt on the part of humans to destroy all Roke civilization, which also relied strongly on artificial intelligence.

The key to the initial misunderstanding had been the Oceanic itself, for which reconciliation was largely an unknown quantity. On Aquamarine symbiotic mutualism had taken precedence over struggles and accommodations of a Darwinian sort. Something either conformed to the Oceanic's rule or was cast out. As much had been bequeathed to the Roke, but through millennia of adaption and change it had come to recognize in humans a seemingly unbounded capacity for reconciliation—hence the Roke's false assumption that humanity would extend itself to help the Roke return home. Nevertheless, in an effort to emulate that perceived capacity for accommodation, the Roke who had returned to Aquamarine had expressed an eagerness to end the war—or, at the very least, make that eagerness known to Periapt and LAW.

"Will you take me with you when you set sail, Chaz?" Dextra asked when they had walked a bit farther down the beach.

"It would be both my honor and my pleasure, madame, though I expect the experience will be less like being buoyed by water than by the hand of some invisible creature. It certainly felt that way to me for the brief period the *GammaLAW* was at sea. Very humbling, actually. More humbling than sailing any normal ocean."

Dextra stopped near the base of the decapitated lighthouse to watch Eyewash drop below the horizon. "Even so, I don't feel the human race is entirely without skills, Chaz. We're certainly the best we've yet encountered at somehow muddling along, cutting love and hate with necessity, practicality, forbearance, wistfulness, need, longing. We're like master toxicologists, balancing poisons with poisons. And you know what?" She turned to face him. "In some ways it's a lot better than using synomes."

They angled for the rocks and sat to watch Eyewash complete its disappearing act. Dextra was feeling brittle and vulnerable but happier than she'd been in some time. It would take time, but Aquamarine would eventually yield solutions to both the Roke Conflict and the Cyberplagues—even though she might not be alive to see the results. Even with the burst they had managed to aim at Periapt with the help of Boon's Optimant antenna, the message would be ten years in arriving, equally slow if the Roke made good on their word to hand carry the message across the stars. Another ten years for a ship to arrive, unless one had already been sent or advances in superluminal travel would permit a swifter journey. In either case she would be an old woman by the time a LAW ship was inserted in orbit around Aquamarine.

She put her hand on Quant's. "I'm fast catching up with you, Chaz. Another couple of months and we're going to at least look the same age."

"Save that you wear your years better than I do mine," he said quietly without looking at her.

She smiled and patted his hand. "The GammaLAW mission's pair of elders, growing old together."

He turned slightly in her direction. "I can imagine much worse things than growing old with you, Dextra."

"And I with you, Chaz. And I with you."

✎ FREE DRINKS ✎

Take the Del Rey® survey and get a free newsletter! Answer the questions below and we will send you complimentary copies of the DRINK (Del Rey® Ink) newsletter free for one year. Here's where you will find out all about upcoming books, read articles by top authors, artists, and editors, and get the inside scoop on your favorite books.

Age _____ Sex ❑ M ❑ F

Highest education level: ❑ high school ❑ college ❑ graduate degree

Annual income: ❑ $0-30,000 ❑ $30,001-60,000 ❑ over $60,000

Number of books you read per month: ❑ 0-2 ❑ 3-5 ❑ 6 or more

Preference: ❑ fantasy ❑ science fiction ❑ horror ❑ other fiction ❑ nonfiction

I buy books in hardcover: ❑ frequently ❑ sometimes ❑ rarely

I buy books at: ❑ superstores ❑ mall bookstores ❑ independent bookstores
   ❑ mail order

I read books by new authors: ❑ frequently ❑ sometimes ❑ rarely

I read comic books: ❑ frequently ❑ sometimes ❑ rarely

I watch the Sci-Fi cable TV channel: ❑ frequently ❑ sometimes ❑ rarely

I am interested in collector editions (signed by the author or illustrated):
   ❑ yes ❑ no ❑ maybe

I read Star Wars novels: ❑ frequently ❑ sometimes ❑ rarely

I read Star Trek novels: ❑ frequently ❑ sometimes ❑ rarely

I read the following newspapers and magazines:

❑ *Analog*	❑ *Locus*	❑ *Popular Science*
❑ *Asimov*	❑ *Wired*	❑ *USA Today*
❑ *SF Universe*	❑ *Realms of Fantasy*	❑ *The New York Times*

Check the box if you do not want your name and address shared with qualified vendors ❑

Name _____
Address _____
City/State/Zip _____
E-mail _____

                                                              daley

PLEASE SEND TO: DEL REY®/The DRINK
201 EAST 50TH STREET NEW YORK NY 10022
OR FAX TO THE ATTENTION OF DEL REY PUBLICITY 212/572-2676

DEL REY® ONLINE!

The Del Rey Internet Newsletter...

A monthly electronic publication e-mailed to subscribers and posted on the rec.arts.sf.written Usenet newsgroup and on our Del Rey Books Web site (www.randomhouse.com/delrey/). It features hype-free descriptions of books that are new in the stores, a list of our upcoming books, special promotional programs and offers, announcements and news, a signing/reading/convention-attendance calendar for Del Rey authors and editors, "In Depth" essays in which professionals in the field (authors, artists, cover designers, salespeople, etc.) talk about their jobs in science fiction, a question-and-answer section, and more!

Subscribe to the DRIN: send a message reading "subscribe" in the subject or body to drin-dist@cruises.randomhouse.com

The Del Rey Books Web Site!

We make a lot of information available on our Web site at
www.randomhouse.com/delrey/

- all back issues and the current issue of the Del Rey Internet Newsletter
- sample chapters of almost every new book
- detailed interactive features of some of our books
- special features on various authors and SF/F worlds
- ordering information (and online ordering)
- reader reviews of upcoming books
- news and announcements
- our Works in Progress report, detailing the doings of our most popular authors
- bargain offers in our Del Rey Online Store
- manuscript transmission requirements
- and more!

If You're Not on the Web...

You can subscribe to the DRIN via e-mail (send a message reading "subscribe" in the subject or body to drin-dist@cruises.randomhouse.com), read it on the rec.arts.sf.written Usenet newsgroup the first few days of every month, or visit our gopher site (gopher.panix.com) for back issues of the DRIN and about a hundred sample chapters. We also have editors and other representatives who participate in America Online and CompuServe SF/F forums and rec.arts.sf.written, making contact and sharing information with SF/F readers.

Questions? E-mail us...

at delrey@randomhouse.com (though it sometimes takes us a little while to answer).